FORSAKEN LOVE

originally written in Armenian
by
Vahram Dadrian

translated and edited
by
Ara Melkonian and Ara Sarafian

Taderon Press
London and Reading

COVER: The cover photographs are representational of the characters Sara and Kirk in *Forsaken Love* while actually being photos of the author's brother and sister-in-law Souren and Bertha Dadrian.

FROM THE PUBLISHERS: *Forsaken Love* was originally published in Armenian and entitled *Kerezmannerou Mechen: Prtsvadz Echer Orakres* (*From the Graves: Pages from My Diary*) (Gotchnag Press, New York, 1945). In this English translation, we have changed the original Armenian title of 1945, as well as some of the personal names in the novel.

Published by Taderon Press, PO Box 2735, Reading RG4 8GF, England.

Printed in association with the Gomidas Institute.

09 08 07 06   5 4 3 2 1

ISBN 978-1-903656-65-6

Distributed worldwide by
Garod Books Ltd.
42 Blythe Rd.
London, W14 0HA
Email: *info@garodbooks.com*

To the memory of a great
Armenian patriot and writer,
Vahram Dadrian (1900-1948),
from loving members
of his family

Table of Contents

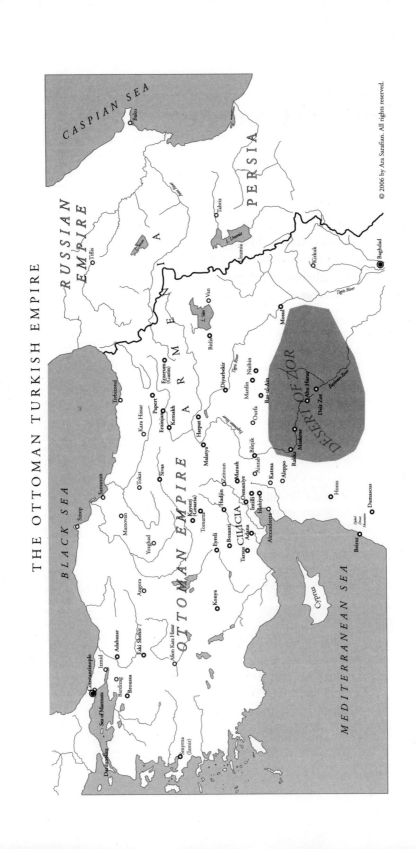

THE OTTOMAN TURKISH EMPIRE

CASPIAN SEA

Baku

RUSSIAN
EMPIRE

PERSIA

Tiflis

Tabriz

L. Urumia

Urumia

Kirkuk

Baghdad

Tigris River

Mosul

BLACK SEA

Trebizond

Kara Hissar

Papert

Erzinjan

Kemakh

Erzerum
(Garin)

ARMENIA

L. Van

Van

Bitlis

Diyarbekir

Mardin

Nisibin

Ras-ul-Ain

DESERT OF ZOR

Abu Hurej

Euphrates River

Deir Zor

Meskene

Rakka

Tigris River

Samsoun

Sinop

Marsovan

Tokat

Sivas

Harput

Malatya

Zeitoun

Marash

Aintab

Birejik

Ourfa

Euphrates River

Aleppo

Homs

Damascus

Kayseri
(Cesarea)

Hadjin

OTTOMAN EMPIRE

Yozghad

Tomarza

Bozanji

Osmaniye

Intilli

CILICIA

Adana

Tarsus

Eyreli

Ekbiye

Alexandretta

Jebel Druse
Mountains

Beirut

Cyprus

Angora

Eski Shehir?

Afion Kara Hissar

Konya

MEDITERRANEAN SEA

Constantinople

Ismid

Adabazar

Bardizag

Broussa

Sea of Marmara

Dardanelles

Smyrna
(Izmir)

INTRODUCTION TO ENGLISH TRANSLATION

Vahram Dadrian

Vahram Dadrian (1900-1948) was a popular western Armenian writer who was born in Chorum (Central Turkey) and died in Fresno (California, United States). For most of his life as a writer, he was known for his detective stories and satirical plays. However, his best known works, *To the Desert: Pages from My Diary* and *Forsaken Love*, were of the different genre.[*] These two books focused on the period 1915-1919 and reflected the author's personal testimony and anguish as a survivor of the Armenian Genocide.[†] While *To the Desert* was an exposition of his teenage diaries, *Forsaken Love* was a novel about the destruction of Armenians.

Dadrian wanted these works to be published because he wanted to bear witness to the mass annihilation of Armenians. The author lost twenty-three members of his family during this period, and he knew of the worse fate of many others. Furthermore, because he kept a diary starting in 1915, he had something substantial to say in the aftermath of this period.

Dadrian began to prepare his diary and novel simultaneously for publication after the collapse of the Ottoman Turkish empire in World War I (1918) and the occupation of the Ottoman capital, Constantinople (modern Istanbul), by Allied powers (1919-23). It was during this period that he, along with his mother and siblings, moved to Constantinople from Jeresh (Jordan) where they had survived the Armenian Genocide. However, Vahram was not able to have these two work printed as he had originally intended because Turkish nationalists

---

[*] Vahram Dadrian (Agop Hacikyan transl., Ara Sarafian ed. and intro.), *To the Desert: Pages from My Diary* (Gomidas Institute: Princeton and London, 2003, 2005). This work was originally written in Armenian and serialised in the newspaper *Baykar* and later published by Gotchnag Press, New York, 1945. *Forsaken Love* was originally published under the title, *Kerezmannerou Mechen: Prtsvadz Echer Orakres* [*From the Graves: Pages from My Diary*] by Gotchnag Press, New York, 1945. The English translation appears under the present new title, *Forsaken Love*.

[†] Dadrian makes his feelings clear in the introduction to *To the Desert*, where he laments that the great catastrophy of Armenians in 1915 was alread largely forgotten by 1945.

regrouped their forces and rose against the Allies, eventually gaining control of Constantinople and founding modern Turkey (1923).[*] Consequently, *To the Desert* and *Forsaken Love* were not published until 1945, after the author had left Turkey and settled in the United States.

Forsaken Love: A Synopsis

Forsaken Love is about the destruction of Ottoman Armenians in 1915, written from the perspective of victims. Though a fictional account, Dadrian stresses that this novel is based on real testimonies which he heard and recorded himself, and many of the scenes in the novel are clearly based on his diaries.[†] *Forsaken Love* is one of the first historical novel about the Armenian Genocide written by a survivor of that event.

Forsaken Love is set in the late Ottoman Empire, where over two million Armenians lived alongside other groups, mainly Turks, Kurds, Greeks, Arabs and Assyrians. Armenians had their own community organizations, ran their own schools, printed their own newspapers, and built their own churches. However, they were second class subjects because they were Christians in a Muslim-Turkish Empire.

The opening political setting of the novel is the Ottoman entry into World War I followed by the decision of the Turkish government to deport and eliminate its Armenian subjects. *Forsaken Love* captures the sense of bewilderment and helplessness of Armenian victims following the victimization of entire communities, the mass arrest, torture and killing of community leaders, the execution of Armenians soldiers serving in the Ottoman army, and the great massacres of Der Zor. Dadrian portrays Armenian criminals, informers and apostates who work with the executioners, as well as others who become slave workers simply to live. Within a single novel, Dadrian presents real scenarios – some simple, others profound – about the Armenian Genocide of 1915.

Dadrian also gives a prominent place to the Arab struggle for independence from the Ottoman Empire. This is first portrayed through a group of Arab deserters, led by an officer from a prominent Arab family, who help to save Armenians in Der Zor, and then other Arab characters from Lebanon and Syria. The presence of the Arab struggle in Dadrian's

---

[*] *To the Desert*, p. 3.

[†] In his introduction to *To the Desert*, the author states that he used ten stories mentioned in his diaries, as well as "assembling hundreds of tiny events" which he had heard about when writing *Forsaken Love*. See *To the Desert*, p. x, p. 4.

novel should not be surprising, given that the author's family survived the Armenian Genocide amongst Arabs in Jeresh (Jordan) from 1915-1919.

The political setting of the novel changes with the end of World War I (1918) and the expectation of Armenian survivors to return to their homes and villages. By 1923, these survivors are abandoned by European powers (most notaby France and Great Britain) when a new Turkish nationalist movement sweeps across Cilicia (and many other parts of the former Ottoman Empire) and seals the fate of Armenians once and for all – both in *Forsaken Love* as well as in real life.[*]

This novel is centered around a main character, Kirk, who survives this period to tell his story. He is a romantic hero who resists his executioners and fights for his people, while his world collapses around him, first with the apparent death of Sara (his financée from Erzeroum), and then the death of his second love and wife, Julia, who dies in his arms. *Forsaken Love* is a remarkable and very powerful novel which reflected much of the reality of the Armenian Genocide, influenced a whole generation of Armenians over the years.

When publishing this work, we chose to change the original Armenian title *From Amongst the Graves: Pages from My Diary* to *Forsaken Love* in order to focus on the poignant love story that is in the novel. We also changed some of the names of individuals to make the work more accessible to an English speaking audience.

Ara Sarafian
Gomidas Institute, London
(September 2006)

---

[*] For a recent work about the political background to this post-WWI period and the condition of Armenian refugees inside Turkey, see Mary Garougian, *Flight of the Dzidzernag: The Autobiography of Varteres Garougian*, (Taderon Press, 2002). Also see Stanley Kerr, *The Lions of Marash: Personal Experiences with American Near East Relief, 1919-1922* (Albany, NY: State University of New York, 1973).

PART I

The Black Hand at Work

One day the people of Garin (Erzerum) read the following notice pasted on the walls:

OFFICIAL NOTICE FROM THE GENERAL SECURITY OFFICE OF THE GOVERNORSHIP

All citizens, without distinction of race or religion, are invited to hand in to the government all manner of lethal weapons – rifles, pistols, dynamite, swords, daggers etc. within three days.

After the deadline expires, the war tribunal will punish those who disobey this order with the severest penalties.

Governor TAHSIN

* * *

That day, Master Christopher Sarkisian returned home earlier than usual. His forehead was wrinkled and his eyes unusually filled with sadness.

"Are you ill?" Margaret asked, putting aside the newspaper in her hand.

"No," answered Master Sarkisian in a hoarse voice.

"What's wrong with you? Why have you returned early?" asked his wife anxiously.

As if he had not heard, Master Sarkisian sat in his usual corner and taking a sealed envelope from his pocket, said, "Where's Sara? There's a letter for her from Constantinople."

"She's gone to visit her friend," replied Margaret. "Is it bad news?"

"I don't know. The letter's addressed to her, so I didn't open it."

"So why are you sad?"

"Don't you know about today's announcement? They are collecting weapons."

"Yes, Diran said so. But not just from us. The announcement apparently said 'without distinction of race or religion.'"

"That is just a smoke screen," Master Sarkisian said. "I'm afraid that today's announcement is only a small precursor to an enormous storm on the horizon."

"But there's no reason to be pessimistic. On the contrary, the government's attitude towards Armenians is very benevolent," Mrs Sarkisian pointed out. "Look at this newspaper from Constantinople."

Master Christopher Sarkisian put his glasses on and taking the paper from his wife held it in the light from the window.

The war was continuing at a furious pace. All the columns of the newspaper were filled with abject descriptions of the dead, the wounded, bombed cities, and burnt villages.

The Dardanelles front, the Caucasian front, the Suez front. Every side of Turkey was a front, or more correctly, every part of Europe was a front, where human blood flowed in torrents, continuously.

What was this fratricidal war for?

Master Sarkisian had no time for analysis. He read the headlines of news items without finding the piece of good news that had made his wife positive towards the Turkish government.

He finally found the news she had alluded to and took it in with a quick glance.

"Enver Pasha, the Minister of War, expresses his thanks to the diocesan bishop of Konya for the services rendered by Armenian soldiers on the battlefield. His Excellency requests that the diocesan bishop passes his deepest appreciation and satisfaction to the Armenian people who for centuries have nourished feelings of loyalty…"

"Has this news made you feel more positive?" asked Master Sarkisian, stopping his reading.

"Yes."

"Your news is quite old," he said, with a chuckle. "Here in Turkey politics change from one day to the next."

He threw the paper on a table with contempt, took off his glasses, and looked dreamily out of the window, apparently examining the garden behind the house, but in reality seeing visions in his mind.

* * *

Master Christopher Sarkisian was fifty-eight years old. His younger brother, Mardiros Sarkisian, lived in Constantinople, while he himself lived in Erzerum. They worked together in the knitted fabrics' trade.

Thanks to their honest activities, they had achieved an enviable position in the knitted fabrics business in both Constantinople and Erzerum.

Master Sarkisian had married Margaret, who was an educated person and the daughter of one of the city's wealthiest families, the Sempadians. They had been blessed with two sons, Simon and Diran: the first was 19, the other 17 years old. He and his wife had taken great trouble over their children's education, as well as doing much for all the poor Armenian children of the city, of whom there were very many in the schools.

Master Sarkisian was, in the real sense of the word, a noble Armenian merchant who knew his national and patriotic obligations, a citizen who enjoyed esteem and honor everywhere.

He was pleased for himself and his family, but he was unhappy because of his concerns for his own Armenian community.

His sensitive Armenian soul became uneasy every time something bad happened to a fellow Armenian. Especially the latest events, the special measures taken against Armenians under the pretext of military requisitioning, the official robbery of Armenian warehouses; the specific oppression of Armenian villages, such as the village where the local priest was tortured on the altar during the Easter Day service and the congregation was gunned down; the public execution of a friend and his 10-year old daughter in another village by the inspector of education and so on – all this made him depressed.

The centuries of torture and persecution, and the constant fear and danger of death, had given Master Sarkisian, as in all honest Armenians, a sixth sense of premonition.

Like the desert camel that can sense an impending desert storm, Master Sarkisian could feel the build-up of a great storm on the horizons of the Armenian world. What the extent of that storm would be, Master Sarkisian was not able to determine, but it was enough that his whole being felt its existence.

Now, in his imagination, he could see that storm suddenly bursting out, shaking Turkish Armenia from one end to the other at its foundations. Dazzling lightning strikes flashed; heaven and earth shook; hundreds of thousands of people – all of whose faces were known to him, all of whom carried the same blood as he did, all of whom spoke the same language and worshipped the same God as he did – were running away in panic; darkness covered everything and the storm carried them all, like sheaves of hay, and cleared them from the face of the earth.

Master Sarkisian was suddenly startled by his son's entrance, the terrible vision in his agitated mind was shattered. Turning to the cold reality of life, he sighed deeply. Oh! Thank goodness that what he saw was only an illusory picture!

"Father," said Diran, greeting the head of the family with respect, "have you any news of today's announcement?"

"Yes," Master Sarkisian replied with an affirmative nod of his head.

"What do you think? Shall we hand in our pistol?"

"Of course, as we can't ignore the government order."

"Father, let's not hand it in," Diran urged in a pleading tone. "This order is a trap for us. They want to take our weapons so that they can kill us more easily later."

"But if the government was minded to massacre us, our pistol wouldn't be an obstacle," Master Sarkisian said angrily.

"No father, if we are to die, wouldn't it be better that we die fighting?"

"My son," Master Sarkisian said, "I've reached this age and so far I have never done anything against the laws of our government. We must obey as long as they order it."

"So shall we extend our necks under the executioner's broadsword?"

"If we don't hand over our weapons, we'll excite the anger of the executioner. Maybe we'll prevent the evil by our obedience."

"I don't believe that."

"I don't either, but we've no other way my son."

"But I don't understand," said Margaret, entering the argument between father and son. "Why are you determined to see a secret agenda in the government's collection of weapons? Don't we read in the newspapers, every day, how the army suffers due to a lack of equipment?"

"So," Diran asked sarcastically, "do they want to equip the Turkish soldiers with our few weapons?"

"Why not? Wasn't it only a few months ago that they collected all the damaged cauldrons from kitchens to make cartridges?"

No one answered the question, and there was an unusual silence.

It was only a quarter of an hour later that a breath of transient life broke that heavy atmosphere, when Sara entered the room merrily.

"Come, daughter," said Master Sarkisian, cutting through the heart-breaking silence. "You've got a letter from Constantinople."

"From Kirk?"

"Yes, here you are."

An angelic smile appeared on Sara's beautiful face. She ran to her father joyfully, took the letter, and tore open the envelope.

A handwritten page emerged from the envelope with a photograph in its folds.

"Oh! A picture of Kirk in officer's uniform," exclaimed the young Armenian girl, gazing ecstatically at the picture of her fiancée.

"Bring it here, let me look…"

Shortly afterwards Kirk's picture passed from hand to hand, accompanied by expressions of admiration, while Sara tenderly read his affectionate letter.

"What's he written?" asked Mrs Sarkisian, after satisfying her need to see him again from the photograph.

"Lots of lovely things," Sara replied, continuing to read the letter in her mind. "He's graduated from the army school and entered the army itself. He's involved with training soldiers in Maltepe (a distant suburb of Constantinople). He writes that he occasionally goes to stay for a night or two with uncle in Pangalti. Uncle's wife, Mrs Soghomeh, had an operation for appendicitis and has recovered. Then he describes his visits with my cousins to the historic Byzantine places and his studies – the naughty boy hasn't stopped thinking about his penchant for archaeology – and finally he sends all of you his loving greetings and kisses. He's added a postscript. Let me see what he's written."

Then a moment passed before Sara paled and uttered a stifled "Oh!"

"What's the matter, daughter? What've you found out?" asked her parents anxiously.

Before his sister could answer, Diran took the letter from her and read, "Having sealed this letter I was going to take it to the post when they said that orders had come to move immediately to the Dardanelles. So we're going to war, my Sara. If I should die, you can be sure it will be with your undying love in my heart and your sweet name on my lips. Goodbye my love."

* * *

On the following morning Harry, one of the employees of the warehouse, came in an agitated state and put a parcel in front of Master Sarkisian, stating, "They wouldn't take it, Sir. They want you to take it personally."

"Did you tell them that you took it for me?" Master Sarkisian asked with a troubled look.

"Yes, I told them, so that they would know that you had handed over your weapon. But when the policeman heard your name, he said, 'Why didn't your master bring it to the police station himself? Won't he lower himself to come to the police station?' He then hit me in the face and gave strict instructions that you were to take it there yourself."

Master Sarkisian took the parcel and after standing for a minute in thought asked, "Was there a crowd in front of the police station?"

"Yes, almost all of them were Armenian. There was no one from any other community bringing weapons at all."

"Which policeman struck you?"

"Ahmed from Terjan. He buys so much on credit from us but never pays his bill."

"Which of them pays his bill?" Master Sarkisian said with a bitter smile. "From the governor and the chief of police down to the lowliest official, they're all my customers. We give them what they want so that nothing happens to us."

"If only those ungrateful people appreciated your generosity."

"What can you do my son? We're born here and will live here. We're forced to accept all the injustices done by them. So it was Ahmed Bey who gave the order for me to take it to him?"

"That is so, Sir."

"Very good. Let it be as he wishes."

Master Sarkisian took the parcel and went to the government building. There was indeed an enormous crowd there, and they were all faces that he knew. The crowd, upon seeing their principal approaching, moved respectfully to one side to allow him to move forward.

"Please, don't disturb yourselves," said Master Sarkisian in an emotional voice. "All of you are heads of households and businesses. I'll wait my turn."

"Please Sir, you go first."

Not being able to deny people's earnest request, Master Sarkisian went forward and entered the police station, where Ahmed from Terjan, seated at a desk near the door, received the weapons, while someone else wrote out the receipts for them. The chief of police, sitting at a desk at the back of the room, watched his policemen's work from a distance.

Master Sarkisian had often entered that official building. On those occasions the chief of police would hurriedly jump to his feet, come to the door, welcome him, and escort him by the hand to an armchair, where he would offer him coffee and cigarettes, even light them respectfully himself. But that had been when relations between Turks and Armenians were different. Now, seeing Master Sarkisian enter, the chief of police went through the papers on his desk, trying to appear that he had not seen him come in.

Not wanting to disturb his friend in his 'many activities,' Master Sarkisian came and stood, as if he were a guilty person, in front of Ahmed Bey's desk.

"You had sent your weapon with your servant," the Turkish policeman said, blushing from shame, "but I couldn't accept it as the law says that we have to give the receipt to the owner after obtaining his signature."

"Please excuse me, I wasn't aware of that," Master Sarkisian said meekly. "Please accept it now. I have brought it myself."

Ahmed opened the parcel and, taking the pistol in his hand, asked, "Only this? Have you nothing else?"

"Why should I have anything else? I bought this for my safety when I went to the villages," the merchant said.

A sarcastic smile slid under Ahmed's moustache. Then he turned to his colleague and said, "Sedki Bey, write a receipt for Christopher, son of Sarkis. A 'Nagant' pistol, serial number 18.214."

Master Sarkisian signed the original receipt in the book, placed the receipt in his pocket, and left.

* * *

The deadline for the handover of weapons expired on Thursday at six o'clock in the evening.

News of the arrest of various Armenian community workers and intellectuals by the police that afternoon left the Armenian inhabitants of the city stupefied.

Master Sarkisian had also on that day returned home earlier than usual and was talking with members of his family about the events of the day when Sandra, the maid, ran into the room.

"Sir, Sir…"

"What's the matter, girl?"

Sandra's hands and knees shook as if she had seen the devil.

"Sir, there's a pistol in the garden."

"A pistol?"

"Yes, under the rose bush, covered with grass."

Master Sarkisian, his wife and children rushed into the garden while the maid ran ahead saying breathlessly, "I was watering the flowerbed when I spotted something white like an egg that was shining under the rose bush. I went to it out of curiosity and what did I see? A rusty pistol hidden under the grass… with its mother-of-pearl handle showing…"

Master Sarkisian reached the rose bush first, picked up the pistol and muttered angrily, "But whose is this?"

"I don't know, Sir. I found it just there and came to tell you without touching it."

"This has been put here for mischief," Diran said, glancing uneasily at the low wall surrounding the garden, "so that they can later accuse us of concealing weapons."

"Fortunately we found it before the time's up," said Master Sarkisian, looking at his watch. "It's 5:30. I'll go and hand it to the police immediately. We'll think about who did this later."

Master Sarkisian quickly wrapped the pistol in a piece of paper and swiftly made his way to the government building. "May God grant that I reach it in time" he said continuously looking at his watch. "Yes, yes, I'll get there in time. There's still a quarter of an hour."

When Master Sarkisian reached the building, the office was indeed still open, and four people were engaged in handing over their weapons.

It was as if a great weight was lifted from his shoulders. Christopher drew a deep breath and stood behind the fourth man.

The task of handing over the weapons was gradually being completed. The owners of the arms handed over their parcels and left. The first man left, then the second, and the third, and the fourth. When it was Master Sarkisian's turn, the corporal shut the office door, announcing that it was six o'clock already.

"Excuse me Sir," Master Sarkisian said respectfully, "I was here before six."

"It's possible," the corporal said coldly, "but it's now six and it's forbidden to accept any more weapons."

"Never mind, Sir, writing a receipt will take less than a moment."

"Who said never mind?" the Turk said angrily, looking at Master Sarkisian with hateful eyes. "Are you going to teach me my business? You should have brought it earlier. What were you doing for the last three days?"

"Excuse me Sir, but I only found the weapon just now. That's the reason I was late," replied Master Sarkisian calmly.

"What did you find?"

"This pistol."

The corporal looked carefully at Master Sarkisian. "Have you come here to make fun of me?"

"No, I'm telling the truth."

"Come with me!"

The police official led Master Sarkisian to a basement room which was furnished only with a table and chair. On the table were an inkwell, some pens, paper and a whip made from ox hide. In other words, all the things necessary to beat a man and make him confess.

"Your problem is quite serious," said the man solemnly while sitting down. "Give me that parcel."

After accepting the parcel, opening it with feverish movements, and superficially examining the pistol, he pulled a sheet of paper towards him.

"What is your name, age, address and occupation?"

Master Sarkisian provided the answers.

"You say that this pistol doesn't belong to you?"

"No."

"Where did you find it?"

"In the garden of my house."

"Did you find it yourself?"

"No, my maid did."

"What's her nationality?"

"Armenian."

"An Armenian's testimony isn't acceptable."

The policeman was writing something with his reed pen and damaging it in the process, when Master Sarkisian protested, "But Sir, I've no reason to lie. If the pistol was mine, I would have brought it in three days ago with my own pistol, which I handed in to the government, and for which I've got a receipt here. I swear that I found this other pistol less than half an hour ago."

"You can swear your oath in front of the war tribunal."

"So you'll hand me over to the court so that…"

"Please be quiet. Don't disturb my writing."

"But…"

"Effendi! Do you understand Turkish? I'm telling you to be silent. If you can't understand what's said to you, I'll make you understand by other means."

"But listen to me for one moment," Master Sarkisian begged.

"Not even for a second. Do you understand, or must I come near you?"

"I understand, but…"

The corporal suddenly picked up the whip and ran at Christopher. "Are you still talking?"

Christopher saw the flash of wickedness in the Turk's eyes, so he thought it best to keep quiet.

The evil man looked at his victim like a crazed animal and then returned to his desk and continued writing his note.

The writing was completed a little later on. The Turk offered Master Sarkisian the pen and said, "Sign your declaration."

Master Sarkisian took the pen and was about to put on his glasses to read the paper which required his signature, when the corporal ordered impatiently, "Sign it, sign it! They'll read it later in court and translate your recollections."

* * *

"What injustice!" Master Sarkisian muttered after the executioner had left and he was alone in the room. "What an unjust manner to a conscientious citizen like me! To make me guilty through defamation…! To obtain a signature from me by force…! What hatred! What devilish machinations!"

The affluent Armenian was greatly affected by the force used against him and paced the length and width of the room with nervous steps while racking his brain to understand the meaning of these criminal developments.

Hours passed but no one came to look for him.

Tired from walking up and down, Master Sarkisian thought of sitting on the only chair in the room but decided not to do so, in case the corporal suddenly burst into the room and made disparaging remarks at him… for sitting on an official's chair.

Every time he heard footsteps in the yard outside, he thought that it was his friend the chief of police who, hearing about his unjust imprisonment, was coming to free him. Indeed, during this wait, he heard, at one time, the familiar voice of the police chief who was having an emotional conversation with someone. "Of course, when he brings weapons after the time is up, he is subject to the law."

Whoever the chief of police's interlocutor was, he was defending someone who had brought in weapons after the stated time. His voice couldn't be heard and a little later he was condemned to complete silence with the chief of police's threatening warning, "Sir, we won't learn what is right or wrong from you. If you have missed your father so much, we can send you to him…"

Your father?

A dreadful shudder ran through his body. Could it have been his son Diran who was arguing with the chief of police?

Oh, the inexperienced boy! It would appear that, worried that his father had not returned home, he had come to the government building to obtain news and was now arguing with his father's one time friend, without taking the delicate situation into account.

Oh, if only he could leave the room he was imprisoned in and run to his son and tell him not to say anything… that he should return home immediately.

But Master Sarkisian couldn't leave because the corporal who had tormented him had locked the door with two locks when he had left the room. He could now see the danger both to himself and to his son. Diran was probably still talking because suddenly a great slap was heard, then others, immediately followed by a scream of agony.

Horrified, Master Sarkisian ran to the closed door. He recognised his son's scream and the sound of further blows and the police chief's frightening voice that cracked like a whip in the air, "Take this lizard and give 100 blows to his feet."

Master Sarkisian heard the sound of many feet moving towards the victim. Then he heard a body being dragged towards his cell. His tongue shrank and his knees became feeble from bewilderment, and he froze where he stood as if turned to stone. Suddenly he received a heavy blow to the forehead as the door was thrown-open, and he fell to the floor unconscious.

When he recovered consciousness, Master Sarkisian felt that there were several people in the room who were busy beating someone. The blows of a stave fell at intervals, while a hoarse voice counted the strokes.

Thud.

"Eighty seven."

Thud.

"Eighty eight."

Gradually recovering clarity of mind, Master Sarkisian straightened himself to see who was being beaten and made no noise at all. He hardly recognised his son who had fainted and was lying in the center of the room as violent blows fell on his naked and bloody feet held in a rifle sling. Master Sarkisian ran madly in front of the policemen, shouting, heartrendingly, "For God's sake, don't beat him… he's my son…"

"The dead man has risen!" laughed the policeman who was counting the blows. "Old man, stay away, or the end of the stave may touch you."

Thud.

"Eighty nine."

"I beg you, I implore you, spare him, he's my son!" sobbed Master Sarkisian holding the hand of the policeman doing the beating. "Don't, don't!"

"Stay there, friend," roared the executioner, punching Master Sarkisian hard in the chest. "Move aside."

Thud.

"Ninety."

Master Sarkisian's fatherly heart couldn't endure the state of his son. Although he knew it was dangerous to interfere with police business, he threw his whole body over his son and covered his mangled feet with his hands.

"Take that!" yelled the policeman, enraged, hitting him on the head with the stave. "Have another and another, four, five, six, seven…"

The blows of the stave landed one after another on Master Sarkisian's head, back, shoulders, sides and legs.

But he made not one sound of pain, nor did he attempt to defend himself, as he had fainted from the first blow and lost consciousness.

* * *

Weeks passed.

The prison filled each day with new people under arrest. On the other hand, every day, 20-30 people were removed in chains, according to a prepared list, to be judged by a war tribunal. In reality, they were taken to an unknown location outside the city and killed.

It's impossible to describe the methods used to extract forced confessions. Those remaining in prison could hear the pitiful screams of their poor brothers from morning till night, until their cries ceased to sound human and became unimaginable groans.

Occasionally a heart-rending lament would split the air, followed by the bitter smell of smoking flesh. People rolled around on the ground like headless chickens. Their dreadful screams made the prison walls shudder, just like the roar of a lion would shake the earth at its foundations.

The prison door would open. New prisoners would be thrown inside. The prison door would open. New victims would be taken out.

Those who were taken out didn't return.

On one of these terrifying days, a group of twenty people was brought in, under the escort of policemen with fixed bayonets. All of them were in a grievous state. Their clothes were in rags, their faces injured. It was obvious from their dress that they were Armenian peasants.

The prisoners surrounded them to understand why those poor people had been brought in, as until then only prominent people of the city were arrested.

"The barbarities taking place in the villages have reached dreadful levels," a black-bearded young man, who was later understood to be a married priest, said. "The police came to our village and demanded weapons. We gave them what we had. Claiming 'You've got others hidden away,' they began to beat, torture and rob us mercilessly. When they stole the earrings women were wearing, they savagely ripped their ears to get them off. When they took possession of the gold coins in their hair, they pulled all their hair out by the roots. Young men who opposed them were killed. Women who protested were laid on the ground with one policeman sitting on their heads, a second on their legs, while a third beat their bellies until they died vomiting blood. They tied me up in my house, dragged my wife into the next room and carried out the worst crime that could ever be perpetrated on the sanctity of the family only a few paces away from me. Then they armed us with knives, swords, rifles and dynamite, brought us to the city and photographed us. Then they beat us again and brought us here."

There was a horrified silence in the room.

Until then all the prisoners had thought that they were sentenced to death but at least there was no danger to their families or the innocent. But it now became obvious that the government's objective was not the destruction of community leaders but the whole Armenian nation itself.

"The situation is far worse than we supposed," Dr. Caloustian said. He was Master Sarkisian's personal friend and now his prison-mate. "When they first arrested us, we said that the government wanted to cut off the heads of the leaders. Then, when they started to arrest merchants with their own businesses such as yourself, we said that the aim was to eliminate the nation's prominent people. But now we can see that the attack is aimed directly at the nation's heart."

"Yes, all the Armenians in Turkey are living a life or death situation," sighed Master Sarkisian who, thanks to his friend's care, had recovered somewhat from his wounds. "God help us in our situation!"

"When they began to collect weapons, it was obvious that it was going to end like this," said Diran, whose feet were wrapped in white cloths. "We shouldn't have handed our weapons in."

"My son," Master Sarkisian said, shaking his head bitterly, "it would be better to say that we should never have had any weapons. People like Dr Caloustian led the nation down the wrong path."

"Master Sarkisian," Caloustian said with a bitter smile, "It's not the fault of the Dr Caloustians. For years we party members preached the necessity of self-defense to the people. The fault is with the nation which didn't prepare for battle."

"Preparing for battle, to the government, was a crime, doctor. If the nation was aware of the scope of that crime, it either wouldn't have committed it at all, or it would have been in a position to resist all approaching dangers. Being in neither one situation nor the other meant that the people were playing with fire like children. You national leaders shouldn't have ignored it."

"We warned of the dangers but no one listened to us, Master Sarkisian."

"But why put the blame on the people or their leaders? Is the desire for freedom a crime, father?"

Diran's question remained unanswered because, just at that moment, the prison door opened and a giant policeman stood on the threshold. "All the people whose names I read out should come out," he said, taking a large sheet of paper carrying the imperial coat of arms from the folds in his sleeve.

With everyone's attention on him, he read out the names on the list, slowly and individually, stopping between each name, so that he could savour, with devilish joy, the hopeless sighs of the victims.

Finally he read the eighteenth and last name, "Christopher, son of Sarkis, merchant."

A deathly pallor spread across Master Sarkisian's face. It was as if a red-hot skewer had been plunged into his heart. Cold sweat ran down his back. In spite of this, his strong will controlled the stormy feelings deep in his soul, and he got to his feet, silently, like a condemned man.

"Be brave, Master Sarkisian," said Dr Caloustian in a manner that was full of feeling. Shaking his old friend's hand, Caloustian added, "Death is the same everywhere."

"I put my son in your care, Caloustian," Master Sarkisian whispered and, seeing that he was going to weep, he swiftly kissed Diran's forehead and left the room in a hurry.

* * *

"Are you Sarkis' son Christopher?" the chief of police asked to complete a simple formality, despite the fact that he had well known his former friend and benefactor.

"Yes, that's me," Master Sarkisian replied, maintaining his proud posture between two men with fixed bayonets. "You have every reason not to be able to recognise me in this tortured state."

"Well, that's how the world is," said the chief of police with false sympathy. "Sometimes the wet also get burned next to the dry" and, looking at the file of papers before him, added "but you've committed a crime."

"No, Sir. I brought my only pistol in on the very first day that weapons were being handed in and gave it to the police. As you well know, my only principle in life has been to obey the government's laws."

"Leave what I know aside, Master Sarkisian. At this moment you're not before me but the law."

"Good, and I say that I've done nothing against it."

"However not? To show your false respect for the law, you handed in your pistol, but kept the Mauser in your possession."

"Which Mauser?"

"Which Mauser? So you've got others at your house?"

"Excuse me, but there's a mistake in all this. First, I've not kept a Mauser in my house, but found a rusted pistol under some grass in my garden, put there out of mischief. I brought it myself to hand over to the police. But the corporal who wrote that report, protesting that the time was up…"

"How can that be?" interrupted the police chief, "You've declared, over your signature, that during a police search a Mauser was found in your garden."

"It's a lie, Sir. The corporal imprisoned me in a room and made me sign it under the threat of being whipped. Then…"

"Enough, enough! You've all learnt the slogan 'I'm innocent… I signed it under threat… I confessed when I was beaten…' But I see that you're all wolves under sheep's clothing. Master Sarkisian, keeping rifles and pistols in your house is proof that you were a political party member and waiting for the opportunity to strike us when our backs were turned."

"Excuse me Sir. You know me very well. I…"

"No, don't introduce yourself. Yes, we know you very well. Aren't you Armenian? All of you – the merchant, the clergyman, the artisan, the worker, the doctor, the lawyer, the man, the woman, the old, the young – all of you without distinction are the enemies of the Turkish nation and fatherland."

"Master Sarkisian, we've followed all your movements, and what you've said and written for years. We occasionally became your friend, played to your vanity and dignity, sympathised with the state you were forced to be in, simply to gain your confidence and to find out all your secrets.

"It's a universal law that, to gain victory over your enemy, you must know him very well. Look at your songbooks. All your desires, ideals, and aims… the feelings you nourish towards Turks. Everything is reflected there, as in a mirror – 'A Call was Made from the Armenian Mountains of Erzerum…' 'Let's take the Bulgarian Nation as an Example…' 'For the Sake of Freedom Much Blood was Spilt…' 'May Turkey be Destroyed…' These songs have been written for years on our soil. You have sung them so we would hear.

"Master Christopher Sarkisian, every Armenian is a revolutionary in his soul. You've confessed that with your lips and pen. To deny it now and say 'I am innocent' is unnecessary. As traitors to the fatherland, all of you will receive your just punishment. Your examination is complete. Get out!"

The two policemen held Master Sarkisian by the arms to take him out. But Master Sarkisian, deeply affected by the unjust hearing, stood erect where he stood and for the first time in his life stood up againt a government official and stated in a bitter scolding tone, "Sir, you obtained a forced confession from me, beat me without mercy, and finally, without listening, judged me and found me guilty. Are you surprised that we Armenians don't like you? I'm not a member of any political party, but I don't reproach those people who are sick of your never-ending harassment and oppression…"

Master Sarkisian wasn't able to finish what he was going to say. Suddenly the hands of the policeman on his right closed in, like pincers, around his throat. The ferocious strength of the policeman made the elderly merchant lose his balance and fall on his back with a strangled cry.

Shortly afterwards, the two executioners, holding Master Sarkisian by his collar, dragged him away from the chief of police and threw him into the dark room where the bodies of the dead were held until the arrival of the mortuary carts.

The following day the giant policeman arrived at the prison with his large sheet of paper emblazoned with the imperial coat of arms and, with 24 others, took Dr. Caloustian too.

Two days later, Master Sarkisian's 17 year-old Diran, a student, left in a group of 30 men.

It was as if the storm that had appeared in Master Sarkisian's vision had actually been unleashed. A week later the black ghost of death spread its wings over other villages and cities of Armenia, and blood flowed under every Armenian's window.

The Curtain Closes

The night when Master Sarkisian and his son Diran were arrested became a night of mourning for Sara and her mother Mrs Sarkisian.

These two women and Diran had waited for hours for the return of their father and husband. Seeing that Master Sarkisian was late returning home, Diran had gone to the government building to see if some misfortune had befallen his father. Hours later, when Diran had also not returned, the maid had gone and returned half an hour later, saying that the offices were closed and she had not been able to get any information about her two masters.

Mother and daughter spent that night sorrowfully, thinking about their loved ones' unknown fate.

Early next morning, Sandra, on her mistress' orders, went to the home of the chief clerk of Master Sarkisian's warehouse, Harold, so that the latter might be able to obtain information about his employer and his son at the government building.

He returned an hour later, stating that Master Sarkisian and Diran were both in prison.

"Did you see them?" asked Sara and her mother in the depths of despair.

"It's impossible to approach the government building," said the clerk in a sad tone. "Everyone who goes to see the arrested is also arrested. The situation is very dangerous. There have been many more arrests during the night. Many have been taken to the prison in their nightclothes."

"What's the aim of these arrests?" Mrs Sarkisian asked anxiously.

"No one knows anything. They say that they will be sent to the war tribunal. It's even said that the general population will be deported."

"Where to?" Sara asked, trembling.

"We don't know. All of this is sheer supposition. I think it would be wise if we didn't open the warehouse for a few days. What do you think, Mrs Sarkisian?"

"Yes, don't open it. The staff shouldn't also move about too much. You look after yourself too, Mr Harold," Mrs Sarkisian said.

Harold left and never returned. He, in his turn, was arrested and imprisoned.

On Saturday the maid – who had gone out to see if she could get any news from the people she knew – returned to the house in a terrible state, shouting, as soon as she entered the door, "Madam, Miss, you've no idea how they've beaten the Master Sarkisian and Diran… Both of them are lying wounded and unconscious in prison."

Hearing this bearer of bad news, Sara and her mother, were stupefied with horror and stood as if turned to stone. Then Mrs Sarkisian, who was not able to withstand this harsh blow, gave out a stifled scream, fainted, and collapsed on the sofa.

"Oh, you thoughtless girl!" Sara exclaimed, hurrying to her mother's assistance at the same time. "Should such hurtful news be blurted out like that?"

"What should I have done Miss? When I heard that…"

"Tell us later. Now go to my room and get the phial of ether."

While Sandra ran to the next room, Sara opened her mother's bodice, sprinkled water on her face, and massaged her forehead and hands. After a short time she was able to help mother regain her senses with the help of the medicine.

"Oh, my husband! Oh, my son!" sobbed the poor woman in a touching tone. "Who knows how much they tortured them."

"Calm down, mother," Sara begged, wiping her wet eyes so that her mother couldn't see. "Don't you know how much our Sandra exaggerates? Who would dare to beat my father and brother when, from the governor down to the lowest official, they are all father's friends? Sandra didn't come from the prison anyway, but from the street, where every kind of rumour is circulating."

Sara herself didn't believe what she was saying, but she said it to comfort her mother.

"It's true, Madam," Sandra confessed, completely regretting not being able to keep the news secret. "When I heard in the street that most of the prisoners had been beaten, I was so agitated that I assumed that the Master and Diran were among them."

Mrs Sarkisian innocently believed this latest lie, stopped her sobbing, and asked her daughter and the maid to move her to bed.

All that day and the following night Mrs Sarkisian lay down in spiritual crises, like someone ill.

Sara, seated at her mother's bedside, kept watch over her until daylight and, looking at Kirk's photograph she held in her hand, cried for hours.

* * *

Sara was a gracefully tall, delicate young lady with a slim, beautiful face.

From the very first moment she left a captivating impression with the nobility of her soul and heart and the sweetness of her looks and speech.

Many of the young men of the city's wealthiest families had already asked for her hand but she had politely refused them all, as she loved a young man who, although not a compatriot or of the same class, had conquered her heart with his irreproachable character.

That young man was Kirk, the son of a humble peasant, who had come from a lost corner of Armenia Minor to study at the Sanasarian School in Erzerum.

With an intrepid and brave nature, Kirk had quickly excited the attention of the teaching staff and students.

It was impossible to joke with him and refer to his peasant origins. One day a student was stupid enough to call him someone "from Kayseri." Kirk had punched that student to the ground and, when he accounted for his coarse action before the principal, he had said, with proud contempt, "We're Armenians. There is no one from Kayseri, Erzerum, Izmir or Edirne. We're all Armenians! We must not laugh at one another and create false barriers between us. An Armenian from any town or village has his blessings as well as faults, but above anything else, he is Armenian!"

Kirk's bold and logical answer had saved him from punishment, and from then on was the school's hero.

Another incident had spread his fame throughout the city. One year the school's students were to present a play with the title "Vartanants." He was to play Vartan. Kirk was so enthusiastic about Vartan's life on the stage that he was about to strangle a boy from Eudocia who had had the stupidity of playing the role of Vasag, Prince of Sunik, opposite him. There was no one in Erzerum after that play who didn't know General Vartan of the Sanasarian School.

Sara had got to know Kirk through her brother, who was also a student at the same school. Although Kirk was five classes higher than Diran, an incident bound them together in close friendship.

One evening, when Diran was passing through a Turkish neighbourhood, Turkish boys surrounded him and were getting ready to beat him with sticks and stones when Kirk, quite by coincidence, was passing that way. Recognising Diran, and seeing the impending attack on him by five or six boys, Kirk ran up and, striking out with his fists and delivering his blows left and right, he chased the Turkish boys away.

Then, taking Diran by the hand, he took him home, and met Diran's parents and sister, who already knew him by name and appearance from his school.

Although he had only spoken to the family for half an hour, Kirk had endeared himself to the family.

Sara, who observed Kirk from the corner of her eye for a long time, thought to herself, "He's the prince I love." However, Kirk, who also felt love at first sight, took account of his own and her father's economic position, and wanted to smother his feelings, thinking that a wealthy merchant like Master Sarkisian would never give his only daughter to a peasant's son like him.

But was it possible to check the love that had been born in the two young hearts? One day, when they met during a school function, they confessed their love for each other and exchanged kisses for the first time in the school garden's enchanted emptiness.

Four years passed since that time, when they also become engaged with Sara's parents' blessing and lived the happiest times of their lives.

The following year the Sanasarian School moved to Sivas. Although parting was difficult, the weekly exchange of tender letters, and Kirk's visit to Master Sarkisian's in Erzerum a few weeks each year, somewhat lessened the aches born of longing and exile.

Kirk graduated last year but he did not have time to get married because of the outbreak of the Great War. As a graduate from a high school he was sent to Constantinople and accepted into a military school to complete his military education.

He often wrote long letters, giving his fiancée news of his life and the work he was doing. The last letter came from him only five days earlier but what dreadful events had happened since then!

The thought of future events appearing on the horizon made the poor girl's soul shudder. "Oh, Kirk," she sobbed continually putting her fiancée's picture to her lips, "If only you were at least with us. My father and brother are in prison, my mother and I in an uncertain position. Who'll look after us? Who'll defend us?"

* * *

Sara, terrified, opened her eyes and it was night. Her heart was beating and her body was trembling as if she was having a nervous attack.

She had had a bad dream, a terrifying dream, whose horrors she could see before her eyes, even though they were open.

A horrific skeleton, standing on the dome of a mosque, was reaping human heads with a large sickle. The heads which separated from the bodies fell down like shaken mulberries, then bounced on the ground, all their faces turning towards her, opening and shutting their eyelids, and moving their tongues in and out of their mouths.

Bewildered, Sara closed her eyes to stop seeing that frightening picture. But alas! That vision tortured her overwrought brain for a long time.

Sara said nothing about her dream to her mother the next morning but immediately sent the maid to the prison to get news of her father and brother.

Sandra returned an hour later filled with terror, her cheeks running with copious tears.

"I wasn't able to approach the government building," she said in a moaning voice. "All the surrounding streets were cordoned off by the army. They have taken the prisoners away in chains and admitted groups of new people. I saw one man in a dreadful state. His face was swollen and blue, his body covered in wounds, and his head covered in blood.

"He was apparently from Erzinjan. The police found an empty water vessel in the house he rented and asked him where weapons were hidden. The poor man, who didn't even know of the water vessel, said that he knew nothing. At that, the police laid him down and stamped many parts of his body with red-hot irons.

"The man, not being able to stand the torture, fainted. The police brought him round by throwing water on his face, then burned and tortured his body again. They were dragging his body, now just a mass of flesh, to the prison, telling everybody about their great deeds and adding that they will treat all Armenians in the same way if they don't hand over their weapons."

"Oh my God!" Mrs Sarkisian muttered, terrified, turning her eyes to the heavens, "Have mercy on us, Lord."

"So you couldn't get any news of my father and brother?" Sara asked impatiently.

"No news at all, Miss. All I learned was that they have taken the old prisoners away to make way for new ones."

"Where did they take them?"

"Out of the city."

"Where outside the city?"

"Nobody knows."

* * *

One morning three policemen armed with axes furiously knocked at the door of Master Sarkisian's house, and as soon as it was opened, announced that they had come to search the house for hidden weapons.

"We have no weapons," Mrs Sarkisian said in a trembling voice. "We had a pistol that my husband handed over to the police. Two days later we found another one in the garden. My husband took it to hand it over, and that was the last we saw of him. My son went after him and never returned either. Please tell me Sir, what happened to my husband and son? Do you have any news about them?"

"How come you don't know," their leader said sternly, "that Master Sarkisian died in prison a while ago. As for your son, I think he was exiled with all the revolutionaries three days after your husband's death."

"My husband is dead…? My son exiled…?"

Mrs Sarkisian was hardly able to say the words before she fainted and fell into her daughter's arms.

"Oh my father! My brother!" Sara sobbed, filled with absolute fear. "Where, oh where was my brother exiled to?"

"Don't worry, miss," the police leader said with cynical coldness, "he too is in a safe place with your father." Then, turning to his men, he ordered, "We've talked far too long… get to work boys!"

Leaving the bereaved women in the room, the three policemen separated through the floors of the house and began the search.

They demolished the walls with their axes, destroyed the ceilings and lifted the floors. Not finding anything suspicious in the house, they went and excavated various places in the garden. Having failed there too, they returned to the house and took out their anger on the furniture, smashing tables and cupboards, the piano and the porcelain stove – all supposedly in the hope of finding dangerous weapons or books hidden in them.

Sara, who was occupied with her ill mother, had no further strength to grieve for anything else. After losing her father and brother, what value did the house, furniture, treasure or wealth have?

Only the maid had the courage to protest for a moment at the destruction of her mistress' piano. She received a blow from a spade and rolled among the heaps of broken chairs and tables.

Having achieved the destruction they wanted, they left and went to the next house to continue their search there for a time.

That night however, they returned to Master Sarkisian's house, where Sara's extraordinary beauty had aroused their animal passions.

But they knocked at the door in vain...

Seeing that there was no one to open the door, they entered through the garden, but it was too late. Sara, her mother and the maid, who had understood the danger that they were facing from the policemen's amorous eyes, had already abandoned their house as it stood and escaped to one of their distant relations.

* * *

The rumour among the general population, after the arrest of the men, was that the women and children were to be deported, and this was finally confirmed as true. In any case, what bad news didn't come true for Armenians?

On a black day, according to government orders, Mrs Sarkisian, her daughter and maid, alongside relatives and many other Armenians, set out in carriages for Arabia, where they were to live until the end of the war.

This caravan of more than 300 families included some men who had escaped arrest and were accompanying their wives and children, taking all their money, jewels, beds and linen with them.

A police detachment accompanied the caravan not only to show them the way, but also to protect them from Kurdish attacks. The government order was clear – the guilty had been punished and the innocent were supposed to reach the places assigned to them alive...

One morning however, when the caravan was getting ready to move as usual, the police detachment commander ordered the men to be separated from the women.

Without becoming suspicious of any devilish plan, the men went to one side, the women to the other.

The police commander looked at the two groups for a moment, then ordered the men to go off the main highway and down a spur road accompanied by a group of policemen, while the women were ordered to continue on.

"But why are you separating us?" the people asked, perplexed.

"Don't worry," the commander said in a civil tone. "I've made this arrangement for your own good. From here on all the roads are dangerous. When Kurdish bandits see a rich caravan such as your one, they attack without hesitation to rob and plunder. They also use the opportunity to kill the men and rape the women. But when they see a column on foot, they do not do anything, thinking it had already been robbed, and wait for rich caravans to pass."

"So will we have to leave our carriages, possessions and food here?"

"Yes, but you can be sure that not even one handkerchief will be lost. I'll personally look after them, while my lieutenants will lead you onward by separate roads. In three days we'll all be reunited."

"But why separate the men from the women?"

"We've split you into two groups, because it's easier to defend small groups than large ones."

"In that case, let's divide into two groups of 150 families each."

"No, that's impossible. When we take the men separately, the Kurds will think that they're army recruits, so won't attack."

"But you've included 13 year-old boys in the men's group."

"They'll walk in the middle. The women and children, as I said, form a contemptible mass, so they won't attract the bandits' attention. But why are you asking all these superfluous questions? Don't you believe what I say? Once we pass the dangerous area you will understand what a great favour I did for you."

Although the people didn't believe the officer's persuasive words, what could they do apart from obey? They had been handed over to the will and whims of the police and had no way of changing the flow of events; so, with tears in their eyes, they all looked at their loved ones, and each group walked towards its Golgotha.

* * *

The women's caravan walked continuously for three days through mountains, valleys, hills and plains without a moment's rest, nor food, nor drink, in the suffocating summer heat.

Sara and Sandra, taking Mrs Sarkisian by the arms, walked in the middle of the caravan. Those who weren't able to walk fell behind and were bayoneted by the police on the pretext that, by their slow progress, they were endangering the caravan, which needed to pass through that dangerous place as quickly as possible. The police told the people they were about to bayonet that they were doing them a favour because, if they were left half dead on the edge of the deserted road, wild animals would tear them to pieces while they were still alive.

Using the same pretext when crossing a bridge, the police would throw old people, little ones, the sick and the pregnant into the river because, having become weak, they could not match the speed of the caravan.

On the fourth day the police handed their remaining charges over to another squad.

"Aren't you going to give us a gift for bringing you here safe and sound?" they asked shamelessly.

"Everything we had remained with our bundles in the carriages," the women declared. "We've nothing to give you."

"Don't say that!" the policemen said. "You're bound to have hidden jewels or money. Give what your hearts dictate."

The women collected earrings, rings and brooches and, giving them to their erstwhile protectors, asked, "But when will our husbands and the carriages join us?"

"*Inshallah* (God willing), when they come to earth for a second time" the policemen replied with insolent laughter and turned their horses' heads around.

After making the women walk for two hours, this time the new group of policemen stopped the caravan in a lonely valley. "So, what are you giving us?" they asked.

"But what can we give you? You saw that we gave your predecessors all we had."

"What you gave them was nothing," the policemen said with evil grins. The people from Erzerum are rich. Give us what you've got."

"But we've no riches left," the women implored. "We left everything in the city and if we were able to take anything small with us, we left those in the carriages."

"You Armenians are like bags of flour," the policemen said in half-joking, half-serious tones. "No matter how much more you are shaken, the more flour dust you give out. Right, shake now, don't waste our time, we have to get moving."

"But we've nothing left to shake."

"Now we have understood! We wanted to deal with you in a humane manner, but we can now see that you understand nothing of sweet words."

Saying this, the policemen grabbed about 50 women and girls and searched them from top to bottom with the hope of finding hidden jewels or gold. But as the Armenian women had told them in the first place, nothing more than a few pieces of silver and small change was found.

The policemen, disappointed in their hopes, moved the caravan on and didn't harm them at all – until the evening.

In the evening, however, when the caravan had stopped on the edge of a wood, the policemen, having become agitated, approached the caravan of women, just like people who enter a henhouse to remove a ready chicken, got hold of some girls they liked, and dragged them out of the caravan.

* * *

Sara had foreseen this danger. While still in the city, she had cut her hair, pulled out her eyebrows and eyelashes and, using pricks from a needle, had wounded her delicate face, giving herself the look of someone with a skin disease.

To make her disguise more perfect, she had worn the dress of an old woman and put on a white wig and a black muslin scarf on her head.

But no matter how careful she was to escape the penetrating looks of policemen, she still attracted the attention of an ill-natured policeman on the road the next day, when he came up to her and said with a mocking tone, "Armenian girl, your disguise is successful, but what shall we do about the freshness of your breast and hands…?"

Sara stopped coldly, apparently not hearing the remark.

"That's not a girl, she's my elder sister," Mrs Sarkisian said.

"Really?" the policeman asked with a laugh. "Why doesn't she tell me that?"

"She can't because she's mute."

"I know what she is," said the policeman, moving his horse forward. "Who knows how beautiful someone is who spoils her face like that. Let's wait. Let the wounds on her face heal, her eyelashes grow again, then we'll look at her."

Indeed, why hurry? There were so many pretty women and girls in the caravan, while Sara's wounds healed before they reached their destination.

But before that awful day, either luckily or unluckily, the inevitable finally happened.

It was a few days after that policeman's remarks, when the caravan was moving along a mountain road, that it was suddenly surrounded by a group of bloodthirsty *chettehs* (irregular soldiers) and Kurdish bandits.

Like the highwayman, whose first words would be, "your purse or your life," the first thing these barbaric robbers shouted was, "your money or your lives."

"We've no money, ask the policemen! They searched us and found nothing!" answered several brave women.

"The police searched you, but they didn't look inside your intestines," the criminals said, chuckling devilishly.

Just then there was uproar. Howls, screams and cries erupted from the rear of the caravan. The villainous robbers, who were later joined by the police, had attacked the people in the caravan with swords and axes and were killing the women and children without mercy. Their victims' cries and laments resounded up to the pillars of heaven.

It's beyond the ability of any pen to attempt to describe the dreadful savagery that befell that defenseless crowd over the next two hours. Let's just say that only around 40 out of 800 people survived. The others were torn to pieces and fell into pools of their own blood.

Sara was among the survivors.

Having seen her mother beheaded, her maid felled by an axe, and the pitiless killing of many of her relatives and acquaintances, she ran madly out of the encirclement, jumping over corpses, and escaped from the blows of bloody axes.

The robbers, who were occupied with looting the dead, and the chettehs and police, who were raping women, let her escape for a short time.

However, as soon as they had finished their lewd work, they pursued the runaways like hunters, firing and giggling victoriously every time they killed and felled a human being who was sliding under a bush or between piles of rocks.

* * *

Sara and eleven other fugitives finally reached Harput in a pitiful state after much wandering and misery.

It was their further misfortune that the population of that city had also been deported and all community buildings and establishments had been emptied. Hearing that the only Christians still in the city were Americans, they approached the United States consulate for help and sanctuary.

The consul, a noble person, fortunately did not refuse their request, and settled them in a house owned by one of his compatriots, promising that he would do what he could to safeguard their lives.

However, less than a week later, he returned with an anxious look and, calling his protégés to him, said, "Girls, I'm sorry I have to bring you unpleasant news. The police have discovered that you're here and they are demanding that I hand you over to them."

A horrified shudder passed through the surviving Armenian girls. Having hardly escaped the clutches of the Turkish police, were they to be handed over to them again?

"No! No!" the women exclaimed with a cry of horror. "We'd prefer to commit suicide as a group rather than be surrendered to the police!"

"Listen to me," the consul said, quietening them with a wave of his hand, "I'm not going to hand you to the police. I know your story. I know what happened to the people of this city, as well as to the people of Armenian-populated towns and villages. The Turks' aim is to destroy all the Armenians. I know that if I surrender you to the police, you will all be exiled and killed on the way. On the other hand I also know that, even though I am a foreigner and a member of the diplomatic corps, I must obey the law of the land. Now, not wanting to hand you over to the police, I have to find a way that won't disturb the relations between me and this country."

"How can you do that?" the Armenian women asked anxiously. "If you are careful not to disturb your relationship, you have to surrender us to the police."

"No, there is a way, but it is 90% doubtful," the consul said.

"No matter how doubtful it is, please use it," the women pleaded earnestly. "Do what you like, but don't give us to the police."

"That way is to help some of you to escape to Aleppo and the rest of you to Tarsus. Then the police would be faced with a *fait accompli*," the

American said. "I can tell the police that you got wind of the danger and escaped without my knowledge. The only thing that concerns me is the problem of your journey, which is full of difficulties."

"We're willing to accept any difficulties. Do what you feel is best," the Armenian women said together.

"I think that," the consul continued, "if you reach where you're going safely, no one will bother you. There's no deportation of Armenians at Aleppo, while the government in Cilicia is comparatively mild in its treatment of Armenians – unlike the eastern provinces. You'll be able to stay in the American institutions there. I'll write to my colleagues that, if there's any danger, they are to take measures and move those of you who are in Aleppo to Beirut, and those in Tarsus to Constantinople."

"Thank you, Mr Consul."

"So, now that I've got your agreement, I'll go and arrange the journey. You decide among yourselves who is to go to Aleppo and who to Tarsus. I'll let you know tomorrow when I've arranged everything. Goodbye girls."

* * *

After a heart-wrenching parting, where the fear of the danger of the journey and the anguish of breaking friendships were evident, seven of the Armenian girls went to Aleppo by carriage, while the other five, including Sara, went to Tarsus.

The latter group had an emotional journey but happily they finally reached their destination unscathed.

Sara spoke good English, so she saw the American consul in Tarsus and presented his colleague's letter to him on the group's behalf. The consul in Tarsus was informed of the Armenian girls' misfortunes and received them warmly. In accordance with his colleague's recommendation he settled them with a missionary named Mrs Christie, whose husband, a friend of Armenians, was at that time in the United States to awaken public opinion to the barbaric deeds carried out by the Turks.

After settling in with the American lady, the first thing Sara did was to write a letter to her uncle in Constantinople, giving him details of all that had happened and asking him to find a way to get her to Constantinople. She wrote a second letter to Kirk and enclosed it in that letter to her uncle, requesting the latter to forward it to Kirk, as well as sending her Kirk's address.

Weeks passed in hope and waiting. However, one day her letter was returned with the following note on it, "Returned to sender as addressee's whereabouts is unknown."

"But it's impossible that my uncle, Mardiros Sarkisian, shouldn't be found in his own home," Sara muttered, turning the letter over in her trembling hands. "Even if he wasn't there, what has happened to his wife and two sons? Is it possible that like us, they were also deported and killed?"

Without being able to answer the various questions in her mind, Sara went to her room, put her head on her pillow, and cried bitterly, mourning the destruction of the one remaining hope that had nourished her innermost heart, with the innocent expectation that she would find her uncle and, through him, her fiancée.

As if the poor girl's misfortunes were not enough, a few nights later a closed carriage stopped at the corner of the street where she was staying.

A corporal and two soldiers, who had been keeping Mrs Christie's house under surveillance, got out of the carriage. Like conspirators, they looked around and advanced towards the American lady's house.

In passing, I shouldn't forget to say that about two months had passed since Sara's deportation from Erzerum and, in that time, her face, formerly covered with superficial wounds, had recovered its former beauty, being more attractive than ever with its pallid, melancholy expression.

All the inmates of the house opened their eyes with terror at the sharp, intermittent sound of the doorbell.

Papadopoulos, Mrs Christie's Greek servant, approaching the door from the inside, asked who was disturbing them.

"Open the door in the name of the law!" the corporal said.

"I hope you're not making a mistake, this is an American's house," the servant pointed out.

"We know whose house this is, open up!" commanded the fierce voice from outside.

The Greek obeyed. But he had hardly half-opened the door when he fell down unconscious, having received several blows to his face and stomach.

The three criminals, their faces hidden behind cloth masks, entered the house and, holding their guns in the air, ran up the stairs, terrifying the women who were in the hall. The women ran to their rooms screaming.

Only Mrs Christie retained her calmness and, standing in front of the masked bandits, asked what they wanted and by what right they had entered her house by night.

"There's a revolutionary hidden here, and we have come to arrest him," the corporal said roughly.

"There's no revolutionary in my house," the American lady said disparagingly. "First take off your masks, then speak."

"Our masks don't concern you," the corporal yelled in a frightening tone. "Show me where the revolutionary is."

"There's no male in this house, apart from the servant you attacked," Mrs Christie declared.

"We're going to search the rooms."

Without wasting time, they entered one room after another, looking at the women who were hiding, rather than looking for the imaginary revolutionary.

When they finally came to Sara's room, they immediately grabbed her by the wrist and dragged her saying, "Come with us!"

"What do you want from me?" Sara screamed, terrified, trying to free herself.

"Come on, don't resist."

"But where are you taking her?" Mrs Christie protested, moving in front of the soldiers. "You were looking for revolutionaries, weren't you?"

"She knows the whereabouts of the person we're looking for. We're going to question her in the barracks," lied the corporal.

"I don't believe it. You're robbers. You're kidnapping the girl! I'm going to report you..."

The American lady wasn't able to say more. A soldier struck her and pushed her into a room. Another stuffed a handkerchief in Sara's mouth and holding her tightly by the arm, ran down the stairs. The corporal and the other soldier, holding their guns ready to shoot, defended their friend's retreat.

The Greek servant still hadn't recovered from the blows he had received. The criminals jumped over his body like supple animals and ran outside.

Shortly afterwards the loaded carriage departed making low creaking noises, while Mrs Christie looked in bewilderment at the Armenian women's faces in her house, not knowing if the things that had happened in the last five minutes were a dream or reality.

The Armenian Officer

A great commotion began one morning at the Dardanelles front. After months of fruitless bombardment, the British had finally been able to land troops.

The Turk's agitation was justifiable. If the British were able to establish a permanent bridgehead, they could consider victory assured, as the gradual reinforcement of British troops would seriously threaten the Turkish Army. Until that day, Turkish supremacy lay in the fact that enemy troops were defenseless in ships, while the Turkish army was protected by trenches. That morning, the Turkish commander, who had foreseen this danger, was very concerned by British successes and hurried to the trenches where he made the following short speech to the troops. "Soldiers! The Turkish Empire is living a life or death moment. Its future will be decided by your selfless sacrifice. The whole nation, whose eyes are upon you, has only one request to make of you – victory – at all costs victory!"

The soldiers – among whom were Armenians, Greeks, Arabs, Albanians and so on – shouted together, "We're ready to pay for that victory with our blood! Command us!"

"Well done, my children!" the commander said with gratitude. "When the signal is given, you'll all come out of your trenches and advance like a tempest on the enemy. You must not give him time to establish himself on our soil. He must be thrown back into the sea at all costs. Your slogan for today is, 'Throw the British into the sea.'"

"Command us. You'll see!"

The order wasn't late in coming. Suddenly, at the signal, cannon boomed. The soldiers rose out of their trenches and began to advance in groups towards the enemy, sometimes crouched, at other times sliding along, and at still others protecting themselves behind mounds of earth.

The British also began to advance, occasionally forming a line behind heaps of stone, occasionally running forward, then lying down once more.

With the two armies continually advancing towards one another, the battle that had started with distant exchanges of fire quickly turned into hand-to-hand combat, in which men struck one another without mercy, both receiving and giving wounds and often screaming with the agony of death as they fell beneath the fighting men's feet.

With the command on both sides being to advance at all costs, the surviving soldiers rushed forward with furious roars, to secure yet another position or trench. Whoever could, immediately sought shelter behind a rampart, thus saving his life. The soldier, who was late even by a second, suddenly found that the enemy had risen from an unexpected corner and fell to the ground dead, pierced by a bayonet or a bullet.

Often the safety of trenches or walls was nullified by the shells and bombs that rained down from the sky, sea and land, creating great holes, burying the living, wounded and dead all mixed together.

It was during the height of battle that a young captain of the Turkish army suddenly advanced, leading a group of selfless soldiers, to recapture a very important position that had been taken by the enemy.

At the same time there was a volley of machine gun fire from the other side, whose bullets seemed to comb the air. In less than a minute the advancing soldiers had fallen on their faces covered in blood.

The enemy, seeing that the officer leading the advancing troops had not died, prepared to kill him with a rifle bullet, when another young officer came from the Turkish lines. Disregarding every danger, he ran with the speed of lightning to his wounded comrade-in-in arms and, taking him in his arms, ran back.

Bullets flew after him. One buried itself in the rescuer's shoulder, another in his leg. The heroic officer tripped and fell on his face after receiving the second wound. But he didn't abandon his comrade. He dragged him with his good arm to a nearby trench and, making a superhuman effort, threw himself and his load into it and remained there unconscious.

When the rescuing officer came to, he found himself in a large tent that was used as a hospital some distance from the battlefield. Red Crescent stretcher-bearers had moved the two unconscious officers there and, after being operated on, the nurses had put them into adjoining beds.

Before he could open his mouth the captain, who had recovered consciousness before him, said, "I heard from the doctor that you saved my life, endangering your own. Will you tell me your name?"

"Sub-Lieutenant Kirk," the rescuing officer said, who was none other than Sara's fiancée.

"Are you Armenian?"

"Yes."

"My name is Seyfi," his interlocutor said in a weak voice. "I'm from Baghdad, from the Ensari family. Kirk, if I survive... Oh... Oh..."

"Captain, are you ill?" Kirk asked, suddenly trembling. "Shall I call the nurse?"

"My wound, my wound," whispered the officer, indicating his thigh from which a bullet had been removed. "The anaesthetic has worn off... I can feel it now... Oh, the stabbing pains hurt very much..."

* * *

The British Army was totally defeated and retreated, leaving thousands of dead on the battlefield.

The warships, collecting the remains of the army, left ingloriously and vanished from Turkish waters.

The joy and enthusiasm in the Turkish Army were boundless. Never mind that thousands had been sacrificed. A threat to the very existence of the fatherland had, at least temporarily, been removed.

In those animated days, the general officer commanding the front received a telegram from the Ministry of War. "Disarm the Armenian soldiers and officers and send them to the interior provinces to be used for road construction."

Kirk had left the hospital on the day the telegram arrived and his left leg was still bandaged. (His shoulder wound was only a slight scratch.) On that same day, when he was handing over his sword to the colonel, Kirk asked the following question, "Why are you disarming us, Sureya Bey? Weren't we able to serve the army worthily?"

"On the contrary," the Turkish officer replied. "But what can we do? The order is from above."

"Why the order?"

"After the revolt in Van, confidence in Armenians has disappeared. The government no longer wants Armenian soldiers at the front, concerned that they'll be in contact with the enemy."

"But you saw how the Armenian soldiers fought against the British! On the day of the advance, 62 men were sacrificed in defense of Turkish soil and fatherland."

"You're right, what is my knowing that worth?"

"What's going to happen to us?"

"You'll be working on the road between Yozghad and Ankara. That too is patriotic work, Mr Kirk."

"The officers too?"

"There aren't any Armenian officers any more. You're all ordinary soldiers. I wish you success."

Next day, the former warriors of the Dardanelles – about 200 men, of whom three were officers – began the march, on foot, to Ankara, under the supervision of a corporal and a few mounted soldiers.

Kirk thoughtfully walked in the middle of the group when he felt a friendly tap on the shoulder. He looked round and recognised Major Sisag from Amasia, a person with greying hair who inspired respect. Lieutenant Zarmair walked next to him, a sympathetic young man who, like him, had only just left school.

"Don't think too much like that," Major Sisag said, directing his words at Kirk. Nothing more will happen than what is already written on our foreheads."

"I don't believe in fate," Kirk said with a bitter smile.

"I'll bet," Zarmair said, "that our friend is concerned about his reduction in rank to that of an ordinary soldier."

"Soldier? Laborer!" Major Sisag corrected.

"I'm not worried about being a laborer," Kirk muttered. "I'm wondering why the government has reduced us to the ranks."

"But Sureya Bey told you the reason. The rebellion in Van made Armenian soldiers untrustworthy," Major Sisag pointed out.

"But that's not a reason, it's a result," Kirk said. "We really know what the problem is. Kurdish bandits and Turkish irregulars have been perpetrating unheard-of barbarities upon the inhabitants of the villages around Van for a long time, burning their homes, stealing what they have, and raping their women.

"To prevent incidents, the people kept quiet and accepted what happened, until one day the oppression reached the city itself. The government wanted to arrest all the young men who had paid tax in lieu of military service. The people understood the government's aim and defended themselves in the Armenian quarter called Aikesdan.

"The army began to move. 20,000 shells were fired at 30,000 Armenians. The Armenians broke out of the siege lines and captured a number of military positions, burnt the Turkish barracks and held out for a month, until the Russians came and saved them. There – that's the whole story of the rebellion in Van.

"I can't understand why the Turks start the story from the time of the fighting in Aikesdan. That fighting wasn't the signal for a prepared rebellion, but a natural response to the violence used against them."

"That means," Major Sisag said, "that the government wants to inflame the Armenian people, so that it rebels, and it then has the excuse to massacre people, saying 'they rebelled.'"

"I also think so," Lieutenant Zarmair agreed.

"So," Kirk concluded, "as the government's aim is to massacre the Armenians, after Van the turn will come for Erzerum, Bitlis, Harput, Diyarbekir, Sivas, Cilicia and perhaps all Turkish Armenian communities. That's what I was thinking about, that's what I see in the disarming of Armenian soldiers."

The three former officers spoke no more. Each was buried in his personal concerns and uneasiness, and they continued the journey silently.

They continued for days in such a manner, until they reached the place assigned to them, where there were about 4,000 Armenian soldiers from different places already working, building roads and bridges, dykes and canals.

* * *

The disaster that the former officers predicted happened a month later.

Only spades and mattocks were left in the hands of the poor soldiers when they heard, during one of their work shifts, that there were no Armenians left in the eastern provinces. The population of all the villages and towns were deported, the men killed on the road, the women with pretty faces kidnapped, and the elderly and children butchered and thrown into the rivers.

Many of them had parents, relatives and people whom they knew from those provinces. So, were all of them in the eastern provinces killed by the sword, raped and destroyed?

No, they couldn't believe that. Their reason denied it, revolted against it, didn't want to accept that such villainy could take place in the twentieth century against a whole defenseless people.

"Sara! Diran! Master Sarkisian! Mrs Sarkisian! All the people from Erzerum! All the people from Armenia! Did they all disappear?" Kirk asked himself, beset by terror. "No! It's not possible, it's not possible..."

"Why isn't it possible?" Lieutenant Zarmair asked, having heard Kirk's monologue. "Didn't we say that tomorrow would be our turn? We should escape from these places, or one day we'll be the victims of the Turk's bloodthirsty hatred."

"Yes, yes, they'll massacre us too," Kirk muttered in a hideous tone.

"It's horrific!" Major Sisag moaned, with his head in his hands. "So, has my wife and my one and only daughter been slaughtered?"

"No doubt, brother, and if we don't escape, they'll do the same to us."

"But how can we escape? The whole length of the road is under police cordon. Anyone who leaves is shot dead."

"But let's not forget that, if we stay here, the executioners will come one day and lead us all like lambs to the slaughter."

"There's one way," Kirk said, joining Zarmair's and Sisag's conversation. "There's 4,000 of us here. We'll all attack the guards with our shovels and mattocks, capture their weapons, and go up the mountain. Even if a thousand are killed, at least the rest will be free."

"For how long?" Major Sisag asked doubtfully. "Government troops would quickly surround the mountain and besiege us."

"But aren't we surrounded now?"

"Yes we are. But we still have one hope."

"Hope?" Kirk and Zarmair asked, looking at their friend.

"Yes, hope" replied Sisag, wiping his brow to remove the sweat that had gathered there with a handkerchief. "Only we have to know whether the government's aim is to wipe out the people only in the Armenian provinces or all Armenians in the whole of Turkey. If it's the first, then we can hope that, having achieved its aim, it will then leave us, and the rest of Armenians, in peace. In that case, our revolt will endanger the survival of the remaining people. But if it's the second, then it won't make any difference whether we rebel or not, as we're condemned to death one way or another."

"I believe that," Lieutenant Zarmair said, "the government's aim is to wipe out the Armenian people root and branch. But I wouldn't like to play with the fate of the remainder of the people for the sake of a one–in–a-thousand chance."

"So," Kirk said, "there's nothing for us to do other than to sit with our arms folded, hoping that the government has achieved its aim, and that there no longer is any danger to us. I don't believe that, but so be it."

* * *

About two weeks after the soldiers in the labor battalion had heard the bad news quoted above, they awoke one morning to find that their spades and mattocks had been removed and about 300 cavalrymen – who had arrived from who knows where – had surrounded the tents.

"Everyone is to get his pack and come out of the tents," the sergeant-major in charge of the police ordered. "You're going to Sivas."

"Boys," the Armenian soldiers said to one another, "they're going to take us to be massacred…"

"But the work here hasn't finished," Major Sisag said, approaching the sergeant-major. "Why are we going to Sivas?"

"There's more important work to be done there," the sergeant-major replied. "But don't delay, line up in fours."

4,000 young Armenians assembled as ordered without complaint.

The cavalry commander – a fat major with glasses – started his horse forward and said to the Armenians, "Armenians from other encampments, taking advantage of lighter guarding arrangements, have deserted. To be careful, you are to be tied together in groups of 16. Let the police do their duty."

4,000 Armenian soldiers, without any resistance, extended their arms to the guards, while the newly arrived cavalry with fixed bayonets took up threatening positions around them.

When the operation was complete the major said, "Farewell," in a kindly voice. Then, turning to his soldiers, he added, "Lower your weapons. About face. Forward!"

300 cavalrymen turned their horses around and departed westwards, led by the major, while 4,000 prisoners, accompanied by 40 policemen, went east.

"There's no doubt now of the government's aims," Lieutenant Zarmair said to his two companions, who were one on either side of him. If only we had rebelled, we would at least have died fighting."

"I suggested that, but you didn't accept it," Kirk said.

"I was sure too, but I didn't want to endanger the people's well being for the sake of a thousand-to-one chance," Zarmair said.

"So, now what?"

A soul-destroying silence reigned. Major Sisag, who had heard the two hotheaded young men's conversation, looked to the front like a defeated general.

They walked a long, long way.

Burning under the rays of the July sun, they passed through mountains, valleys, passes and rivers. Every time they went through an uninhabited place, they were afraid and held each other's hands, thinking that it was there that they would be slaughtered. When they left it, they were very affected, comforting themselves with the thought that they really were going to Sivas.

Their police guards halted them one day outside a village. The sergeant divided the prisoners into four equal groups and, under the guard of ten policemen for each contingent, sent them in different directions, saying that all of them would be working on the same road, but would camp about one hour's distance from one another at different points.

The group with the three officers in it went for a considerable distance along a proper highway then, moving off it onto a narrow path, went on to a mountain road.

The boys' hearts started beating hard with terror. Were their guards duping them, or were they really going to a camp?

They went for two hours along rocky paths, climbing the slopes and going down the mountainsides. They finally reached a valley, in whose bottom was a fast-flowing river. Following its bank, they entered a lonely vale where, as if by command, they all stopped together.

A dreadful smell percolated from the depths of the valley.

"They've thrown the carcasses of dead army horses up there," the policemen said to calm the Armenians. "Let's go through this place quickly."

The young Armenians quickened their steps. Shortly after however, a horrifying scene chilled the blood in their veins.

A group of animal-featured people looking like woodcutters – whose clothes consisted of white pantaloons, red fezes and simple sandals – were sitting at the water's edge and were sharpening their axes or securing the stocks.

The Armenians sweated with the dread of death until they passed those wicked-looking individuals. But their relief only lasted for a moment. They soon joined a narrow road, one side of which rose towards a hill, the other being the swiftly flowing river. Then many other woodcutters advanced down the hill, all of them holding swords and axes.

Their route was closed. Caught between swords, with their hands bound together, the imprisoned Armenians, in groups of 16, didn't know what to do.

Suddenly they heard the cry *"Ya'allah!"* and then saw white shirted, red fezzed and sandal-wearing men advancing from all directions, striking arms and legs off with their weapons right and left, splitting skulls and breasts.

A heavy sword hit the nape of Major Sisag's neck, the blow of an axe smashed Lieutenant Zarmair's backbone and Sub-Lieutenant Kirk received a blow from a scythe to his stomach.

Kirk instinctively held the wound closed and fell on his face, between his two lifeless friends' bodies.

As he fell, he momentarily realized that other hot and wet bodies were falling on him. Then he closed his eyes and everything went black.

* * *

When Kirk awoke from his death-like state, he turned his eyes in every direction and was extremely surprised to find himself in a cart that was moving along a potholed road to melancholy creaking noises.

An old but very healthy peasant, who was walking next to the cart, seeing Kirk come to, crossed himself and with a cry of joy and shouted, "Yeghsa, Yeghsa, come here, the boy's woken up!"

Kirk wanted to ask where he was, but found that no sound came from his dry throat. It seemed as if a large heavy stone had been put on his stomach and had fixed him to the floor of the cart. His body was covered with cuts, bruises and abrasions and hurt terribly. His heart was beating in an unusual manner, his cheeks were burning, and his head was spinning as if he was seasick, the more so as the cart bounced and swayed along the poor road.

Shortly afterwards an old woman came running up and cleaned the black dust that had settled on his forehead. Then other women, men and children surrounded the cart and enclosed the 'recovering dead man' with their anxious glances.

Kirk looked into their eyes silently, making a supreme effort to collect his wits, but without success. Fainting shortly afterwards, he once more closed his eyes and was buried in the pit of unconsciousness.

When Kirk opened his eyes once more, it was dark. He was lying on his back in the cart, but this time it was stationary in a field.

The same old peasant and old woman were sitting near the cart and were busy milking a black goat. Seeing that their invalid had woken up, they quickly got to their feet and tenderly asked how he was.

Kirk couldn't speak. He opened and closed his mouth, to make them understand that he was thirsty and wanted some water.

"No, I can't do that," the old man said, shaking his head in a negative way, "Let tonight pass and I'll give you three drops tomorrow."

"Water, water!" Kirk begged, putting his whole effort into his expression. "Give me some water, my insides are burning!"

"Have patience, my son," the old woman said, comforting him, wiping his dry lips with a wet cloth. "We'll give you some tomorrow."

Putting his tongue out, he touched the wet cloth that was wiping his lips, with the hope of cooling his burning heart. Then he closed his eyes and slept in a weakened, broken state.

When Kirk awoke from his long spell of drowsiness the following day, he saw that the sun had risen and the peasants were already on the road.

"Who are you? Where are you going, and where are you taking me?" he asked, finding the ability to speak for the first time.

"Quiet! Don't talk, be still," chided the old man in a fatherly voice. "We'll tell you later."

"But what's on my stomach that's stopping me from getting up? Why have you tied me to the cart?"

"Shush…" said the old man, putting his finger to his lips.

Kirk closed his mouth and turning his head right and left looked around with the hope that he would understand something from what he heard and saw.

About 250 people of both sexes, mixed up with a herd of foals and goats, was moving along the edge of a dusty road, some on foot, some on donkeys and others in carts. Two policemen on horseback followed the crowd, continually scolding those people who, tired from walking, sat at the side of the road to rest.

"Come on, come on! We humoured you, and now you're taking advantage," they said, waving their whips.

"What's the matter, Ismail Bey? Let's take a rest. Our feet are swollen," those who were sitting down begged.

"You've taken too much time. We'll use the whips on you next!" the policemen said.

The exhausted travellers would get to their feet and limp after the caravan.

Who were these people? Where had they come from and where were they going? How come the police treated them with such familiarity? Also, how did he come to be among them?

Kirk tried to understand what had happened to him. He remembered walking a long way with his military friends and their entering the valley; the dreadful stench of corpses; the swiftly running river; the shout *"ya'allah!"*; Major Sisag's head being lopped off by a sword; Lieutenant Zarmair falling with his back shattered; and then he himself receiving a tremendous blow to the stomach with a scythe...

Then? What had happened after that? How was it that he found himself with these strange people? "But who are you? Where did you find me? Why don't you answer my questions?" he asked the old man who, just then, was making a shade to keep the sun off him.

"I'll tell you in a few words," the old carter said, "but on the understanding that you won't ask any more questions. We are Armenian sieve makers; my name is Jivan. We lived near Kastamonu and were deported too. We found you alive, among other bodies thrown there, on the sandy bank of the Kizil Irmak river three days ago as we were crossing it. There was a large wound in your stomach and part of your intestines were hanging out. You had fainted, holding the wound tightly closed with your hand. We have no idea how long you had been in the water or where the waves had brought you and your comrades from. Holding you by your shoulders and legs, we put you in our cart. We replaced your intestines, washed and bandaged your wound, and we are pleased to have saved your life."

"I'm greatly obliged to you for all you've done for me," Kirk murmured, deeply affected by these noble actions. "How is my wound? When will I be able to get to my feet? I ask because I see that I'm occupying your one and only cart. Because of me, despite your advanced years, you have to walk."

"Don't worry about that, son. We're used to walking. As for your wound, we're hoping that it'll close in a week."

"Please excuse my asking you one more question. Why did you say 'they deported us too'? Aren't you Armenians that you say 'us too'?"

The old man didn't like the question. He sighed deeply and said, "Didn't I tell you not to ask me anything else?"

* * *

Two weeks later the caravan of sieve makers reached Oulou Keshla station.

An enormous number of people had pitched tents near the station and were waiting their turn for transport to take them to Aleppo.

Kirk's traveling companions made camp in the plain and pitched their tents.

They sold their carts and oxen, donkeys and fowl the next day and, in their turn, awaited the government order to continue their journey by train.

Kirk stayed with his saviours in their tent for another week and was looked after by Mrs Yeghsa who fed him milk from the black goat and meals she cooked.

He had hardly recovered some of his lost strength when a policeman appeared one morning and announced that they were leaving for Aleppo in half an hour.

"Are all the Armenians going?" Kirk asked worriedly.

"No, only those who are camped in this plain," the policeman replied.

This pleased Kirk because, no matter how difficult it was to part from his benefactors without compensating them in any way for their kindness, his state of health didn't allow him to undertake a long journey – especially in a crowded train. "I need some time to recover," he said to his hosts when they were tying up their bundles. "I'm sorry not to be going with you. But I'll remember what you did for me until my dying day. If I stay alive and join you in Aleppo, I promise that I'll repay your kindness a hundred-fold."

"There is no need to say that, my son," the old people protested. "We didn't do anything special, only what humanity demanded."

"No, no! What you did for me is impossible to emulate," Kirk said. "You saved my life by pulling me from among dead bodies, sacrificing your comfort, transporting me for long distances and looking after me for weeks."

"Please forget it," the old sieve maker said with obvious unhappiness. "What will you do here? You have no money or anything! Tell me what!"

"I'll find work; I'm sure that I'll be able to earn enough to eat."

Just then the train whistle sounded in the distance.

"Come on, hurry up!" the policeman ordered.

Kirk came with the old couple to the station. His attention was drawn to a large sack on Mrs Yeghsa's back in which something was moving.

"Mother, what's that?" he asked, amazed.

"It's the goat," the old lady said with a smile. "If the police see it, they'll take it away. That's why I put her in a sack. I'm taking her with me to Arabia. If we find bread there, our nourishment will be secure."

Kirk laughed at the woman's alertness and, after expressing his thanks again and again, helped them to embark and settle themselves and their possessions in a goods' wagon.

The engine's whistle sounded once more.

"Goodbye, goodbye!" the travellers shouted.

"Goodbye, goodbye! Have a safe journey…"

Old Jivan extended his hand to shake Kirk's for the last time.

When the train was moving, Kirk felt something in his hand. He looked and couldn't restrain his feelings. The noble-hearted sieve maker had put a silver piece in it.

Recollections from the Past

Seated under a tree in a distant corner of the refugee camp, Kirk thought about the incomparable misfortune his fellow Armenians were suffering.

During the time he was trying to recover his health, he had no time to think about anything other than the villainous events which had succeeded each other with great rapidity in the last few months.

What a horrific situation!

He had traveled for days with the Armenian sieve makers along bloody roads, at every step seeing distressing, horrifying scenes.

He had seen an abandoned child, an exhausted sick person, a famished orphan or crazed mother under every bush and rock. And everywhere corpses, corpses, corpses – in the bottom of valleys, in the plains, in hollows, on the banks of rivers – all of them victims of dreadful barbaric criminality, intolerable privation, or ferocious beatings.

Sometimes there were no corpses to be seen in desolate areas, but there were black splashes of blood betraying where bloody carnage had taken place. They had passed those places, treading and squashing that blackened soil under their feet, where shortly before their kith and kin had fallen with their veins emptying blood and their brains leaking from their skulls.

And what happened to them?

4,000 young men – who had been brought up by 8,000 mothers and fathers with great sacrifices – had been led, hands bound, to the banks of the Kizil Irmak river, to be axed to death by bloodthirsty peasants, who cut heads off, broke backbones, and split stomachs open.

Kirk desperately tried to wipe that frightful vision from his mind, but it was impossible. No matter how he tried to forget it, that vision, whether he was awake or asleep, was constantly before his eyes, fresher and even more alive every day.

"Let's consider for a moment that it's useless to mourn the dead," he said to himself, "so what will happen to those left alive, the dispersed remnants who have escaped the massacres, and who, exhausted, struggle to survive in their ragged tents, or on the long roads under the burning sun? What will happen to the women and girls who, although they were lucky enough not to fall into Turkish harems, now roam the streets naked and destitute? The orphaned children – the one-time jewels and pride of Armenian families – who now cried hoarsely 'we're hungry'. The old fathers crushed by sorrow, whose hearts have been deeply pierced and who, after losing status, wealth and children, hold out their hands to passers-by. The pain-afflicted mothers tortured by sorrow who, standing at every corner, beat their breasts and sob soundlessly."

Kirk had a grandfather too – his father, having died years before, fortunately hadn't seen these days – as well as a grandmother and two young sisters, one 15, the other 17 years old. What happened to them? Where did they go? Which stone were they under?

During his journey he had come across hundreds of caravans and questioned thousands of people, but had not found one person who could give him news not only of his family and birthplace, but also of the 48 villages in the whole area, which he had once jokingly called 'Little Armenia'.

What had happened to the population of that Little Armenia, for whose education and progress he had vowed to devote his whole life?

Thinking about those active and peaceful peasants, his own home and birthplace, Kirk's vision flew with imaginary wings back to the past, and for a moment he had the illusion that he was seeing himself as a little boy playing carelessly and happily in the fields around the village. "If only it was possible to turn back the wheel of life, and leave it forever in that time," he murmured sadly and sank deeper and deeper into those sweet memories of the past.

* * *

Their's was a village of 200 houses, populated completely by Armenians, in the Yozghad area, spread along a stream and surrounded by gardens and pastures. It had a breezy position and was famous for its hot springs which were to be found only a few hours' distance away.

Among the single-storied village houses, two newly built and white plastered buildings attracted the attention of the visitor: the village school and the church.

Kirk had opened his eyes in that church and, in the school, constantly practiced spelling the characters of the Armenian alphabet, created by St

Mesrob, from his *"Ayp-Pen-Kim"* book on a slate with a piece of chalk, then wiping them off.

His grandfather was the village priest. Every morning when the bell tolled, he would go to the stable with him, collect the oxen and take them to the church, where his task was to look after the animals in the church yard, until grandfather had completed morning worship.

Many devout old women would arrive at the church before them. Some would be on their knees praying, in front of the closed doors, that their hens would produce eggs every day, while others, sitting on the tombstones, chatted, waiting for the service to begin.

Kirk sometimes listened to what they said. The things the simple village women told each other! One would say that her 'Lord's Prayer' was sometimes short, sometimes long, because she would jump from 'Give us this day our daily bread' to 'Yours is the power.' Another old woman would confess that she had no 'trespasses,' while a third would declare that she always forgot 'And lead us not.'

The woman who had no 'trespasses' one day related how, early one morning on her way to church, she had seen a group of spirits in the street who, dancing in the moonlight, were eating nougat. The old woman, hidden in a corner, had watched their dance until a cockerel in a nearby henhouse had started to crow. The fairies, hearing the crowing, disappeared at once, leaving, however, the nougat dish, which the old woman had brought to the church, and which was now kept with the vellum Gospel near the stream.

The old woman whose 'Lord's Prayer' was short said that at one time their house was filled with benevolent spirits of which one – a beautiful bride swathed in white gauze – went to the stable every day and plaited the horse's tail. And a white-bearded old man always left one silver coin in the larder, which she would find when she swept it out the following day. One day the good woman had told her neighbour the secret, and after that neither the horse's tail was plaited, nor were any more silver coins found in her larder. "Yes, the secret shouldn't have been divulged," said the old lady who forgot 'And lead us not.' "The spirits don't like a lack of secrecy."

"Also the light from the sun," said the fourth old woman from the place she was sitting – who was known by the villagers as 'before or after?' because, one day, with much effort, she had cooked a wonderful meal, but had no time to eat it as she had the misfortune to lose her mother, thus putting her in a difficult position: should she mourn the dead before or after she had eaten. As the question was very difficult to answer, the poor woman went to her neighbours to ask their advice, thus gaining her nickname.

"My son," continued the fortunate one, "when he was returning from town one night, he saw a white lamb in the Turkish cemetery that was eating grass insatiably. Thinking that it had got lost, my son dismounted from his horse, caught it and put it on his horse's crupper, to bring it to the village. But there's an amazing thing! As he was riding along, his horse began to whine, as if it was carrying a tremendous load. My son, wonderingly looked behind him, and what do you think he saw? The lamb had swollen up, had got much bigger and put its legs, which now reached the ground, over the horse's flanks. My son, very frightened, threw this monster off his horse and galloped away from it. At dawn the shepherds found, at the spot where the lamb had fallen, the shrouded dead body of a man who had not been given the last rites."

The old women would continue to tell improbable stories as if they were the truth, until the priest made his solemn entrance into the yard. Then they would all be silent and stand up with respect.

Rev. Aristages, greeting them, would go and open the church door with a large key. Continually muttering prayers under his breath, he would put on the cassock that was hanging on the wall, put his black hat on his head, and go towards the altar as the people filled the church in awe-filled silence.

Three or four boys in the chancel – all wearing pantaloons and shirts – would begin singing the canticles in their treble voices. The congregation would cross themselves on their knees and with their arms wide open.

What the priest said, what the choir sang, and what they prayed, they didn't know, nor did they wish to do so. They only knew that by going to church every day, they did something pleasing to God.

One day a young man who had a wonderful voice arrived in the village. The villagers, who thought that a good voice was enough to make him a chorister, invited him to church and begged him to sing.

However, the young man only knew ordinary songs, so he put his hand over his face and sang, "Don't cry, girl, your tears will spoil your eyes, your eyes…"

Hearing this, as if angels had descended from heaven, the devout villagers began to bow and cross themselves.

* * *

When the church service was over, the priest would bless the churchgoers who kissed his right hand and the hem of his robe. He would then hang his cassock and hat on the wall, put his faded, ancient fez on his head, take his oxen and, shouting "Doha! Doha!" would go to the fields, while he and his friends of the same age would run to the stream, either to watch the ducks swimming or to throw stones the croaking frogs.

That was the liveliest time of the day in the village. The cockerels would throatily call from every pile of dung, inviting everybody to start work.

The men would go to the fields, the women to the stream to wash their white knitted linen using large mallets. Those remaining at home would be kneading flour, milking sheep or using churns.

The old women, having gone up onto the roofs, with their spinners hanging from those roofs to the ground, would spin wool or, using long poles, would scare away the lazy birds which, leaving the plentiful seeds in the fields, would come in small flocks, to steal the boiled grain that was spread out to dry in the sun.

Kirk would play with his friends until midday, making whistles from the branched of willow trees, hunting birds with catapults, climbing tall poplar trees, or riding on the backs of buffalos grazing near the stream. These buffalos would sometimes, to cool of, enter the stream and, lying down, spill their riders into the water, much to the amusement of the those watching on the bank.

At midday, tired and sweaty from play, he would return home. His mother would put the bread, hot from the oven, in front of him with honey, butter, eggs and fruit. What should he eat? Which one should he enjoy? All those appetising things would bewilder him; but he would eat and, after his stomach was satisfied, he would run outside again.

The evening calm would descend on the village. The peasants working in the fields would return talking gaily and singing, their sickles on their shoulders. In the distance dust would rise from the edges of the roads. The goats and sheep, cows and calves would come, lowing and making their bells ring. Heavily laden carts would follow, filling the streets with their deafening noise.

Kirk sometimes went with his grandfather to the fields and vineyards where he did more harm than good with his wicked play. But with the setting of the sun, he would recline on top of the golden corn or the different kinds of fruit that filled the cart and enter the village like some victorious Caeasar.

After midday on a Sunday, the villagers – sometimes from distant places – would come to their house and, saying "Bless us lord" to the priest, crouch down under the walls. Those who had a question to ask would do so. Those who dissented explained their position.

Rev Aristages would listen attentively to both sides' of arguments, smooth problems out, give them advice and send them away.

His advice was sensible, trials fair, and his judgements inviolable.

* * *

One year three mounted travellers came to their house late.

That day they were celebrating the Start of Spring: a festival left over from pagan times, when it was customary for the region's Armenian inhabitants to congregate in the area surrounding a half-ruined and abandoned hermitage to celebrate the miraculous awakening of the soil.

After the conclusion of church services, young girls, in multicolour dresses, with their hair decorated with spring flowers, and painted with henna, danced, sang, played musical instruments, ate and drank with the young peasant lads in the shade of the centuries-old oak trees around the monastery.

It was during these celebrations when the inhabitants of the villages got to know one another, arranged marriages for the girls, and established new friendships and relationships. The greatest amusement of the day was to have those who didn't go to church on Sundays be taken through streets riding on a donkey, facing the donkey's tail, to the laughter of the crowd.

There then followed the pivotal event of the whole festival: the game of mall, in which all the vigorous young men on wonderful horses, from all the villages, took part.

The picnic ended in the evening with circle-dances, after which everyone returned to their villages happily, with the intention of doing the same, on the same day, in the same place, the next year.

It had become evening and the centuries-old hermitage resumed its usual peace and quiet, when the three unknown horsemen had entered their yard.

The three of them were lively, healthy and fiery, especially the one with a bushy moustache and a long scar on his left eyebrow made by a dagger.

They were sitting cross-legged in a corner of the room and had begun talking to the priest about a serious matter. At that time the grandmother, indifferent to their conversation, was seated and spinning wool in the light of a lamp. His mother was making coffee at the stove. Kirk, with his two sisters, had retreated to another corner and was playing with a newly born calf, which they had brought in from the stable to make a fuss over.

During their game – in which they made a lot of noise and were often told off by the priest – the animal escaped from them, and stood in the middle of the room, looking stupidly around it and lowing piteously.

Kirk tried to grab the calf but, shying away, it escaped once more and fell with the whole of its wet body on the open prayer book in front of the priest's knees, making Rev Aristages angry. He got to his feet and, asking his guests' pardon, took the calf back to the stable, to leave it with its mother.

Taking advantage of the priest's absence, the man with the long scar called over Kirk and asked, "My son, what's your name?"

Despite his frightening appearance, he had a sweet voice and hypnotic eyes. Kirk quietly approached the guest and gave his name.

"How old are you?"

"Eleven."

"Do you go to school?"

"No, I've finished it."

Kirk's reply brought a smile to the guests' faces.

"You have finished? Well done! So you know how to read and write?"

"Yes."

"What do you read?"

"The Book of Psalms."

"Do you understand what you're reading?"

"No."

"Do you know science, mathematics, geography and history?"

"Pardon?" Kirk looked stupidly at the man with the bushy moustache, wondering what he wanted from him.

"My son," said the latter with a serious expression on his face, "What you've not learnt is important in a man's life. I've a son named Arshavir, two years older than you; the things he knows…! In spite of that, he's going to the Sanasarian School this year to widen his education."

"What does your son know?"

"He knows the names of all the countries where there are big cities with beautiful houses, and where people travel by steamship, trains and balloons. But first let's see. Do you know what a steamship, train and balloon are?"

"No."

"Fine. Let me explain what they are. A steamship is a large ship that can carry all the houses and gardens of this village. There are hundreds of rooms, halls, even shops and places for amusement in it. People sit in these great ships and, cutting through the waves, travel over the unlimited extent of the waters, without seeing land for days, only seeing the blue sky above and the green sea below.

"A train is made up of 10-20 carriages linked together, each one of which can carry 30-40 people with their bundles and bags. These carriages run along specially made iron roads at a dizzying speed, without a horse or ox pulling it. The travellers sit in front of windows and travel looking at the fields, villages and towns that continuously follow one another. Sometimes they go over high bridges, thrown across rivers and chasms; sometimes through long, dark tunnels that are bored through enormous rocks.

"A balloon is a large house which is suspended below a rubber sphere a hundred times its size. People sit in this house, slowly rise through the air and then, flying over the clouds, go where they want."

Kirk, completely astonished, listened to the scarred traveller, who continued, with a gentle, slow tone, "My son Arshavir knows all this. He's got books with pictures in them of all the world's wonderful places. Reading them, he knows that at one end of the world there are people who, wearing thick furs in winter and summer, live in houses made from snow; at the other end of it there are people who live almost naked on sands that burn like fire.

"My son knows the history of great cities too, where people live in a civilized way. There are tens of thousands of houses in these cities. People walk through the streets shoulder to shoulder. Omnibuses, horse-drawn carriages and bicycles travel the roads continually. Girls and boys, cleanly dressed, carry their bags under their arms, go to school. Young men go to places of amusement or factories. Women go to the markets, theaters or public gardens.

"My son also knows how, in those civilized cities, rooms are lit by pressing a button, or how, by pushing another, they cool rooms down in summer. And how they speak to people in distant cities using electricity; how they have sound recording machines that speak like men, or sing and play music. Or about fantastic machines that show, on big, white screens, people moving, walking and dancing."

It was as if he was listening to the story of a magical world; Kirk hung on every word, absorbed and entranced by everything that was said and, at the end, whispered, "I also want to got to school and learn all that."

"No, you're still young. Let a few years pass, and then you'll learn everything," the man said, putting an emphasis on his words.

The conversation came to an end with the priest's return and Kirk, having retreated to his corner, rapturously thought about all the wonders he had heard about.

So there was another world outside his village, where people flew like birds, where carriages moved without horses, where pictures moved, machines spoke, and buttons lit things up.

In his sleep that night, and until morning, Kirk wandered through that enchanted world. When he opened his eyes in the morning, he saw that the three strange horsemen had disappeared, like the spirits the 'no trespasses' old woman had seen.

* * *

The following year, one day before the festival of the Start of Spring, the same horsemen came once more to the village.

Kirk, seeing his friend, ran towards him with affectionate joy and, holding his hand, shouted with a genuine outburst, "I've been thinking about you for a year. Where did you go? Please take me to that school!"

"No, you're still young," said the guest with the bushy moustache, stroking his hair. "Your grandfather won't let us take you. But next year, when you're much bigger, we'll definitely take you."

"Where is this Sanasarian School?"

"In Erzerum, a city a long way from here."

"Are you from that city?"

"Yes, were cattle dealers.... We bring cattle to Kayseri to sell and then we go round these villages.

"Why?"

"So that we can make the villagers understand that outside the narrow confines of their lives there's a world of light, where men study, become educated, progress and enjoy life in a far more comfortable position. We're always telling the great notables and priests, but can't make them understand. They stubbornly insist on staying in their primitive state, preferring the dark to light, ignorance to science, serfdom to freedom."

"But why?"

"Ask your grandfather."

"Please excuse me, but what is your name?"

"My name is Vartan. This strong, tall friend of mine is Mourad, and the other with the blond beard, Kenneth."

That evening, all the young men and the wealthy householders of the village came together in their house. Vartan spoke to them at length. Kirk didn't understand much of what he said this time, when the words 'crime', 'oppression', 'aim', 'revolution' and 'freedom' were frequently used. But magnetised, he watched his eyes, which sparkled every time he used one or the other of those words.

Mourad spoke after Vartan, telling of brave Armenians, and of three freedom fighters who, persecuted by Turkish policemen, had found sanctuary in an Armenian monastery on the top of a mountain.

This monastery was famous not only for its ancient artefacts but also for its hospitable monks, who with Christian hospitality, kept the doors of their monastery open to all travellers.

On the day the freedom fighters obtained sanctuary, a rich Turkish merchant was also lodging there, who, according to his story, had come from an Aleppo fair with his servant and six boxes of costly fabrics he had bought.

The way the boxes had been arranged in the monastery's courtyard – put next to one another and not piled up – had excited the attention of the leader of the three freedom fighters who, taking advantage of the merchant's and servant's inattention, went towards them to find out whether they really did contain bolts of cloth.

He had hardly got ready to take the lid off one of the boxes when suddenly a voice from inside the box said, in Turkish, "Shall we come out?"

The Armenian immediately grasped the situation. There was a thief in each of the six cases – as the question was in the plural – and they had come under the leadership of the false merchant, like the 40 thieves in the *Thousand and One Nights*, to rob the monastery and possibly kill the monks.

So, imitating the merchant's voice, he said, "Wait," and explaining to his companions what was happening, said to them "Boys, one of you go and keep the merchant and his servant talking; the other come with me to sort out the thieves."

The freedom fighters' leader then went to the first box and, saying, "Get ready," took the box outside the monastery with his companion's help, as if they were moving a military rampart. They strangled the thief inside it, then returned the box to where they had found it.

After doing the same with the other five, the leader and his companion returned to the monastery's refectory, where the Turk and his servant were talking innocently with those present and waiting for the delicious meal that was being prepared.

After eating their meal and drinking their coffee the Turks realized that they were not going to be able to carry out their plan as the fighters were present, so they rose and, after thanking the monks for their hospitality, left, promising to return soon with large gifts with them.

The fake merchant and his servant with their mules had only gone as far as sound could carry, when the leader of the fighters related the danger that had been averted, and how careful the monks would have to be in future with regard to who their guests were.

The story hadn't quite ended. The two thieves returned and, galloping their horses, rushed at the Armenians, shouting and cursing at the same time.

The monks, in panic, escaped to their rooms. The three fighters however, took up positions behind the monastery door and held out against the thieves, who hid themselves behind the trees with thick trunks at the side of the road. They fired continuously and smashed all the monastery's windows.

The fighters' leader, seeing that it would be very difficult to beat the enemy in those circumstances, ordered his two men to leave by the door at the rear of the monastery's courtyard and get behind the thieves, while he kept them busy, continually changing his position and firing quickly, thus giving the impression that they were fighting the three of them.

The fighters carried out their leader's instructions and, trapping the thieves between two lines of fires shortly afterwards, killed them stone dead, thus saving a historic monastery from robbery and bloodshed.

Mourad's story created great enthusiasm among the listeners. Then Kenneth told them of an incident that had happened to him, how one day, a policeman, out of enmity, had cut his moustache, and in revenge, he had cut the policeman's head off. "They consider Armenians as sheep,"

Kenneth said, finishing his story. "The more we stay silent, the more they tyrannise us. We must make them understand that we're not sheep, and can become lions when it comes to the defense of our lives, honor and property."

They continued their preaching in the yard of the ruined monastery the following day, where, as was the custom, thousands of peasants had arrived to celebrate the festival of the Start of Spring. Then they played skilful games with horses and pikes, and finally departed, while the enthusiastic people shouted after them, "Next year, come again next year."

* * *

Vartan, Mourad and Kenneth returned the following year.

Kirk joyfully welcomed them and, throwing himself in his friend's arms, loudly shouted, "My grandfather has given permission... I'm going with you!"

"I'm pleased that we were finally able to plant a seed in this fertile soil," Vartan said, hugging him.

After the Start of Spring festival was over, they sat Kirk on a horse and took him with them to Erzerum, to the Sanasarian School.

It was as if a new world had opened before his dazzled eyes. The school, desks, books, teachers, surroundings, life... everything was new for him. The desire to get to know these new things fired his imagination and whipped up his interest.

Buried in learning and reading books, he studied continuously, researching and learning so much that before five years was up, that uneducated and naughty village boy had completely changed in mind and character.

He never saw Vartan and his companions in all those five years, simply because they went to his village in the spring and he had his vacations there during the summer.

In his fifth year however, he had the pleasant surprise, when he returned to his village, and found his three old friends there.

"Kirk, is that you?"

The three braves, delighted with their protégées progress, ran to him, hugged him and planted kisses on his forehead.

"Kirk," said Vartan, when they were leaving the following day, "There's nothing more for us to do in this region. We leave the care of this 'Little Armenia' to you."

"Yes, yes," replied Kirk, controlling his feelings, "I promise you. Just like you brought me out of the darkness, I'll work to bring my brothers out of ignorance. Your mission is finished now. Goodbye!"

Kirk never saw them again. The next year he met Sara. A year later the school transferred from Erzerum to Sivas. He continued his education for some years, until he graduated, followed by the war and military call-up.

The last time he parted from the village to go to military school in Constantinople, the whole village gathered outside their house to wish him a safe journey.

He said goodbye to them in turn, kissing the hands of his grandfather, grandmother and mother, kissing his two sisters' foreheads and squeezing the hands of all his friends and relatives.

When he mounted his horse, the villagers, proud that one of their sons was going to be an officer, shouted, "Well done Kirk" three times and fired guns in the air, while the church bell tolled with the joy of a feast day.

Then about 20 young men, also on horseback, went with him to the edge of the village, wishing him, in their simple words, their heart-felt good wishes.

"What healthy young men," Kirk murmured, looking after his compatriots for a moment. "What miracles could be performed with them, if it becomes possible to put pen and paper in their knobbly hands."

For a final time, he looked with great emotion at the fields surrounding him, without a weed or stone, as if the soil had been sieved by its owners; then there were the bulls and horses, cows and sheep that were calmly grazing in the green pastures. Last of all, he looked at the babbling stream, and his home village which stretched along its banks. Clouds of smoke arose from individual roofs, below which lived families from heaven.

* * *

Where were those families, those people, and those inhabitants now? Who knows what harem those village women who washed clothes in the stream using a mallet were imprisoned in. Who knows in which valley those brave young men who played with their sticks were slaughtered.

What was the fault of those poor people, who knew nothing beyond working day and night in the fields or at home? They had harmed no one, stole nothing from anyone, and took no one's rights. Taxes were demanded – and they gave. They tortured them – and they accepted it.

They dishonored them – and they remained silent. They struck them on one cheek – and they turned the other cheek.

All this because they felt themselves content with their work and fields.

To massacre such a humble and tough people, to destroy such a blooming country, oh what an injustice! What barbarity, what a terrible crime!

Now what would the surviving people do? What would happen to him – yes, to him – one part of a massacred people, when the curtain of tragedy had just opened over the tombs?

An Unbelievable Revelation

Kirk remained still for hours, submerged in these dark thoughts, without finding answers to the questions that were troubling his mind. "I'll throw myself under a train and free myself from all this," he eventually said to himself. "The only way to endure a disaster on this scale is to die."

But he gave up the idea, thinking that suicide was what wretched people did. Abandoning the nation in face of danger was the action of a despicable person.

Not to run away… But what could he do, alone, against a powerful empire? Could he, with his powerless arms, stop the unbridled evil that flowed like an avalanche, smashing every obstacle and barrier?

Even if he couldn't stop it, couldn't he at least save one or two people? And wasn't whatever that was saved from the claws of the enemy a benefit to his people?

No, it wasn't time to die: it was time to live!

Kirk was thinking all this, when a deep sigh cut through his thoughts, bringing him back to the real world.

"Oh! Curse you," said a trembling voice from a nearby tent. "Curse you a thousand times for bringing us to this state."

"Oh, I'm burning," said another voice from the same tent. "Haigouhi, please, give me some water."

"I'll go and get some yoghurt," a gentle female voice said. "Be patient, Harry, I'll be back in a quarter of an hour."

A little later a young woman, her head covered with cloth, left the tent and, with hurried steps, went towards the camp's market.

"There must be someone in that tent who's very ill," Kirk said, getting to his feet. "I'll go and see who the poor person is."

But there was a reason other than curiosity that made Kirk go to that tent. He had, at that moment, thought and realized that, in order to bear his personal misfortune, and the best way to forget and not feel it, was to help other unfortunate people.

The former officer, entering the tent, saw a sick young man who was lying practically at death's door on a bed on the ground.

A thin, barefoot little girl sat at his bedside, driving the flies away from her father's face. A little further away was an old man who, panting, moaning and occasionally sighing, was repairing the sole of an old shoe.

"Oh, I'm burning, give me water," sobbed the sick man, suffering the effects of a very high temperature.

"Have patience, my son," the old man said, exactly as old Jivan had said to him when he was burning with fever about four weeks earlier.

Kirk thought he saw his own one-time state in the sick person's face, which was just skin and bone. He felt as if an invisible hand was squeezing his throat to the point of strangulation.

"What's he suffering from?" he asked the old man sadly.

"Three dagger wounds," the latter replied, lifting his head from his work for a moment.

Kirk looked sympathetically at the wounded man, the little girl, and the old man. "Did you survive a massacre?"

"No, thank God we didn't see one," the tent owner said with a sigh. "But what we didn't see in Broussa we saw in Oulou Keshla."

"Why, what happened?" Kirk asked curiously.

"There's a hyena of a traitor here."

Thinking he had misheard, Kirk doubtfully asked, "An Armenian?"

"Yes, unfortunately an Armenian," the old man said with disgust. "Damn his mother's milk, damn the Holy Chrism on his forehead!"

"I don't understand, what are you saying?"

"I'm telling you the truth!"

"But who is that wicked man?"

"We don't know who he is, where he was born, where he comes from, or what his real name is," explained the old man, inviting him to sit down with a motion of his hand. "We only know that, to save his own miserable life, he changed his religion and calls himself Nouri Osman. In other words, 'Nouri de sang' – his kindred call him the murderer 'nourished on blood'. He's a sergeant major, with a swarthy complexion, and small, deep eyes. He has committed every crime to please his superior officer, the bloodthirsty Khalil."

Kirk looked astonished at the old man. Was it really possible for there to be an Armenian in the world who would pour molten oil on painful wounds? No! It wasn't possible, but a seventy year-old man had no reason to lie.

"He kidnaps women," he continued, "he makes children Muslim, has all the families that have succeeded in one way or another in staying in Konya or Bozanti, subject to his usury, or exiled. All in all his is a black soul, an evil spirit sent from hell to complete what the Turk hasn't finished."

"But where is he?" asked Kirk, gradually developing a feeling of abhorrence towards this wretched person with Armenian blood in his veins.

"Nowhere and everywhere. His field of activity is very wide and stretches from Konya to Adana. One day you'll see him in Konya, another day in Oulu Keshla, another in Eyreli, another in Bozanti, or in Tarsus. In effect everywhere where there is a household to be destroyed or a girl to be kidnapped. But his real center is Eyreli, where he's the governor's, chief of police's and military commander's – the three evil men of that region's Armenian population – docile agent.

"To satisfy his superiors, so that he can keep his position, he enters the caravans or refugee centers, has the children collected, and hands them over to Turkish orphanages. He looks at the beautiful women and girls and, with the accusation that their father, brother or husband is a revolutionary, arrests them and imprisons them in his house, where his superiors come every night to arrange drunken parties.

"In orderto keep the supply of women fresh, if he can't find beautiful girls in the caravans, he has beautiful women followed who are under the protection of Greeks, Germans and Americans. With their dirty faces hidden behind masks, he enters their houses with one or two soldiers and, frightening the inhabitants with pistols and daggers, kidnaps his victim."

"Did you say that animal with an evil soul is Armenian?" Kirk asked with an outburst of hatred.

"Yes."

"How do you know he's Armenian?"

"His many victims, who now wander the pavements, swear that he's Armenian."

"Those victims, who were accused of being the wife, sister or daughter of a revolutionary and then arrested?"

"Yes, but as I said, that accusation was for appearances' sake only. Having imprisoned them for a few days or sometimes a week, he frees them, and then the daughter or fiancée of another 'revolutionary' is arrested."

"But you didn't say who had injured your son."

"That accursed betrayer."

"Why?"

"Because he wanted to prevent his wife's kidnap."

"His wife? So your daughter-in-law has also been kidnapped?" Kirk asked, astonished.

"Yes. My daughter-in-law has been imprisoned in that animal's house for five days."

There was a heavy silence for a time, during which Mrs Haigouhi returned to the tent.

Before she arrived however, Harry had already lapsed into deep unconsciousness.

The young woman, who really was blessed with extraordinary beauty, greeted the guest with a nod of her head, and then sat sadly near her husband, waiting for him to wake up so that she could give him the yoghurt she had bought in the market.

"We're so taken with our sorrow that we forgot to ask who you are, where you're from, or which tent you live in," the old man said, finally cutting the soul-destroying silence.

Kirk briefly told his story.

"So you're also unfortunate," the tent owner exclaimed sympathetically. "You've no parents, know no one, haven't any money and nowhere to stay. So stay here with us, my son, at least you can spend the night here in this tent."

"Thank you for your hospitality," Kirk said, "but…"

"But what?" the old man interjected with a sad smile, "Do you think you make my daughter-in-law uncomfortable by your presence? Don't worry, son, we travellers have become used to that. All the men and women used to sleep next to one another in the plains. Our hearts are pure, all of us are Armenian Christians."

"I know that we're all brothers and sisters, but that's not what I meant."

"So what do you mean?"

"I'm going to find that despicable Nouri Osman," Kirk replied decisively.

"Find him, Sir, find him!" cried the young woman, shaking like a lioness. "I beg you, in the name of God, save Armenian womens' honor!"

"Don't worry, madam, I'll find him," Kirk exclaimed.

As he was beginning to get to his feet, the old man grabbed his hand and said, "Sit down, son, at least stay with us tonight."

* * *

Harry never recovered consciousness. He gave up the ghost in a coma.

Kirk and the old man buried him the next morning and, without returning to the tents, he left Oulu Keshla, having forgotten his sadness and sickness.

He wandered for a month between Konya and Adana, quizzing every Armenian he met as to the whereabouts of the traitor Nouri Osman. But whomever he asked, he received the same answer: "We don't know. Maybe he's dead. It's been a month since we last heard of his assaults."

Indeed, since the day that Kirk had set out to find the Armenian traitor, it was as if he the latter had sensed the danger he was in and so had disappeared from sight.

Not one kidnap, rape or incident of exile took place that would have allowed Kirk to follow that traitorous dog's trail.

One day however, when he was walking about in the refugee camp in Eyreli, he heard that Nouri Osman had been seen in Bozanti.

Kirk went there and, questioning the Armenian railway workers, learnt the address of the man he was seeking and hurried there.

The house had two stories, had been repaired and painted, and was located in quite a good street. Kirk, standing in the vestibule of a nearby house, carefully examined the house, when he heard someone approach him from behind.

"Who are you looking for, son?" The question had been in Armenian.

Kirk quickly turned round and saw a man of over 50 years old with a respectable face, whom he would have likened to an apostle if he had worn a robe, rather than the tattered clothing of a deportee.

"The traitor Nouri Osman," the former officer replied, thinking that someone with a noble face like his couldn't be someone bad.

"What are you going to do to him?" asked the unknown man with a mysterious curiosity.

"That's my affair."

"I know what you've come here for… but I won't allow you to do it!"

"Why not?" Kirk asked, annoyed.

"Come with me," the Armenian said gently. "I can see that you're very upset. Come to my house and I'll explain it all to you."

There was such an air of assurance in his eyes and speech that Kirk, without demur, walked silently with him, until they reached a small hut at the edge of the town.

"May I ask who you are and why you want to stop me carrying out my aim?" he said, finally breaking the silence.

"Sit down," the elderly personage said, first sitting down and having Kirk sit down on a large beam that stretched the length of the hut. "The nobility of your aim and the boldness of your character make it obvious that you're a patriotic young man, so I've no hesitation in answering your two questions. But first – who I am – provided that it remains between us."

"I promise on my honor!"

"Thank you" – and the mysterious man whispered a name.

Kirk suddenly jumped up and respectfully bowing before his host, said, "But you..."

"Calm down, my son, said the apostle-like man," taking Kirk by the hand and sitting him down next to him. Here I'm called Charles, and I want you to call me that without giving me a title. Now let's come to your second question. You want to know why I prevent you from carrying out your aim?"

"Yes," Kirk whispered, gradually calming down from his agitation and wonderment.

"It's a long story. Let me just say that I'm dealing with that traitor."

"Why don't you then?"

"Because I gave him his life in return for a promise that he'd leave the Armenians alone. Now I follow his actions step by step. He was in Eyreli, and then he came to Bozanti. If he goes against his promise in the least way, I'm ready to stab him to death with this dagger."

"So that's why there's not been any kidnaps... I was surprised..."

"Don't be surprised, son, I've removed that hyena's teeth, so he can't bite any more."

"But how did that happen? Please tell me."

"Yes, I'll tell you," Charles said, and – after lighting a cigarette – "don't you smoke? That's good, my son, if only I hadn't got used to them. But let's turn to our story."

"I too followed Nouri Osman for a long time and, like you, had decided to kill him to stop his dreadful torturing of abandoned orphans and girls. I gave him the French 'Nouri de sang' name, and swore that I'd repay him for the blood he was weaned on.

"A month ago I heard that abominable man had planned to kidnap an Armenian girl who had found refuge with an American woman in Tarsus. As soon as I heard the news, I set out and, after walking for two complete days, arrived late at night on the third day at Tarsus station.

"I first thought of going to the American woman's house to warn her of the danger she was in. But I decided not to, thinking that if Nouri Osman had kidnapped the girl the day before, my warning would be of no use; if he was to kidnap her the following night, then I'd still have time to do what I had to. If however, he was to kidnap her that very night, wherever he was he would come to the station, as there was a train leaving half an hour later.

"I'm please to say that I'd thought it out well. I'd hardly waited for a quarter of an hour when I heard a loudly creaking carriage stop at the station entrance.

"Two soldiers alighted from it, holding a woman who'd fainted by the arms between them. Nouri Osman got out behind them and who, after giving the soldiers orders, went to the ticket booth, to buy two tickets.

"The two soldiers had taken the woman who'd fainted to the train and settled her in a first-class carriage. Nouri Osman joined them shortly afterwards and after speaking to them separately – during which time he gave them money – sent them on their way, thanking them.

"Then, turning to the train official, who'd hurried to him, said, 'My wife has appendicitis and fainted in the carriage a few minutes ago. Please don't let anyone sit in her compartment.'

"'Very well, my Bey,' the official said obligingly. 'I'll call the station doctor if you would like me to.'

"'There's no need, I've got the medicines needed. Please clip the tickets and leave us alone.'

"He palmed some money into the hand of the official with his tickets and closed the compartment door.

"The train left five minutes later. Ten minutes after that, the door of Nouri Osman's compartment opened and a man, wearing a handkerchief over his face and holding a dagger in his hand, entered. I was that man.

"'Don't make a sound, Nouri Osman Bey,' I said threateningly standing in front of him. 'Don't be surprised, I'm just copying what you do.'

"Nouri Osman, taken aback, looked once at the dagger in my hand and once into my eyes – they were the only part of my face that could be seen – and began to move his hand towards the back pocket of his trousers, when I suddenly leaned the point of my dagger on his chest and said, 'Don't move, or I'll kill you!'

"The execrable being understood my resolve from the tone of my voice and decided not to resist.

"'But what do you want from me?' he asked in Turkish.

"'Speak Armenian you disgusting man!' I chided him. 'Speak Armenian! Who is that unconscious woman? Answer me!'

"'She's my wife.'

"'You're lying, you low traitor. You haven't got a wife.'

"'I swear on my honor that she's my wife.'

"'You've no honor to be able to swear, you shameless liar!'

"'But I assure you she is my wife.'

"Enough, you betrayer of your nation. You kidnapped this girl from an American teacher's house and are taking her to your masters, to receive Judas' 30 pieces of silver. Nouri Osman, this is not the first time you've done this evil. I've been following you for months. You'll drop dead and expiate all your sins.'

"Say I'll thrust this dagger into your chest very hard.

"'Don't! Don't! Don't, for the love of God' he screeched, twisting about like a snake. 'I swear on Jesus Christ that I won't hurt the Armenians any more.'

"'How can you swear on the Christ you've disowned, you apostate ruffian!' I said between my teeth.

"'Forgive me, I'm sorry for all I've done,' he bawled in pain.

"'You're not sorry. If I let you live, you'll start again tomorrow, you wicked dog!'

"'I swear I won't!'

"'So what are the things you've done now, you cursed criminal?'

"'What could I do, brother? My superior forced me to do it. "If you've become a real Turk, bring me Armenian girls" he'd say.'

"'And you would take them to save your own skin?'

"'I said that I regret what I've done. Yes, I should have died, and shouldn't have committed crimes against my fellow Armenians. But life is sweet... I went as low as becoming a betrayer.'

"'You'll die, you unfeeling wretch,' I said pushing the dagger a little more into his chest 'as your sins are very heavy to forgive.'

"'I beg you, I implore you, spare my life! I repent! If I do even the smallest thing against my fellow Armenians, kill me. May my blood be yours!'

"'Will you return to your religion?'

"'Yes, but not now. As you know, thanks to changing my religion, I'm serving in the army as a sergeant major. Until I return to my former religion, I'll use my position to lessen the results of my crimes.'

"'I give you your life,' I said, 'but be sure, Nouri Osman, you can't escape my vengeance.'

"'Do what you like if I don't keep to my promise!'

"'And if your superior demands an Armenian girl from you?'

"'I won't obey. Let him send me to a labor battalion! From now on I won't hurt a hair of an Armenian's head.'

"'Nouri Osman, are you saying this under duress, or have you really repented?'

"'I swear by the most sacred holiness of the Armenian Church. I've truly repented.'

"'I repeat: you should know that, if you cheat me, wherever you hide, whatever you do, you can't escape me. As you don't know my face, I'll appear before you like the angel of death at the most unexpected moment.'

"'You'll see that I'll keep my promise.'

"'Now let's come to the real issue. Does your commander know that you've come to Tarsus to kidnap this girl?'

"'Yes, he does.'

"'What's your superior's name?'

"'Captain Khalid.'

"'Your name?'

"'Oh, I can't tell you that.'

"'Very well. I'll call you by your Turkish name, Nouri Osman Bey. If I return this girl to her American protector, can your commander kidnap her by any other means?'

"'Yes he can as he knows the place.'

"'Now you'll give me your tickets, as well as all the money you've got, so that until I find a safe place for her. Then you get off the train at the first station and disappear from my sight.'

"'As you wish; here's the tickets and all the money I've got – 12 liras.'

"'Keep the two and give me the ten. But I remind you again and again, I spare your life as you've promised to make redress for the crimes you've committed. Be careful Nouri Osman, don't try to follow me or take revenge. We've reached the first station. I now say go in peace. See that you return to your religion at the first opportunity, and from today begin to help your fellow Armenians. They've suffered a great deal from the Turks, at least may they suffer no more at your hands.'

"When Nouri Osman left the train, my first action was to remove the handkerchief from my face and quickly go to the kidnapped Armenian girl, who was still unconscious on the opposite seat.

"Fortunately there was a carafe of water in a corner of the compartment. I immediately sprinkled some water on her face and, rubbing her hands and neck, I was able to bring her round.

"'Who are you? Where am I?' the poor girl groaned, as soon as she was able to speak.

"'Don't be afraid, my girl,' I said, taking her trembling hands in mine. 'I'm an Armenian. I've rescued you from your captors and am taking you to Adana, to put you in a place of safety.'

"'Oh, I can't believe my happiness. Who were the masked men?'

"'Didn't you see their faces?'

"'No, they were always masked. I don't know what happened after they put me into the carriage.'

"'It's good that you don't know. Don't worry any more, you're safe.'

"'Are you my rescuer? Let me kiss your hands!' she said suddenly, madly taking my hand.

"'There's no need,' I said. 'Tell me, do you hurt anywhere?'

"'I'm not in pain, but I'm frightened that my captors may return.'

"'Don't worry, my girl, two of your captors were hired soldiers; they received their rewards and stayed in Tarsus. As for their leader, he gave his word of honor that he'll not hurt you any more.'

"'Word of honor?'

"'Yes, my girl, believe me. That man won't harm you or any other Armenian.'

"'Please tell me your name, so that, until the end of my life, I can remember you with thankfulness and pray for you.'

"'Leave your prayers,' I said with a laugh. 'I spent the whole of my life in prayer, but it was of no use. My name is Charles. Your name?'

"'Sara, Sara Sarkisian.'

Kirk, who until this point had listened with rapt attention to the story, suddenly uttered a roar, "Did you say Sara? Sara Sarkisian? But where was she from?"

"From Erzerum," murmured Charles. "But why do you tremble, do you know her?"

"She's my fiancée, my fiancée!" Kirk shouted, jumping to his feet. "Where's she now?"

"I've a compatriot in Adana named Lutfik who, with my approval, has apparently become a Turk. He runs a pickle factory. About 50 women that I've saved work in that factory. I took Sara there too. I gave her the ten liras I took from Nouri Osman and told her to look after herself."

"Is she there now?"

"Of course!"

"But I don't understand. How did she get from Erzerum to Tarsus?"

"Sara told me everything that had happened to her. Her father, the wealthy Master Sarkisian, was killed during a beating. They handed her brother to the 'chettehs'. They were deported from the city and her mother was killed before her eyes. Twelve of them escaped from the massacre and went to Harput. From there, with the help of the American consul, some of them went to Aleppo, the rest to Tarsus."

"Enough!" cried Kirk with an affected voice. "Give me your hands, at least let me kiss them, my friend. You didn't save the life of only one person, but two."

* * *

A few days later, when Kirk stopped in Adana, in front of Lutfik Effendi's pickle factory, he saw that the door was closed.

"Is the factory closed today?" he asked a refugee Armenian woman who was passing.

"No, it's been closed for a week, due to the death of the owner," she replied.

"Did Lutfik Effendi die?" Kirk asked, concerned.

"Yes, apparently he committed suicide, but that's a lie; they killed him so that the factory would close and the women protected there would be abandoned in the street."

Kirk's blood rushed to his head. "But who killed that good man?" he asked with a horrified look.

"Who else but the bloodthirsty Khalid."

"Who's Khalid?"

"Sir, you must be new in this city if you've not heard of Captain Khalid."

"One of the three evil men of Eyreli?"

"Yes, that's him. That Armenian-hating monster came here ten days ago. Hearing that there were beautiful Armenian girls working in Lutfik Effendi's factory, he visited it, apparently to make an important purchase for the army. We don't know what happened between Khalid and Lutfik Effendi. Only, a few days later, Lutfik Effendi was invited to Khalid's house for dinner. His body was found in the river the next day. It was said that he'd left Khalid's house drunk and had either fallen by accident into it or had thrown himself in deliberately. It's a lie! Those who found his body said that there were stab marks on it. But who can accuse Khalid? They buried the body without a medical examination."

"What happened to the women working in the factory?"

"They scattered…! When they heard that criminal Khalid's name, they disappeared like chicks that had seen a kite."

A shudder of anger and rage went through Kirk's body from head to foot. "Madam," he said with a voice as heavy as lead, "I had a fiancée in this factory, named Sara Sarkisian from Erzerum. Do you know anything of her?"

"I don't know, my son," replied the Armenian woman. "There are quite a number of Armenian families in Adana; you should ask among them."

* * *

Kirk asked everyone and went to every house in Adana for three whole weeks. He found one or two people who had worked in Lutfik Effendi's factory who knew Sara, but they didn't know where she now was.

"She's probably left the city," Kirk said to himself. But where could she have gone? Had Khalid kidnapped her?

It was also surprising that Khalid had also disappeared too. A week after Lutfik Effendi's death, no one saw him in the city.

When Kirk had given up hope of finding Sara in the city, he went to Bozanti to find out from his friend Charles if he knew where Khalid was. He also wanted to know what the traitor Nouri Osman was doing, as he was suspicious that he was Khalid's accomplice in this crime.

Indeed, wasn't it possible that the sly traitor had told his commander that as he was under a mortal threat and was being watched, he couldn't take a direct part in the kidnapping of girls, nor prepare drunken parties in his house, but could show where they were hiding, thus continuing his service under the guise of an innocent man?

Yes, it was important to keep Charles informed of these latest developments, and together take measures against those lawless thieves, who after a month's respite, had once more begun to carry out their crimes. Who knows, maybe Charles was deluding himself, seeing that degenerate Armenian's apparent obedience, while in fact he had not stopped, by one iota, his work of betrayal.

Reaching Bozanti, Kirk went to Charles' hut.

An old woman opened the door, which surprised Kirk, as Charles was unmarried and lived there alone.

"Where's Charles?" he asked, his heart beating as if he was going to hear bad news.

"Who's Charles?"

"An old man lived here about a month ago."

"I don't know. When we arrived here two weeks ago, the hut was empty. Ask the landlord."

Kirk got the landlord's address from the old woman and asked him the same question.

"I don't know where Charles is," the latter said. "He left three weeks ago and never returned. It appears that the poor man was arrested and deported with one of the caravans to Aleppo, as there were some old shoes and underclothes which were his left in the hut that he never came back for."

Kirk's heart broke when he heard of his friend's disappearance. Was he killed because Nouri Osman discovered his identity?

Kirk went to the latter's neighbourhood to find the answer to the secret. He had hardly reached the house when a maid came out of it.

"Is this Nouri Osman Bey's house?" he asked, as if he had important business with him.

"Nouri Osman Bey no longer lives here," the maid replied, continuing on her way.

"Where does he live now?"

"We don't know. He went away three weeks ago. We're new tenants."

Nouri Osman had gone three weeks ago! On the same day that Charles had gone… The fact that both had gone on the same day reassured Kirk somewhat, as Charles hadn't been deported to Aleppo or killed as he had thought.

It appeared that Nouri Osman had changed his address for various reasons, and Charles had gone after him. But where?

Kirk left no stone unturned in Bozanti, but he found no trace of either Nouri Osman, Charles or Sara.

Continuing his journey, Kirk went to Eyreli, to see if Nouri Osman had returned there. No, he wasn't there, nor were two of the three evil men – by order of the central government the chief of police had been sent to Beybazar, and Captain Khalid to the front at Baghdad.

The wasps' nest had been upset, which pleased Kirk somewhat. The governor had been denied his two helpers, and no longer showed severity towards the Armenians. More than him, or the chief of police, it was Khalid who was the driving force behind the crimes, and if he closed his eyes to the assaults, that was simply because he joined in the parties and shameful activities. ·

But as much as it was pleasing that the organizer of the bloody drinking parties had been distanced from the Armenian refugees, it didn't explain Nouri Osman's disappearance for the simple reason that he had vanished ten days before his superior.

Where had he gone? Kirk went to Oulu Keshla, with the hope of getting some information from his friends from Broussa. But he found no one he knew. All of them had been sent to Aleppo, and there were now new refugees' tents where theirs had been.

Having lost hope of finding Nouri Osman – and reassured for a time that Charles was on his trail – he went to Konya, to try to find Sara among the Armenians remaining there. Having no success there either, he returned to Eyreli, Bozanti, Tarsus, Adana and other centers; but wherever he went, he couldn't find any information about his fiancée.

Hearing that many Armenian men and women were working on the railway line at Amanos, Kirk began to search on the line, and found a woman who knew Sara from Lutfik Effendi's factory.

"We lost each other after the factory closed," said the woman, "but I heard that Sara was working on this railway, although I don't really know on which part."

Master Sarkisian's one and only daughter a worker...! So, was that slightly-built girl who had been brought up among silks and satins, now under the sun, in the dust from the roads, using a spade or mattock, breaking stones or carrying heavy loads on her back?

Anyhow, Kirk wasn't upset; on the contrary, he was pleased that she was alive and hadn't fallen into Khalid or Nouri Osman's ravenous claws.

Sara was alive and working!

But where? Which part of the railway, whose length was a ten-day walk from one end to the other, and on which 20,000 Armenian workers labored.

Looking for Sara over that distance and among that many people was like looking for a needle in a haystack. But Kirk didn't lose hope because he knew that what he was looking for wasn't a needle, nor an expensive bodkin, but a priceless being.

Explosion

All those who've passed over the Taurus mountain chain during the war years know the feverish pace at which work progressed to complete the construction of the railway that had become vital for military transport.

More than ten tunnels were under construction simultaneously in the heart of those mountains. The workers – among whom were vigorous women – went up, entered, and came out of dark holes like ants, moving earth, rocks, cement and other building materials.

They were mostly Armenians – those not exiled to the deserts – as the government couldn't find laborers from among the local Turks who, enriched from the things the Armenians had left behind or by looting the caravans, refused to lower themselves to be laborers. It was the Armenians who worked for the German company.

Kirk entered the ranks of these laborers to be able to find Sara, as otherwise he couldn't remain as an escapee for long in that restricted area of Cilicia.

One day he was pushing a barrow filled with bricks in the tunnel, when a young man appeared in front of him. "Kirk, is that you?"

Hearing that seemingly familiar voice, Kirk was startled and looking directly at the lightly bearded laborer's face, recognised his one-time friend from Constantinople, Mardiros Sarkisian's younger son Henry. "But what are you doing here?" he asked, astonished. "You're not that old for me to say that you've been a soldier. Have the Armenians of Constantinople been deported too?"

"No," Henry said sadly. "But they deported our family because we were from Erzerum. They sent us to Trabzon by steamship, disembarked us at Samsun and exiled us, with the local Armenians, to Malatya. On the way the chettehs massacred our caravan. My father, mother and my elder brother were killed. I was somehow able to escape and ended up here. What happened in Erzerum I wonder, have you any news?"

"They suffered the same fate. Only Sara escaped."

"Really? Is my cousin alive? Where is she?" Henry exclaimed joyfully.

"She's on this line apparently. But I don't know where."

"Is Sara a laborer?"

"Yes. I'll tell you everything later. We'd better not stop here too long. The foreman is very strict. He might say something. We'll meet this evening. What's your tent number?"

Henry was about to give his tent number when he suddenly cried, "Look at that!"

On the slope of the mountain opposite – where a tunnel was being bored – a sudden, powerful tongue of flame flared, followed by thick smoke that, gradually getting larger and spreading, filled the whole atmosphere.

Kirk had hardly looked in the direction shown him when he felt a powerful earth tremor as a tremendous explosion shook the mountains.

"Help! Help! An accident's happened in the next tunnel!"

All the laborers, hearing the cry, ran towards their injured brothers. Kirk and Henry, who were among the first, saw, when they reached the site of the accident, that the smoke still obscured the mountain like a black curtain. The acrid smell of gunpowder made it impossible to breathe.

Many laborers, because of their nearness to the scene of the accident, had reached the place sooner, and were occupied in collecting the people in the accident, who despite being outside the tunnel at the moment of the explosion, were wounded in one way or other. Their bodies had been smashed by the shock when they fell onto rocks, or crushed by the heavy loads they were carrying.

Kirk and his friends immediately got to work, moving the victims to the first aid station where, after receiving first aid, those needing surgery were sent to the hospital in the nearby town on stretchers.

Other laborers, wearing gas masks, entered the thick fog and reappeared moments later with bloody and asphyxiated bodies in their arms.

Those who had arrived first found themselves in front of a pile of rock. As a result of the explosion, which happened in the depths of the tunnel, the entrance arch had collapsed. There was neither sound nor movement behind the pile, nor any sign of life.

Seeing that it was no use in trying to save those imprisoned in the tunnel, the laborers waited until the smoke cleared.

Then all of them, as one man, attacked the pile of rock and removed hundreds of bodies of both men and women, with bruised heads, broken legs, burnt hands, frozen eyes, straining mouths and transformed faces;

some were mixed with the soil like crushed worms, others were piles of flesh, blood, intestines and brains.

It wasn't possible to lift them from the ground without being horrified or their hair stand on end.

The laborers worked for three hours, removing bodies from under piles of soil and rock. They laid them out in an open field and, bareheaded, paraded past them, with the dread of seeing a friend or someone they knew there.

* * *

About a month after this horrible event, one rainy evening – heavy, continuous rain, the harbinger of an early winter, that had already started – Kirk, seated in front of a tent was drying his clothes before a fire, thinking about Henry who, the day after the explosion, had gone to Aleppo with a few others, preferring to die hungry there than to be in danger of being blown up.

Henry had also gone to find Sara around Aleppo, and promised to write to Kirk as soon as he found out something important. But he had not written a word since he had left. At the same time Kirk's search along the railway had brought no results either.

Kirk, giving up the hope of receiving news from Henry, was thinking of moving to look somewhere else, when the postman held out a sealed envelope to him.

He had no one in the world who knew his address to write to him apart from Henry, so he quickly tore open the envelope and took out his friend's letter.

After letting him know that he and his friends had reached Aleppo without any trouble – there was no obstacle to Armenians going there, it was the return that was prohibited – he wrote:

> ...So after fruitless searches in the camps at Osmaniye, Allahiye and Katma, my only hope was Aleppo itself. When I reached the city, I made my first task to go to the church, to continue my search.
>
> I'm pleased to tell you that I found a young woman named Mrs Dikranouhi who knew Sara in Lutfik Effendi's factory. I heard from her that they – four friends, in other words Sara, Mrs Dikranouhi, a girl named Arshalouis and a 40 year-old woman from Biledjik named Mrs Anna – left the factory the

very next day after it closed, frightened of the traps Khalid would set. They escaped from Adana and worked as laborers on the railway in the Amanos area.

Arshalouis died there. Mrs Dikranouhi, not being able to do heavy work, became ill and came to Aleppo. Sara and Mrs Anna remained there, in your immediate area.

So, dear Kirk, it's up to you to find Mrs Anna from Biledjik as soon as you can and send me the results using the Armenian church's address.

By the way, it's impossible to work here. Any Armenians the police catch are sent to Der Zor. My friends have already been exiled. I've been able to stay as I'm hiding in a Christian Arab's house. I'm impatiently awaiting your news…

When Kirk finished reading the letter, he immediately jumped up and, entering his tent, where a group of laborers were seated and talking, he asked, "Boys, is there anyone among you who knows Mrs Anna, a 40 year-old woman from Biledjik?"

"Mrs Anna…? We don't know her," more than ten voices said.

"As you're looking for someone from Biledjik, you should ask Ashod," said a laborer from the corner.

"Who's Ashod?" Kirk asked, with little hope.

"He's from Biledjik, and is in the seventh tent in the last line."

Kirk flew like an arrow from the tent, and drew breath at the tent he had been directed to. "Friends! Who among you is Ashod from Biledjik?"

"That's me," replied an elderly laborer, who was busy at that moment sewing. "What's up?"

"Excuse me, brother, I'd like to know if you know a lady named Mrs Anna from your town."

"We grew up in the same street. But why are you so affected. Has something happened to her?"

"No, nothing's happened to her," Kirk assured him. "I'm looking for my fiancée… I heard that she was apparently with her."

"I've not seen her since the explosion. I've no idea if she's alive or dead."

"After the explosion? Mrs Anna worked in that awful tunnel," Kirk murmured, looking into his eyes frantically.

Ashod, seeing he had done the wrong thing by thoughtlessly giving him the news, tried to redress the situation and said to comfort his young fellow-laborer, "But I didn't see Mrs Anna much before the explosion either. It could be that she's moved elsewhere since I last saw her. You know what its like here. They don't leave the laborers alone. They keep moving them about like chess pieces."

"I was at the explosion," Kirk growled in a horrified voice. "I saw the lacerated bodies of the women laborers… I'm worried that my fiancée was among them."

"As you didn't see your fiancée, it means she wasn't among them."

"But there were such unidentifiable mounds of flesh that it was impossible to even tell whether they were male or female."

"I pray that your fiancée wasn't among them," Ashod said in an affected voice.

"Oh! May you be cursed, Nouri Osman, you Armenian traitor; and may you too, bloodthirsty Khalid, be cursed a thousand times," Kirk cried in deep sorrow as he returned to his tent. "You destroyed my home. Turks, may you be cursed forever!"

* * *

Kirk finished work with the company the next day and set out to find Mrs Anna.

He first went to the tunnel where the explosion happened to ask among the women laborers there. He found a woman from Tomarza who not only knew Mrs Anna, but had seen her alive after the explosion.

A trace of hope and happiness crossed Kirk's face. "Do you know Sara as well?" he asked worriedly.

"No, I don't."

"Did you see a young woman with Mrs Anna?"

"I may have done, but I don't remember."

"Do you know where Mrs Anna is?"

"She's probably somewhere around Entili, as the laborers who survived the explosion were sent there."

Walking along the railway and constantly asking Armenians he met, Kirk one evening finally arrived at the camp where Mrs Anna was working.

"There you are; the woman who's washing clothes in front of the third tent is her," said the last female laborer he asked.

Kirk rushed to the woman pointed out to him and, grabbing her hand, cried, in a choked voice full of emotion and urgency, "Sara! Where is Sara?"

Surprised by Kirk's mad conduct, Mrs Anna cried out in alarm.

"Don't be frightened, madam," Kirk murmured, gradually recovering himself. "I'm Sara Sarkisian's fiancée. I heard that after Lutfik Effendi's factory was closed, you worked together on this railway. I came to ask you news of her."

Mrs Anna looked at Kirk sympathetically and, after looking him up and down, said, with a voice trembling with emotion, "I don't know her, my son."

"No, madam, you do know her," Kirk said. "I know from a well-informed source that before the tunnel explosion she worked with you there."

Two tears slid down Mrs Anna's cheeks.

"But why do you cry? Please tell me the truth."

"Come inside," said Mrs Anna, inviting Kirk into the tent. "Sit down, I'll tell you the whole story."

"She died, didn't she?" the former Armenian officer said in a depressed voice.

Mrs Anna, without replying to Kirk's question said, "I got to know Sara in Lutfik Effendi's factory. She'd been through many bad times. She too, like us, was a victim of that traitor Nouri Osman. Sara was an immature and inexperienced young girl when she joined us in the factory. She became friends with me first, perhaps because I was the oldest among the women there. It was as if she was looking for a mother so that she could put her head on her breast and cry. The poor girl worked during the day and would tell me of her sorrows and torments until very late at night. She talked a lot about you to me. Your name's Kirk, isn't it?"

"Yes," whispered Kirk, nodding.

"When our factory owner was killed by Khalid, that criminal born of a viper," Mrs Anna continued, "Sara ran to me, put her arms round my neck and said 'Mrs Anna, I think there's treachery in Lutfik Effendi's death. Let's escape from this city. I've got ten liras with me and we can go a very long way and disappear.'

"'Yes, let's run away,' I said, and we, with two other friends, did so the very next day. After we reached Amanos, we met, quite by chance, one of our friend Arshalouis' relatives who had a position with the German railway company as a translator. Thanks to his intervention we registered as workers and were able to work on that line. Ten days later poor Arshalouis became ill and died, and our other friend, Mrs Dikranouhi, not being able to stand the tough life, and having resigned from her job, joined a caravan and went to Aleppo."

"I know," Kirk said, sighing deeply. "I got news of you through her."

"So she's alive? Oh, I'm so pleased!" cried Mrs Anna joyfully – then, remembering the dreadful ending to her story, she checked her happiness and said in a lamenting voice, "Sara and I, feeling quite strong, stayed where we were."

"On the wretched day of the explosion, we were carrying a large beam on our shoulders to the tunnel, where scaffolding was being built, so that they would be able to brick the inner walls and dome. We'd hardly reached within 20 paces of the entrance to the tunnel when a Turkish foreman came up to us and said to me in a reproving manner, 'What's this? Does it take two of you to carry a small beam?'

"'What do you mean, small? Can't you see, Sir, that two of us can hardly carry it?'

"'It's the company's fault that weak women like you are made work in this sort of trade,' the man said.

"'But what are women to eat, if they don't work?' I asked.

"'This is not a charity, madam, we want work.'

"'There we are, we're working.'

"'Yes, but if it takes ten people to handle one beam, the work won't be finished. Give it to you friend. She can drag it. You go and get another.'

"Seeing that there was no point in arguing – because the man could write a report and have us dismissed – I passed the beam to Sara and went to the store to get another.

"But I'd not gone 30 paces when I saw the ground slipping from beneath my feet. Then I heard a terrific explosion and was thrown to the ground with great force. What happened after that, I don't know. When I opened my eyes, I found myself in the first aid station, where there were many injured men and women. A nurse was binding the wound in my shoulder, while another was washing the blood from my forehead."

"But Sara?" Kirk asked, shivering. "What happened to Sara?"

"She was nowhere to be found. Of course, she'd gone into the tunnel."

"Oh! I knew it! I knew it!"

Kirk could not stand this terrible blow to his heart. He emitted a heart-rending scream and, taking his head in his hands, for the first time in his life, wept like a little boy, sobbing and shaking.

PART II

PART II

Death's Door

A long, long way away, beyond the deserts, in an arid place devoid of humanity, where plants couldn't take root or birds build nests, there was a wedge-shaped rock that, with sphinx-like mysteriousness, silently guarded the surrounding areas and emptiness.

It was the only thing that was raised above ground, and to which the lost travellers' steps were directed, with the hope that, if they did not find a drop of water to drink to soothe their thirsty heart, at least they would find a shady place where they could rest their weary bodies.

Coming closer to that wedge-shaped rock, travellers would see a building made of black stones and, at the middle of the front, a large door with a semi-circular top, with a high window on either side of it.

It was possible to find many buildings like this in the depths of the desert on a direct line from Damascus to Baghdad, and Aleppo to Baghdad, about three or four days' march from one another. They had been built many years before as resting places for long-distance camel caravans.

With the passing of time however, as civilization advanced, cities were linked to one another with iron rails, and such buildings lost their importance and were left to their fate.

There were only a few of these abandoned and ruined buildings still standing and, due to their geographical position, they were turned into guardhouses.

Five, ten or even up to thirty border guards under the command of an officer lived in those guard posts, watching over military transport movements or looking for smugglers, bearing in mind that beyond where they were stationed, untrodden Arabia began, stretching to the Persian Gulf, the Red Sea and the Indian Ocean.

This building, leaning against the wedge-shaped rock at the southern end of the desert between Mosul and Der Zor, was converted into a military post.

Passing through the great door with the semi-circular top, one would see nothing untoward at all; just a large square yard, in the middle of which rose a well, while in the distance there was the black rock, with a strong iron door closing and opening in it.

On two sides of the yard, as well as in the front, were rooms supported by tall pillars and gave the appearance of being guest chambers. Under these rooms, in other words on the ground floor, which was part of the yard, was the area where horses and camels were tethered.

The tall door to the building separated these upper chambers into two separate sections, which were accessed by a staircase on each side of the door.

Each upper chamber comprised of six rooms, with a balcony at the front. Four of these rooms were to be found at the sides of the building, the other two at the front. Each room had a window looking into the yard. The rooms immediately on either side of the main door actually had an extra window each, looking outward, and were used to see who was coming or going.

As ordinary as it looked from the inside, from the outside it seemed to be a mysterious place, especially since, apart from the great door and the two windows, there was no other opening in the fortress-like walls.

It was especially fearsome at night, seeming like an enormous skull put on a large tray, whose forehead was the black rock, the nose cavity was the door, and the eye sockets were the two outward-facing windows.

Captain Khalid, on his way to the Baghdad front – the most brutal of the three evil men of Eyreli – had established himself in this military post, transforming it into a most disgusting theater of debauchery and dreadful crimes.

It was Death's Door, the slaughterhouse of tens of thousands Armenian deportees, the grave of thousands of Armenian virgins.

* * *

One day in May 1916, at about 2:00 o'clock in the afternoon, the bloody-jawed monster walked up and down like a wild animal in his office – the room on the left-hand side of the main door – making the floorboards under his feet squeak.

He was tall, with a swarthy, pockmarked face, a large moustache and red eyes that gave him a terrible appearance, especially when he was in a rage.

This coarse, clumsy son of a Turk, beside whose barbaric nature Genghis Khan and Tamerlane would pale into insignificance, still could not accept the attempt on his life by a young Armenian.

Six days before, according to habit, he had gone to the camp at Der Zor to get a caravan of 1,000 people and to bring them to imprisonment under the black rock. Before that day he had brought many, many caravans of Armenian deportees there, with no one making any protest.

That 'cursed' Armenian however had dared not only to shout at him ferociously, but also to raise his hand against him, rushing at him with a dagger. Although the Armenian had paid for his sin under the bayonets of selfless soldiers, the boiling, tremendous poison of hatred in his soul had not yet abated.

Although he had returned from his tiring journey only a quarter of an hour earlier, he still had not sat down and, with his hands in his pockets, walked up and down the room, thinking of new plans. At the same time he was indirectly frightening the 30 or so beautiful women and girls who he had had imprisoned in the 'women's cage'. (That was the name given to the room, number 3, next to Khalid's bedroom.)

"Hammed!"

The monster's deep voice rang out suddenly, frightening the imprisoned women.

His faithful servant came out of the room, which was against the black rock at the other end and ran to his master. He gave a military salute and stood still.

"Hammed, I'm tired. I want to go to bed. Is my meal ready?"

"In five minutes, Sir."

"Give the women some food. Send Corporal Reza Bey to me."

"Immediately, Sir."

Shortly afterwards a short military man, burnt by the sun and as black as an Arab, entered and, bowing low, said to Khalid, "Welcome back, Sir. How are you?"

"Thank you," Khalid replied. Did anything happen during my absence?"

"Nothing, Sir."

Khalid felt pleased at this answer. "Have the camels returned from Der Zor?"

"Yes, Sir, a week ago."

"So they must be quite rested. Can Rasum leave tomorrow?"

"He can, Sir."

"Is there much left?"

"Yes, Sir."

"Open the storeroom."

"Yes, Sir."

The two soldiers, passing the 'women's cage', entered Room 5.

"How many bales will they make?" Khalid asked, showing, with his foot, a heap of clothing – every colour and size, old and new, men's and women's, piled up in the middle of the room.

"Ten or twelve, Sir."

"How much is in the next storeroom?"

"Let me open it and you'll see. It'll make five or six boxes."

The quartermaster Reza Bey opened Room 4 and invited Khalid in.

There were different kinds of underclothes thrown in one corner; shoes of every colour and size in another; in a third there were hats, socks and handkerchiefs; and in the fourth razors, cigarette boxes, pipes, wallets, pencils, notebooks and other things.

"Good. Parcel these all up. A thousand people are on their way… the place should be made ready."

"Yes, Sir."

"What's that?" Khalid cried, suddenly frowning. "I can see a watch among the pencils."

Confused, Corporal Reza Bey bent down and picked up the watch. "Please excuse me Sir," he stuttered, "it's slipped through without us noticing."

"How many slip-ups have there been, Reza Bey? I gave you strict instructions that any money, jewellery and similar items are to be stored in the box in my bedroom."

"You're right Sir, but…"

"There are no buts! Be careful. If we sell watches at the price of pencils, it's not worth carrying on with this business."

"Please excuse me, Sir! I swear that from now on there will be no more mistakes… I'm personally going to check their pockets."

"Begin tying up the bales immediately. Rasum can take them tomorrow."

"Very well, Sir."

While Corporal Reza Bey ran down the stairs to give his men their orders, Khalid passed the window of the 'women's cage' like a blood-thirsty hyena, glancing horridly through the window.

The table was laid in his apartment, and his servant was respectfully standing near it.

"Hammed, did you give the women some food?" Khalid asked, sitting at the table.

"Yes, Sir," the servant replied. "But they won't look at it, although they've not had much to eat on the journey for six days."

"They'll behave better later," said the monster. "Pull my boots off."

* * *

The situation in the 'women's cage' was terrible.

Khalid, with ten soldiers, had come to their refugee camp six days earlier. Presenting himself as the deportee inspector, he had already been there four times and put four caravans of 1,000 people each on the road, apparently to take them to Mosul and to put them to work there.

All of them, without being suspicious of Khalid's nefarious activities, had registered and joyfully started out, thinking that they would escape the murderous camp life.

But one Armenian, who had gone with the last caravan and was thought to have died on the journey, had solved the mystery of the deportations and returned, telling everyone that Khalid wasn't taking the caravans to Mosul but to Death's Door.

Four days after this dreadful revelation Khalid had come once more and ordered 1,000 people to get ready to set out.

Seeing that no one moved, he dropped his mask of friendliness to Armenians and, with his soldiers, he entered the tents to forcibly put the caravan together. It was then that a young man, armed with a dagger, had rushed towards the mass killer. The man had hardly got near Khalid when he fell, bayoneted, under the horses' hooves.

Khalid and his adjutants, even more enraged by this attempted assassination, had got the caravan on the move with beatings and torture.

They had walked for five days through deserted dry plains, burnt by the sun and parched with thirst. On the sixth day, in other words, that morning Khalid, seeing that the caravan was marching very slowly, he had separated himself and his devoted servant from it with the women he had chosen and gone on ahead, leaving his lieutenant and soldiers to bring the caravan after them.

On the way Khalid had got drunk, continually taking a bottle of *oghi* from his pocket and drinking. He had taken his revenge and anger out on the poor Armenian women, who couldn't keep up with his and his servant's horses.

They had finally brought and imprisoned them in that evil-smelling room, from where they could hear, from one side, the animal-like sound of Khalid's snoring – assuredly to gather his monstrous energies – and from the other side, the noise of the soldiers' feverish efforts to fill the boxes and nail the lids on them – to make room, of course, for clothing taken from new deportees.

Poor women! They didn't know for whom to cry and for whom to grieve. For themselves, who would shortly be sacrificed to animal lust, or their loved ones who, very soon, would be entombed beneath the black rock?

Towards evening they heard a sound like thousands of voices from the depths that gradually became clearer as the minutes passed.

The caravan was approaching. Their parents…!

In less than half an hour, the atmosphere was filled with the sounds of weeping, and the shouts and screams of the song of death, as well as of whips and swearing.

The caravan had seen Death's Door and did not want to enter it. The soldiers, with fixed bayonets, drove the people forward, bayoneting anyone who stopped.

"Have mercy on us for the love of God! Don't kill us! Spare us!" cried many suffocating voices.

"So move on!" the thunderous voices replied.

"Where are you taking us?"

"Inside… Inside… the courtyard."

The people, with despairing cries, entered the courtyard. The outer door was closed behind them, and the black rock's solid door opened before them.

"Forward!"

"Where?"

"There, there, the cave!"

"But are you going to bury us alive in that tomb?"

"Walk on, you wicked people!"

It was Khalid who was yelling, having woken from his sleep. Leaning on the upper floor's balcony-handrail, he roared like a rabid animal,

"Walk if you don't want me to order all of you to be bayoneted to death here! You dared to raise your hands against me, didn't you? See what I'll do to you! If your gods came, they'd not be able to save you from me. Walk! There! There... your mausoleum!"

There were shouts of protest from the crowd, heart-rending pleas and sobbing whispers.

The soldiers, unfeeling and merciless towards the people's sea of torment, began to strike out, beat and whip.

Shortly after that, Khalid, Hammed, Corporal Reza, the camel driver Rasum and six other soldiers ran down the stairs and, helping their murderous friends, succeeded, after killing a few people, in getting the remainder into the cave.

Then the iron door to the cave was closed with a squeaking noise, and the silence of a cemetery replaced the hellish noise of the people.

"Clean the ground!" Khalid ordered.

A group of soldiers dragged the bodies away, while others got pails of water from the well and poured them on the ground, and others cleaned the bloody places with fern brooms.

Five minutes later, heavy footsteps went up the stairs and stopped outside Room 3.

"Hammed!"

"Yes, Sir!"

"Open the cage!"

The women, having heard, seen and understood all that had happened, held one another and retreated, as far as possible, to the depths of the room, thus making a solid mass of 30 people.

Then the door opened and Khalid entered and looked at the women, huddled together on the floor, with reddened eyes like those of a mad bull.

"Stand up!" he ordered a young girl who was hardly 20 years old and who, humbled and reduced by terror, had tried to maker herself invisible...

The victim, bewildered, looked up.

"Get up!" Khalid roared, cracking his whip in the air. "Did you hear me? I'm the god of this place. Anyone who doesn't obey me is crushed under the steel heels of my boots. Get up and walk in front of me!"

* * *

In the right-hand upper room, which had been assigned to Khalid's 24 soldiers as their mess, joy reached its zenith that night.

A dinner table had been set in the hall next to the great doors, around which the soldiers ate, drank and sang continuously.

At a high point in the jollities, the door to the hall opened and Hammed entered, holding the half-dead body of a young girl in his arms.

"Is she dead?" asked the soldiers, seeing the girl's closed eyes, disarranged hair and ripped clothes.

"No!"

"So why's blood coming out of her mouth?"

Without replying, Hammed took his burden and laid it down in the next room that, like Khalid's bedroom, opened on the hall.

"Well done Hammed!" cried the soldiers, chuckling with pleasure. "Take and drink this cup, my friend."

Cups were offered to Hammed from all sides.

Khalid's devoted servant took the cup nearest him and, putting it to his lips said, "To your good health!"

"Have a cup from me, Hammed!"

Hammed drank a second cup. "Thank you!"

"A cup from me too!"

"To your health, my brother!"

While Hammed was enjoying the plaudits proffered by his comrades-in-arms and was drinking cup after cup and enjoying the food on the table, a thin officer in a lieutenant's uniform came in from the adjoining room and, addressing those present, said, "She's a lovely piece, boys. Hammed, how many have we got tonight?"

"I really don't know. The second one's in my master's room."

"Long live Khalid, long live Hammed!" the soldiers cried, lifting their cups in salute. "Another, Hammed."

"Thank you boys, I must go. My master may need me."

Hammed descended the stairs with quick strides and, going up the opposite one he stood outside his master's door like a faithful dog, so that if he called, he could enter immediately.

Inside, the tiger-like monster was wrestling with a woman.

From the woman's cries of pain it was obvious that Khalid had knelt on her and was biting her arm, shoulder, breast, face and wherever his sharp, ravenous, animal teeth could reach.

"I'll tear you to pieces with my teeth," he growled in a frightening voice. "You must submit to me. Here in the desert there's no god but me. Every resistance must be smashed before my will."

Then taking her neck in his strong hands, he squeezed it and said, "I'll kill you like this, like a kitten. Do you understand? You must obey me. There's no other way."

There was a deep silence.

In all probability the woman was lying unconscious on the floor.

All that the women held in the 'women's cage' could hear was the wild beast's debauched murmurings.

* * *

12 days after these barbaric crimes, a caravan of camels nonchalantly entered Death's Door. Three soldiers, who were riding on camels, got down. While two of them were untying the loads of provisions, the other hurriedly ascended the left-hand room's staircase and respectfully stood before Khalid.

"Welcome back, Rasum," the latter said. "You went and returned safely?"

"Yes, Sir. Colonel Hamdi Bey has a letter for you." He held out the letter to his superior while he put a heavy money belt on to the desk.

"Is that all?" Khalid asked, referring to the money belt.

"Second-hand dealer Selim hasn't paid the major part of his debt," Rasum said.

Khalid silently read the letter. "Yes, from now on we shouldn't do business with him," he said, throwing the letter on the desk. "You can sell the goods to whoever pays in advance. Thank you, my son, you must be tired. We'll talk again later."

Saluting, Rasum left the room.

Khalid walked up and down the room for a while, and then raising his voice, shouted, "Hammed!"

"Yes, Sir?"

"What news from below?" he asked the servant as he entered.

It's as silent as the grave, Sir. There were sounds of crying until yesterday evening from the depths of the cave... but there's no sound today."

"Are you sure they're all dead?"

"Yes, Sir."

"Go and open the door and air the cave well. Tell Reza's men to strip the corpses tomorrow."

"Please tell the soldiers yourself, Sir. If I tell them, they'll complain."

"Very well. Go and do as I ask. Send Lieutenant Mahir Bey to me."

A thin officer with a pale face entered shortly afterwards.

"The soldiers are right if they don't want to enter the cave to remove the dead people's clothes," Khalid said, offering his associate a cigarette. "I think that the Armenians should be stripped before they go into the cave."

"It's not easy to make thousands of people naked," Mahir pointed out, crossing his legs as he sat down opposite Khalid. "Can't you see how much those worthless people resist?"

"There's another way," Khalid said. "We'll keep ten people from the next caravan aside, and give them the task of moving the bodies. When they've finished, we get rid of them too."

"That reminds me of something we did," laughed Mahir. "Last year I was stationed in the Khnous area. They sent thousands of male deportees to be killed there. The most tiring thing was, after they were killed, their burial. But after much killing we learnt our lesson. We selected 50 of the strongest telling them that they were innocent. We had the rest dig a great pit and, when they'd finished digging it, we'd kill them all and tell the 50 men still alive that, as a thank you for the favour we'd done them, they should put all the bodies in the pit and bury them. After the job was completed, we had them dig their own graves, this time holding one man alive. We had him bury his friends, then killed him too."

"We could do the same here too. Take 15 soldiers with you to the camp tomorrow to lead all the refugees here."

"Aren't you coming with us?"

"I'll accompany you as far as Der Zor," Khalid said. "But then I'll be going further with Hammed."

"Where are you going?"

"I understand from Hamdi Bey's letter that a new refugee camp has been set up between Rakka and Der Zor filled with refugees from Ba'ab, Hammam, Meskeneh and Ras-ul-Ain. They're probably Armenians from the Roumeli, Izmir and Cilicia regions and, compared with those from the eastern provinces, are richer and have more beautiful girls."

"Of course, they've been robbed fewer times and had fewer kidnaps on the way."

"There are very beautiful women, especially among those from Broussa, Adabazar and Adana. Eight months ago, when I was in Eyreli, I had one every night. Many of them were deported to Aleppo. My aim is to find out what state that camp's in."

"That's a good idea."

"Hamdi Bey also wants a… maid. He says that she should be the most beautiful woman in the desert. I'll take one from there to him."

"Of course, of course! He closes his eyes to our illegalities. He deserves not one, but a thousand maids."

"Before I forget, Mahir Bey, when you lead the refugees here, don't forget to remove the clothing from those who've died on the way. Take everything."

"But if we begin to loot the corpses, the people in the caravan will become suspicious," Mahir pointed out.

"Don't rob them. Let the poor people in the caravan do that," Khalid said. "At the end, aren't they all ours? Hamdi Bey writes that there's great demand for underclothes and clothes on the market. In this trouserless country every piece of cloth sells at the rate for silver. When you lead the caravan here, do as I say; in other words keep ten of the strongest and imprison the rest in the cave after, of course, putting the most beautiful in the 'women's cage'. Reza Bey will stay here and prepare the bales. A week later Rasum will load the camels and leave. Go and tell the soldiers to get ready for tomorrow's journey."

* * *

When Lieutenant Mahir told the soldiers the news of the marauding party, they threw their caps in the air with joy.

"Mahir Bey," asked a soldier who was sitting in a corner playing cards with three others, "are we bringing another thousand again?"

"No, this time all the refugees remaining in the camp," replied Khalid's right-hand man, with a devilish sense of pleasure.

"Hurray!" shouted all the soldiers together. "Why didn't you say that there'd be a lot of booty?"

"And don't think this is the last! Khalid Bey is going to look at a larger refugee camp."

"Where is it?" the intrigued soldiers asked.

"It's like the refugee camp beyond Der Zor, but further away."

"Lieutenant," said camel driver Rasum, raising his head from beneath the bedclothes, "You go and bring the caravans and enjoy the women… but also think of us. Don't forget that we're God's creatures too."

"Be quiet, you lecher!" Mahir cried jokingly. "We've kept a wonderful surprise for you and your two companions."

"A surprise?"

"Yes. We brought the last 'bird' to Khalid Bey's room from the women's cage and have kept her specially for you."

"Are you joking?"

"It's not a joke. But sleep now, have a rest. The girl is very tired. She's sleeping like the dead next door."

"I thought that the Armenians were people who lasted," said a soldier, taking down a rifle that was hanging on the wall and wiping it with a cloth dipped in olive oil, "they've become so delicate, especially the women! Brother, you love them for one night and find that they've become ill and die two days later."

"The reason is their mental anguish," said the soldier sitting next to him.

"It's not their mental anguish," Corporal Reza corrected them. "Hunger and privation have weakened them. Here they're stubborn, they won't take nourishment, so they die for the smallest reason."

"Really, Corporal? We know these people from the old country," exclaimed the card-playing soldier. "They weren't hungry or suffering from privation there. They can't stand as rough a life, because the boys from Constantinople are brought up on milk-soup. They're a feeble people. Last year, in Veghir Keopru, I axed 150 of them to death on my own. Despite the fact that their arms were only tied with thin rope, not one of them tried to free himself. You see, tomorrow 16 of us will go and bring 3,000 people here. You'll see that they'll shout, cry, and weep, but we'll drive them ahead of us here like a flock of sheep."

"Why… didn't a youth resist last time?" asked the soldier cleaning the rifle, sarcastically.

"Damn that young man's bravery!" replied the card-playing soldier with disdain. If, instead of 3,000 Armenians, there were 3,000 Turks, Kurds, Lazes, Cherkez or even gypsies, they'd scatter us and eat us alive with their teeth. What I mean to say is that it's stupid to say that hunger, misfortune, mental torture are the reasons. The Armenians aren't a fighting people."

"Long may they continue like that!" Lieutenant Mahir said, rubbing his hands. There's no need to spill blood to be victorious."

Queen of the Desert

Ten dreadful months had passed from the day that the people had been exiled from their homeland and had come to the Der-Zor desert.

All of them were remnants of hunger and massacre – robbed many times and tortured in unspeakable ways on the journey – and were already on the edge of death when they reached Arabia.

The passing winter and the famine and sickness that followed had completed their misfortune.

To give an approximate idea of the scale of the death-dealing misery, it's worth mentioning here that 60,000 died of hunger and illness in Meskeneh during this period. 400 people a day were dying in Ba'ab from famine and sickness. The starving people in Rakka and Abu-Harar attacked the cemeteries to exhume and eat the flesh of newly interred bodies.

The wretchedness and illnesses eventually became so widespread that the government was forced to protect the local population from attacks by the starving and from the sickness borne by bacteria. They collected all the Armenians – wretched and well-to-do, beggars and artisans – and drove them away from the towns and villages to distant places, leaving them to feast on one another as much as they liked, without harming the local people.

This is how the refugee camp Khalid mentioned was set up. Khalid was going to check this new camp after sending the remaining people to his mausoleum, to see what hellish plans he could also impose on the Armenians there.

It was Saturday evening when his carriage stopped in front of the camp. (Khalid, tired from the long journey on horseback, had bought a carriage in Der-Zor a few days before, which was driven by his devoted servant Hammed.)

The hyena alighted alone from his carriage and, seeing a hunchbacked old man – who was hurrying to the carriage in the hope of receiving alms – asked, "Hey! Grandfather, where's the police chief of this camp?"

The old refugee pointed to a wooden house built above the camp with his bony hand and, with a trembling voice, murmured, "They're all there."

"What's the police chief's name?"

"Sergeant Major Kiazim."

Khalid went towards the place pointed out to him, giving the old man, who had dared to ask him for alms at the last moment, a thunderous look.

Cracking his silver-mounted whip, jingling the metal spurs on his jackboots, with his chest thrust out, his moustache rolled upwards, he entered the police station and, representing himself as the general inspector of refugees, sat in Sergeant Kiazim's place, while the latter, seeing him enter, already stood up to attention.

"How many people are here?" asked the fake refugee inspector, after going through a notebook on the desk.

"When we brought them here 15 days ago," Sergeant Kiazim replied, always in a respectful pose, "there were 6,200. Since then about 600 have died, so at present there are about 5,600."

"Then according to those figures there won't be anyone left here in four to five months."

"It won't take even that long."

"We must think of a way to save these poor people from death," Khalid said with feeling. "It's good that I called here on my way. When I return to Der-Zor I'll report on the situation to the General Administration for Resettlement."

"Please speak well of us too," Sergeant Kiazim said with a pleading look on his face. "Living among these people we've become like them. I had 20 policemen under my command; two of them died and five others are in bed sick."

"It really isn't possible to live in this infected atmosphere," Khalid said. "I promise to make arrangements for you."

"Thank you, Sir."

"Kiazim Bey," the monster asked, changing the subject after a moment, "have you got a girl here suitable to be a maid?"

"We've got plenty, but they're all in an emaciated condition," the man in charge of the camp said, sadly.

"Never mind. My superior needs a maid. The woman who serves in his house eats well and quickly gains weight."

"In that case, Khalid Bey, I have a very suitable girl here."

"Is she beautiful?"

"I've not seen another one as beautiful as this in my whole life. You could call her the queen of the desert. I saw her yesterday quite by accident. She's hardly 18 years old and has a high temperature. She was lying in a tent and had thrown off her coverlet because she was so hot. Seeing her beautiful height and face, her fair hair and her sea-coloured eyes, I bit my lip and marvelled how such a beautiful piece has ended up here. I inquired and learnt who she is. She's from Adana and her name is Julia Aghasian."

"Her name tells us she's beautiful. Who's she got?"

"A mother and a brother two years older than her. There's also an old man in the tent who's mute. Before they were deported, they were apparently very rich in Adana. The mute man seems to have been their servant who they're keeping with them."

"Please take me to this tent."

"This way, Sir."

* * *

The queen of the desert, Julia Aghasian, was lying ill in a neat white canvas tent.

Outside, Mrs Zarouhi – a lady about 50 years old with a patrician face – was busy lighting a fire under a large pan settled on two big rocks.

"Mother," Julia asked in a worried voice, "Has Alex returned?"

"No, daughter."

"I wonder where he's got to," she said, sighing with concern. "He should have returned today, shouldn't he?"

"Yes. A day to get to Der Zor and a day to return is more than enough. We must be patient, my girl, maybe he'll arrive later."

"I'm frightened that something's happened to him. My heart's burning. Please give me some water."

"Don't drink water, my girl. I'm making you some tea. Wherever Alex is, he'll bring your medicine. Tonight we'll make you sweat and tomorrow you'll be better."

"Oh, never mind my medicine. My brother's lateness worries me very much."

"I'll go and have a look, my girl. Ah! Samuel is coming here at a run. Maybe he's seen Alex in the distance and is coming to let us know."

But Samuel – the old mute – didn't have the air of bringing good news. He came to his mistress bowed down by terror, and asked something using sign language.

"What's he saying, mother?" Julia asked curiously. "Isn't my brother coming?"

"No," Mrs Zarouhi replied, sobbing. The refugee inspector is here again. Cover your head with the coverlet. He may come this way."

The poor woman had hardly finished what she was saying when Khalid and Sergeant Kiazim appeared in front of her, one hand in his pocket, the other clutching his inseparable whip. "Good day, madam. Where are you from?" he asked with a friendly smile.

"Adana."

"Your name?"

"Zarouhi Aghasian."

Khalid took a piece of paper out of his pocket and, having examined it for a moment, said, "That's correct. Where is your esteemed husband?"

"He died."

"He died? Oh dear!" Khalid exclaimed with false feeling and uneasiness. "You may not know me madam. When I was the chief of the gendarmes in Adana, I was very close to your husband. Did the deceased mention me to you? My name is Khalid."

Mrs Zarouhi, without suspecting that he was lying, thought for a few moments and replied, in a sincere tone, "No, I don't remember."

"It's not important," Khalid said. "I'm now the general inspector of refugees and have taken up the post of checking the state of your community. I regret the misfortune that's befallen you with all my heart. It isn't possible to redress the past; what's happened, happened. But I'll try with every means at my disposal to relieve the present, to at least save the remainder of the people from certain death. I heard from Kiazim Bey a little while ago that 40 people a day are dying here. This is dreadful, madam."

"Yes, our situation is dreadful, Khalid Bey."

"I'll write a report to the appropriate authorities about what I've seen and have all the arrangements made to improve your situation."

"Write, Khalid Bey! You'll have saved thousands of people," Mrs Zarouhi sobbed, completely deceived by his honeyed words.

"You can be sure of that, madam. I'm going to do you a favour first of all, because I can't ever forget your deceased husband's generosity.

During my time as general inspector of refugees I always asked myself 'Will I ever meet my friend Aghasian or a member of his family so that I repay his good works?' You can imagine my pleasure when, examining the list of those living in the camp I saw your name. From now on you've no need to worry, madam. You're under my protection."

"You're very noble, Sir," Mrs Zarouhi murmured, beginning to be suspicious that there was a hidden purpose under all these flattering words.

"If my memory isn't at fault, you had a son and daughter. Yes, yes! I think your daughter's name was Julia," cried Khalid, apparently suddenly remembering. "Is she alive?"

"Yes, she's lying ill in the tent," Mrs Zarouhi replied, glancing at the tent hopelessly.

"Oh dear. What's she suffering from?"

"Malaria. Nearly all of us suffer from it."

"Naturally, madam. This place is very bad for the health. Men with iron constitutions turn into rags in a month."

Mrs Zarouhi didn't reply, with the hope that Khalid Bey would finish his conversation quickly and go on his way.

But was it possible that the monster in human form would go somewhere and leave that place without destroying it? So he resumed his conversation, always with polite and false formality. "Arabia is a charmless country, madam. Oh for our home country's air, water, people, civilization... compared to this. I say this to my wife every evening; there's nothing to eat or drink, nor people to see. I've an eleven year-old daughter... she's growing up like a shepherdess. There's not even a regular school to send her to."

"Hmm."

"It was good that I met you, madam. On my way here I said to myself, 'There are so many educated families among the Armenians. Their daughters speak one or two foreign languages, know how to play the piano, to sew and to cook delicious meals; in short they know all the things needed to run a house. Why shouldn't I bring one of them into my house, saving her from famine, wretchedness and, at the same time, give my daughter a proper education?' I consider it having been arranged by providence that I've discovered you on my way and think that I should take Miss Julia to my house, so that I can repay at least some of her father's generosity."

"Thank you for your noble interest in our family," Mrs Zarouhi said, making a supreme effort to control her inner emotions. "But I regret that my daughter can't be a teacher to your little girl, as she's not received the education you suppose, nor can she play the piano, and doesn't know any European language."

"Never mind, madam. When I said piano and European languages, I didn't mean that it was a condition to teach them to my daughter. In other words I meant to say that the friendship of an educated Armenian girl like Miss Julia is sufficient for my daughter's education."

"It's possible, Khalid Bey, but my daughter is ill and can't go anywhere."

"It's exactly for that reason that I want to take her and save her from this cursed place, where you're all destined to die in a few months. Your daughter will rest very well in my house, madam. My wife and daughter will lovingly look after her and do what they can to make her forget these bitter pains. I will look after her like a father, even bringing doctors from Aleppo if necessary to cure her. I shouldn't forget to say, here and now, that if you don't want to be parted from your daughter I'll take you as well."

"Thank you, Khalid Bey, but it's better that you leave us in our present state."

"You really are surprising people. I'm telling you that you'll all be destroyed in a few months. Instead of begging me to save you from this hell for your husband's sake, I'm begging you, and still you refuse."

"God is great, Khalid Bey. Death comes to all of us; we'll have no more than fate has in store for us."

"So you put your hopes on tomorrow?" Khalid asked, showing signs of impatience.

"Man lives in hope, Khalid Bey."

"If you think that the British will come and save you from here, you're mistaken, madam. You'll all die here. Consider yourselves fortunate that in your present straitened circumstances you've met someone who wants to do something for an old family friend."

"We're very grateful to you, Khalid Bey. But if you want to do something for an old family friend, please do so by leaving us alone here."

"So you refuse to let me take your daughter with me?"

"No, I'm asking you."

Khalid couldn't restrain himself. It was a miracle that he was able to play his well-known role of friend of the Armenians for so long, so he suddenly became angry and, raising his voice, shouted in a terrifying voice, "The fault is mine that, despite knowing how stubborn and ungrateful your people are, I begged you to let me do you a kindness. Get out of my way!"

He pushed Mrs Zarouhi in the chest and, with one bound, entered the tent.

"But Khalid Bey," Mrs Zarouhi protested, entering after him, "how do you dare to enter a place where a woman is in bed?"

"Madam, I see that you still haven't heard who I am," Khalid growled horrifyingly. "Don't come too close to me. I smash the heads that are raised up in front of me!"

Mrs Zarouhi looked in bewilderment at her husband's 'friend's' eyes that sparkled with wickedness. "Khalid bey, you don't act as a friend with us."

"A friend...? Me, a friend of bad Armenians? Take that as a friend...."

Khalid prepared to whip Mrs Zarouhi, when suddenly the mute – who until then had been listening to the conversation carefully, completely understanding what was going on from the facial expressions he could see – threw himself forward in protest, shouting "Ehbe...! Beh...! Ehbe! Beh..."

The whiplash, meant for Mrs Zarouhi, fell on the poor old man's face. Holding it, he uttered a dreadful cry and rolled to the floor.

"Khalid Bey..." Mrs Zarouhi exclaimed with a pleading movement.

"Get up, girl!" Khalid Bey yelled, going towards Julia's bed. "Why are you playing at being sick, lying there? Get up!"

Horrified, Julia looked at the beast that had come to take possession of her. The heat had coloured her cheeks and given her beautiful eyes an extraordinary sparkle.

"Can't you hear my voice?" Khalid asked, holding her hand with a desire he found impossible to resist. "Get up, I tell you!"

"But how can I get up?" Julia stammered, terrified. "You can see I'm ill."

The heat of the girl's hand made the blood in the beast's veins course strangely. Filled with the fire of lust, the savage strongly yanked the girl's trembling hand, pulling her out of bed.

"Get dressed and come on!"

"Help, help! They're kidnapping my daughter!" cried the mother madly holding on to her loved one.

"Stay away, woman!" roared Khalid in a horrid voice. "There's no one born in this world who can force me to do something against my will. If you love your life, your religion and your God, get out of the way!"

"Kiazim Bey, Kiazim Bey! What are you standing there for? He's taking my daughter!" protested the mother, screaming helplessly.

"Let him take her, if she stays here she'll die anyway," the police chief replied indifferently.

"No, I won't, I won't…"

"Oh, yes you will…!" Khalid swiftly struck the poor woman's face, forehead and head again and again with his whip.

Holding her daughter with her two hands, Mrs Zarouhi accepted all the blows rained on her until her arms weakened and, sighing, she fell to the floor on her back, covered in blood.

Khalid, with the air of a man gaining a great victory, pulled the fainting girl from her mother's arms and, a few minutes later, put her in the carriage brought up by Hammed. Then they drove away quickly, at the same time giving the police chief the false promise, "Don't worry, Kiazim Bey, I noted your request."

* * *

When Julia's brother Alex arrived an hour later at the camp, he found it in a state of considerable ferment.

"What's up, boys?" he suspiciously asked people from the camp who came up to him.

"Didn't a carriage go past you?" the Armenians asked.

"Yes, what about it?"

"Didn't you see who was in it?"

"No, I didn't see anything, as it was dark inside. The only thing I noticed was that the driver was a soldier."

"And who was in it?"

"I didn't see, it was closed. But please tell me quickly, what's happened?"

"Julia was kidnapped."

Alex shuddered with horror. "My sister…? By whom?"

"By the officer in the carriage."

"Oh! The cursed dog!" Alex exclaimed, suddenly turning and running in the direction the carriage had gone.

He had hardly gone ten paces when someone shouted from behind him, "Alex! Alex!"

Julia's brother turned and saw a man of middle height, about forty years old, with deep scars from burns on his face, coming towards him quickly.

"I too heard, a littler while ago, of the misfortune," the unknown man said reaching him. "Running after that officer is the same as throwing yourself in a fire. Like killing a rabid dog, he'll pull out his pistol and coldly kill a man. Rest for a few hours, and we'll go and act prudently together."

"This is not a time for rest, brother!" Alex cried impatiently. "The more time we take, the greater the difficulty of catching up with it."

"But our hurrying doesn't help, my son," said the man with the burnt face. "The carriage left an hour ago and is traveling very fast. We'll never catch it by running after it. It's not the time to waste our energies. I know where he's gone. It doesn't make any difference if we follow it in a few hours. In any event we shouldn't act rashly."

"What a disaster!" muttered Alex, putting his hand to his head. "My sister was ill in bed. Did they get her out of bed and take her away?"

"Yes my son. You don't know that monstrous beast."

"Who knows, my mother's probably gone mad with grief," Alex muttered, in the depths of despair.

"Your mother!"

From his interlocutor's expression, the young man, with a premonition of disaster, ran madly back to the tent and, finding his mother's lifeless body surrounded by crying and lamenting women, fell upon it and wept bitterly.

After a while, when he calmed down, he looked sadly around him as if to find someone, and then asked the women gathered in the tent "But where's Samuel...? What happened to him?"

"The mute? He's disappeared," they replied.

"I know," said a small girl, who had been the first to enter the tent. "When I came in, I saw him lying unconscious in a corner. Just at that moment he recovered consciousness and began to rub his forehead, from which blood was running. After looking at his blood-soaked fingers, he got up and ran to Miss Julia's bed. Seeing the bed empty, he looked around him in horror and saw his mistress' dead body. This time he rushed to it like a madman. He held it, moved it, leaned over it and looked at the face and, finally seeing blood oozing out of Mrs Zarouhi's ear, cried piteously and, beating his breast, escaped from the tent."

"Where did he go?" Alex asked, his throat tight with sobs.

"I don't know, he was running towards the camp gates," the little exile said.

"He obviously went after the carriage," said the man with the burnt face. "Alex, didn't you see him?"

"No."

"Let's go," his comrade said. "But first let's make arrangements for the poor woman's eternal rest."

* * *

Just after midnight Alex and his unknown friend left the refugee camp extremely quietly and took the road to Der-Zor.

Although Alex hadn't completely rested from his two day journey, he walked with sure and swift steps, thinking that he was going to free his sister and exact revenge from the hyena who was her kidnapper and their mother's killer.

The same feelings and thoughts had strengthened his friend's legs and, although he looked badly hurt, proved to be even fitter.

They had walked for a considerable time in silence when Alex turned to his companion and said, "In the emotional turmoil of those criminal acts we didn't have an opportunity to introduce ourselves. It would give me great pleasure to know who you are, as you're so selflessly giving your blood and life for me."

"Yes we must get to know one another, because we're on a path without knowing what awaits us at the end," his fellow traveller replied calmly. "My name is Paul, and I'm from Kayseri. Until three weeks ago I lived in the camp near Der-Zor. I know that officer from there. He came five times to take caravans of people apparently to Mosul, to work in factories there; but in reality to take them deep into the desert, to bury them alive under a big black rock and to arrange bloody orgies with the women.

"The last time, an inexperienced young man, with the object of killing him, attacked him with a dagger. Before he achieved his aim, he was torn to pieces and crushed under the officer's companions' horses' hooves.

"I saw that crime and was bad enough to run away and come to your camp. But I now see that our salvation is not in running away.

"It seems that this beast, thirsty for Armenian blood, honor and possessions, having devoured the heads of the remaining 3,000

Armenians, has come here to do the same. He won't be satisfied with the kidnap of one Julia. Tomorrow he'll come to take more Julias and one day to get the whole of the camp on the road. Expanding his field of activity ever wider, one day he'll go even further, who knows, probably to Aleppo, so as not to leave one Armenian alive in the Arabian deserts. Until we kill him, there's no freedom for us. That's why I'm giving you my life and blood."

Alex listened to his friend's words with admiration, happy to know that there were high-minded spirits within the Armenian nation ready to give their comfort and lives for the well-being and freedom of others.

"I understand that," Paul continued, after breathing deeply, "we must, to protect our existence, not only unite, help and work with each other, but also fight bravely to carve on the enemy's skulls this truth: before you strike, think carefully, because we'll return the blow, and in a more deadly way."

"That's true," Alex affirmed, "if the enemy is convinced of that, then he can't hurt us."

"Twenty centuries have passed since the day when they preached, if struck on one cheek, one should turn the other. We've turned the other cheek many times; and despite staying silent and complying many times, the blows have been struck harder and harder, until they brought us to this state. It's about time we awoke from our sleep and thought about ways to return the blows, otherwise there's no salvation for us."

"I'm sure that," Alex said, "individuals – and also nations – that don't fight in this world can't maintain their existence."

There was a deep silence between the two traveling companions. As they walked, each was buried in his own grief and worries.

The moon rose from the edge of the plain, lighting up the surrounding regions, where there was a thin, silver-like ribbon that edged part of the horizon then disappeared behind the rugged terrain.

"It's the Euphrates," Alex sighed, pointing at the shining ribbon.

"Yes, that cursed river, that swallowed 100,000 innocent women and children," murmured his companion through his clenched teeth.

"Please excuse my curiosity," Alex said, looking at his friend's face closely. "Did you have an accident, or are your burn scars the result of a barbaric act?"

Paul smiled bitterly. "Do you want to know how I got burnt?" he asked. "Very well, I'll tell you. One needs conversation to dispel the monotony of the journey." Then he told his story.

"About a year ago, when the police began to search for dangerous weapons and books, my house was full of books on history and revolution. I didn't belong to any political party, but because I was interested in the community's woes, I always bought and read all those books and papers that were concerned with the battles for freedom.

"Hearing that people were being hanged for the sake of a songbook, one evening I had the evil thought of burning all the books in my library, to free myself from pursuit by the courts. In my haste however, I threw all my books into one brazier, without thinking that the thick smoke and smell rising from the chimney would attract my Turkish neighbours' attention.

"Indeed, before even a quarter of an hour had passed, the street door began to be pounded continuously. Shortly afterwards my wife, frightened out of her wits, ran to tell me that five or six Turks, led by a policeman, had surrounded the house. 'Don't open the door until I destroy the books,' I told her.

"But it wasn't an easy task to burn a large pile of paper in a few minutes. While I poured oil on it to speed up the burning of the paper, the crowd broke the door down and entered.

"Hearing their footsteps, I immediately jumped out of the kitchen window and, going through the yard, hid in our hayloft that was at its far end.

"Crouched down behind a small window, I began to watch our house, to see what would happen.

"The Turks immediately saw the pile of books burning in the brazier and, saying 'one of their leaders is here', arrested my wife.

"'By burning those books you wanted to remove traces of your guilt, isn't that so?' the policeman asked my wife.

"'Why am I guilty if I burn books that are superfluous in my house?' my wife boldly asked.

"'Let's see what sort of books they are,' the policeman said, bending down and retrieving a half-burnt picture of a freedom fighter. 'Hmm... so you're one of them. Where's your husband?'

"'I don't know, he's not at home,' my wife replied.

"'Don't lie, he is at home,' chided the policeman.

"The Turks had scattered through the rooms to try to find me. I had a six year-old daughter, who was lying down ill upstairs. I suddenly heard her scream of terror from her bedroom. It would appear that my daughter, seeing fierce-looking people enter her room, thought that they were thieves, and was now shouting 'father, mother!' for us to help her.

"My wife ran after the Turks and begged them to leave the room and not frighten our daughter.

"'You're traitors to the fatherland; may you all die!' the policeman roared shaking my wife. 'Where's your husband? Tell me where he is, or I'll trample you!'

"My daughter, seeing her mother being tortured, began to cry even louder. Not able to stand my wife being tortured or my child's screams, I came out of my hiding place and said to the policeman, 'I'm here; why are you beating my wife? Why are you frightening an innocent ill child?'

"Before I had time to finish what I was saying, the policeman and the Turks with him rushed at me like rabid wolves, knocked me down using blows with sticks and fists, and began to rain blows to my face, chest and stomach using the steel heels of their shoes.

"Of course I lost consciousness under this inhuman beating. When I came round a few days later I saw that I was in prison; my broken bones ached, my flesh was swollen and twitched with pain, my ears buzzed, and inside my skull it was as if I had mill wheels grinding away; one of my eyes had been damaged and was shut tight. I couldn't breathe, speak or get up.

"But my wife's state was even worse, as she'd tried to intervene to stop them beating me: they'd tortured her barbarically and she'd become mute in front of her child.

"Her face was black and blue and swollen, her forehead tied with a piece of cloth, her left arm held in a sling; she'd come to the prison to bring me medicine and yoghurt.

"'I came to see you yesterday and the day before, but the police wouldn't let me in,' she said in a faint voice. 'I went to the chief of police's office today, stood waiting for an hour and cried and begged until I got permission to see you.'

"My wife came to visit me twice more after that. On the tenth day of my imprisonment, she came to see me, dressed in black, and told me that my daughter, terrified out of her senses from seeing our beatings, had died two days before. My wife, with a few relatives and the priest, had buried her in the Armenian cemetery. On their way back, a group of

Turks confronted them and declared that from then on dirty Armenian bodies should not be buried in Turkey's sacred soil.

"'So where should we bury our dead?' the priest asked innocently.

"'Throw them in the fields and let the dogs eat them,' the Turks had answered. 'If not, you can be sure that we'll bring the body from the grave and leave it in your yard.'

"I was in prison for a month and a half. During all that time no one questioned me nor did they put me in court. One night however, they took us – 22 people – out of the prison and, saying that they were sending us to Diyarbekir, made us set out on the road in chains.

"We'd hardly left the city limits when the commander of the police accompanying us ordered us to halt. 'We're going to get some more prisoners; you wait for us here,' he said. He handed us over to three policemen, and he and the rest of his men hurriedly went back to the city.

"'We'll wait in this building then,' said the policemen left with us shortly afterwards.

"We went to the building they'd pointed out; it was a workshop without any roof tiles. There the police removed our chains and made us go into a room. Two hours later some of the police who had gone to the city returned with 14 new prisoners. We still had to wait for the rest. Because the room was too small to shut us all in, they took us out and put us in a larger one that had a strange, low door.

"After they'd shut the door on us, we realized that we were held in a pottery kiln. 'Boys! These men are going to burn us in here!' we exclaimed in unison.

"We definitely heard the policemen having logs and brushwood piled up against the door. It isn't possible to describe the dreadful moments we lived each time we heard them bring in pieces of wood and throw them to the floor with an awful noise. Shortly afterwards we heard the lighting of a match and the crackling sound of dry leaves and branches burning.

"At the same time the police, using a long pole, opened our prison door, and we found ourselves faced with an enormous flame and black smoke that gradually filled the interior, making it extremely hot and with an atmosphere that was impossible to breathe in.

"Horrified, we retreated and, with our backs to the far wall, we watched the approaching flames that were devouring our hair, moustaches, eyebrows, faces, hands and clothing. In less than a minute we had all fallen to the floor, shrieking with pain, with many of us badly burnt and suffocating.

"When I fell to the floor, I saw that the air was relatively easier to breathe at that level than higher up. The idea that I may be able to survive suddenly gave me hope, and I said to myself, 'I must move forwards. If I can get through the fire, I may be saved; if I don't, I'm a dead man.'

"Some of my poor companions seemed to have had the same idea as, at the moment that I threw myself into the fire, I saw that others were following me.

"Our coming out of the fire alive astonished the police, who hadn't envisaged such courage. They immediately picked up their weapons and began firing after us. I saw one or two people fall, but fortunately the bullets didn't touch me and I was able to escape thanks to the darkness.

"So, having saved myself, I returned to the city and hid in one of my relatives' houses. They immediately called an Armenian doctor, at the same time sending news to my wife. They bandaged me and had me lie down on a bed, whose comfort I'd long forgotten in prison.

"I stayed there for two weeks. Then, with the rest of the community, I was deported from the city. They'd already taken away most of the men some considerable time before that and killed them in the uninhabited valleys and plains several days march beyond Kayseri. Our caravan, mostly made up of women, old people and children, fortunately wasn't massacred, although hundreds died from privation and exhaustion before we reached Aleppo.

"The story from Aleppo to this place is that of every Armenian, my son. We were exiled from there to Der-Zor. My wife died from illness in winter. I made my living in the camp by making cutlery until the day that Khalid's terror appeared, and I escaped to your camp."

* * *

The two walking travellers – who had become very close friends – walked and talked all night, and reached Der-Zor, the capital of the desert, on the following day.

Seeing a dilapidated hovel at the edge of the town, they directed their steps to it to ask for water to drink.

A simply-dressed 50 year-old Armenian refugee woman with a kind face opened the door and, seeing the travellers' tired state, said, "Please come in and rest for a while."

Alex and Paul went in and sat on a mattress on the floor. "Do you live here alone, Madam?" Paul asked, seeing the room's emptiness.

"Yes," replied the lady of the house, filling a metal cup with water from a broken water pot. "My husband, my two grown-up daughters and my son died. I live here alone, and earn my living by doing the washing of the families of government officials."

While Paul was drinking, Alex asked, feeling sorry for the woman's poverty, "Where are you from, Madam?"

"I'm from Hadjin," the woman refugee answered. "And you? I see that you've come from a distance."

It was Alex's turn to drink, so Paul answered for him. "He's from Adana, I'm from Kayseri. We were in the upper camp. Last evening an officer named Khalid came and kidnapped my friend's sister."

"Khalid? Captain Khalid?" cried Mrs Iskouhi, suddenly crossing herself, as if she had heard the name of the devil.

"Yes, do you know him?" Paul asked.

"Who doesn't know that bloodthirsty beast, who only two days ago took all the remaining Armenians from the camp to his slaughterhouse in the desert."

"Khalid?" Alex asked with feeling.

"In other words his soldiers," Mrs Iskouhi corrected. "Hearing about his absence, we were all delighted that he was ill or was dead. Now I see that he's gone to you camp to kidnap girls. Be careful, brothers, if that monster has learnt where your camp is, he'll not leave one person alive there tomorrow."

"We know he's like that, and that's why we followed him. Where can we find him now? We think because of my sister's illness, he couldn't have gone further than Der-Zor."

"Whenever Khalid comes to Der-Zor he stays in Colonel Hamdi Bey's house," Mrs Iskouhi replied.

"Where is that house? Can you take us to it?"

"I can. But we must be careful. That house is not like any house you've known. Many skulls of poor Armenians like yourselves, who've gone there to demand their kidnapped loved ones, have been smashed there."

"No matter how great the danger is, we must rescue my sister from that beast's hands," Alex said.

"You're right, my son. If Khalid leaves the town, you'll not be able to find any trace of him. You stay and rest here for a while, I'll go to the town to see if he is still there."

"How will you be able to find that out, Madam?"

"I have a 12 year-old compatriot named Sepon, who's been adopted and made a Muslim by Hamdi Bey's housekeeper. That boy can go in and out of Hamdi Bey's palace as much as he likes. I hope I'll find out about the situation through him."

"Oh, Madam, God led us here!" Alex exclaimed happily. "Please, do us that favour. If it's possible, I'd like to give you a note to be passed to her, so that she knows that apart from her brother there are other noble and selfless souls who are working for her salvation."

"Yes, write your note. I'll take it straight away," the lady of the house said.

"Thank you very much, Madam!"

"There's no need for thanks, my son; in these times of crisis, it's our duty to help one another."

* * *

The few hours that passed after Mrs Iskouhi left seemed like years to the two friends.

Finally she returned smiling and with a letter in her hand. "Thank God!" she cried from a distance, "Khalid hasn't gone yet and here's the answer to your letter!"

Alex grabbed the letter from the lady's hand and wept tears of joy as he read out the following lines.

> My dear brother,
>
> I can't describe, on this piece of paper, my feelings learning that you're alive and have come to save me.
>
> But no matter how unacceptable my situation is, I can't ask you to help me. Be careful, my dear Alex; you must realize that any attempt will be tantamount to suicide.
>
> Khalid kidnapped me to give me as a maid to his superior Colonel Hamdi Bey.
>
> When we reached here that night, the latter had left an hour before to chase a regiment of cavalry that has rebelled under the command of an Arab from Baghdad named Seyfi.
>
> Khalid will wait for Hamdi Bey here until tomorrow evening. If he doesn't return by then, on the following morning, in other

words on Tuesday, Khalid will be taking me to his camp, the whereabouts of which he won't tell me.

I spent the night in a separate room in the company of an Ethiopian maid, who watched over me until daylight.

Apart from Khalid and his servant there are five soldiers and servants in the house. I repeat, you must be careful.

I'm sorry that I don't know your friends Mr Paul and Mrs Iskouhi personally. I don't know, if one day I will enjoy freedom, how I'll be able to repay them for what they're doing for me.

Please express my gratitude to them.

With longing kisses,

Julia

"This is good news," Paul said, after Alex had finished reading the letter. We've got until the day after tomorrow to act."

"It's also a stroke of good fortune that Colonel Hamdi Bey is absent," Mrs Iskouhi said. "When he's in residence, the house is as crowded as a barracks."

"So we'll go straight to Hamdi Bey's house tonight," Alex cried with a tone of hatred in his voice.

"Yes, but let's check on the house and street," Paul said. "Mrs Iskouhi, can you show us the house?"

* * *

It was as if the two brave-hearted Armenians' breaths caught, when they saw Colonel Hamdi Bey's palace. It gave the impression of a fortress which took up the entire block.

Although Paul had a fearless character, he was noticeably annoyed at seeing the building's extraordinary defenses. "Alex," he said, turning to his companion, "if we make an attempt to enter the house at night, you can be sure that death is inevitable."

"So what shall we do?" Alex asked, looking concerned.

"I think we'll have to wait until Khalid begins his journey back to his lair. We've a greater chance outside than here, in this fort, to corner him."

"But if Hamdi Bey returns, won't we be forced to attack the building to rescue my sister?"

"Yes, we will, but do you really think that we'll be able to enter it at night, overwhelm the soldiers and servants, and free Julia?" Paul pointed out.

"No, but we should think of another way," the young man said. "Anyway, we shouldn't wait for Khalid to leave."

"There is one way, but it's very difficult," Mrs Iskouhi said.

"What way?" both friends asked, their hearts in their mouths.

"To dress Julia in men's clothing and get her out of the house."

"A brilliant idea!" Paul cried, suddenly enthusiastic. "I'll give my jacket towards it."

"And I'll give my trousers," Alex said. "But how will we get the clothing to her? That's the question."

"That's not important," Paul said, "as we've got Sepon."

"No, it's dangerous to do it through Sepon," Mrs Iskouhi said. We'll throw the bundle of clothes over the wall, then we'll send Sepon to Miss Julia and tell her to wear them and leave the house."

"But let's think carefully," Alex said, "wouldn't she attract the guard's attention as she comes out of the house?"

"She won't, because in the evening the Arab water carriers bring water to Hamdi Bey's house. Julia, in those old clothes, would leave disguised as a water carrier."

"So as to make the disguise complete, we'll throw a pole and two tin containers into the garden," Paul suggested.

"Yes, it'll work that way." Alex said spiritedly. "I'll write a letter to give my sister the necessary instructions. Let's move away to a corner somewhere."

They went to a safe place, where Alex took a piece of paper from his pocket and hurriedly wrote the following lines:

My dear sister,

Don't worry about our undertaking being dangerous. We've come here knowing that we might die. Be brave and carry out these instructions to the letter.

When the Arab water carriers start to bring water, go into the garden using the excuse that you need to get some air, without worrying if the Ethiopian maid is with you. To obtain her trust, walk about with her for a time. Then make an excuse and leave her for a minute. Go to the bottom of the garden where, under the pomegranate tree, you'll find some men's clothes and two tin containers fitted to a pole. Put those clothes on immediately and, putting the pole with the two containers on your shoulder, leave through the door. The guard won't pay you any attention if you carry out your role boldly.

So, Julia, success is dependent on your cleverness and coolness. Once you've left the house, don't worry. We'll meet you at the street corner with open arms.

Your brother,

Alex

Alex read his two companions what he had written and, having got their approval, said to Mrs Iskouhi "Here you are, Madam, it's up to you to get it to my sister. Then go to your home and wait for us there. Mr Paul and I are going to the market to buy what's necessary."

* * *

The same evening, Alex and Paul were standing, like begging refugees, on Hamdi Bey's street corner and saying:

"She's late."

"I'm afraid that something's happened."

"Surprisingly the Arab water carriers haven't come out either."

"Here they come. Is one of them Julia?"

"No, that's not her."

"I'm afraid that Julia wasn't able to go into the garden. Let's go, Alex. Tomorrow we'll find out through Sepon what happened."

"But if Hamdi Bey returns?"

"I don't think it's possible that Hamdi Bey, who's pursuing a rebel regiment, will return so quickly. Come on, let's go. We'll wait again tomorrow and, if we don't succeed, we'll try our luck in the open plain the following day."

"Look there! A shadow has left the house and is coming in our direction... Is it Julia...?"

"Yes, Julia!" the shadow muttered in a hoarse voice, and then, suddenly producing a pistol, ordered, "Surrender! Otherwise I'll kill you both, you bandits!"

A Traveller in the Desert

A young traveller was walking along a dusty road, having given his final farewell to the Der-Zor desert one boiling hot day in May.

He had left Aleppo two weeks before. Gradually leaving the centers of civilization behind, he had gone through the villages inhabited by the *fellah* (peasants) and the half-wild Bedouin tents, and was now entering the uninhabited plains region, beyond which assuredly the real desert, in other words the ocean of sand, began.

Concerned to find a place to shelter before nightfall, he was examining his surroundings when he heard the sound of small bells coming from behind a hill in front of him.

"A flock of sheep's passing," the traveller said joyfully. "The presence of animals tells me that there's human habitation nearby, so I've not lost my way."

Before he had finished these thoughts, he was struck with strange emotions, because the air resounded with a sweet-sounding melody, whose words could be heard clearly in the silence which was like that of a cemetery:

"If our sons forgive you for so much evil,
May the whole world shame Armenians...."

The young traveller, hurrying his steps, climbed to the top of the hill and saw a young shepherd, wearing a white shirt, holding a staff and carrying a sack on his back. He was driving 50-60 sheep in front of him and was heading, as he sang, towards black tents which were visible in the distance.

The traveller was sure that he wasn't the victim of a mirage, so he raised his voice and shouted, "Hey! Boy! Are you Armenian?"

Hearing a stranger's voice, the youth shuddered, then, satisfying himself that he wasn't seeing an illusion, collected himself and replied, "Yes, but what're you doing round here?"

"I lost my way," the young man said. "I don't know where I am."

"In a savage place," the shepherd declared unhappily.

"So what're you doing in this wild area? Are there other Armenians around here?"

"There were some in the villages six hours from here, but all of them were destroyed."

"Where are you from? What's your name?"

"I'm from Papert. My name was Kegham, but I'm now called Hassan."

"Have you become Muslim?"

"I was forced to be one. What's your name?"

"Kirk. I had a friend in Aleppo and heard he'd been exiled to Der-Zor. I was going to find him. So there are no Armenians here?"

"You may find Armenians in the Ras-ul-Ain, Nisibis, Mosul and Der-Zor areas. All the Armenians here were massacred."

"Who massacred them?"

"Hunger, sickness and wretchedness. Whatever was left was finished off by the Enezenis."

"Who're the Enezenis?"

"Half-wild Arab raiders of the area."

"Is the Der-Zor area peaceful at least?"

"Khalid's there."

"Who's Khalid?"

"Haven't you heard about Captain Khalid?"

"How can I have heard of him. I've only just come from Aleppo."

"You're right. But if you go deeper into the desert, you'll begin to hear about him."

"But you've still not said who Khalid is."

"No one knows who he really is. Apparently, he's a refugee resettlement official, but it would be more accurate to call him the refugee disappearance official."

"What sort of talk is that?"

"It's not talk, Sir. It's the truth. He goes to a refugee camp with ten soldiers, gets a 1,000-person caravan on the road, apparently to take them to Mosul, then makes them disappear."

"Does he kill them?"

"No one knows, because not one of his victims' bodies has been found."

"So he drowns them in the river."

"There's no river, lake, mountain or valley where he takes them."

"Where is the place he takes them?"

"It's supposed that it's a desert somewhere between Der-Zor and Mosul, to the south."

"How does he make his victims disappear in the desert? Does he bury them in the sand after killing them?"

"No, he apparently makes them go into a building with a large door. What happens after that we don't know. The Armenians have called it Death's Door, as those who cross it's threshold never return."

"It's good that you told me. If no one returns, how does anyone know of its existence?"

"An Armenian from one of the caravans was left for dead. He saw Death's Door and told everything."

"So why do you say that no one knows where Death's Door is, when that man saw it and knows where it is?"

"The man, not having eaten for days, didn't live long; he's dead."

"That's a fable, my son. Terror sometimes makes people imagine horrible things."

"It's not a fable, Sir. What I'm telling you is the real truth."

"But I can't believe that an officer in the desert can settle himself in such a mysterious building and commit crimes like that under the nose of the government."

"You don't believe me? Then let me talk to you in terms of dates and numbers that can easily be proved in Der-Zor. On April 15th four caravans totalling 19,000 people were assembled and set out for Mosul. The number of people who reached their assigned places was 2,500, the remainder having disappeared en route. On 30th April another 20,000 people set out, once more to go to Mosul, but nobody arrived. Apart from these 39,000, every day for about a month a small caravan of 500 people set out from Der-Zor in a southeasterly direction and disappeared. Khalid, after carrying out these official massacres with the government's knowledge and with the help of the Cherkez and chettehs, seeing the profits to be made, began to utilize Death's Door for his own benefit."

"Forgive me, my friend, how do you know all this, as you say you live here alone?"

"I know because another traveller lost like you passed here and told me everything. He said that after Khalid established himself in Death's Door, he'd taken five 1,000-person caravans from the camp at Der-Zor.

Recently someone tried to kill him. On that occasion the mad beast shouted that he'd not leave one Armenian alive in the desert. The man had been frightened by that threat and, escaping from the camp, was going towards Djaraboulos."

The young shepherd's words were so genuine and full of proof that the traveller began to be persuaded as to their truth.

"But isn't there anyone who knows where this beast stays?" he asked in a frightening voice. "As he's a soldier he must be linked to an army unit."

"Yes. Everyone knows that Khalid's crimes are protected by a merciless soldier named Colonel Hamdi Bey, who lives in the town of Der-Zor," the youth replied.

"Can't the location of Khalid's lair be found out from this wretched Hamdi?"

"That's impossible, because Colonel Hamdi Bey lives in a fortified house that no one can get near."

"Boy! What are you saying?" exclaimed the traveller, shaking his fist at an imaginary enemy. "You're telling me so many stories that I think you're exaggerating!"

"Sir!" the youth replied, feeling his honor besmirched, "I've told you what I've heard accurately. We're still talking, but mustn't go beyond this point because if my master sees me with another Armenian, he'd be angry. You stay here. Do you see that small hut near the sheepfold behind the black tents? That's where I live. When it gets dark, when I whistle three times to call the dog in, go there from behind the tents. I'll give you something to eat. Bye!"

* * *

After the young shepherd had left, the traveller sat down on a rock and fell into deep thought.

As was obvious, the traveller was Kirk who, after hearing of Sara's tragic death, had come to Aleppo to join Henry and work out a new plan of action.

In Aleppo however, before he even had time to find his friend, he had collapsed from mental and physical exhaustion brought on by the distress and crises he had suffered. He also suffered an attack of typhoid fever which almost killed him if, through good luck, he had not encountered a local Armenian woman who had nursed him for two months in her house. So, after the sieve-makers from Kastamonu had saved his life for the first time, he had been saved a second time by an Arabic speaking Armenian woman.

After he had recovered, he looked for Henry with great caution, because the police were arresting any Armenians they met and sending them to Der-Zor.

It was only months later that he heard that Henry hadn't escaped his fellow-Armenians' evil fate.

At the same time the horrifying news about the dreadful situation in the Der-Zor desert had reached his ears.

"Famished hyenas and vultures gather where dead bodies are scattered," he said one day to his benefactress. "I won't allow those beasts, ravenous for Armenian blood, to tear apart the bodies of my brothers and sisters without being punished. So I'm going to Der-Zor to exact revenge for my dear parents, my 4,000 comrades-in-arms, and my adorable Sara."

The Aleppo Armenian woman's advice and warnings were in vain. Kirk, with a dagger in his belt, had gone towards Der-Zor but, before he got there, was hearing about an infamous Khalid who, like a dragon of legend in his lair in a corner of the desert, demanded blood, Armenian blood, every day.

Khalid…!

Who was this Khalid? Was he perhaps the terror of the Armenians of Eyreli who had gone to the Baghdad front? But how could an officer who was to go to the front be found in the Der-Zor desert? Could it be that Colonel Hamdi Bey's intervention had kept him in Der-Zor to manage the destruction of the Armenians?

According to the young shepherd's declaration, he had already massacred about 50,000 people, and threatened that not one Armenian would be left alive in the Der-Zor desert, where there were still 200,000 left.

So was the fate of 200,000 Armenians dependent on the whim of a bloodthirsty massacrer whose whereabouts no one knew?

Kirk, given over to indescribable feelings and agitation, was thinking like that when, in the stillness of the night, he heard three blasts of a whistle.

It was the young shepherd. Overcome, he got to his feet and went towards the sound.

A quarter of an hour later, when he reached the hovel without incident, he saw that Kegham had set the table consisting of milk and bread in a wooden dish.

"If you don't like milk, I'll make it into cheese," the youth said, inviting his guest to sit at the head of the table.

"Don't worry," Kirk said, tearing off a large piece of bread, "I'm very hungry. Who's going to wait for four hours to make the milk into cheese?"

"Four hours? It doesn't take four minutes!" Saying this, Kegham took a piece of cloth from a bag and dipped it into the milk. In less than a minute the milk curdled and became cheese.

"That's amazing," Kirk murmured, dumbfounded.

"There's nothing amazing about it," the shepherd said, smiling. "There's juice from unripe figs dried on the cloth. That's what thickens the milk. The Arabs have many tricks like this."

"But tell me," Kirk said, after finishing his meal, "when we first met in the plain you said that the Enezenis had massacred all the Armenians who were here. Were your father and mother killed too? How did you end up with these people?"

"I never knew my father," Kegham said sadly, "because he was killed when I was still very young. The Kurds killed my mother while we were on the march. My younger sister was kidnapped and my elder brother was shot dead by the police in the city."

"Wait a minute," Kirk said. "I would prefer you not to tell me your story in a superficial way. Every Armenian who was deported, and who's still alive, has his or her hellish moments. I want to hear all of them in detail."

"As you're interested, let me tell you my odyssey," Kegham said and continued:

"Many years ago, one evening, our friends and relations gathered in our house to celebrate my uncle's name day, which was on the feast of Vartanantz. My uncle was unmarried and was living with us at that time.

"After our meal, the young people began to sing patriotic songs, dance and enjoy themselves. At one point, when we were really enjoying ourselves the window was suddenly smashed and a large muddy stone landed in the middle of our living room.

"Joy and laughter stopped immediately. While all the guests were frightened and had fallen silent, my uncle, rushing down the stairs, went into the street and ran after the unknown man who, after deliberately spoiling our celebration, was running away.

"My uncle reached the man with one bound and, holding him by the collar, shook him several times. He then hit him and knocked him to the ground. The man, who was a puny Turk, was frightened that he'd be beaten, began to shout in the street, yelling 'Mohammedans, Mohammedans, help! They're killing me!'

"Upon the Turk's shouts, the police and night guards arrived and arrested my uncle for the crime of 'attacking a peaceful pedestrian'.

"Just at that moment my father and many of the guests arrived at the scene and, showing the police the Turk's muddy hands, swore that he'd stoned their house without any reason.

"But the guilty man, saying *'vallahi'* (God is my witness), was able to free himself, while they took my uncle to prison.

"The following day the chief of police, deciding that my uncle was innocent, freed him, but before sending him home, had his long whiskers cut off out of devilish envy, saying that unbelieving Armenians had no right to have luxuriant whiskers.

"My uncle couldn't stomach the insult. He didn't leave the house for a month, not wanting people to see him without his moustache. During the days and nights that followed, while seated or pacing the room, he gradually became agitated. But his anger had a reason other than that of his lost whiskers. He couldn't understand how it could be that, after all the statements by Armenians and proof of the Turk's guilt, he was released after swearing an oath, and my uncle went to prison instead. Also, in which law book was it written that a government official could, at a whim, cut off people's hair and beards? So if there was no law and justice, then that same official could, the following day, cut people's heads off.

"All the thoughts that ran through my uncle's head became reality two months later. One day my father went to the baths to bathe. Apparently he looked very like my uncle. Two men, encouraged by the chief of police, took out their daggers and attacked my father there, in the baths, thinking it was my uncle and stabbed him, mortally wounding him.

"My uncle tried in vain to have the two criminals arrested and punished. Not only didn't the police chief arrest them, but he warned my uncle to stop his pursuit.

"My uncle, coming to the realisation that the author of the crime was the chief of police, secretly followed him and, one day on the road to the village…"

"…finding him alone, cut his head off and escaped to the mountains, didn't he?" Kirk asked, suddenly interrupting the story he was so avidly listening to. "Boy, are you Kenneth's nephew?"

"Yes," Kegham answered, "do you know my uncle?"

"I know him very well, as well as his two comrades Vartan and Mourad."

"But how?"

"They were cattle dealers and went around the villages in our region, warning the villagers to be careful and alert. They were deeply convinced that the Turkish government persecuted, harassed and oppressed us, and that is why we are weak. 'Using these policies', they'd say, 'the Turks will one day exterminate us. But if we take up arms and become stronger, then they can't cause us harm and would live with us like lions and tigers, without thinking of hurting one another'. Do you know what happened to them?"

"I don't know what happened to Vartan and Mourad. But my uncle was beheaded before the deportations," the young shepherd replied.

"Kenneth beheaded?" Kirk asked, shuddering with his whole body, "But how?"

"As you know, after the proclamation of the constitution, my uncle was pardoned and returned to the city. He often came and went to Erzinjan on business. He'd gone there last year again, promising to return to the city before Vartanantz week. Unexpected work having come up, he telegraphed us that he'd return on the evening of his name day.

"Our friends and relations were gathered at our house once more and were sitting round the table, everyone waiting for my uncle's arrival. But minutes and hours passed, and he still didn't appear. Could it have been that he'd had a carriage accident? May it have been that the roads had deteriorated due to the rain and snow? Everyone present supposed something and anxiety and concern grew hour by hour, when suddenly the noise of the wheels of a carriage turning the corner dispelled the worry.

"'It's Kenneth! It's Kenneth!'

"All of us got up from the table with glad cries; some ran to the windows, some hung over the banisters of the staircase, and others rushed down into the yard, waiting for the carriage. It stopped in front of our door with a quiet squeaking. 'Come and get him down!' said the coachman to my brother and a few friends who had come down to the street with lanterns.

"'Is he ill?' my brother asked, running to the coach.

"'Worse than that… Look at my wounds…' (Saying this he showed the wounds on his hands in the lamplight.) 'Bandits attacked us on the road… They spared me because I'm a Muslim…'

"'Oh my uncle!' my brother suddenly cried in a horrified way. 'Bring the light here, bring it here!'

"They took the lamp and what did they see? My uncle was lying in the coach headless, with his shirt and collar covered in blood. 'His head is in my horse's nosebag,' the coachman growled. 'I got it back from the bandits with difficulty.'

"You can imagine the terror and anguish among those present, and the heartrending cries and screams. The house of joy had become a house of mourning and sorrow.

"Hratch – that was my brother's name – and his two friends took the carriage, just as it was, to the government building. The coachman was questioned by the police and the identities of the criminals established; but despite that, the police made no attempt to apprehend them. The situation changed so much that a few months' later killers of Armenians were considered to have done good work, rather than commit crimes.

"Despite all this we didn't completely give up hope and waited for justice to be done. At the same time my brother continued to approach the appropriate people. One night, just before we went to bed, there was a terrific pounding on our front door. My brother looked out of the window and, turning to us, said that there were two policemen there who had probably come to ask us something about my uncle's death.

"Indeed, when he opened the door, the police stated that they'd come to see us about an important matter. My brother led them into our living room and shut the door.

"The visit lasted for a considerable time. Curious as to the subject of the discussion, leaving my mother and sister in the bedroom, I carefully went to the living room door and put my ear to it and listened, but I could only just hear my brother say 'No, I can't'. The police said 'Very well' and got up to leave. Knowing they were coming to the door, I immediately escaped and returned to my mother and sister.

"My brother and the policemen came out of the living room and, carrying a lamp, went down the stairs with them into our yard. 'Put your lamp down and follow us,' one of the policemen said, as they got to the door opening on the street.

"'Why?' my brother asked, 'Am I under arrest?'

"'Yes, be quick!'

"'Then please allow me to go upstairs and tell my mother of my arrest.'

"'There's no need, she'll hear later.'

"The police took the lamp from my brother's hand and put it on the ground. They then pushed him into the street.

"Seeing my brother's arrest, I got dressed immediately and went down into the street. It was empty. I ran into the next street that went to the government building and, when I saw that it was empty too, I stopped. If the police were going to take him to the government building, it was impossible that they'd have disappeared so soon. So they'd taken my brother in the opposite direction, towards the edge of the city.

"I then remembered a crime that had happened only a few days before: saying that he was a member of a political party (a revolutionary), the police had arrested one of my brother's friends and, to free him, had demanded a large sum of money. The poor young man hadn't paid it. They then took him out of the city on the way to Erzinjan and, after traveling for a quarter of an hour, killed him. They then returned, saying that a 'revolutionary' had tried to escape from them, and they'd been forced to shoot him dead.

"Were they taking my brother the same way? The arrival of the police at night, their meeting with him secretly, his 'No, I can't' response to their offer, then their arresting and taking him away, all looked exactly the same as the crime that had happened a few nights previously.

"So horrified, I retraced my steps and entered that street that went towards the fields. After running for quite a distance, I saw my brother walking between the two policemen, his hands tied behind his back, and his jacket torn from top to bottom.

"'Help! Help!' I cried, suddenly raising my voice. 'Help! Help! They're taking my brother away to murder him!'

"The police, hearing my shouting, immediately turned back. One of them ran towards me and hit me on the mouth so hard that I lost my balance and fell on my back. When I got to my feet some time later, I saw that the policemen and my brother had disappeared. The back of my head hurt very much. I automatically put my hand to it and felt a large bump, the summit of which had split open. From the matted and sticky state my hair I realized that I had lain there for some time unconsciously. Then I felt a foreign body in my mouth and put my hand to it to find a broken tooth in my palm.

"Limping, I dragged myself home and told my mother and sister, who'd been crying bitter tears since my brother and I had left the house, what had happened. Seeing me return alive they calmed down a little and took me to the kitchen to wash my wound.

"They'd hardly wet my head when there was a knock at the street door once more. I immediately washed off the soap and ran and hid in the cupboard in the kitchen, under the floor of which was a secret passage to our larder. My father had it built at one time, so that in the event of a massacre, the women and children in the house could escape and hide in the larder.

"I'd hardly pulled the cover over my head when my mother opened the street door. The same policemen entered and began to search for me. Coming to the kitchen, they asked my mother why she'd got hot water in the sink.

"'I washed my daughter's apron,' my mother said calmly.

"'Why is the water reddened?'

"'The apron was red, and the colour ran.'

"It seems that the policemen looked around them suspiciously, because they then asked, 'What are those drops of water that start at the sink and extend as far as the cupboard?'

"'I went to the cupboard with my wet hands to get a towel,' replied my mother with great presence of mind.

"The police opened the cupboard door and looked at it from top to bottom, without wondering what a towel had to do with a cupboard full of flour, vegetables and oil.

"Disappointed at not catching me, they slammed the cupboard door, left the kitchen and went to the rooms on the upper floor. The search of that floor, needless to say, produced no results. They came down the stairs swearing and went away slamming the street door behind them.

"I came out of my hiding place after the departure of the executioners and told my mother that I should hide in one of our relatives' houses, as the police may return and try to find me. 'But going out into the street now is dangerous,' my mother said. 'Maybe the policemen are waiting at a corner. It's better that you rest. I'll wake you up early and take you to your aunt's house.'

"I agreed with my mother and got into bed. But I'd not even closed my eyes when the police, opening the door with a shove of their shoulders, rushed upstairs shouting, 'Woman! You lied to us... The reddish water in the sink was blood... Show us the apron you washed!' Then suddenly seeing me, they yelled, 'You spawn of the devil, you're lying down are you?"

One of the policemen pulled me out of bed and threw me against the wall like an old rag, pointing his pistol at my chest and shouting, 'I'll kill you like a dog so that you'll understand what it is to fool us!'

"My mother rushed in front of the policeman and holding his hand, begged him to spare my life. 'Get away, woman, or I'll kill you too!' the policeman threatened.

"But my mother wasn't one to be frightened by threats and, holding on to his hand with all her strength, cried, 'For the love of God, spare my son!'

"'Very well, we'll spare him,' said the second policeman, as if he was sympathetic towards me, 'but on one condition. Until we leave, you stay in this room and make no noise.'

"'Yes, yes!' my mother groaned, falling to her knees, almost fainting.

"During all this my younger sister was in a corner, rigid with fright, while I was up against the wall, as if nailed there, like the crucified Christ.

"The policemen left the room and, after closing the door, went to the living room. Shortly afterwards we heard the noise of furniture being moved and the sound of carpets being taken up and removed from the walls. They went from one room to another; it was obvious they were parcelling up all the valuables.

"It was almost dawn when they finished their home-destroying work. They rolled four large bundles down the stairs, took my brother's horse from the stable, and then called us to help them load two of the bundles on to it.

"We obeyed immediately. One of the policemen, taking part of their loot, left. The other stayed with the two remaining bundles, waiting for the other to return with the horse.

"'Pray, woman; today you saw my good side,' the policeman said, 'or your son wouldn't have escaped me.'

"'Good health! May you have a long life!' said my mother.

"'Of course, if anyone asks – although we don't think anyone will – you'll say that we bought all these things from you and you received payment.'

"A quarter of an hour later the policeman who'd taken the first load returned with the horse. Having loaded the remaining two bundles on it, they reiterated, many times, as they were going, that should we protest to the government, they would come and shoot all of us one night.

"'No, no, we won't protest,' my mother said. 'We're not lovers of furniture or material goods. But just tell me, where did you take him and what did you do with my elder son Hratch?'

"'Your son was a fanatical revolutionary apparently. We'd arrested him and were taking him to Erzinjan when he tried to escape, so we...' The policeman closed one eye and, with the index finger of his right hand made the action of pulling a trigger, thus completing his sentence.

"Two days later we heard that the Turks had hanged the diocesan prelate of the Armenian Apostolic Church as well as the notable men of the city. Between 70 and 80 people had died during beatings in prison too.

"A few days later the deportations began. We left with the third caravan. On the journey we saw the bodies of those who'd gone before us – men, women, little children – all mixed up and lying next to one another.

"We walked for days, being attacked at every step by Kurdish bandits, who stole our clothes, shoes, food, money, jewellery and finally all the beautiful women and children.

"At Kemakh Gorge the Kurds stole my sister, who was a year younger than me, and killed my mother, who had tried to resist the kidnapping. Then they separated the old people, the sick and the incapable, and threw them into the Euphrates.

"The rest of us continued on, always subject to killings and massacre, and reached Edessa, where, joining other caravans, we came to Ras-ul-Ain.

"I stayed in that town for six months, where 20 people a day died from starvation and epidemics. It was at the beginning of April when they forced 12,000 of us onto the road to move us to Der-Zor. When the caravan entered the desert, mounted Enezenis – among whom were government mounted units – surrounded us.

"Seeing that they were going to massacre us, I immediately left the caravan and began to run back the way we'd come. A bearded robber pursued me, who, eventually reaching me, was about to stab me in the neck with his dagger when I suddenly threw myself into his arms and cried, 'Don't kill me! I'll become your son!'

"'Will you accept Islam?' the savage asked, threatening me with his raised dagger.

"'Yes!'

"'Come on then,' he said, 'kill someone from your accursed race so that I can believe you're sincere.'

"'But I can't kill anyone,' I said, trembling.

"As you can't kill people, what am I supposed to do with a useless Muslim like you?' my executioner said with contempt.

"'You're right; give me your dagger,' I suddenly said, having an idea. 'I'll show you what a valuable Muslim I am!'

"The Enezeni gave his only weapon and, before he realized his mistake, I rushed at him and buried the blade in his chest up to the hilt. 'Now do you believe how I can kill people,' I said – then, horrified by what I'd done, I ran like a madman into the distance, while the other wild killers, crowing, struck left and right.

"Traveling alone in the desert for several days and nights I finally reached Rakka in a completely emaciated and weakened state.

"About five weeks ago, when I was in front of the town bakery, I saw a rich Bedouin who was buying bread. I went up to him to beg for alms because I was dreadfully hungry.

"The Bedouin looked me up and down and said, 'Boy, if you accept Mohammedanism I'll take you to my tents, where you'll look after my sheep and be freed from hunger.'

"'Where are your tents?' I asked, hopelessly.

"'A very long way away, to the east.'

"For a moment I could picture the state of my fellow-Armenians dying of hunger, then the ever-present threat of massacre, so I replied, 'I'll go.'

"'But don't escape after you've eaten,' the Bedouin threatened, looking me straight in the eye.

"'No, I won't run away.'

"We left Rakka on the same day and reached here two days later. My master has 3,000 sheep. All the tents in the area used by the shepherds and their families belong to him. Everyone's affectionate to me. My master loves me very much, as does his wife and daughter, who's about my age."

"You're only just 15 years old, but the things you've suffered are more than 15 men will have seen," Kirk said at the end of the tale. Then he said to himself "…and I thought that I was the only unfortunate person in the world."

* * *

At dawn the following day Kirk said goodbye to the hospitable shepherd.

"You must go in that direction," Kegham said, pointing to the south with his staff. "You'll reach Der-Zor in three days. If you go to the east you'll be in the empty desert in a day."

"So you're right at the edge of the plains?"

"Yes."

"But what's that?" Kirk asked, suddenly pointing to a company of mounted soldiers that was passing at a great distance heading east. "You said no one lived there."

"It really is surprising," murmured the youth. "I'm sure that there's only desert in that direction."

"Have soldiers passed this way before?" Kirk asked.

"No, it's the first time I've seen them," Kegham said. "Soldiers, police and government officials don't exist here. All the land belongs to my master. All the people you've seen and will see are either my master's shepherds or servants" – then he suddenly cried – "but Mr Kirk, I hope they're not Khalid's soldiers!"

"I thought of that too," Kirk said, "but first, there aren't any Armenians around here – as you yourself have said – for them to have any business here. Then, as there are about 30 mounted soldiers with about ten mules loaded with supplies and food, this company appears to be a military unit, rather than that of a massacring party. But where are they going in that direction, as there's a sea of sand in front of them?"

"They've probably lost their way," Kegham said. "Aren't they Turks? Let them go to hell!"

The Rebels

Kirk had only traveled for about a quarter of an hour when he heard a galloping horse behind him.

"Hey! Compatriot, a moment!"

The former officer looked round and saw a youthful captain who drew up beside him. "Do you know anything of this area or where we are?" the mounted officer asked.

"I'd lost my way too," Kirk answered. "A little while ago a shepherd told me that Der-Zor is three days' journey south from here."

"Thank you!" The captain began to pull on the horse's reins when he suddenly yelled out in amazement. "Kirk, is that you?"

Kirk, hearing his name, was startled, and then looked at the officer's face carefully. "Seyfi!" he cried, running madly towards his former comrade-in-arms.

The soldier threw himself off his horse and embraced Kirk warmly, kissing him on both cheeks. "What sort of state are you in?" he asked, after calming down. "I knew that you were an Armenian refugee from your appearance, but I never expected that under that refugee's garb I'd find the man who saved my life."

"Seyfi, the government has committed many crimes against us," Kirk said in a dull voice.

"I know, I know! What happened to our other comrades from the Dardanelles?"

"All of them were axed to death."

"Axed to death… Major Sisag! Lieutenant Zarmair…!"

"Yes, all of them – 4,000 men: officers and soldiers. Only I escaped. But let's leave that story for now. What are you doing in these parts?"

"I'm not alone. My company is resting behind the hill. We lost our way and I left them to get some information."

"Where are you going like that?"

"Basra."

"What are you going to do there?"

"Kirk, I know you're a brave and honorable young man, and you also saved my life in the Dardanelles, so I don't expect you'll betray me. So let me tell you that I've rebelled against the government."

"Really?"

"Yes, against that unscrupulous government that, after destroying your race, has started to do the same to ours. Did you know that they hanged my father?"

"Your father? But why?"

"Apparently my father was conspiring against the government to set up an independent Arabia under British protection. They hanged more than 30 patriots in Baghdad, Aleppo and Damascus. Hundreds, after unbelievable tortures, are held in dark prisons. Thousands have been exiled to the depths of Anatolia where, unused to the climate and local conditions, they're dying every day from sickness and hunger, just as your's are here, in the Arabian deserts."

Seyfi's lips trembled with a nervous movement. He managed to pull himself together and continued, "To die or shed blood for the sake of such a government is sinful. But I was going to continue to do my military duty without complaint, if one day I hadn't heard that they were going to disarm the Arab officers.

"I was posted to Diyarbekir at that time. In that dreadful action by the government I saw the second act of the Armenian martyrdom that was to be visited on the Arab people. Just as your patriotic people were arrested, imprisoned and then hanged, so have ours. Just as they deported the Armenian inhabitants of border villages allegedly for military reasons, so have ours. Just as they disarmed the Armenian soldiers and officers, so they want to do the same to us. Without doubt those horrible crimes, which were carried out so savagely on your defenseless people, would begin again.

"I heard, from an Arab intellectual who was exiled to Diyarbekir – who was a friend of my father – of the extraordinary persecution that was being meted out to the Arab people, supposedly looking for deserters, or under the excuse of requisitioning supplies. He told me of the circumstances of the hanging of my father, uncle and their four friends, without basic proof or witnesses to their guilt.

"'Seyfi,' I said to myself, 'escape, or one day they'll kill you too.' Yes, escape! But how? First I thought of escaping alone but rejected that idea, thinking that I'd soon be captured and shot. I thought it better to rebel with my entire company, but to do that I'd need to prepare the soldiers. Fortunately most of them were Arabs, the majority of whose families had been deported. It wasn't difficult to persuade them, especially as the example of the Armenians was before them. If they were disarmed tomorrow, they would be condemned to breaking stone at the sides of roads and then one day to be massacred like the Armenian soldiers.

"They began to preach to the other soldiers. At the same time I told an officer named Khoulousi Bey my secret who, although a Turk, was opposed to the present government leaders for the treacherous killing of his uncle, because he was a member of the 'Italaf' (political movement). Khoulousi Bey undertook to prepare all the papers we needed to show on our way that we were going to the Baghdad front as arranged by our army corps. He also prepared a fake order that gave us the right – a rebel cavalry company – to pursue rebels, in other words ourselves.

"We set out with those papers and reached Ras-ul-Ain with all our equipment without hindrance. There we heard that the government had discovered our trick, and had sent soldiers after us. Many of the soldiers – including Khoulousi Bey – hearing this, escaped, frightened that they would be captured and shot. Others also ran away as they'd arrived at their villages and didn't feel it was necessary to continue the journey. But Sergeant Major Rifaat and 27 loyal soldiers stayed with me, swearing to die rather than surrender.

"Avoiding villages and towns as far as possible, in other words keeping to the edge of the desert, we've continued our journey, always heading south. We've a considerable amount of provisions and military stores and have the capability of defending ourselves against pursuing forces."

Seyfi ended his story by saying, "I'm delighted to have found you on my way, Kirk. In these difficult moments I've great need of the advice of a friend of the same heart and as clever as you. I hope that this meeting will be an opportunity you would have wished for to escape from the hell that is Turkey."

"Thank you," Kirk said, deeply touched by his friend's offer. "Only, my friend, I'm sorry I won't be able to accept the offer of accompanying you. More than saving myself, I'm thinking of the salvation of 200,000 of my people at the moment."

"Have you any backing?"

"No."

"So how will you save hundreds of thousands of your people?"

"How? That's the problem."

"Forget it, friend, now is not the time to follow unrealisable dreams," the Arab soldier cried.

"Seyfi, what I'm talking about is not an impossible dream," Kirk insisted. "In an unknown corner of this desert lives a Turkish officer named Khalid who, after having about 50,000 Armenians massacred, has now started to have caravans taken to his Death's Door, to have them robbed, raped and buried alive under a great black rock. This monster has sworn not to let a single Armenian remain alive in the desert. If I manage to kill him, I'll have saved 200,000 Armenian lives."

Seyfi shook his head with annoyance and asked very angrily, "Where is this animal?"

"I don't know. No one does. That's where the difficulty lies," Kirk replied.

"As you don't know, how will you kill him?"

"I'll search for him. According to what I've heard, his lair is south of Der-Zor."

"So it's on our way, as we're going south to Basra. Listen, Kirk, come with us. On the way we'll deal with him."

"And if we don't find where he is?"

"Then you'll return to the place you came from."

"True, but where will I return from? Death's Door may be only a day from Der-Zor, perhaps two days, or a week. Before I set out, I must learn where it is."

"How will you do so, when you say that no one knows?"

"There's a colonel in Der-Zor named Hamdi Bey, Khalid's superior. I'm hoping to learn Khalid's whereabouts from him."

"So you'll force Colonel Hamdi to tell you where he is?"

"No, that's impossible, but there are other possibilities. In other words Khalid may visit his superior. He may go to the camp at Der-Zor to lead another caravan to Death's Door. Finally, there are many ways to find his trail there."

"Let's suppose that you met Khalid in Der-Zor. What will you do? Do you have a weapon on your person?"

"Yes, a dagger."

"Kirk, a man who's massacred thousands of people will have taken the greatest precautions. That sort of monster won't be killed with your dagger. Come with me!"

"No, Seyfi, I've sworn an oath. I must kill that bloodthirsty monster."

"Have you got any money?"

"Yes, about 40 keroush."

"Now I understand… you really have lost your mind, friend. Do you know what they do to madmen like you? They put them under supervision, so they won't hurt themselves. Choose, Kirk: either you go to Basra in chains, or you take up an officer's position with my company."

"Don't joke, Seyfi!"

"I'm being serious, Kirk. Either one or the other!"

* * *

The meeting between Kirk and his comrade-in-arms Seyfi took place on a Saturday morning. On the evening of the same day Khalid killed Mrs Zarouhi and kidnapped Julia.

At the time that Khalid was traveling from the refugee camp to Der-Zor to place his precious gift at Hamdi Bey's feet, the two young officers were riding ahead of a company of mounted men, talking at the same time.

"This is where our points of view differ, Seyfi. Having been successful in your aim until today is not a surety for continued success. The work is very complex and weighty. To travel in uninhabited plains resembles playing blind-man's buff. You don't know where your enemy will appear from."

"But if we travel through inhabited areas as you suggest, government forces will quickly find our trail."

"And how do you know they're not already on our trail?"

"Leave that to me. Look, maybe another army has set out from Der-Zor and, with the soldiers from Ras-ul-Ain, they will catch us between two fires. The real strategy, Seyfi, is to avoid an ambush. And to avoid that you must know the direction the enemy's coming from. And to know that you must visit the odd village and learn about the enemy's movements."

"But your advice creates difficulties for your other aim, as we'll be looking for him in uninhabited places."

"You're right, Seyfi. But we can only get information about Khalid from inhabited places. Once we've learned where he is, we'll return to the desert."

"But what if the village we want to visit has soldiers in it? Won't we have entered a trap?"

"Before we enter a village we'll ask the peasants about that."

"Say we entered a village; how will we get information about any government force following us?* We would no longer be in the desert but in settled areas. Do you see the smoke that's rising from behind the hill?"

"Yes. But I hope there are no soldiers there, Kirk."

"I don't think so, as we can see farmland in the distance."

"That's right. There must be villages around here. But where, I wonder?"

"A young shepherd told me this morning that it took three days to walk to Der-Zor. We've been traveling for over ten hours on horseback. Judging by that, I think we're about 4 – 5 hours north of the town, near a village. Would you lend me your map for a moment?"

* * *

The company of rebels entered the village on the other side of the hill an hour later. It proved to be five hours north of Der-Zor.

The two young officers went directly to the government building and asked the three or four policemen who appeared for information about the village commander. "Your servant, Sergeant Seghayi," replied an old soldier, running forward and standing to attention.

"Seghayi Bey," Seyfi said in a serious tone, "You know, of course, about the rebel detachment led by Seyfi."

"Yes, Sir," replied the police officer. "We've received an order addressed to all units that states that we're to use every means available to arrest those treacherous people."

"Have you got their description?"

"Yes, Sir. There are 92 soldiers, with 18 mules carrying a field artillery piece, 3 machine guns and quite a large quantity of provisions."

"Correct. Our duty is to pursue them. Have they passed this way?"

"Who'd be bold enough to come through here Sir? The town is only five hours that way. If we shout, they'll hear us over there."

"Very well, Seghayi Bey. Have you anywhere for us to rest here tonight?"

"Yes, with pleasure, Sir."

"Then send someone immediately to obtain the necessary food for the soldiers, horses and mules."

---

* There seems to be a break here in the original Armenian text, which we have smoothed in the English translation. —Translator.

"Immediately, Sir!"

Sergeant Seghayi and his men were about to leave when Seyfi called him. "Wait, where are you going without money?"

"Why do we need money, Sir?" Seghayi Bey cried, wanting to help. "We'll commandeer it from the peasants in the army's name."

"How can you commandeer the bread that's been produced by the sweat of the peasant's brow?" Seyfi asked, surprised. "Don't you feel sorry for them?"

"Feel sorry for them? They're Arabs!" the Turk replied, with a contemptuous look on his face.

"No, no! Its against my conscience," Seyfi said, holding his feelings in check. "Take this money and buy what's necessary. Don't just take it."

"Very well Sir. Please go in and have a rest. We'll bring the necessary food shortly."

Kirk and Seyfi went up several steps and entered a large room, in one corner of which was a bed, while in another were several decrepit chairs and a table covered with a mat. There was a telephone, an oil lamp with a dirty chimney, an inkstand, a reed pen, paper and notebooks on the table, and five rifles and their bandoliers hanging on the wall. There were various cigarette paper covers stuck behind the door with flour, apparently as decoration.

"Did you hear that worthless man's excuse?" Seyfi said, nervously sitting at the table. "'Why should we feel sorry for them? 'They're Arabs' indeed!"

"The police did the same in Armenian villages too," Kirk said, sitting, in his turn, on the strongest chair. "They'd eat without paying, they'd drink and, not satisfied with that, they'd rape their host's wife and daughter... saying, 'Why should we feel sorry for them? They're Armenians'."

"I know, my friend, now the Armenians have been destroyed, it's the Arabs' turn to be oppressed."

Just then the telephone on the table rang with a shrill sound.

"A telephone call!" Seyfi cried, looking at it askance. "I wonder where it's from?"

"Let's answer it and see," Kirk suggested. "Put yourself in Seghayi's place and take the orders."

The leader of the rebels lifted the receiver and listened with surprise for a few moments, occasionally saying, "Yes, Sir... Very well, Sir... Don't worry, Sir…" and other polite expressions. He eventually put the receiver down and, wiping the sweat from his forehead, said, "Guess who I spoke to. With your man, Kirk."

"With Khalid?" Kirk asked, shuddering.

"No, with Colonel Hamdi. The man was telephoning from Der-Zor and said that two companies of soldiers from Ras-ul-Ain and Rakka are following us. He's making preparations to leave Der-Zor at midnight to surround us tomorrow morning. He orders Seghayi Bey to be alert and to notify Der-Zor of any suspicious incidents."

"Is that all?"

"What more do you want, friend? We're surrounded by enemies. We didn't do well to come here, Kirk."

"On the contrary, it's good that we've found out about the enemy's movements," the Armenian officer said. "If we'd blindly continued our journey through the desert, tomorrow we'd have fallen into Colonel Hamdi's arms."

"What shall we do now?" Seyfi asked anxiously.

"What we have to do is very simple," Kirk replied. Forces are coming from the north, from Ras-ul-Ain; from the west, from Rakka; and, from the south, from Der-Zor. So the east is open to us."

"So let's leave immediately!"

"No, that would arouse suspicion. We'll leave early in the morning. But we've got something to do here first. Give me that fake order."

* * *

Sergeant Seghayi returned from the village half an hour later. "We brought the provisions," he said, taking an official stance. "Your dinners will be ready shortly. Have you any other orders, Sir?"

"Thank you," Seyfi said. "Please sit down."

"Never mind, Sir; we sit down all day."

"No, sit down. I've important things to say to you," Seyfi ordered in a serious voice. The old sergeant obeyed and sat respectfully on the chair near the door.

"Seghayi Bey," Seyfi said after a moment, "do you know what the punishment is for a soldier who fails in his duty?"

"Please excuse me Sir, if I unknowingly failed in my duty," the Turkish soldier stammered, annoyed.

"Not unknowingly, but knowingly," Seyfi corrected. Sergeant Seghayi looked into his superior's eyes, confused. "When we told you," Seyfi continued, "that we were following the rebel Seyfi, shouldn't you have checked our papers?"

"But Sir, of course I wouldn't have doubted your announcement," Seghayi Bey stammered.

"It's not a question of doubt. You're the village commander and, as such, have the right to examine every military man's papers, even if it's the War Minister."

"I know that's the military law."

"You know it, but don't carry it out. Please read this order," Seyfi said, offering him an official document, in which the Fourth Army Corps commander, Fakhri Pasha, ordered all military authorities to assist the bearer, Ekrem Bey, who had the duty of pursuing the rebel Seyfi's mounted company. "The rebels came from Diyarbekir as far as here," Seyfi continued, after the sergeant had finished reading the document, "because they represented themselves as a regular unit chasing the rebels, and no one doubted their word. We've reached this state through blind confidence, Seghayi Bey."

"You're right, Ekrem Bey," the elderly sergeant muttered guiltily.

"Have you any idea what documents the rebel Seyfi uses on his travels?" the rebel leader asked.

"No Sir, that wasn't in the order to all units," Seghayi said.

"Because," Seyfi said, "he always uses false names. Around here, according to what we know, he represents himself as Colonel Hamdi Bey of Der-Zor. Do you know the colonel?"

"Not personally."

"Your not knowing Hamdi Bey personally is a very bad thing," Seyfi said, appearing in deep thought. Take care, Seghayi Bey, that the imposter doesn't take advantage of your lack of knowledge."

"Don't worry, Ekrem Bey," the old sergeant said with a wolfish smile. "Now that I've found his secret out, if he passes through my hands, I'll know what to do with him."

The Deaf-Mute

Who cared what happened to him?

When the whole world was weeping blood and tears, no one would be interested in a decrepit deaf-mute.

But that individual, scorned by all, didn't think like that.

When he had seen his senior mistress killed, he had run after his junior mistress to at least rescue her from the criminal officer. He had run for more than half an hour, always keeping the swiftly escaping carriage in view.

At one place, where the road skirted a hill, he had left the carriage and followed a short trail, with the hope of getting ahead of the carriage on the other side. (That was why he had not met Alex). But through his bad luck, when he reached the other side of the hill, he found that the carriage had completed the circuit quicker than him and was continuing on its way.

Thinking that it would stop somewhere, Samuel ran after it without stopping.

* * *

He had served in the Aghasian's household in Adana for fifty-five years. He had virtually opened his eyes in the bosom of that family.

He had brought up Julia's father, Manuel, on his lap. When Manuel had grown up, he had married Zarouhi. She had given birth, in turn, to Aghasi, Vazken, Alex and last of all, Julia.

He had brought up the three children on his lap too. He had followed their footsteps day by day; when they were very small he led them by the hand, taking them to, and bringing them back from, the sweet shop; then to school; finally serving them as a servant.

On one black day terrified people had escaped from the streets. His senior master had returned home very pale. Outside men were killing one another with knives, axes and bullets. Aghasi wasn't to be found anywhere. Everyone had waited anxiously. Two days later they had brought his stabbed, dead body home.

Three years passed. Men with trumpets and drums wandered the streets. Vazken, dressed in his army uniform, left one day. Months passed. The postman brought them a letter one evening. Shortly afterwards mourning began. Vazken had been killed on the battlefield.

Two more years passed. Once more men were in the streets with trumpets and drums. The poor deaf-mute had gone to Alex and asked him if he was going to be a soldier too. "No, I'm not yet of military service age," Alex told him, and he had been as happy as a child.

A year later, in other words last year, the police had come to their house. The following day the entire household had set out in a carriage. But where to? Why? He hadn't understood.

Poor Samuel had never been able to understand why, if they were going on holiday, they had left their furniture behind. Why didn't they roll up the carpets in the rooms, cover them in naphthalene and put them away? Why hadn't they put white dustsheets over the red velvet armchairs and settees? Why had they left the chickens hungry in the garden when they left? Why didn't they let him take his personal possessions that he loved so much?

Could it be that they weren't going a long way away, and would return in a few days? But why were hundreds of other families like theirs also going? Then, why were people crying, and why were the cruel-faced police going with them, whipping those who couldn't walk or who couldn't keep up with the caravan?

His senior and junior masters had tried to make him understand, but no explanation had entered his brain. "Where are we going?" he would ask with his usual hand signals.

"We don't know."

"Very well" – pointing to someone he knew – "doesn't this gentleman know either... doesn't that lady know... doesn't the priest know?"

"He doesn't know."

"You're all mad to go! Let's return to the town! I had no time to lock the door to my room; the washing I'd done is still on the line; my trunk hasn't got a key; thieves will steal my brass dishes, as well as my fur coat that I'd left hanging on the wall."

Although no one felt like laughing, they unwittingly did so at his innocence, and had then comforted him, saying that they would return soon.

They had traveled for months until late one night they had reached a large city (Aleppo). Their carriage had traveled down winding, paved streets until it had stopped outside a stone-built house. They got down carefully and moved everything they had with them into a gloomy, damp room.

So, they would be living in this dirty city, in this room like a prison cell. He really didn't understand why they had made such a stupid journey.

And while he had worried, waiting for their return to their beautiful town, the police had come and led them to a barren and waterless place, where strange people, with black faces and bodies, glanced at them with wild eyes.

Fortunately the journey hadn't been long. They had come to a small town (Meskeneh) and settled in a narrow, low hut.

Samuel had thought that the town was their final stop and they would return from there to their home. But his senior and junior masters had opened a grocer's shop and begun to work.

Had these people gone mad? What had such a rich man as Aghasian to do with opening such a poor shop, whose contents wouldn't fill two sacks and a case? Then, why had they left their palace-like beautiful house and furnishings and settled in this charmless place inhabited by primitive people?

Winter had come. Their senior master had become sick one morning and couldn't get out of bed. Every day his temperature had risen and his energy lessened. They hadn't called a doctor, nor brought any medicine. One night they had woken him up: his master had died...

The cold was replaced by hot weather once more. One day the police had arrived and, removing them from that town he disliked, brought them to the camp, where they had pitched their tent surrounded by absolute wretchedness and poverty.

As if all these evils weren't enough, that day that cursed officer had come and got into an argument with his senior mistress. At one time the officer had wanted to whip her and, when he had come forward to protect her, he had received a blow on the head. He had become unconscious after that and, when he had recovered after a time, he had seen the body of his senior mistress lying dead on the ground. His younger mistress, the criminal officer and the carriage had disappeared.

Thinking like this, Samuel had run after the carriage, never mind that he had lost sight of it.

Totally bereft of any knowledge of basic science, he believed that the world was a very small place, and that they lived near its very edge… So the kidnapping officer with his prey couldn't go very far. If he could just get past this hill, he would probably reach that final edge…

But no matter how many hills he crossed, neither the horizons had ended nor could he see the trail of the carriage carrying his mistress.

* * *

Samuel continued for the whole night and the following day in this manner, sometimes stopping to catch his breath, sometimes walking and running.

On Sunday evening, tired and weakened, hungry and thirsty, he had reached a village. He sat on a stone at its edge, sighing and crying. He didn't know where to go, what to do, or what to say to anyone.

There were little children, dressed in rags, a short distance away from him – whose white skin showed that they were Armenians – who were running and jumping about, without paying him any attention. Then one of them saw him, stood in front of him and said something.

Samuel didn't understand what he said – did he want alms? – and while he looked blinking at the child, the boy called his friends, who scampered around him, making funny movements and expressions.

The poor man was so deeply sunk into his sorrows and trouble that he didn't even tell them to go away. What did it matter that they laughed at him… being the subject of ridicule was nothing compared to his sea of troubles.

The mischievous boys, seeing that the deaf-mute, instead of being angry, was crying… felt sorry for him and went back where they had been, continuing their game, occasionally interrupting it and holding out their hands to Arab passers-by who had fruit or vegetables.

Through his tears Samuel could see the boys' parents who, sitting outside hovels built from dry branches and tin sheets, were spinning and knitting, while their children were playing carelessly, without the knowledge of the terrible fate that awaited them. Poor little souls, who had learnt to walk in the burning deserts and thought that this was the whole world and normal life.

Who knows, maybe the police would come and drive them with cracking whips to the refugee camp too. Or perhaps that evil-looking monster would come and kill their mothers and kidnap their elder sisters.

Samuel, with his head in his hands, was in these thoughts when he saw that the boys were running, frightened, back to their hovels, shouting, calling and, with their tiny fingers, pointing at the bend in the road.

Although the deaf-mute didn't understand anything of the boys' shouts, he quickly understood the reason for their alarm when he automatically turned in the direction they had pointed and saw a group of mounted soldiers coming in their direction at the gallop.

Oh! Was the frightening thing he had thought of about to happen? Were the soldiers going to drive the Armenians out of the village into exile in the uninhabited desert?

Samuel saw a small boy, hardly more than four years old, at the side of the road. The boy, unable to run away like his friends, had remained there, looking at the approaching horsemen in terror.

There was no doubt that the soldiers would trample him under their horses' hooves. Samuel jumped up and ran towards the child, trying to get him to safety. But he was very, very late… Before he got there a young officer had already jumped from the saddle and grabbing the boy… stroked his face and hair, at the same time asking him something.

On the boy's positive answers, the officer turned his head and, pointing at the village, once more asked a question. The bashful little boy replied once more. This time the officer squeezed a coin into the child's palm and leaving the soldiers – who were slowly continuing their journey under the command of another young officer – went towards the village, leading the little boy with one hand, and the horse's reins with the other.

How strange! Samuel remained frozen where he stood. It was the first time since they were deported that he had seen a soldier who spoke kindly to an Armenian refugee, who stroked a boy's face and hair, who had given him money and, holding him by the hand like an elder brother, was going to his parents.

Had the officer given the boy money specially, so that he could make friends with him, learn where his mother was to kidnap her later?

But no! There was the boy's mother running towards the officer and, after hearing an explanation, clapping her hands with joy. Shortly afterwards all the old people, the young, girls, even those who were sick came out of their huts and surrounded the officer, exclaiming with surprise.

The young officer spoke with them for some time. Then, handing a purse to an old man, he mounted his horse and galloped away in the direction that his companions had taken.

Samuel, seeing that the old man who had received the purse was distributing money to the people, approached him and, in his unique way, asked who the beneficent officer was.

The old man, thinking that the deaf-mute was asking for money, put a quarter silver piece in his hand.

Samuel shook his shoulders and protested. He didn't want money; just to know who the officer was. But the old man replied, "Have patience, friend, if there's more than enough, I'll give you some more."

"Grandfather, he's deaf," said one of the children playing by the roadside.

"Very well, what does he want? I gave him some money, but he wouldn't take it."

"He's asking who the officer was," said an old woman. Then, shouting at Samuel, she said, "He's Armenian! Do you understand? Like this (crossing herself), he's Armenian!"

Samuel' eyes sparkled with unusual feeling and, fearing that he had misunderstood the old woman's signs, repeated his question.

"Yes, it's true, he's Armenian!"

Seeing this, Samuel gave a horrifying yell and ran after the receding officer, while the people laughed, saying, "Run, old man, it looks as if your share wasn't enough!"

* * *

With the inner satisfaction of having done a new good deed, Kirk whipped his horse and caught up with his companions. "Seyfi, thank you for letting me have that money," he said to his friend. "You won't believe how much good we've done."

"But what's the use? They'll be hungry again tomorrow," Seyfi replied with a voice full of feeling. "What we've done is like putting a single drop of oil in their lamp that's burning low."

"You're right. Did you see how scared the little ones were, and how they ran away when they saw us?"

"Yes I did. We create panic everywhere among these poor people. They've seen so many criminal acts committed by soldiers and policemen that they think we're like them. Did you find out anything about Khalid?"

"They've heard his name, but don't know where he is. 'Go south' they said."

"Fine, we're already going south. But what's that noise? The soldiers are laughing out loud; something funny must have happened." Saying this, the two officers turned back and saw an exhausted and dust-covered old man who, crossing himself, was asking the soldiers something. The latter, while laughing, pushed the old man forward so that he could speak to the officers.

Samuel, recognising Kirk, ran joyfully to him and, kissing his knee, began to make gestures, at the same time making crying noises and weeping.

"He saw you giving the refugees money, and maybe has come to ask for more," Seyfi said smiling. "Give him a 'hundred' coin so that he leaves us alone."

Kirk tried to give the deaf-mute the large copper coin, but the latter, instead of taking it, continued to make his poor gestures.

"He doesn't want money," Kirk said. "He's trying to make us understand something, but I can't understand what it is. Look, he's showing us killing and then escaping gestures."

"He's saying that he's escaped the massacre and run away. Don't you understand, friend? He's trying to make you feel sorry for him, so that you'll give him more money," Seyfi concluded.

"You're wrong!"

"Give him a *mejidieh* (coin) and you'll soon see that I'm right."

Kirk gave the deaf-mute a silver piece and whipped his horse.

"Ehbe... be..." Samuel ran shouting after Kirk and held his horse's bridle. "Ehbe... be! Ehbe... be!"

"We've got trouble," Seyfi said, turning to the sergeant behind him. "Rifaat Bey, is there anyone among you who understands this deaf-mute's language? Ask the soldiers."

"My brother was deaf-mute," said a soldier who came forward shortly afterwards. "I understood what he said, but this man is Armenian. I don't know how I'll understand what he says."

"A deaf-mute's language is neither Armenian nor Arabic," Seyfi said, laughing at the soldier's innocence. "Ask him, let's see what he's got to say."

The soldier turned to Samuel and almost immediately a conversation began between them using gestures. Samuel, seeing he understood what he was trying to say, explained the crime committed in the refugee camp with all its details.

"He says that," the soldier translated, turning to the commanders after a while, "an officer came to their refugee camp last night who, after beating him and killing his mistress, kidnapped her young daughter who was in bed. He asks that we go and save the girl."

Samuel nodded his head positively, realising from the expressions on the officers faces that they had understood what had happened.

"Eh! Where did the kidnapping officer go?" Kirk asked with interest.

"The translator asked Samuel in his turn and, having received the answer, said, "He doesn't know. He says that the girl was kidnapped and taken away in a carriage and that it should be possible to find traces of it."

"Where are the carriage's traces?"

The translator asked the deaf-mute the question. "He doesn't know. He lost it in the dark."

"What was the officer like? Let him describe him."

"He says that he was tall, swarthy and with a pockmarked face."

"It's Khalid!" Kirk murmured hotly. "So the criminal was in this area last night. Ask him where his camp is."

Samuel pointed vaguely.

"What does the poor man understand of geography?" Seyfi pointed out. "He doesn't know village or town names either, otherwise he could give us some idea."

"How long has he been walking to get here?" Kirk asked.

"Twenty hours," the soldier replied.

"So the camp is twenty hours away," Seyfi said. "But twenty hours in which direction?"

"The deaf-mute has walked for twenty hours, but that doesn't mean that he's walked for that long in a straight line," Kirk said. "Maybe he's walked in circles during the night."

"It's probable. What are we going to do now?"

"Continue on our way. Maybe we can get more information from the neighbouring villages." Turning to Samuel, Kirk made hand movements meaning, "Very good, we'll save the girl. You go to that village".

"No!" Samuel protested – and pointing to himself – "I'm coming with you."

"You can't come with us. Go to that village. When we find your young mistress, we'll bring her to you," the officer repeated.

"No, no! I'm coming too."

"This man won't leave us," Kirk said, speaking to Seyfi. "Let him come with us. We'll leave him in the first village we come to."

"Rifaat Bey," Seyfi ordered his bodyguard, "please bring a lightly loaded mule and sit him on it."

* * *

The rebel army left the inhabited region and entered the desert on Monday. Now the desert landscape stretched before them, covered with rocks, thorns and useless plants.

"We're in the desert," Seyfi said. "Government forces can't follow us now."

"But we can't travel eastwards all the time," Kirk pointed out. "It would be a good idea if we turn southwards."

"To inhabited areas again?"

"Yes, always between the desert and inhabited areas, but never the desert alone."

"I understand your point. It's to find Khalid, isn't it?"

"Yes."

"I agree with you, Kirk. But do you understand how dangerous a game we're playing, trying to satisfy our two opposing aims? We want to steer clear of government forces pursuing us and also to find Khalid. If our aim was either one or the other, it would be relatively easy to be successful. But when military units from Ras-ul-Ain, Rakka and Der-Zor are following us, I consider it dangerous and a waste of time to search for an animal in his den in an unknown place."

"You're right, Seyfi. It's difficult to pursue two opposite plans at the same time, but let me control the effort in my own way. We don't lose much by visiting unimportant villages and tents; on the contrary, finding out about government troop movements, we can plan our route accordingly."

"But don't forget that the government forces, finding our trail, can also pursue us in the same way."

"It's true that it'll be dangerous, but nothing ventured, nothing gained, Seyfi."

They came to farmlands once more that evening.

"There must be a village nearby," Kirk said, pointing out a well at the side of the road."

"Yes," agreed his companion, as he looked on the horizon with binoculars. "Someone's coming this way on foot."

A quarter of an hour later the traveller, who was an Arab peasant, reached them.

"Compatriot!" Seyfi asked him, "Is there a village around here?"

"Yes. Go straight on and you'll reach it in an hour," the fellah said.

"Any soldiers in the village?"

"Our village is small. Soldiers and police don't visit us."

"Can we get food and supplies for our soldiers and animals there?"

"Of course, if you can pay for it."

"Do you see," Seyfi said a little later, speaking to Kirk, "how far the Ottoman Army lives off the people? Here, at the edge of the desert, the fellah says, 'Of course, if you can pay for it', as if monetary payment is an anomalous law."

"Because it really is," Kirk replied. "Just as I was telling you the other day, Turkish soldiers would commandeer everything in the Armenian provinces in the name of the army, despite the fact that the Armenian peasants paid regular taxes to the government as well."

"The fellah is within his rights not paying taxes here," Seyfi said justly. "For what road, water channel, school and hospital is he going to pay taxes here in the desert? The Turkish government spends nothing for the well-being, education and health of the people here. The sums collected and stolen go to the pashas, high-ranking officials, viziers, and the sultan's wasteful spending. The Arab villager can't satisfy the parasites sticking to his skin forever.

* * *

Kirk, hearing that there were Armenian refugees in the village, went to the quarter where they lived to obtain the information he wanted and to make arrangements for Samuel to stay there.

On the other side of the village where the soldiers were camped, he saw an old, white-haired man, dressed in rags, sitting at the roadside, begging for bread.

"Father, are you Armenian?" Kirk asked, approaching the beggar.

"Yes," replied the old man, looking at the young officer in astonishment.

Kirk shook his head bitterly. "How did you get here at your advanced age?" he asked in a sympathetic voice.

"Like everybody else, my son."

"Where are you from?"

"Gurin."

"Are you alone, or do you have relatives in the village?"

"They all died," the old man replied, sighing deeply. "God left me alone to expiate I don't know what sin."

"Are there other Armenians in the village?"

"Yes, about a hundred, old and sick, like me."

Seeing the old man's wretched state, Kirk's heart contracted and he said to comfort him, "Have patience, father, these days will pass too."

"We've grown up with these vain hopes for centuries my son," the old man said, sighing again – then, to release all his heartaches, he added – "I opened my eyes 84 years ago to misery... I grew up, became old and have reached the edge of the grave... and the dark days are still to disappear for us Armenians.

"I was a very small boy when one day my father came home with a head wound. When we asked what had happened, he told us that when he was buying meat from the butcher, he'd asked for a fatty piece, and the Turk had hit him on the head with a weight from the scales, saying that the fatty part was too good for the dirty mouths of infidels.

"My father told us that my grandfather had been beaten by the Turks one day because he'd carelessly trodden on a piece of paper. They'd beaten him, saying that treading on a piece of paper was a criminal act, as a portion of the Koran could be written on it.

"When I was a child, we children couldn't go into the street to play. As soon as we went into the street, Turkish youths surrounded and stoned us, saying we were the young of *giavours* (a derogatory term for non-Muslims). There was no school at that time. Only the old people went to church, because the women and girls were, like us, frightened to go into the street, where Turks, like dogs foaming at the mouth, waited for them.

"Gradually times changed. The Janissaries disappeared during my grandfather's time and were replaced by *nizamis*. The nizamis went and the Hamidiyes arrived. The hamidiyes went and the zaptiehs came. They went and the gendarmes arrived... but nothing changed from the Turkish sultans. On the contrary, persecution, oppression and massacre increased, until they removed us from our houses and brought us here and flung us to the four winds like ashes. Don't wait for happy days under those cursed people, my son. That which comes makes you long for the past."

"You're right," Kirk said, with deep anger. "The Talaats made us pine for the Hamids. Now a Captain Khalid has appeared; have you heard of him?"

"Who hasn't heard of that animal?" the old man cried with disgust. "It was only this morning that an Armenian who escaped from his claws arrived here. Khalid's put the camp's last 3,000 people on the road."

"So he's carried out his threat!" Kirk murmured through his teeth. "Where's that escaped Armenian now?"

"He went to Meyadin, and from there in the direction of the river, to Baghdad."

"Where did he escape the soldiers from? Did he give any real directions?"

"He couldn't. All he said was that he came from the east."

"When did he escape?"

"Last night."

"When did they leave the camp?"

"On Saturday morning."

"So the caravan walked all of Saturday and Sunday, and still hadn't reached Death's Door. Where is that place? Is there anyone in the village who knows?"

"No one knows."

"Thank you for all the information you've given me," Kirk said, putting a silver piece in the old man's hand. "Where are the other refugees in the village? I want to see them."

"They all live in the caves you can see in the distance," the old man replied – then thanking him for the money he had received, he added – "May God help you my son."

* * *

When the soldiers woke up on Monday morning, they saw that Samuel had got up before anyone else and was sitting on his mule.

"Get down!" Sergeant Rifaat ordered, using his whip to make an understandable gesture. "Go into that village. There are many Armenians like you there."

"No," Samuel said, shaking his shoulders.

Seyfi, who had seen this from a distance, shouted angrily, "What a stubborn man he is! Boys, take him off by force."

Four soldiers went towards Samuel and after a fearful struggle got him off the mule.

Samuel, desperate, ran to Kirk, to ask for his intervention.

"Go there, to the village," the Armenian officer said, putting a gold coin in his hand.

"No, I don't want money," Samuel protested.

"Don't take any notice of him," Seyfi said to the soldiers, "mount your horses and gallop off."

All of them did so, while Samuel ran after them like a madman, shouting and waving his arms.

"Don't look back," Seyfi ordered. "He'll tire shortly and leave us alone."

But Samuel didn't get tired. He followed the mounted soldiers for an hour, always begging them, crying and making movements.

"This man's not frightened of beatings, nor threats," Seyfi said after a while, turning to Kirk. "What shall we do now?"

"Let him come with us," Kirk said, smiling. "Maybe it's for our good."

"Rifaat Bey, sit him on the mule again," Seyfi ordered his bodyguard. "He's like an old, faithful dog. No matter how fed up his master is of him, he won't leave him."

When they started off again shortly afterwards, Kirk brought his horse near Seyfi's and said, "This animal called Khalid hasn't only kidnapped the deaf-mute's mistress, but on the same day, using his soldiers, has put 3,000 people from the camp on the road to Death's Door too. Based on the information I've culled from the refugees in the village, I can say that either tomorrow or the following day we'll find that cursed man's lair."

"How?" asked Seyfi, glad that an impediment to their escape would finally be removed.

"Get your map out and I'll explain," Kirk said.

A few minutes later, having brought his horse next to Seyfi's, and putting his finger on a place on the map Seyfi was holding, he continued, "At this moment we're at this point. The night before last an Armenian from the caravan escaped and yesterday morning arrived at the village we've just left to go to Baghdad using the Meyadin road. Assuming the man walked for six hours, and during that time covered 30 kilometres, it means that on Sunday night the caravan was somewhere 30 kilometres away from the village. But where? 30 kilometres north? South? East or west? The man came from the east, but it's not clear if it was from north-east or south-east. There's only one thing we can do to check that. Noting that the caravan has been traveling for two days, and that 3,000 people couldn't have walked more that 25 kilometres in one day, it's possible that the place the man escaped from is 50 kilometres south of the camp, at the intersection of the two lines 30 kilometres to the east, in other words about here."

"Your logic isn't bad," Seyfi admitted, "but it all falls to pieces if the caravan didn't travel 25 kilometres a day and if the escapee hasn't come 30 kilometres."

"Yes, but not altogether," Kirk said.

"Very well, let's assume, for a moment, that the caravan was here on Sunday night, where is it now, on Monday morning?"

"Now that we've found, more or less, the direction the caravan has taken, we can extend the line towards the depths of the desert for each day by 25 kilometres," Kirk said. "From Sunday evening the caravan has only traveled on Monday, so at this time it must be 25 kilometres below, about here."

"How many days will it take us to reach that point?"

"We'll not go there, as the caravan always continues its journey," Kirk said.

"I understand. Like a hunter, who takes aim at a bird, we must go further down, taking the movement of the caravan into consideration. But tell me, how many days will it be before we cross its path?"

"By Thursday evening, I hope."

"Don't you think that the caravan will be locked under the rock by then?"

"I don't think so, and here's why. According to what I gleaned from the refugees, after Khalid took the first caravan, it was 15 days before he went to Der-Zor to get the second one, and the third caravan was 20 days later. The fourth was 10 days later; the fifth, 14 days later; this last one, the sixth, 23 days later. From this we can determine that it takes ten days – the timescale between the third and fourth caravans – to go from the camp to Death's Door and return from it. If we allow the monster two days rest out of the ten, then we are left with eight days."

"So Death's Door is four days from the camp, and according to your logic, the caravan will get there this evening," Seyfi pointed out.

"No," Kirk said. "Don't forget that Khalid and his soldiers go to the camp from Death's Door on horseback, while the caravan goes from the camp on foot. If we say that the journey takes two and a half days on horseback, the time taken by the caravan is five and a half days, so it'll arrive by Thursday midday or evening."

"By that calculation we have time to prevent the crime."

"I think we will. But it's different for the deaf-mute's mistress, bearing in mind that she was kidnapped on Saturday evening by carriage from the camp, one day further from that at Der-Zor. If Khalid brought her to Der-Zor that night and left there on Sunday morning, he'd have reached Death's Door that evening. But if, due to the girl's illness, he stayed in Der-Zor for a day or two, he may, for example, instead of leaving on Sunday, have left on Monday morning. I think we'll have time to rescue her from that animal's claws."

* * *

Wednesday had passed without incident until late.

To free themselves from boredom, the soldiers had taken to joking with Samuel, threatening to take him off his mule.

At first the poor man believed their jokes and became angry and shouted at them, but later, seeing that they were joking, he laughed as well, and seated on his mule, continued on the way, always looking at the hills and flat areas in the hope of finding his mistress' trail.

Late that evening, a Bedouin shepherd's announcement that he had seen about 20 soldiers that morning traveling south spoiled the soldiers' mood.

"Do you know," Seyfi said at one point, bringing his horse close to Kirk's, "there's discontent among our soldiers but they don't want to talk about it yet. Several of them, using indirect explanations, wanted me to understand that they didn't agree with our action against Death's Door."

"Very well, let them stay away," Kirk said.

"But the problem is not of staying away," Seyfi pointed out. "They're muttering that they're wasting time going east when our route is south."

"Give me one more day's grace, Seyfi," Kirk said. "If by tomorrow night we don't find Deaths' Door, well continue south. Let me also say that it's good fortune that we've come east. If we'd gone south, we'd have come up against the government soldiers seen by the Bedouin shepherd."

"Yes, I told the complainants that we'd chosen this route for their safety," Seyfi assured him.

"What's the noise?" Kirk asked, suddenly turning round. "Why's the deaf-mute shouting again?"

"The soldiers joke with him and he shouts," Seyfi laughed.

"No, look. He's showing us something on the ground."

The two comrades rode their horses where the deaf-mute was. He was looking at the ground amazed, where carriage wheel tracks had made deep ruts in the dust that stretched onward in the direction they were going.

"Judging from the horseshoe marks we're on the right track," Kirk said joyfully. "You can see that the carriage has gone in the direction we're traveling."

"Yes, I can see," Seyfi said. "But when did they go?"

"There's the answer to your question," Kirk replied, pointing to a pile of horse manure between the ruts about 20 paces away.

"Your discovery, although not the subject, is brilliant," Seyfi cried, laughing aloud. "Now the problem is to know when it was left there," and turning to his bodyguard, Rifaat Bey, he added "you've been looking after horses for years… can you give us an idea?"

"It's from this morning," the sergeant replied, carefully examining… the subject.

"So if the carriage belongs to Khalid, he's eight hours ahead of us," Seyfi concluded.

"This means that Khalid left Der-Zor on Monday morning," Kirk pointed out. "Seyfi, I'll lay a bet that this parallel line is the string that will get us out of this labyrinth."

"Yes, let's follow it."

But unfortunately the detachment was only able to follow it for an hour. Then it got dark, and everything was lost to sight.

* * *

When the rebels set out on Thursday morning, they found that the wind had eradicated the carriage tracks they had been following.

After traveling for an hour, in place of the flat country they had been going through for days, the landscape was now made up of such rocky terrain that it would have been difficult for even cannon wheels to leave traces on the hard ground, leave alone a light carriage.

"I've great hopes that we'll get to Death's Door by this evening," Kirk said, encouraging his comrade who, happy for a time to have been following the wheel tracks, had now given way to despondency.

"Your time will be up this evening," Seyfi said. "If we don't find Death's Door, we'll turn our horses south."

"Don't lose hope, friend. I'm sure we're on the road to victory."

"But where are we going like this, as we can't see wheel tracks in front of us?"

"We're following the line we drew on the map. It's not important if the carriage has gone a little above or below. It's going in the same direction."

Near midday the soldiers spotted the corpse of a woman at the side of the road, covered with thistles.

"She's totally nude," Sergeant Rifaat said, bringing the news to the two officers. "But it's obvious from her face that she's Armenian."

The two comrades rode quickly to the corpse and, dismounting, examined it silently.

"She died only about three or four hours ago," Kirk said, finally breaking the silence. "The presence of an Armenian woman's body means that the people from the camp passed here a few hours ago."

"Right! Forward!" Seyfi commanded.

The horsemen advanced, and half an hour later found themselves faced with another surprise. A camel caravan was coming in their direction from a great distance away. It was unexpected, as there were no habitable places in front of them.

Seyfi looked at the caravan with his binoculars for a few moments, then turning to Kirk, said, "There are about ten camels loaded with bales. Three soldiers are accompanying them. What do you think, friend? Do they belong to the military units that are after us?"

"Let's be patient," Kirk said. "We'll know shortly."

Indeed, with the horsemen moving forward and the camel caravan coming towards them, they met very soon afterwards in the middle of the desert.

"What's the load and where are you coming from?" Seyfi asked the camel drivers' leader, who was none other than Rasum, Death's Doors transport organiser.

"Uniforms," the criminal replied, without suspecting who he was dealing with.

"Where are you bringing them from and where are they going to?" Seyfi asked again.

"We're bringing them from a military post five hours from here and taking them to Der-Zor."

"What's the use of having uniforms in a military post?" asked Kirk, joining the conversation.

"Military movements go through that post," Rasum replied.

"Who's the post commander?"

"Captain Khalid Bey."

Seyfi looked meaningfully at Sergeant Rifaat.

A moment later the soldiers, taking with them the captured camels and their drivers, quickly went towards Captain Khalid's military post.

The Home-Destroyer's House

The final group of people from the camp at Der-Zor had almost completed their arduous journey when, towards evening, they saw a great black rock. In front of the rock was Death's Door that seemed to rise out of the emptiness like a hideous guillotine.

Although just a little while before they had been wishing with all their hearts for death, the frightening aspect of the black rock horrified them and they all stopped as one in their tracks.

"Walk on!"

The whips, that had for a time been unused, cracked once more. The bayonets glittered. Bullets whistled through the air.

To avoid the merciless blows, people began to run forward, terrified, when they stopped unnerved. They had seen a black cloud on the horizon that gradually got bigger...

It was a company of about 30 soldiers that was hurtling towards them with the speed of lightning.

"Soldiers! Soldiers!" the poor people screamed, staggering and falling to the ground. "They're going to massacre us!"

Khalid's criminal mounted soldiers, who never expected to see a mounted unit in those parts, stopped their beatings for a moment and were bewildered to understand who these horsemen were and what they were coming for.

The answer to their question wasn't long to arrive.

"Surrender!" a young officer commanded, who was none other than the commander of the rebels, Seyfi. "Hands up!"

The criminals, at first glance not understanding the situation, hesitated. They had hardly reached for their weapons when they found rifles pointing at them from every direction.

The disarming and arrest of the murderers took but a few moments.

The Armenians, amazed at this unbelievable development, looked blinkingly around them – not knowing if they were in a dream or living in reality – when another young officer, whose eyes were sparkling with an unusual flame of vengeance, rode up to them. "Don't be afraid!" he said, putting his hand on the first refugee's shoulder. "I'm Armenian… my name is Kirk. We're going to break down Death's Door. Don't stay here; run away, as far away as you can from here. Don't go to Der-Zor; go towards Aleppo! Take this money and go at once! Run away without looking behind you! Run away with all your strength!" And handing a purse to the first refugee, he continued, "We've got about ten camels carrying loads of clothing. Divide the clothing among those who are naked. Then put those who can't walk on the camels and go at once."

It was as if fire was going to break out in this second Sodom and Gomorrah. The people, as one man, got to its feet and, with renewed energy and spirit, escaped without looking back, while Kirk whipped up his horse and returned to his comrade-in-arms who was, at that moment, busy tying the hands of the arrested men.

* * *

"Seyfi," the Armenian officer said after a moment, in an outburst of gratitude, squeezing his friend's hand, "Thank you so much… You saved the lives of 3,000 people."

"Now its only Khalid, isn't it?" the Arab soldier said with a victorious smile.

"Now it's the turn of that rogue," Kirk muttered with deep anger.

"We'll deal with him. Don't worry, friend." Saying this, he gave Sergeant Rifaat a series of short orders. He put the prisoners in Rifaat's and the others' military charge, and then he left to go to the distant Death's Door with Kirk.

They reached their destination an hour later. Although it was now dark, the two officers, so they wouldn't be seen, approached the building from the rear and dismounted.

After a short examination, they were convinced that it wasn't possible to enter Death's Door without drawing the attention of the people inside.

"There's only one way," Kirk said, "we'll have to climb down the rock face."

"I was thinking the same thing," Seyfi said and took the first step up it.

After some time, the two officers had climbed up like gymnasts and, passing over the roof of the soldiers' quarters, entered the building.

They had hardly descended to the balcony in front of the upper storey when they saw two soldiers in the yard below, one of whom was carrying a lamp and the other a human body, moving slowly towards the iron door set into the side of the rock.

"Oh!" Kirk muttered, shaking and startled. "The monster's killed his victim."

"Don't make a sound. Let's go and see where they're taking it," Seyfi whispered, squeezing his friend's hand.

After a short interval they descended the right-hand staircase with great care and quietly followed the deathly procession, at the same time listening to the two soldiers who, without any suspicion of the presence of outsiders, were talking to one another.

"As she's not dead, we ought to keep her."

"What're you going to do with a dying girl, friend? Didn't you hear? The caravan will arrive soon. There are hundreds of girls you can choose from it."

"But I don't understand. Why all the hurry? When the caravan arrives, we'll throw her in then."

"I think you're in love with the girl, Khayri!"

"Don't forget that Rasum gave her to me when he left."

"I understand, friend! There's no famine of Armenian girls. Did you see the bit Khalid Bey brought? Wasn't she beautiful! She'll be ours tomorrow."

"But until he tires of her and leaves her to us, a week will have gone by."

"What else have we got to do? We'll wait. Until then, may the women in the caravan be alive!"

Reaching the rock, the soldier carrying the lamp, who was called Khayri, opened the iron door. Holding the lamp, he went into the depths of the cave, while the soldier carrying the body followed him, panting.

They had hardly gone forward ten paces when a horrifying sound came from behind them. "Put your hands up!"

The order was so unexpected and frightening that the two criminals were shaken. However, while one dropped the dying girl, the other dropped the lamp, thus creating pitch darkness in the cave, much against his will.

"Light the lamp," Seyfi ordered, "and explain to us who you are and what you're doing with this woman here."

Not a sound, not a movement.

What had happened to the soldiers? They hadn't escaped, nor fallen to the floor, as the two officers hadn't heard their escape or the sound of them falling down. Was it possible that they had become tongue-tied from fright and frozen there, or were they coming towards them to suddenly attack them?

The latter was the most probable, because it was so dark in the cave that if they put their fingers in their eyes, they wouldn't know it.

"Where are you? Have you dropped dead that you make no noise?" Seyfi shouted impatiently. "Light the lamp, or we'll smash your heads in!"

There was the sound of a match being struck in the distance. One of the soldiers, bending down, picked up the lamp and shortly afterwards lit up the cave's interior, the air of which was heavy with a sickly stinking smell.

"Who's this woman?" Kirk asked, terrified, leaning over the dying girl. "Why did you bring her here?"

"She's an Armenian girl, Sir," the soldier who had carried the girl's body replied, thinking that answer would negate their crime. "We'd brought her from the refugee camp, so that she could do our washing and cook our meals... She became ill as soon as she got here. We saw she'd die, so we brought her here."

"But look over here!" Seyfi suddenly shouted, using a terrible swearword, and pointing towards a corner of the cave. "What're these?"

Kirk glanced in the direction Seyfi was pointing and was stunned, as if turned to stone, upon seeing many human corpses – all of them completely naked. They had been piled one on top of another. He stayed silent for a moment then, conquering his feelings, asked, "Who are they and who killed them?"

"They're Armenians, Sir," stammered the soldiers, very frightened. "We didn't kill them... They died of natural causes."

"Natural causes?"

"Yes, Khalid Bey imprisoned them here... and they died of hunger."

"But they don't have that appearance. They've been killed and piled on top of each other," Kirk growled, looking at the criminals with blazing eyes.

"We swear we didn't kill them," stuttered the soldiers. "When they died, we took off their clothes and piled them up like that."

"Didn't you ever pity them when you imprisoned them here alive?"

"What could we do, Sir? We're soldiers and have to obey our officers' commands."

"You're not soldiers; you're unfeeling criminals," Kirk yelled, pouring out the venom of hatred from his soul for the first time on the heads of the two animal-like beings. "You've made this post into a slaughter house, to bring caravans of Armenian refugees here, to kill them, rape their women and girls, and then to steal everything they possessed. We saw the bales of clothes that you were sending to Der-Zor and forced your camel drivers to tell us of your crimes. A little earlier on we saw your 16 bandit comrades who, using their bayonets, were bringing a 3,000-person caravan here. You've become so stone-hearted from drinking Armenian blood that you'll be the first to pay for your crimes, then we'll deal with your officer, Khalid Bey."

"Don't, don't...!"

The sound of two gunshots silenced the two criminals who had fallen to the floor screaming.

"Come on, Seyfi," Kirk said, pulling his comrade by the arm. "Justice was done here. The time has now come for the cursed Khalid and his henchmen. But before that, let's get this girl out of this place that smells of death. Although she's in agony, maybe we can bring her back to life."

* * *

Khalid had returned from his journey two hours before and, having his devoted servant lay a table immediately, had seated Julia opposite him, to make her a participant in his drunkenness.

He filled a cup with *oghi* from a flask and offering it to his victim, said, "Here, let me see you drink this."

"I'm not used to drinking spirits," Julia said, refusing his offer with great loathing.

"You'll get used to it. Here, take it."

"I can't take anything from the hand of my mother and brother's killer."

"Was it my fault that I killed them? They shouldn't have gone against me."

"Did you want them to be indifferent to the kidnap of their daughter and sister?"

"Was your brother an indifferent onlooker? The idiot had the audacity to come to Der-Zor with a friend, to the house where I was staying, to steal you away. We caught them in the act, and taught them a lesson, just as I teach lessons to all those who dare to oppose my will. I told you to drink it!"

Julia pushed Khalid's hand away with disdain, spilling the cup's contents.

"No Armenian woman has ever been so bold with me," Khalid growled, biting his lips with anger and filling the cup once more. "But what can I do when I've got to hand you over untouched to Hamdi Bey. I repeat, Julia, pray that no other woman more beautiful than you is in the caravan that's due. If I see a more suitable girl to give to Hamdi Bey, then I know how to make you obedient to me. Here, drink this."

"No, I won't."

"Listen, Julia, my patience is very limited. If I get angry, then I take no notice of Hamdi, Enver, Talaat, Mohammed or God. Do you understand? Don't make me angry. I'm telling you to drink it!"

"Even if you were to kill me, I won't drink it."

"I can see that you're a very stubborn girl. But look, do you see the room next door? I've imprisoned hundreds of rebellious girls like you in the 'women's cage' and crushed their bones under my feet. Do you understand? I don't like your attitude."

"I believe what you say. Without doubt you've proved that you're a bloodthirsty criminal!"

"So be afraid of me."

"I've got one soul to give to God. I'm not frightened of men."

"I'll take that soul of yours simply to make you understand that the person opposite you is the god of the desert Khalid," the monster cried, giving out a fierce growl. "Come and sit next to me."

Julia, seeing the monster's amorous looks that were like that of a lynx following her, screamed with terror and swiftly jumping up, ran towards the door.

Khalid reached her with one bound and taking her by the hair, threw her to the ground, chuckling hellishly at the same time. "Where are you running to? Don't you know that the person who enters Death's Door never leaves it alive?" Then bending over his victim, driven by madness, he started biting her cheeks and shoulders, saying, "Don't shout, or I'll strangle you like I would a kitten."

* * *

Just then Hamid's voice was raised outside. "Hey! Who're you?"

"Us... Here's who we are!" The sound of a shot finished the sentence.

The Armenian girl, struggling under Khalid's enormous weight heard a scream and the sound of a body falling by the door, then she saw the door thrust open on itself and the entry of a young officer who, aiming this firearm at the executioner's chest, cried, "Leave her alone, animal!"

Khalid immediately straightened up and confused, at the same time angry at being disturbed in his pleasure, said, "Who are you, and by what right do you come into my room?"

"I'm the vengeful Armenian nemesis," Kirk replied, looking his enemy up and down with hatred. "I've arrested the soldiers who were bringing the caravan and have come to destroy Death's Door on top of you." Then seeing that Khalid was making a quiet attempt to pull his pistol out of his pocket, the heroic Armenian shot him first and cried, "Die, you disgusting criminal!"

He then jumped over the mortally wounded evil man's body on the floor and went towards the Armenian girl who, leaning against the wall, was trembling with terror. "Don't be frightened Miss, I'm Armenian."

"You're Armenian? Impossible!" whispered the poor girl, almost losing her reason.

"Come with me," Kirk said, taking her out of the room. "You're not in danger any more. My comrade-in-arms Seyfi and I came here to destroy Death's Door."

"I'm eternally grateful to you, Sir," Julia exclaimed, impulsively throwing her arms around her saviour. "But how did you know I was here?"

"We found out from your deaf-mute servant."

"Samuel? Where is he?"

"He's with our soldiers."

Seyfi, at the same time, had dealt with Reza and his two soldiers who, at Hamid's cry, had come out of their room to see what was happening. "There's no one left alive in Death's Door," he said, greeting Kirk and Julia at the bottom of the stairs. Then, giving Julia a respectful greeting, he said, "It's all over now, Miss."

"Let me introduce you to my noble friend, the Arab Captain Seyfi," Kirk said, introducing the two. "We owe your life and those of the people in the caravan to him." Then, when he had finished, he suggested, "Let's go to the other Armenian girl."

"There's no need," Seyfi said in a sad tone. "I've just come from her. She gave up the ghost with a smile on her lips."

"What are you saying? Was there another Armenian girl here?" Julia asked, bewildered.

"Yes," Kirk replied, his moist eyes downcast, "another victim like you… because she was dying, two soldiers wanted to throw her into the cave. We surprised and punished them."

"Please take me to her," Julia begged. "I'd like to say the Lord's Prayer over her."

While Kirk took her to the last victim of Death's Door, Seyfi left the building and gave a prearranged two-blast signal to his soldiers using his whistle.

An hour later, Lieutenant Mahir and his robber band – 19 people altogether, including Rasum and his men – were brought to Death's Door under Sergeant Rifaat's guard and taken to the black rock where they had led 5,000 Armenian refugees without any compunction.

"Sub-Lieutenant Kirk," said Mahir, the last person to cross the threshold, "you're powerful at the moment and you can deal with us as you wish. I don't rely on your forgiveness, but before entering the tomb I warn you that this crime of yours won't go unpunished."

"You're right, Lieutenant Mahir, crime doesn't remain unpunished," Kirk said. "I'm dealing with you just as you did with thousands of defenseless Armenians when you were powerful. As a number of your friends had sudden deaths, they couldn't regret their crimes. I hope that you'll have a lot of time to understand what it's like to bury innocent people alive."

"Life is a wheel, Sub-Lieutenant Kirk. It'll turn again," Mahir muttered through his teeth.

"It turned, Lieutenant Mahir, go in." Mahir entered the cave with a show of bravado.

While Kirk closed the cave door, Seyfi and Rifaat set a number of explosives under the rooms.

Shortly afterwards the sound of a tremendous explosion shook the wide expanses of the desert.

When the smoke and dust lifted, the rebels saw that the black rock remained, but Death's Door in front of it had vanished, just as all its criminal owners had.

* * *

The rebels moved off at dawn the following day. The two young officers went in front, with Julia between them. She was also on horseback. Behind Julia came Samuel, who like an adjutant wouldn't leave his mistress. And behind the deaf-mute came the soldiers under the command of Sergeant Rifaat. The loaded mules and the animals taken from Death's Door followed them and formed part of the great procession.

"So," Kirk asked, turning to Julia, "was there an attempt to rescue you in Der-Zor?"

"Yes," Julia replied in a strained voice. "My brother and an Armenian from Kayseri named Paul, hearing that I'd been kidnapped, left the refugee camp straight away and, walking all night, reached Der-Zor the next day to rescue me from the monster's claws. They got to know an Armenian woman from Hadjin named Mrs Iskouhi, and through a boy that she knew got in touch with me. Paul and my brother got men's clothing and tin containers to me, so that I could leave the house disguised as a water carrier. But Khalid found out at the last minute and arrested my brother and his friend. He brought them to the garden, got them down on their knees, and executed them before my eyes."

"Let's leave this sort of conversation," Seyfi said, seeing that Julia was very affected from the recollection of those sad events. "That bloodthirsty hyena committed many crimes against the Armenians and finally received his just reward. Now, tell me Miss, are you comfortable on the horse?"

"Yes, very, Seyfi Bey."

"Were you used to riding?"

"I often rode on our farm in Adana."

"Do you know why I asked?" Seyfi asked. "As we told you, we've embarked on a long, dangerous journey. It could be that we travel for days and nights in the desert without seeing a village or even a tent. So, until we can leave you in a safe place, Baghdad for example, where I've a mother and a fiancée, will you be able to come with us?"

"I can travel for weeks on horseback if necessary," Julia confirmed. "I was already used to the saddle and deportation made me used to a harsh life, so you've no need to worry about that, Seyfi Bey."

"Wouldn't your illness be an impediment to a long-lasting journey?" Kirk pointed out.

"No. I feel better today," Julia replied. "My weakness was not so much from the illness I suffered from, as the results of my misfortunes. Now I've been saved, I feel that a heavy load has been removed from my shoulders."

"Right, let's consider this subject closed," Seyfi said. Turning to Kirk, he commented, "Eh, friend, the first part of our plan was successful. The second's still to be tackled."

"Yes, the most difficult and complex part," Kirk murmured thoughtfully.

"What do you mean?" said Seyfi amazed. "I thought all that's left is the easy part of the plan."

Kirk smiled bitterly. "Until now the most difficult thing we've done was to find the lair of a group of robbers," he said looking thoughtful. "Once we'd found it, the task of destroying it was as simple as drinking water. But now..."

"Now what?" Seyfi interrupted, "We'll head south without wasting time, won't we?"

"Of course we will," Kirk said. "But Seyfi, let's suppose that by evading government forces we reach Baghdad or Basra one day... After that how are we to join the British? If we assume that the difficulties getting from here to the front are the same as those we encountered trying to find Death's Door, which one of the things we've yet to do is the easiest? To blow up a nest of vipers with explosives or making our way through the lines at the front and joining the opposing forces?"

"Of course the second is difficult, but not impossible to achieve," Seyfi pointed out.

"It's not impossible for one or two people who make the journey through the mountains and valleys, avoiding the rearguard and the forward regiments, to join the enemy after many difficulties," Kirk said. "But it's not the same for our company. If we're to cross the frontier secretly, there are too many of us, and if we're going to fight our way across, there are too few."

"They're only a few soldiers, but I'm sure of their devotion."

"The soldiers' devotion is questionable," Kirk said. "I've been observing them for six days and do you know the most significant thing I've found out? These men follow you, Seyfi, not out of devotion, but because it's in their interests."

"What does that mean?"

"You left Diarbekir with 92 men and reached Ras-ul-Ain with 28," Kirk continued. "Why? Because the other 64 deserters had reached their villages and had no reason to continue the journey. I found out, through indirect questioning, that these men's villages are further south... Rest assured Seyfi, the moment that you reach their lands, you'll not see one man by your side."

"Why are you so pessimistic, friend?"

"This is the truth, Seyfi. Let's be realistic."

"So what shall we do?"

Kirk was silent for a moment to gather his thoughts, and then replied, "Seyfi, to go through the front lines is an unrealistic plan, bearing in mind that we haven't got sufficient strength, nor can we rely on what we have got. There's only one way to go. We should disband the company, give animals, military supplies, provisions and money to each man from what we've got with us and let the men go where they want to. If the aim really is to go over to the British, it can succeed better on an individual basis rather than as a body. If the aim is to desert, what responsibility do we have to go along with it as far as individuals' villages?"

"Oh! What's going to happen to us?"

"It's better to say what are we going to do? Seyfi, we can do one of two things: either stay in this country or leave it. To attain either of these aims we've no need of armed force. Let's examine why we want to go over to the British, and what protection there is if we stay here. If we want to go over to the British, to serve with them as volunteers, the reception they'll give us is uncertain. If we want to save our skins from the Turkish yoke, that's easier here – for example, to take refuge in Lebanon's mountains, where no Turkish soldiers have been able to set foot for years – than getting through the front lines at Baghdad."

"That's not a bad idea," Seyfi said, gradually becoming convinced by Kirk's logical thinking. "Especially as I've an aunt in Damascus, whose husband – hanged with my father – had a close relationship with the independent tribal leaders of the Druse Mountains."

"So, if our aim is to be free of Turkish persecution," Kirk said in an animated tone, we can seek shelter with one of those tribal leaders. If our aim is to help our own people, then we'll be of more use by remaining in our country, than entering British service."

Seyfi, looking at the ground, thought for a long time and, breaking the silence, said, "Kirk, that's a serious matter. We'll talk of it again. Tell me where we're going now, will you?"

"South," Kirk replied. "That's what the compass shows us."

* * *

The rebel unit continued southwards without incident on that and the following day.

At midday the following day, they left the dry plains and once more entered a mountain plain, covered with bushes, thistles and innumerable piles of rocks.

In the evening they noticed a line of dirt hills, like black clouds, on the horizon.

"The Euphrates is behind that mountain range," Seyfi said, looking at the hills with his binoculars. "We'll camp tonight at the foot of those hills, go through the mountains tomorrow, then follow the river's current south, and reach Baghdad on horseback."

"How long will that journey take?" Julia asked, with a curious look.

"Why do you ask, Miss? Have you got tired?" Seyfi asked.

"No, simply for my information," Julia said.

"The Euphrates is naturally nearer to Der-Zor than to Baghdad," Seyfi replied, "But if there are no problems, I think we'll reach Baghdad in a week."

"Seyfi, when you talk of problems, I can see a problem," Kirk said, suddenly joining the conversation. "What's that dot that's coming towards us?"

Seyfi suddenly jumped and, aiming his binoculars in the direction Kirk pointed out, said unhappily, "Cavalry!"

"Really?"

Kirk took the binoculars from his friend's hand and in his turn looked at the moving black dot and said, "Yes, about twenty of them. Their commander is looking at us with binoculars too."

"Let him look. There are thirty of us; we'll soon beat them," Seyfi said, quickly regaining his composure. Then, turning round, he commanded the soldiers to halt. When they had carried out the order, Seyfi rode his horse into the middle of them and said, "Comrades, get ready for battle. Government soldiers are coming this way."

The rebels, surprised by the news, looked around them for a moment to see the approaching enemy.

"They're over there," Seyfi said, pointing with his sword at a black dot. "It's difficult to see them individually with the naked eye, but they can be seen clearly with binoculars; there are 20 of them."

A low murmuring began among the soldiers. It wasn't clear what they were saying, but almost all of them were complaining.

Seyfi, seeing that they had not said 'we're ready to fight', asked crossly, "Why are you silent? Aren't you sure of your strength?"

"Of course we're sure," Sergeant Rifaat said, speaking for the soldiers. "But as the enemy is so far away, why should we fight? Isn't it better to…" – he was going to say "escape", but was ashamed, and said – "retreat."

"Where shall we retreat to?" Seyfi asked, astonished at his most trusted bodyguard's attitude. "Wherever we go, we'll be persecuted by the enemy."

"Let him. When we're in difficulties, we'll fight."

"But where else will we find such favourable positions as these?" Kirk asked, pointing out the piles of stones. "Here victory is ours a hundred times out of a hundred, Rifaat Bey."

"Especially as," Seyfi added, "we have the advantage of numbers over them."

"Don't rely on numbers," Rifaat said. "These troops may be the advanced guard of the real army."

Seyfi, seeing that it was useless to argue with his sergeant, turned to the soldiers and said, "Comrades, speak out. Do you want to fight or run away?"

"We want to fight," said seven or eight voices.

"It's not shameful to escape when we're in danger," 12 other voices said.

The remainder gave no answer, not knowing whether they should say yes or no.

While they were arguing in a state of indecision and uncertainty the government forces came closer, and suddenly a horseman carrying a white flag rode out from the mass of cavalry and galloped towards them.

"Soldiers, take up your positions!" Seyfi ordered.

All of them, even those who were in favour of retreat, finding themselves in a position of fait accompli, immediately obeyed and, dismounting, took up positions behind rocks.

"Don't worry, Miss," Kirk said to Julia, as he helped her dismount and sat her behind a rock. "I'll always be looking after you, only don't move from where you are and, especially, keep your head down behind the rocks just as our soldiers are doing."

Kirk settled Samuel behind another rock and gave him the same instructions, saying by hand signals, "Stay here. Do you understand? Don't move from here!"

Just at that moment the messenger with the white flag approached, courteously greeted them, and handed Seyfi the following letter:

> "If you want to avoid unnecessary bloodshed to both you and us, surrender. Resistance is futile. You are surrounded. Think well. I await your answer with impatience.
>
> (Signed) Colonel Hamdi, Commander, 3rd Cavalry Regiment."

After showing Kirk the letter, he wrote on the back, in pencil:

> "If you think we'll surrender to a criminal government, you are sadly mistaken. We, who are not afraid of death, are not frightened of threats. Only the sword can be victorious over us.
>
> (Signed) Captain Seyfi, Commander of the rebels."

The messenger, taking the answer, returned to his unit at the gallop. Shortly afterwards the sound of rifle fire shook the area.

* * *

The battle continued for about half an hour, without either side gaining an important victory.

Kirk, while he fired from behind his rock, gave Julia, who was hardly 15 paces away behind another rock, constant encouragement, saying, "Don't be frightened, Miss, we won't let them advance."

"Where are they?" Julia asked in a touching voice.

"50 paces away. They're hidden behind rocks just like us."

"But look this way," Julia suddenly exclaimed, pointing to three soldiers from their company who were escaping rapidly on horseback.

As Kirk turned his head, he saw Seyfi, who had left his post, run towards the other soldiers – probably to prevent them running away. However, he received a bullet in the head and immediately fell to the ground as if struck by lightning.

At the same time, the government forces, seeing the demoralized state of the rebels, immediately took to the offensive and, leaving their defensive positions, advanced ten paces to take cover behind more rocks.

Two minutes later they moved forward another ten paces and once more took cover. Five minutes later they had advanced towards the rebels so much that the latter were obliged to leave their positions and withdraw to find new ones.

"Take up positions!" Kirk ordered, running after the retreating soldiers. Before the soldiers were able to, Hamdi's troops, who were waiting for this opportunity, ran forward and killed two of those retreating, although they lost a soldier too, until they were able to take cover.

Kirk had only just taken up a position with the soldiers when he saw the deaf-mute, who had got to his feet, start to run in their direction. "Lie down! Lie down!" he shouted, making hand signals as well. Samuel lay down, but not in response to Kirk's order, but because he had been wounded, and the bullet had thrown him to the ground.

Kirk, seeing the deaf-mute's fall, looked with horror at the rock behind which Julia had hidden. But he saw no one there. The government troops had passed beyond those positions, and Julia, dead or alive, was now behind them. "I wonder what happened to the poor girl?" he said to himself.

But he had no time to think. The government troops attacked for a second time. The rebels, seeing the government troops' advance, deserted their posts once more. As this time they had retreated more than 100 paces, they lost seven men, although the enemy also had losses because they had taken no precautions when chasing the rebels.

Kirk had hardly collected his soldiers when the third and final attack started.

Seeing a few soldiers were treacherously trying to relinquish their positions, Kirk pulled out his pistol and threatened to open fire, when he suddenly let out a cry of pain and, holding his chest, fell down.

The rebels looked back and saw that there was no one to stop their escape. So they got up from their places, mounted their horses, and began to escape like a disorganised rabble.

The government troops, seeing the rebels escape, also left their positions, mounted their horses, and followed the rebels, firing and whooping with victory as they went.

A quarter of an hour later the sound of horses' hooves and gunfire died out in the distance, and darkness, like a black veil, fell over the battlefield.

PART III

A Night Among the Exiles

About eight months after these events one evening a train stopped at Damascus' Kadem Station.

About 30 travellers – mostly Arab peasants and soldiers on leave – disembarked from the carriages and, with their bundles and baskets went to nearby villages. Only two people directed their steps towards the refugee camp set up under the olive trees.

"Compatriot," said one of them, directing his question at an old Armenian who was busy collecting cuttings from the ground, "Is there somewhere we can sleep?"

"You can sleep in the coffee house opposite," the exile said, straightening up. "Where are you from?"

"From Djebel Druse. The police wouldn't let us go into Damascus."

"They won't. Armenians are forbidden to enter the city."

"What do you do here?"

"Every day we bury three or four people."

"How many of you are there?"

"About 400."

"Haven't they settled you in the villages yet?"

"They did. But in villages there were no Armenians, nor any work. We were forced to escape and come here with the hope of entering the city. But apparently it's forbidden, so we couldn't. We haven't the means to return, so we live here in tents in the cold and stormy weather, in a very bad state."

"But I don't understand," the traveller said, "why do you talk about going back when you were dissatisfied with the villages you were settled in?"

"What can we do, my son? In Havran we could at least beg or graze like animals in the hills. We haven't even got that freedom here. Enclosed by an iron fence, we can't go forward or back. We're all sentenced to die if a miracle doesn't happen."

"Did you apply to the governorship about your return?"

"We did, and how many times! The railway is being used for military transportation; when our turn comes, they'll take us."

Conversing like this, the two travellers and their interlocutor reached a hut made of flattened oil drums. "This is the coffee house," the old refugee said, opening the door wide and bowing courteously. "Have you any other orders?"

"No, thank you. Take this money. It'll serve for something you need." The two young travellers said goodbye to him and entered a fairly large room that although hot, was filled with the sharp smoke of wood fuel and cigarettes.

Four people who were dressed in rags were seated around the brazier in one corner of the room to get warm. Seeing the new guests, they rose to their feet and offered the newcomers their chairs.

"Please, don't put yourselves out," the travellers protested in an obliging tone.

"The chairs are for customers, while we come here to get warm," the refugees said and went to another corner of the room where a young man was sleeping on a mattress.

The travellers had hardly sat down near the brazier when a barber, a man of medium height, who was cutting a customer's hair in the third corner (the fourth corner had the oven and the sideboard for cups), left his half-finished work, approached the newcomers and, with a smile on his face, said, "Welcome, Sirs. What would you like?"

"Finish your work, then bring us two teas and biscuits," said the first traveller. "But, compatriot, what's your name and where are you from, if you don't mind my asking?"

"My name is Ardash. I'm from Bardizag."

"Thank you."

After Ardash had left, the second traveller, who until then hadn't opened his mouth once, turned to his friend and said, "I really admire your race's strength of will and belief in living. They've got to this state and still they work to get their bread out of stone. Not one person from any other race would remain alive if they were subject to the same misfortunes."

"Be assured, friend," his comrade declared, "if the government lets them alone, not one person would die of hunger in Arabia. Look, these poor people have come from the desert of Havran to work, but the police won't let them enter the city. They haven't the means to go back there, so they'll all die in the mud here."

"Tomorrow, when we've made our arrangements with the police, we'll divide all the money we've got among them," the second traveller said in a sympathetic voice. "We've no need of money any more. My aunt in Damascus is extremely wealthy."

"Do what your heart tells you, my noble friend."

* * *

It is obvious that this conversation was between Kirk and Seyfi, the one-time commanders of the rebel company.

After the break up of their army, they had the good fortune not to fall into the hands of the government troops. This was helped by the darkness and the shameful rout of their soldiers because, if Colonel Hamdi's soldiers had not pursued them, both officers, who had fallen wounded on the battlefield, would have been captured.

Seyfi was the first to recover consciousness. His head hurt terribly. Putting his hand where it hurt, he found that he had an open wound the thickness of his little finger on his right temple that was extremely painful, especially when he put his finger on it. A rifle bullet had grazed the skin on his head, damaging the skull at the same time.

After remaining motionless for a time, he had recovered and looked about him. First he had not been able to see anything in the dark, but as his eyes gradually adjusted to it, he saw Kirk, who had fallen down unconscious a short distance from him.

Seyfi had wanted to stand up and rush to his comrade's aid, but he saw that it wasn't possible because he couldn't hold his head on his shoulders. He wanted to say Kirk's name, but his mouth and throat had dried up and he couldn't make a sound.

After resting motionless for a time, Seyfi had slid towards his friend and, putting his hand on his chest, had listened to see if Kirk was dead or wounded. Feeling a slight beating under his hand, as well as the wetness of the clotted blood, he had shaken his wounded friend while calling his name.

Not receiving an answer, he looked around him in a bewildered state and saw a mule that was standing next to a medicine chest. Making a superhuman effort, Seyfi went to it, opened it with trembling hands, found a flask and put it to his lips. Drinking the life-giving liquid gave him new strength and spirit and the Arab soldier hurried to his friend and put a few drops of liquid in his mouth.

Shortly afterwards a light rosy colouring appeared on the injured man's face and his breathing also became more regular. With his eyes partly open, and as soon as he was able to speak, he asked in a strangled voice, "Julia...? What happened to Julia?"

"I don't know," Seyfi had replied. "I've only just recovered myself. What have you got, Kirk?"

"My chest!" Kirk had coughed and blood had flowed.

Seyfi immediately opened his chest and carefully looked at the wound. "The bullet has remained in your chest, but don't worry, friend, it's not touched your heart or lungs," he said comfortingly.

"Seyfi, if I die, don't leave Julia without any protection," Kirk whispered.

"Don't be stupid, boy!" Seyfi said, telling him off. "There's nothing wrong with you. Look, I've been wounded in the head. In a little while, when we've recovered our strength, we'll go to one of the nearby villages and have ourselves treated."

"Where are the soldiers?"

"I don't know. In the emptiness of the plain, apart from a poor mule and us, there's no other living thing. Everything – the soldiers, horses and the mules have all run away in terror."

"Julia, Julia, what's happened to her?" Kirk sobbed.

"Wasn't she with you at the start of the battle?"

"Yes, but when we retreated, she stayed behind the rock where she was. I saw the deaf-mute fall down wounded, but I don't know what happened to Julia."

"Get up and let's look for them. Can you straighten up?"

Kirk made an effort, but his face immediately creased with pain, and tears came to his eyes.

"No, no, don't move," Seyfi cried, and handing him the flask, said, "Drink some more of this medicine."

* * *

A few hours later, the two wounded comrades, holding each other's hands, made their way with trembling steps to the positions they had first occupied. Although there was no moon, the star filled sky had lit up the area sufficiently to distinguish one thing from another.

They first came to the place where Samuel had fallen, but couldn't find him. "I'm sure that he fell here," Kirk had said. "Look, there are traces of blood on the rock."

"So he was wounded like us and, when he came to, must have run away," Seyfi pointed out.

"Where?"

"Who knows? Maybe to his mistress."

"But where is his mistress?"

Kirk had gone and looked around the rock that Julia had been hiding behind. "There's no sign of blood," he had cried happily. "She must have escaped, but where to?" Then, raising his voice, he had tried to shout "Julia!" but couldn't. "You call her, Seyfi, my voice has gone."

"Julia…! Julia…!" Seyfi had called, as loudly as he could. But not receiving an answer apart from the echo of his voice in the desert, he had concluded, "They must have escaped together."

"But where could they have escaped to, when they don't know their way?" Kirk had asked.

"Julia knew from our conversation that the Euphrates flows behind the mountains opposite and that there are villages along its banks," Seyfi had replied. "They probably got hold of two horses and escaped in that direction."

The two friends had looked for a long time, behind every rock and bush in the area. They had found the bodies of all the dead soldiers – scattered on rocks and the ground – but there was no sign of Julia and Samuel.

"Not finding the deaf-mute's body is proof that they've escaped," Seyfi had said. "Let's go on, and not waste any more time here. The government troops may return to collect their dead. Let's go straight away. Look, there's a loose horse grazing here. You mount it and I'll use the mule. Maybe Julia hasn't gone very far and, if we hurry, we may catch up with them."

Shortly afterwards, unable to do anything, they had mounted the animals and, having gone round the battlefield again, they had pressed on, completely convinced that, alive or dead, Julia and Samuel weren't there any longer.

Kirk and Seyfi continued on their way for many hours, continually looking round them and shouting Julia's name in the hope that she may answer from behind a rock or bush. But it was dawn; the sun had risen and still there had been no response to their heartfelt calls.

The following day they had seen a small village in the distance. Before they entered it, they had thrown away their uniforms so that they would be thought of as peaceful travellers who had been robbed by bandits.

Kirk had been under the knife of an Arab barber who, without anaesthetics, had so skilfully removed the bullet with the cut of a razor that it would have invited the admiration of the world's most skilled surgeons.

They had stayed in the village for three days and during that time they had sent horsemen in every direction to try to find their erstwhile traveling companions. Three days later the horsemen had returned empty handed without finding any sign of them.

After recovering somewhat, the two friends had departed to personally continue the searching. First, they had gone for days along the river in the same direction as the current. Then they had turned and gone against it, but without result. It was as if, with the wave of a magic wand, Julia and Samuel had disappeared from the face of the earth.

Continuing their journey, they had reached Der-Zor, at least to gain knowledge of their soldiers' fate. But they had no luck on that score either, because the newspapers had been forbidden to publish news of military rebellions.

They had gone to Julia's refugee camp. Maybe she had gone there. But the people there knew nothing more than her kidnap and her brother's and Paul's departure.

The two travellers had visited, in the same way, every village and town, questioning every traveller and refugee. They had given gifts of money to all kinds of wretched people, be they Armenian or Arab (they had taken the money from Khalid's treasury) and had reached Meskeneh, then Aleppo where, on the day they entered the city, they heard of the dreadful massacre of the Armenians in Der-Zor.

The carnage wasn't a surprise for Kirk and Seyfi, but their hearts were affected, thinking that all the Armenians they had seen and comforted in their wanderings, and for whose safety they had struggled and worried for so long, were all dead.

There was no doubt that if Julia had survived the night after that terrible battle, she had been killed with all the other Armenians. Her loss had affected Kirk very badly who, after his fiancée's unlucky death, had become specially attached to that girl. Unfortunately, however, the time they knew each other was less than that of the life of a rose.

With sorrow and anguish in their hearts, the two former officers, always disguised, had continued their journey, and finally found sanctuary in Lebanon, with a Druse tribal leader who was a very close friend of Seyfi's uncle, the late Wahab.

They had enjoyed the noble sheik's hospitality for five months.

Despite the fact that they were, in every way, safe and comfortable in that land of brave warriors, at that time Kirk had been in a strange psychological state. He had gradually stopped taking pleasure in anything. He neither spoke, nor walked about, nor ate, only wanting to be alone and, with his head in his hands, to meditate and sob.

One day, Seyfi, seeing that the developing melancholy was eating into his friend's health like a worm, said, "Kirk, I've decided. We're going to Damascus. When I was 15, I once visited that city; it's wonderful. My aunt has a wonderful palace there – in an extensive garden shaded by tall trees – where she now lives alone, surrounded by her cook, gardener, servant and two maids. The late Wahab lived for many years in Egypt and London, and was well educated and lived a modern life at home. There's a piano in the house, a good library, an exercise hall, a billiard table and other means of enjoying yourself. No one gets bored there. I'll write and get my mother and fiancée there too. We'll go and brighten the place up."

"Thank you for your concern for me," Kirk had said, "but leaving aside the danger, don't you think that it would be inappropriate for me to be in your aunt's house?"

"Eight months have passed since the time of our battle against government forces. Our names have probably been forgotten by now," Seyfi had said. "Coming to the other question, it may be said that my aunt's house is my house. You can live there for as long as you like. My mother and aunt regard you as a son, and my fiancée, as a brother. Our hearts, door and treasury are always open to you; you may be sure of that, friend."

Seeing that Kirk still wasn't sure, he continued, "You'll die here of sadness and loneliness, boy. I feel your dreadful hurt. After losing your family, fiancée, home, your homeland and more than a million of your compatriots, without realising it, you gave your heart to a woman and, like a nightmare, you lost her too. No, Kirk, don't try to protest; you think about *her* night and day. Let's speak openly: Julia's memory tortures you. Time will heal this open wound and the emptiness in the depths of your heart. But until then you need comforting people, my friend. Come with me; my mother, aunt and fiancée will do all that they can to make you happy."

Kirk hadn't been able to refuse his friend's plea, especially as he had be able to help his poor fellow-Armenians in Damascus. So the next day they said goodbye to the mountains that had given them sanctuary and come down into the lap of 'civilization'.

* * *

While Kirk and Seyfi were drinking their tea, they involuntarily heard a conversation carried on by the refugees in the corner, who were relating events from their lives, probably to drive away the monotony of the winter evening. "…On the road," a young man said, "I met a pregnant woman who was rolling about with birth pains, crying piteously and scraping at the ground with her fingers. There was no one with her. The caravan she was with, it appears, had been driven on by the police who'd left her to her fate. Seeing us – a battalion of laborers – she understood we were Armenians, so held out her hand to us, begging us to free her of her pain.

"A young man named Taniel from Constantinople, who'd previously been a captain in the Ottoman army, was walking next to me. Hearing her heartrending cries for help, he immediately left the ranks to go and help her. But the police commander, a sergeant with a bad reputation, spurred his horse forward and, waving his whip, shouted, 'We kill them off and they increase in numbers! There's no end to this cursed race.' Taniel, looking at him straight in the eye said, 'Effendi, have pity on the woman; she's one of God's creatures too.' 'Oh, excuse me Taniel Bey,' murmured the police commander, suddenly lowering his voice, 'I'd forgotten that I've got a "captain" over me. Please go and help your fellow-Armenian.'

"Taniel, without taking any notice of the sergeant's sarcasm, ran to the woman, who was still rolling about at the side of the road and making terrible roaring noises. He'd hardly leant over her when the sound of a rifle shot was heard and we saw the poor man spread lifeless over the body of the woman who'd also died. 'My name is Suleiman' the executioner said, putting his rifle on his shoulder once more. 'I killed three Armenian dogs with one bullet like this.'"

Seyfi, seeing his friend's face tense with hatred, and frightened that he could set out this time to find the chief monster Suleiman… immediately called the coffee house owner-barber, to distract Kirk's attention. "Mr

Ardash," he said, talking to the latter, "You must, of course, know the law here. What way is there of entering Damascus?"

"There's only one way," Ardash replied, rubbing his index finger with his thumb. "May it protect us from temptation."

"We're ready to pay. How much is necessary?"

"One gold piece per head."

"We agree. Who do we have to pay it to?"

"The refugee camp supervisor, Mahir Bey. But before you offer him money, I'll have to talk to him first."

"Do you know him?"

"Yes. He sometimes comes and sits here in the coffee house. He's an anti-Armenian dog. But what can we do, brother? We're forced to talk to him."

"Fine. Arrange it tomorrow. We'll pay you well for your trouble, Mr Ardash."

"Please, Sir, it's not important."

Although Kirk was listening to this conversation, his attention was centered on the refugees squatting in the corner like a hypnotised man.

A second man was saying, "There was a man of over 70 years old called 'crazy Agop' in our town. This man had spent his whole life as a servant in wealthy houses. He kept all the presents he received in a place that couldn't be found and wandered the streets hungry and in rags. People knowing of his madness, never gave him money, but paid for his services in food, clothing and other useful items. Instead of eating or wearing what he'd been given, mad Agop would sell them and hide the money in a secret place. When we asked him why he lived in poverty, as he'd got quite a lot of money to spend, he'd reply that he was saving the money for a more important purpose. When we'd ask him what the purpose was, mad Agop would smile and say that he'd sworn an oath that, when an Armenian government was formed, he was going to give each soldier in the Armenian army a box of cigarettes.

"When the deportation order reached our town, they first exiled those wealthy families that had 'crazy Agop' in their service in the past. His benefactors' exile had such an effect on the poor old madman that he'd go to the edge of the sea to cry alone every night. One day the police saw him wipe his eyes with a red handkerchief and, thinking he was signalling to an imaginary Russian fleet with it, arrested him. His trial didn't last long. A week later we saw that the poor harmless man had been hanged in the main square as a spy and traitor."

"Kirk," Seyfi said, holding his friend's hand, "I can see that those stories are affecting your nerves. Get up and let's get some air outside. Let's see who out of your compatriots are in the camp."

Kirk didn't reply but got to his feet subdued with his head hanging.

Outside, Seyfi's calculations proved to be completely wrong. If there were sickening stories being told inside the coffee house, outside, in the camp, there was one horrible scene after another.

First, they had hardly walked ten paces when they saw an old woman lying on the ground, shaking in her death agony.

The two friends began to go towards the dying woman, when people began to cry out from every side, telling them not to go near her. "Don't, don't go near her… Her sickness is contagious… Leave her, she's dying now…"

Kirk and Seyfi stopped, confused.

"What's she suffering from?" Kirk asked a refugee who had come up to him.

"Typhoid fever."

"Hasn't she got any relatives? Why's she lying in the mud?"

"She's got no one. She lived in a hovel with some other old women at the edge of the camp. During the night, in her crisis, she escaped and fell down here."

"She's been lying here for 20 hours; won't anyone take her to her hovel?" Kirk asked, angry at his fellow-Armenians' indifference.

"Who can go near her, brother? Every family has had two or three victims of this dreadful sickness. We're frightened of catching it and passing it to our families."

"They're right," Seyfi said, pushing Kirk forward. "This is a question of death or survival; you can't lightly judge people guilty."

Then they saw three or four children, who were eating pistachio nut husks that they had collected from the ground, cleaning each one of mud by wiping it on their ragged clothing.

"Children, how can you eat those?" Seyfi asked, pitying the poor children.

"What can we do sir? We're hungry."

"Take this money and go and buy bread," the former officer said, giving each a silver coin.

While the children, with the coins in their hands, raced off to the shops still open at the station, more than 50 wretched individuals of both sexes surrounded the beneficent guests, crying, "Help us, sirs, we're poor too, we're also hungry! Help us, for the love of God!"

Kirk and Seyfi opened their purses and gave each of them a generous sum. Then, seeing that thanks to their rashness the whole camp would be aroused, they gradually retreated and returned to Ardash's coffee house.

* * *

The refugees in rags had changed the subject of their conversation now.

"...When I was a small boy," one of them said, "my father would call me to him and advise me, 'Learn a trade, my son. A trade is a golden bracelet. Someone with it on his wrist will never die hungry.' I followed my father's advice and learnt to be an upholsterer and, really, while I worked I never went hungry. But I can see with experience that having a golden bracelet is not enough to allow one to live, if the environment doesn't value it. Who cares if I can make beautiful furniture? You can repair broken watches; you can make elegant shoes; while you, Mr Koladji, can starch and iron shirts very well. But what will a fellah who doesn't wear trousers do with the bookcase I can make, or with the watch you've repaired, or with shoes and a starched collar?"

"It's true," the watchmaker agreed. "Our fathers taught us the wrong ideas. To be able to live, before any skill, the environment must exist that values that skill."

"Because, if the environment doesn't exist," the upholsterer continued, "your being a scientist or merchant means nothing. Our fathers, not given the land, taught us the way to improve it. It's for that reason that we're like landless farmers, who know how to sow and reap, but suffer from hunger because there's no land to cultivate. In the last one and a half years the number of dead in the Havran desert has exceeded 100,000. All of them were merchants who had hoards of gold in their baggage or artisans with golden bracelets on their wrists."

"Brother, why go as far as Havran to quote an example?" the shoemaker said. "Are there not, under our noses, in Damascus, thousands of families in a wretched state in the streets? Don't 50-60 people die of sickness or wretchedness every day? They too were merchants and artisans. The conclusion that emerges from all this is that the land you live in must be your own fatherland. Otherwise all the successes achieved are like unstable, temporary palaces built on sand."

"Your fellow-Armenians are correct in their logic," Seyfi said, agreeing with the refugees' words. "People can only live and progress in their own country. People living on foreign soil are destined, sooner or later, to wither and be destroyed."

Just then the young man who was lying on the floor, and who until then had remained unmoving and silent, began to groan with pain and made attempts to move.

Everyone fell silent and, turning to the sick man, asked what he wanted.

"Water," begged the man in a faint voice.

The young upholsterer ran to the sideboard, picked up a teacup and, after dipping it in the water jar, quickly went to the sick man.

The others, taking him by the arms, sat him up and carefully helped him drink the water.

"Is it typhus?" Kirk asked the coffee house owner, who was looking at the young man compassionately.

"No, he's not sick," Ardash replied. "This morning he tried to escape to Damascus and the police caught and beat him."

"But why do the police beat people so savagely?" Seyfi asked, scandalized.

"Sir, they openly shout at us, 'Drop dead, then both you and we shall be free,'" the coffee house owner said. "If Miss Julia doesn't get us out of here, we'll be finished."

"Who's Miss Julia?" Kirk asked suddenly with curiosity.

"We don't really know," Ardash replied. "She's a young, very beautiful Armenian girl who arrived here about a week ago, asked about our lives and said that if we wanted anything we were to tell her, because she means to help us morally. We told her that there were two things that concerned us: first, this impossible life and, second, the inhuman way the police treat the Armenians.

"She said, 'There are two ways of escaping from here. The first is to secretly get you into Damascus and the second, to return you to the villages you came from. The first is a little difficult, but I'll try. If I don't succeed, I'll have you sent to Deraa. As for the inhuman attitude of the police, I'll have the necessary orders sent to the camp commander, so that they'll deal with you with humanity.'"

"Incredible," Kirk murmured. "Who is this Armenian girl who promises such arrangements? Is she an official?"

"No, she's got no official position. She said that she enjoyed the protection of an influential person and wants to utilize that unusual position to help her fellow-Armenians."

"How was she able to obtain that unusual position?"

"The Turkish police immediately found an explanation, but I don't believe their bad allusions. That girl appears to be extremely honorable and modest. It's her modesty and the simplicity of her clothes that bear witness to her virtue. The mistress of a high-ranking person wouldn't wear darned socks, would she?"

"There's no doubt of that. So Miss Julia dresses poorly?"

"Yes, but it's obvious that she's the daughter of a rich family. Whoever Miss Julia's benefactor is, he must have received help from her father, and is now repaying her."

"Well done, Mr Ardash!" Kirk cried, pleased about the coffee house owner's impartial thoughts about Miss Julia. "I think that the protection Miss Julia has is because of gratitude rather than for any other reason."

Kirk and Seyfi spent the night stretched out on chairs in the coffee house.

Apart from the two of them, the only other person staying there was the young man who had been beaten, as the four refugees and the coffee house owner had left to go to their tents late. During the night the young man woke up and asked for water. Kirk gave him some, and Seyfi gave him a gold piece, comforting and telling him not to worry; he would recover in a few days and be back on his feet.

The Armenian refugee, receiving the gold piece – which would relieve him from worrying about food for a month – was extremely pleased and slept peacefully, if that could be said for a man with broken bones.

The coffee seller Ardash came to the coffee house in the morning with a smile on his face and told his noble-hearted guests that he had arranged things with the camp supervisor, so they could go directly to the office and, handing over the bribe, receive a permit to enter Damascus.

Kirk and Seyfi did so at once and obtained the necessary document. When they left the supervisor's office, Kirk pointed out to Seyfi, "Seyfi, did you notice how that man resembled that criminal Khalid's military commander?"

"Haven't you heard the saying," Seyfi said with his people's carelessness, "men are always born on this earth with a double."

"What do you say about Miss Julia?"

"I say that she's got the same name as the girl we rescued."

The Secret of the Double and the Namesake

Mrs Makbouleh was a 55 year-old freethinking, educated woman and Seyfi's maternal aunt.

Having lived with her deceased husband for many years in Egypt and England, she had rid herself of the prejudices that are peculiar to Muslim women.

After her husband's tragic death, she lived a self-contained life, dedicated to reading and good works.

Not having had children with her late husband, she had concentrated all her love on her sister's son Seyfi, who was also the heir to her immense fortune. So the wonderful reception she gave him, as well as his friend, when they reached Damascus, can well be imagined.

It was as if they had brought life and energy back to Wahab's lonely and grieving mansion.

The noble Arab lady, hearing their story, was extremely affected, then was delighted with the thought that they had emerged alive from everything that had happened to them and were now free from any threats that had hung over them.

Mrs Makbouleh settled Seyfi in her husband's quarters, giving Kirk two comfortable rooms nearby that looked out over the garden.

"The dark days have now gone," she said, giving her precious guests a loving look. "Rest here and try to forget your troubles and exhaustion."

Indeed, there was nothing missing in that princely mansion for one to be totally happy. The two former officers now had clean beds, delicious meals, a rich library, exercise and amusement halls as well as servants and maids ready to serve them at all times.

There was music in the evenings too when, a few weeks later, Mrs Sabiha and Fehimeh, Seyfi's mother and fiancée, arrived from Baghdad.

Mrs Sabiha was just like her older sister in looks and character. Their faces were so alike that Kirk was often confused as to who was who, giving rise to much merriment.

Seyfi's fiancée Fehimeh was an attractive and educated girl, an orphan from a tender age who was brought up in Seyfi's parents' house, who were related to her through her mother.

From the very first day the two women, like Mrs Makbouleh, liked and respected Kirk, treating him like a son or brother.

Fehimeh knew how to play the piano very well. The evenings were spent pleasurably in singing and with music. During the day, when the two sisters sat apart in a corner of the hall, to relate to one another all the things that had happened to them since they had parted, Kirk, Seyfi and Fehimeh occupied themselves with various pleasant games, or took long walks in the garden that was as large as a small wood at the back of the mansion.

Kirk, to leave the engaged couple alone, would withdraw to the late Wahab's library and for hours study historical, geographical and ethnographical books, with which the library was richly endowed.

The Armenian officer had shown great interest in the history of ancient nations from an early age. This interest had awakened a love of archaeology in him that would probably have led him specialising in it, if misfortune hadn't upset his plans for his life.

Now that he had nothing to do, he devoted himself to studying his preferred subject, in the hope that he would forget his troubles and worries. Unfortunately, however, despite his and the household's efforts, he couldn't find spiritual peace, as he couldn't turn aside from thoughts of Julia and the tragic state of the mass of his fellow-Armenians who, one or two streets away, were suffering in the claws of extraordinary misery.

When he went into the city he had seen, under the walls, the wretched, the sick and those who rolled about from hunger, bled and gave up the ghost under the merciless eyes of passers-by.

He had seen the orphaned, helpless children who collected the roots of plants and mouldy leaves from the mud and filth to eat.

He had also seen a local shopkeeper who, instead of giving the skin of the orange he was eating directly to the little orphans around him, threw it at them in such a way that the pieces hit their faces or fell in distant places, so that he made them run like hungry dogs to get them. As if the joke wasn't enough... the unfeeling man tore the skin into pieces as small as lentils, so that he could enjoy his game with the boys for as long as possible.

Being a witness to this was in a way good for the Armenian refugees as Seyfi, to right the wrong done by his fellow-Arab, had asked his aunt to add the poor Armenians to her list of those receiving charity from her.

Mrs Makbouleh followed her nephew's request and on the following day had a list of needy Armenian families brought from the Armenian church.

Now every Saturday an official came from the diocesan authorities and received a sum of money set aside for poor Armenians. Kirk was very pleased, but what was the use? He knew that it was impossible to put out a fire with a drop of water.

* * *

In Wahab's mansion the days, weeks and months slid by one after another without a serious incident disturbing the lives of the two voluntary prisoners.

One day Kirk was seated in the library and, as was his wont, studying palaeontology, when Seyfi came in with a sympathetic person of about 50 years old. "Kirk, I'd like you to meet one of our family's noble friends, Mr Haroun Libani, who's an authoritative scientist living in Beirut," he said.

And while Kirk was respectfully shaking his hand, Seyfi continued, "Mr Libani was a close friend of the late Wahab and, like him – and I can say like you – is a lover of archaeology. The work done by French and German antiquarians in the Baalbek area are very famous. At the beginning of the war Mr Libani, as an Arab intellectual, was arrested and imprisoned. You know my father's and uncle's tragic story; they were hanged as traitors with many others. But Mr Libani, who had never in his whole life had anything to do with politics, was fortunate to escape with only two years' imprisonment. Today, having served his sentence, he was released and, before he returns to his family in Beirut, he had the nobility to come and visit his friend's widow. When Mr Libani heard of you, he expressed the wish to meet you as a family friend. He's staying with us as a guest for two days. I hope that during this time you'll benefit considerably from his scientific knowledge."

"I'm delighted to meet a scientist like Mr Libani," Kirk said respectfully. "At the same time I sympathise with the long distress he suffered in prison."

"Thank you, Mr Kirk," the Lebanese scientist said in an emotional voice. "I too am pleased to meet such a valuable young man like you who saved Seyfi's life in the Dardanelles and later, in the Der-Zor desert acted as a guide and advisor to our much-loved son of the Estari noble family – the Estaris are descended from the prophet Mohammed – and who is the last of the line."

"Mr Libani, you've praised me far too much!" Seyfi protested in a half-joking way.

"Be quiet, you prodigal!" Libani said in a fatherly way, reproaching him mildly. "It wasn't you, it was Mr Kirk I was praising."

"I'm not worthy of praise," Kirk murmured, lowering his head. "On the contrary, I owe all my happiness to Seyfi."

"No, no, don't say that," Libani protested vigorously. "You saved Seyfi's life; that will be remembered forever with gratitude by the members of this family and its friends."

"I agree with what Mr Libani has just said," Seyfi said, regaining his usual seriousness. "But why are we standing up? Let's sit down. Kirk, do you know what I asked Mr Libani a little earlier? I asked that he sacrifices one day of his stay here to give us a tour of the famous Baalbek ruins."

"Speaking frankly, I find that idea a little dangerous," Kirk said, after thinking for a moment.

"I thought the same," the scientist from Beirut said, agreeing with Kirk's reply. "I'm quite happy to give all my time to please and be helpful to you, but I think it's dangerous for you to go into the street."

"But who'll recognise us?" Seyfi asked ingenuously. "We'll leave the city early tomorrow and return home late at night. There are no spies after us who would betray us straight away."

"Don't say that, Seyfi," Kirk said with a gloomy expression. "Don't forget the refugee director at Kadem."

"You're a strange lad, Kirk. Do you still insist that he's Khalid's lieutenant?"

"Yes, I'm quite sure of it."

"But eleven months have passed since their bones whitened in the Death's Door cave."

"Could it not happen that after we left they were freed?"

"Who by?"

"I don't know. But someone who went there after us, for example."

"By those calculations then, there's not one but 19 Mahirs out there."

"And that means we must be 19 times more careful," Kirk pointed out with a bitter smile.

"There's an easy way out of this," Seyfi said, suddenly having an idea. "Instead of worrying and having suspicions, we'll send our servant Izzet to the camp at Kadem to find out who that animal Mahir is and when he took up his present position."

"That's not a bad idea," Libani said. "The servant will have to be very careful, or instead of getting information, he'll have given information without realising it." Then, turning to Kirk, he asked, "What's the book you're studying, Mr Kirk?"

* * *

After Haroun Libani was released from prison, the chief of police Sherif Bey had given the secret policeman Haidar the responsibility of keeping the former prisoner under surveillance to find out where he went and who he saw.

It was the responsibility of the Public Security's secret branch to keep those guilty of political offences under surveillance, to spy on their least movement, with the directive that they should identify any new plots. So policeman Haidar followed Libani's movements like a shadow, without Libani knowing that even after serving his sentence the police were still interested in him.

Secret policeman Haidar saw the intellectual from Beirut enter Wahab's mansion that day. Hidden at a corner of the street, he waited for a very long time, under the impression that Libani was making a courtesy call on his late friend's widow, and that he would leave the house a little later on.

But hours passed, it got dark, night fell, and still the political prisoner didn't leave the house.

Secret policeman Haidar returned home impotently at midnight, thinking that the residents had kept him for dinner and given him a bed for the night.

When he presented his report to the chief of police the next day, the latter, frowning, thought for a while then asked, "Haidar Bey, Wahab's widow, Mrs Makbouleh lives a lonely, withdrawn life doesn't she?"

"Yes sir."

Who else is in the mansion?"

"Apart from her, a cook, a servant and two maids."

"Anyone else?"

"No one else, Sir."

"I can see that you're a skilful secret policeman, Haidar Bey," the chief of police said ironically. "The information you've given me was known two months ago. Since then two travellers have been there."

"Two travellers?" Haidar asked, annoyed.

"Yes, one elderly, the other a young woman. And do you know who they are?"

"I've no idea," the Public Security official said, affected by his boss' irony.

"Let me teach you then," Sherif Bey said in a calm voice. "The elderly lady is Mrs Makbouleh's sister and the widow of Ensari of Baghdad who, as you know, was hanged with four others and Wahab as traitors to the fatherland. Haroun Libani was arrested with them but because there was no proof of his guilt, he saved his skin by serving two years in prison. Now, don't you find Mr Libani's meeting with two widows of convicted men, on the very day that he's released from prison, strange?"

"So your conclusion is that Ensari's widow, knowing the day that Libani was being released, came specially from Baghdad to consult with him?"

"Yes."

"So who's the young woman?"

"Her coming to Damascus is interesting, as she's the Ensari boy's fiancée."

"Seyfi, the one who got a regiment to revolt in Diarbekir?"

"Yes, that traitor Seyfi, who hasn't been arrested yet, despite the fact that 17 of his soldiers have been captured both dead and alive."

Secret policeman Haidar turned pale and looked at the toes of his shoes. It was a shame that his superior was giving him the information rather than the other way round!

"Let's sum up," the chief of police said, mechanically screwing up the report presented to him. "We've got three people accused of being traitors to the fatherland, of whom two received their punishment on the scaffold, the other escaping with a short jail sentence. This third traitor, as soon as he's released, goes to a house where the widows of his two comrades sentenced to death are to be found. A young woman, whose presence would have been meaningless, is to be found in the same house where the fourth traitor, Seyfi, is staying. I think there's enough information here to set you right, Haidar Bey. Go back to work immediately and do what's necessary. It's no time to sleep; you must be totally alert."

* * *

On that same day Kirk, leaning over a map in Wahab's study, was listening to one of the Lebanese scientist's important reports, when Seyfi entered in an emotional state and said, "Friends, I'm sorry that I must give some bad news" – and to soften the listeners anxiety – "but then a piece of good news that's of interest to Kirk."

"What news?" the latter asked, his curiosity aroused.

"One at a time," Seyfi replied. "First, the bad news. It's probable that the director of the Kadem camp is Khalid's lieutenant that we killed."

Kirk and Libani grimaced, as if they'd been struck an invisible blow.

"Here's how our servant unravelled the mystery," Seyfi continued. "According to my orders he went, last evening, to the Kadem camp and went to stay in the famous barber-coffee shack of Ardash as if he was a traveller, to find out in some way from the refugees who came there, about director Mahir.

"He heard this morning, from Ardash's own lips, that Mahir was given the position in the camp five months ago, and that he was in Der-Zor before that.

"When Ardash was giving this information about Mahir, a very beautiful girl entered the coffee house, who immediately asked what had happened in Der-Zor.

"Ardash, who had taken a respectful position with regard to the young lady, explained that the person he was talking to had wanted information about director Mahir, and that he'd replied that he'd been in Der-Zor at one time.

"Hearing this explanation, the young lady had turned pale for a moment, then taken Izzet to one side and asked why he was interested in Mahir's identity.

"The servant hadn't, of course, revealed that he'd been sent by us, but couldn't provide an answer justifying his curiosity. The young lady, seeing that the person she was talking to was an Arab, who wanted to get information about a Turk he didn't know, had become suspicious about his mixed answers, and asked if he was asking on behalf of other people.

"Izzet had at first denied the truth, but seeing that the young lady had come to the Kadem camp with the aim of helping Armenians, had confessed everything, and at the request of the young lady has…"

"...been led here," Julia completed, entering the room in the company of Mrs Makbouleh, Mrs Sabiha and Miss Fehimeh, and squeezing Kirk's and Libani's extended hands with great feeling.

* * *

Shortly afterwards, when they had all sat down, Julia told her story from the end of the battle, at their request, as they all knew what had happened before that.

"When the battle between the government forces and the rebels began, I hid behind a large rock that was between the positions held by Kirk and Seyfi, about 20 paces away.

"They'd advised me not to move and to stay there until the battle ended. So, crouched behind the rock, I waited for the battle to end, when I saw three soldiers from our regiment running away on their horses, while Seyfi ran after them, ordering them to stop.

"After Seyfi left, I remained under Kirk's protection. I won't say anything about our deaf-mute servant Samuel, as he wasn't armed and also because he was hiding some distance from me and therefore couldn't see or protect me.

"At that point I heard the enemy's fire closer to me. There was no doubt that the government troops, encouraged by the flight of our soldiers, were advancing towards us. My supposition proved correct, because a little later I saw our soldiers retreating, having left their positions, while Kirk, following Seyfi's example, followed them, ordering them to take up new ones.

"Samuel, seeing Kirk's departure, thought that the army, and I, were retreating, so he got up to go to Kirk when he was hit and fell to the ground.

"Horrified and bewildered, I didn't know what to do, when I saw the government forces had suddenly begun to advance and were pursuing our retreating soldiers. One of the government soldiers passed close to me but, in his advance, didn't see me. Taking advantage of this, I went round the other side of the rock, and so remained behind the advancing enemy.

Now I was able to raise my head occasionally and watched the battle. I could see how our soldiers took up positions and defended themselves; how the government forces moved forward step by step; how our soldiers forsook their positions for a second time; how they defended themselves in new positions further away, and how they eventually broke before the enemy's charge, and ran away in a disorganised manner.

"When everything was buried in darkness and silence, I left my protection, terrified. My first move was to go the place where our deaf-mute servant had fallen.

"Seeing him lying face-down and not moving, his face covered in blood, one leg shattered and similarly covered with blood, I stepped backwards with horror. When doing this, my feet hit a strange obstacle that made me fall down. Straightening up I saw that it was the body of a soldier, who'd been hit in the forehead and thrown to the ground.

"While, bewildered, I got to my feet, I heard a strangled cry and, running towards the sound, saw another soldier who was rolling about on the ground in his death agony and moaning.

"I saw a third soldier near him who was lying on his back and was still clutching his rifle in his stiffened hand. He was looking at me with frozen eyes.

"Those cold looks of death and the dying soldier's throat flapping in the dark of evening filled my soul with unspeakable terror. It seemed to me that those bodies lying in the plain were going to get up and wrap themselves around my neck. It was impossible for me to stay there any longer. In any case there was no sense in staying there any longer as Kirk and Seyfi, having retreated with their soldiers, couldn't return and join up with me. On the contrary, the government forces could return for their dead and arrest me. As soon as I appreciated the probability of the danger, I mounted a loose horse and galloped towards those mountain chains that I'd heard were inhabited by fellah peasants.

"After riding all night alone, I reached a Bedouin shepherds' camp the next day. I presented myself as the wife of an officer, who was going to the first village to join my husband who was camped there and, for good measure, added that I'd been accompanied by a soldier who'd deserted.

"The innocent shepherds believed what I said and treated me with great respect. Some of them were even prepared to accompany me to my 'husband''s camp, but I refused their offer, saying that I could protect myself from robbers with my Manlicher pistol that I'd found in a holster on the saddle.

"This extraordinary boldness had a great effect on the Bedouins, and they didn't dare hurt me, thinking that my 'husband' who was awaiting my return, seeing that I was late, could begin to search for me and, with his cavalry regiment, could put all the robber-like people living in the tents to the sword.

"Encouraged by the effect my story had, I repeated it every time I met shepherds, Bedouins and fellahs on the road. All of them, frightened of my 'husband', entertained me with lavash bread and milk.

"Travelling upstream along the Euphrates, and continually asking directions of people I met, I was able to reach Der-Zor one day without incident. I met Mrs Iskouhi there, who'd helped my brother and his friend when they tried to rescue me from Khalid's hands.

"I told her all that had happened to me, saying that I wanted to escape to Aleppo and, if she wanted, she could go with me. I had a considerable sum of money that Kirk and Seyfi had left with me, so that I'd be ready for any eventuality.

"Mrs Iskouhi, whom I now call mother, joyfully accepted my suggestion and, immediately giving what she had in her hut to a refugee woman, went with me.

"After a long and difficult journey, bribing the police and government officials, we reached Aleppo some time later. Let me say in passing that only 120 *tahegans* remained of all that money we had when we entered Aleppo. Fortunately however, before we were reduced to wretchedness, we heard that the government had opened a workshop in Hamaa, where work was given to women who knew how to sew. We immediately shouldered our loads and set out for Hamaa.

"We stayed in that town for two months. We rented a small house with other Armenian women, where, for a pittance, we sewed all sorts of things that the military authorities gave us. I can say that, despite the heavy work, we were happy as we'd a piece of black bread to eat and a roof over our heads.

"But our happiness didn't last long. A few Turkish officers had seen me and began loitering around our house, sometimes whistling, sometimes making rude remarks, and sometimes looking at the windows and winking.

"Seeing that no one paid them any attention, they had the boldness one night to knock at the door and make attempts to enter the house. Fortunately there were quite a few of us women and the criminals were frightened of the noise we made. They ran away without forgetting to make threats against me.

"Under those circumstances it wasn't possible to stay in that house. The neighbours suggested that we go to another safe place. So the next day my mother and I moved to a house rented by an Armenian refugee from Arabkir. Hardly a week had gone by when the officers found our address and started following me again.

"'My girl,' our landlord Mr Melkon, who was a very good and noble man, said to me one day, 'these ruffians won't leave you alone. You must leave Hamaa.'

"'But where can I go?' I asked anxiously.

"'Two months ago,' our landlord told us, 'we lived in a village of Alewis near Homs, where we had the opportunity to get to know a very rich and influential, as well as pro-Armenian, tribal leader. Over 80 Armenian refugees work in his fields. I worked there too for a time, but because of my wife's illness, I was forced to leave my work and come here. I think he'd be able to find suitable work for both of you in his house. Sheikh Razak hasn't been to school, but appreciates education and is an educated man. He once looked for a lady to act as a teacher for his two daughters among the refugees in the camp at Homs. If he hasn't found the person he wants yet, I hope he'll give you that position. As for your mother, maybe he'll giver her work in the kitchen. If it works, you can be assured that you'll be secure with that noble old man.'

"There was nothing else we could do; we accepted brother Melkon's advice and went to the village where he had lived. Indeed Sheikh Razak was a good old man, accepted us and, after a short interview, gave me the responsibility for the education of his 10 and 12 year-old daughters, and the running of the kitchen to my mother; that was a responsible position, bearing in mind that there were 5 – 10 guests at his table every day.

"Sometimes high-ranking government officials, army commanders, Maronite, Druse or Arab tribal leaders from distant places with their 20 – 30 followers would arrive and remain as guests in our master's house for days. Preparing food for all of them and setting table wasn't an easy task, but my mother and I were pleased to carry out the work, having many servants and maids at our disposal.

"We spent three peaceful months with Sheikh Razak's family. Our noble master, our mistress and the two children were extremely pleased with our service, and we were pleased for the protection they provided.

"One day we heard that Djemal Pasha had set out on a regional inspection, and on his way would be calling at our village, to stay the night at my master's house.

Although Sheikh Razak hated the Turkish government – and was therefore a natural ally of the Armenians – he nonetheless maintained good relations with government officials. So when he heard of Djemal Pasha's visit, he called me to him and asked me what sort of hospitality he should provide to especially honor his guest.

"I recalled a time in my childhood when an extraordinary reception was given for the newly-elected Catholicos of Cilicia.

"'Have the road to the village, from the fountain that's half an hour distant, swept and watered, I said. Then have all the streets down which the Pasha is to ride, carpeted.'

"'A wonderful idea,' the sheikh exclaimed, delighted. 'What else?'

"'There is something else, but leave it for me to prepare it myself as a surprise.'

"And while Sheikh Razak sent about ten workers to prepare the streets, I took two servants and the things I needed to the large open space below the balcony, in the middle of which a beautiful dovecote had been built.

"It was midday, and the pigeons had retired to their nests, so I had all the dovecote doors closed and got to work.

"My task was to write four words in huge letters on the ground, then cover them with pigeon food.

"When I had finished what I had to do, I returned to the house, telling one of the servants to stay near the dovecote and, when I waved my handkerchief, to open it's doors.

"By about four o'clock in the afternoon everything was ready. The sheikh and his followers mounted their horses and went to the fountain, which was at the village boundary, to welcome Djemal Pasha.

"An hour later, the sound of shots fired into the air told us that the guests were coming. Indeed, when we went up onto the roof, we could see many horsemen galloping towards us. Djemal was in front, accompanied by three high-ranking officers and the sheikh, and followed by about 30 soldiers and peasants.

"The procession stopped shortly afterwards in the courtyard of my master's house. The pasha, the sheikh and their followers dismounted and, clanking their swords, came up the stairs to sit on the balcony and rest.

"The pasha seemed very happy and on his way up congratulated the sheikh on his unusual idea of carpeting the ground. At the same moment I signalled the servant to open the dovecote doors.

"The guests had hardly sat down in comfortable armchairs when they saw a white cloud of pigeons that, after flying for a minute or two, alighted on the food on the ground, making, with their beautiful bodies the words, 'Welcome Djemal Pasha'.

"Djemal Pasha – as well as everyone else – was astonished at this extraordinary surprise that surpassed the inspiration of carpeting the streets.

"'Who thought of this?' asked the pasha, after looking, charmed, at the good wishes made around his name on the ground.

"'There's an Armenian girl in my house, Pasha; it was probably her idea,' the sheikh said respectfully.

"'An Armenian…?' Djemal Pasha exclaimed, astonished. 'I thought that this reception was the work of a refined person. Call the girl to me!'

"I was before the pasha shortly afterwards.

"'Your idea moved me very much,' the pasha said gently. 'I remember, when I was in Adana many years ago, an Armenian friend did the same thing for me on his farm.'

"'I know, pasha,' I said; 'and I'm the little girl who you sat on your knee and whose hair you stroked when I welcomed you with a recitation.'

"The pasha looked at me, upset. 'Really?' he exclaimed. 'Are you Manuel Aghasian's daughter?'

"'Yes.'

"'Where are your father, mother and brothers?' the pasha asked, annoyed.

"I couldn't answer. Suddenly my heart broke; I burst into tears and ran away.

"The next day, when the pasha was leaving, he had me called to him and said, 'I heard your story from Sheikh Razak. From now on you and your adopted mother are under my protection. Take this letter and go with her to Damascus straight away. Give this letter to the person that it's addressed to, and he will provide you with a comfortable house, and a suitable monthly allowance. Every time you have a request, come to my official quarters and, giving the sentries my name, come in. Be assured that you won't find a Djemal Pasha, but a concerned father, who wants to redress some of the injustice done to your family. Go on, my girl, don't cry, do as I say.'

"I kissed my benefactor's hand and, thanking him, took the letter.

"A week later we were living in a modest part of the city. A policeman gave us 50 liras and said that, if we needed money, we should go, without worrying, to the nearest police station.

"It was as if we were in a dream. From one day to the next we'd become house owners and were under powerful protection, while a week before we were servants in someone else's house, and a few months before that we were running from house to house, village to village to escape from the pursuit of callous men.

"When we'd settled in, I said, 'Mother, what'll we do with such a large house with seven rooms? We only need two for ourselves. Let's give the rest to refugees sleeping in the street. Let them come and live here. You only need 20 liras of the 50 lira monthly allowance; let's distribute the rest among them. I'll start working again and will earn a daily wage through sewing.'

"My mother agreed with me. We did as I suggested and continue to do so to this day.

"As for Djemal Pasha, we've enjoyed his protection for 5 months, and I've only asked to see him once. Three months ago I heard that there were many refugee families at Kadem who were bereft even of the basic means of living and who existed in circumstances worthy of compassion.

"I went to see him to find out what I could do to help them. Since entering the city was forbidden, all of them wanted to return to their villages in Havran, considering that eating grass in the mountains was preferable to dying there of hunger.

"Thinking that if they returned to the villages they'd still die in wretchedness and of hunger, I asked the Pasha to permit them to enter the city to work, with the proviso that they didn't live there.

"It was agreed immediately and that written order is valid until now. The refugees had another complaint about the camp director Mahir Bey, who callously tortured them. I had orders issued concerning him by the appropriate authorities too. I saw him this morning and he was as dejected as a wet cat."

* * *

When Julia had finished her story, everyone present congratulated her on her success and for her humanitarian feelings towards those in need.

"But tell me how you escaped," she asked Kirk and Seyfi with interest.

Kirk briefly told her what had happened after the battle and, ending his story, said, "The most surprising thing was not finding the deaf-mute. We thought that you'd escaped together."

"But wasn't Samuel dead?" Julia asked, astonished.

"No, it would seem that seeing him unconscious, you thought, in your frightened state, that he was dead. We went to the place he'd fallen, found traces of blood, but not him."

Where is he now?"

"Who knows?"

"There's no doubt that, if he remained alive, he got lost in the general melee," Seyfi said sadly. "The poor man was so happy when we freed you from Death's Door. He continually wanted to kiss our hands to express his gratitude."

"Let's leave such words," Libani said, completely overcome by the stories he'd heard. "I can see recollecting the past distresses you. Be comforted that you three have been freed from those dreadful trials. Let's now talk about the present."

"That's right; let's return to the present," Seyfi said. "Miss Julia, what do you think of Mahir? Do you think he was Khalid's lieutenant?"

"I don't know," Julia said, confused. "I heard quite by accident this morning that he'd come from Der-Zor. I was so emotional on the day Death's Door was destroyed that I didn't have the time to even look at those executioners' faces. But anyway, I don't see any reason to be concerned, because first, his coming from Der-Zor doesn't mean that he's come from Death's Door, and even if he is the one from there, I don't think he's got the opportunity to see and betray you.

"He did see us once," Kirk said worriedly.

"When?"

"Three months ago, in the camp."

"So why are you worried? As he saw you and didn't betray you, it means that he didn't recognise you so he can't be the person you thought. Anyway, if you want me to, I'll get precise details about him," Julia said, getting to her feet.

"We'd be very grateful," Kirk and Seyfi said together. "But why did you get up?"

"In truth, it's difficult to leave you, but my mother will be concerned. I've been absent from the house since this morning."

"So, friends," Libani announced, getting to his feet too, "let me go to my family in Beirut. When your suspicions about Mahir are laid to rest, write to me, I'll come and we'll do our tour of Baalbek."

"Very well. I don't want to keep you any longer," Seyfi said, putting his hand on his Lebanese friend's shoulder. "After such a long absence, it's right that you join your family as soon as possible. But I await your return visit. What I say is also for you, Miss Julia. This house is open to you at all times. You'll always find two loving mothers, a sister, and two brothers. I hope you won't forget us from now on."

"Forget you…? Is it possible to forget what you've done for me?" Julia exclaimed in a heartfelt way. "No! No! I can never forget you."

"Do you see, Miss?" Seyfi said with a mischievous smile on his face, "Our friend hasn't forgotten you from that day."

Julia, troubled by this revelation, looked at her rescuer's eyes and saw sparkles of love in them that were apparent for only a second.

But that moment was enough to fill her soul with endless longing.

That Which Was Feared

An hour later, secret policeman Haidar submitted the following report to the general security director Sherif Bey:

"Today, in accordance with your order, I went to Wahab's street to closely watch what happened there.

"On three occasions I tried to obtain secrets from the servants. On one occasion I got into a conversation with a black maid under the pretext of asking for a neighbour's address. I approached the gardener once with the aim of lighting my cigarette. I also met the cook returning from the market to ask the time. But every time I tried to turn the conversation in the direction I wanted, I saw that their mouths closed up like oysters.

"Not to awaken the suspicions of those I talked to, I left them politely and began to watch the house furtively, to see who entered and left.

"After lunch the young servant – whose departure from the house I reported yesterday – returned to the house with a young lady. Both of them were in an excited state, especially the young woman, who was obviously, by her dress and face, an Armenian.

"There was no movement in the house until late. When it got dark, Mr Libani, the young lady and the servant left the house. The servant was carrying Libani's bag on his shoulder. The three of them strolled to the station. Half way there the young lady said goodbye to Libani and, wishing him a safe journey, went away. Shortly afterwards Mr Libani reached the station. The train going to Beirut was ready. He purchased his ticket and got into a first class carriage. The servant put the bag near him, received a tip, and returned to the house."

"Who is this young lady?" the police chief asked, annoyed, throwing the report to one side.

"I don't know. I couldn't find out who she was."

"You did the wrong thing, Haidar Bey. When you saw Mr Libani go straight to the station, you should have left him and followed the young lady."

"But sir, Libani could have met suspicious people in the station," the secret policeman pointed out. "My responsibility was to follow him."

"Armenian! Arab! Lebanese! I can see that this house is a nest of international conspirators," the police chief exclaimed, slamming his fist on the table, and adding after regaining his composure, "But who is that Armenian woman?"

Her house must be some distance away, sir," the secret policeman pointed out, "because the servant left yesterday and returned with her today."

"Haidar Bey!" the police chief cried angrily. "Send the policemen Saadek and Abdul Rahman to me. I can see that a police visit is necessary tonight to solve the riddle of this house."

* * *

Kirk couldn't sleep that night.

The idea that he hadn't been able to destroy the nest of vipers worried him, but not for personal, but for the safety of his community.

There were 19 young vipers, who were now scattered across the desert, without doubt spreading death and destruction around them, and spilling their poisonous anger on helpless refugees.

Had he done right or wrong in sweeping away their lair? He didn't really know the answer, but he definitely knew that he hadn't completed it, and that he had to take action once more to save his fellow-Armenians.

Considering this, he thought about Julia, and how he would lose her again when he resumed the unequal war.

When he thought about Julia, he couldn't forget his own tragic fiancée, whose memory would be forever carved in his heart. There was no way the emptiness left by Sara could be filled, but he needed someone who would stimulate him, understand his pain, and appreciate his struggle.

Kirk had never thought about, or could think about love when he was dedicated to the holy work of punishing the enemy who carried out genocide. But the day he met Julia in Khalid's room, it was as if a storm had loosened the chains in his empty soul.

The feelings of pain and sympathy towards the powerless girl in the first moments they met were quickly replaced by respect and admiration for her heroic battle against the claws of the debauched monster. A girl who was ready to save her honor by sacrificing her life was worthy, not only of compassion and tenderness, but of love and adoration.

The sad events that took place after the destruction of Death's Door, the final parting and the time that had passed hadn't been enough to make Kirk forget that magic charm that Julia had left him with. He had often thought about that vigorous and courageous soul, that noble and sensitive heart, that beautiful and delicate being who was almost the victim of the fury of the monstrous and debauched Khalid – if his intervention hadn't punished the maddened hyena foaming at the mouth.

Julia's loss had opened a painful wound in his already bloodied heart, and her reappearance today seemed to send a ray of sunlight into his darkened soul.

A mysterious force seemed to propel him towards that woman who was not only like him in heart and character, but had a similar unhappy past, the same spiritually tortured existence, and the same encouraging sacrifice and longing for her comrades.

He could only be happy with Julia, and Julia with him…

* * *

Lying fully dressed on the settee, he was thinking in this vein and looking at the trees that were rustling with a mysterious sound in the light of the moon.

He wondered what he had to do and where he had to start to begin a new struggle, when he suddenly straightened up with a sudden shudder.

He had seen a shadow in the garden that was moving towards the house with very great care and hiding behind thickly growing bushes.

Who could that be? A thief or a policeman? Kirk suddenly got up, moved towards the window and looked from behind the curtain to ascertain who the mysterious person was.

Shortly afterwards the shadow came out from behind the thick trunk of a tree. Kirk, seeing the yellow colour of his buttons shining on his clothes, rushed out of the room. "Seyfi, Seyfi!" he called, entering his friend's bedroom. "Get up, there's a policeman in the garden!"

Jumping out of bed, Seyfi ran to the window. "Where is he?"

Kirk went to the window as well, but saw no one in the garden. "He must have entered the house," he replied in a low voice. "But I'm sure. I saw him clearly."

"Was there only one?"

"Yes."

"He must have come to conduct a search. Let's go to our cupboard." Saying this Seyfi quickly dressed, got his pistol from under his pillow and was sliding it into his pocket, when suddenly the door opened wide and two policemen entered, threateningly.

"Don't move!"

"What do you want?" Seyfi asked coldly, stopping.

"We want to know who you are and what you're doing in the widow of Mrs Wahab's mansion," policeman Saadek said.

"That doesn't concern you," Seyfi replied calmly.

"You're wrong, sir. On the contrary, it concerns the police to know who's living in the house of a man who was hanged for being a traitor to his country."

"Is this house forbidden to have friends and acquaintance visit it?" Seyfi asked.

"Please forgive me. The widow Mrs Wahab is free to have whatever friends and acquaintances she likes to entertain in her house," Saadek replied. "But it's our job to know who they are."

"So you want us to introduce ourselves?"

"No, introductions aren't enough. Please come to the police station. We'll establish your identities there."

Seyfi exchanged a meaningful glance with his friend who hadn't spoken in front of the policemen, so they wouldn't know he was Armenian. "Very well, let's go."

As they were descending the stairs, Seyfi's mother, aunt and fiancée, woken by the unusual noise in the house, had come out of their apartment very frightened, crying, "What's this? Where are you going?" and other similar things.

"Don't be frightened, it's nothing," Seyfi said, deliberately quieting them. "The policemen are taking us to the police station to confirm our identities. Go inside. We'll return as soon as we've satisfied the chief of police's curiosity."

* * *

Wahab's mansion was situated at the edge of the city, among other mansions that, surrounded by evergreen trees and woods, gave beautiful Damascus a charming appearance.

The streets of that wealthy part of the city were lined more with garden walls than with houses. They were only animated during the day and almost deserted at night. But one of the city's busiest boulevards, where there always was movement, especially during the hot summer nights, was only a few streets away, where one could find the Arabs' favourite cold drink shops, clubs and coffee houses with singers.

When Seyfi was going through the deserted streets of summer residences, he thought that it was only in that area that they could escape from the policemen otherwise, when they entered the boulevard, any attempt at escape would be impossible. He quickly made his friend understand with an eye movement. His friend, in reply, indicated his readiness in the same way.

Seyfi, after receiving Kirk's assurance, continued walking like a confident man who had become a victim through mischance. But when he came to a particular place, he stopped to light a cigarette. Policeman Saadek, who was walking next to him, also stopped, while Kirk and the other policeman carried on.

Everything was going according to plan. Seyfi lit a match and at the moment he was going to put it to his cigarette, he punched the policeman in the face with such force that Saadek cried with pain and fell to the ground.

At the same time Kirk punched policeman Abdul Rahman in the chest so hard that he felled him in the same way.

Leaving the two policemen to recover from the sudden blows, Kirk and Seyfi began to run along the street.

Shortly afterwards the shrill sound of a whistle broke the silence. The policemen, having got to their feet, were running after the two escapees, continually firing and calling for help.

Just as Kirk and Seyfi were going to turn the corner, they came face to face with a night watchman and a third policeman who, hearing the loud sounds of the whistles and firing, were running to help, one with a cane, the other holding his pistol in the air.

The road was closed before them. The two friends immediately turned back, running the way they came, preferring to deal with policeman dizzy from their blows, rather than fresh forces.

They came face to face with their former enemies once more. One was bleeding from his nose and mouth, the other who had met Kirk's iron fist, was coughing dreadfully, holding his chest. Their hands were trembling due to the stress and pain they were in, when they fired towards the escapees coming in their direction. Fortunately the bullets missed and the two fugitives were able to get through the cordon the policemen formed.

They had hardly gone twenty paces when Kirk slowed, screamed with pain, and fell forward. "Escape, Seyfi!" he cried with a weak voice. "I've been hit in the knee, save yourself!"

But Seyfi, without listening to his friend, bent down to pick him up. As he did so, the night watchman and the policeman with him rushed at Seyfi like mad bulls. He moved quicker. There was an explosion, and the policeman fell on Kirk, dead.

* * *

When Kirk opened his eyes, he saw a nurse bandaging his injured knee, while three people were talking near the head of the bed.

"...The police are already on his trail. We'll soon arrest him dead or alive."

"But I don't understand, Sherif Bey; had they entered Wahab's house to steal?"

"To plot treachery, Doctor."

"But how have you decided that they are plotters, as you've not identified them?"

"If they were innocent, why didn't they come to the police station to prove their innocence?"

At the same moment, the police chief, seeing that Kirk had come to, asked in a gentle voice, "Have you recovered, friend? Don't try to escape again. Come on, sit up and answer my questions."

While the police chief was getting ready to question the wounded man, a third person, who until that time hadn't spoken, took a piece of paper and a pen from his pocket and got ready to record the interrogation that began shortly afterwards.

"What's your name?"

"Kirk."

"Your age?"

"Twenty five."

"Nationality?"

"Armenian."

"Your trade?"

"I don't have a trade. I'm a sub-lieutenant."

"You're an officer? So what are you doing here?"

"I was in the Dardanelles and, because I'm a Christian, they …exiled me."

"How do you know Wahab's widow?"

"I saved the life of an Arab officer in the Dardanelles campaign. I met him by accident in Damascus three months ago. Seeing my parlous financial state, he took me to his aunt's house, where I was a guest until last night."

"So your friend was Estari's son Seyfi?"

"Yes."

"Do you know who he is?"

"I told you. He was an officer at the Dardanelles."

"Then?"

"I don't know."

"Didn't he tell you that he'd got a cavalry regiment to rebel?"

"He'd no reason to."

"Did his mother, aunt and fiancée know of his guilt?"

"I don't know."

"Didn't you ever wonder why an active service officer was imprisoned in the house?"

"He told me that he was on leave."

"Do you know Haroun Libani?"

"Yes, we met three days ago."

"Did you know he was a political prisoner?"

"Yes, he told me."

"Why did he stay for a night in Wahab's mansion?"

"The residents wouldn't let him leave."

"Who is the young lady who visited the house yesterday?"

"A refugee lady I know."

"What's her name?"

"Julia."

"Why did she go there?"

"I asked her to see me, when I found out she was in Damascus."

"How did you find out?"

"From refugees who'd come to the house asking for alms."

"When the police arrested you tonight, why did you try to escape?"

"……"

"Answer! If you're an innocent refugee, and your friend is an innocent officer, why didn't you want to come to the police station and prove your innocence?"

"I don't know why my friend didn't want to come. But I know from experience that an Armenian has never been able to prove his innocence in any Turkish police station."

"Do you think that it's innocence to wound two policemen and kill a third when they're doing their duty?"

"I know nothing of the death of a policeman."

"Didn't you kill him?"

"No."

"So your friend did?"

"I don't know. I had fallen wounded. The incident must have happened after I lost consciousness."

"The questioning's finished. Sign your statement."

The policeman acting as secretary offered him the report and pen. Kirk, with the doctor's and nurse's assistance signed the paper; on the same day he was thrown into the cell reserved for murderers in the central prison.

The Prisoner

Julia had never forgotten, nor could she ever forget, the bold officer who had suddenly appeared before her at the worst, most desperate time of her life.

A hideous criminal had kidnapped her, killing her mother.

Her brother and a self-sacrificing Armenian had come to rescue her. The wretch had, in cold blood, also killed them both, destroying any hope she had of being rescued.

The bloodthirsty beast had then taken her to his lair, to slaughter her with impunity. But hardly had he bared his bloody fangs when a vengeful bullet felled him.

Forget…? Was it possible to forget the heroic officer who had saved her life and destroyed Death's Door, and who had left such a deep and permanent impression on her?

Often, when she struggled with nightmares, she had to call the brave officer for help and, hardly having called "Kirk…!" her nightmare would disappear and she would wake to a light world.

During the day too, she would often think about him: the man who had exacted his and his people's vengeance on a violent murderer.

Only three days before, when she had heard, in Kadem station, that he was still alive, she had run madly to the house where he had taken refuge and would have hugged and kissed him – as she had on the day he had rescued her – if conventional formalities hadn't prevented her heartfelt desire.

When Julia had returned home that evening she thought about Kirk for a long time. She had seen his loving and the tender smile that had lit up his handsome face when she had appeared. She had also seen the ray of love that had sparkled in his eyes with the speed of lightning when she left.

Being a young man of strong will, Kirk had immediately controlled himself, so as not to betray the secret feelings buried deep in his heart. But what Julia had seen was enough to fill her soul with delight.

But Kirk's concern that he had not completely obliterated the nest of vipers had affected her badly. If Mahir was really Khalid's lieutenant, then there was no doubt of great danger from the 19 criminals who had been released, not just to Kirk – and therefore to her happiness – but also to all surviving Armenians in the desert.

To understand this, the following morning Julia went to the local police station, whose director was Behidj Bey, who had had a specific order to satisfy all her requests immediately. "Very well Miss," the police officer said, hearing what she wanted. "I'll write immediately where necessary and let you know the result."

"When will you be able to let me know?" Julia asked.

"Today's Thursday and today is impossible. Tomorrow is a rest day; I hope to let you know on Saturday."

"Shall I come here on Saturday to receive your answer?"

"Please don't inconvenience yourself, Miss. I'll send a policeman to your house with the reply."

A policeman came to Julia's house on Saturday and told her that the refugee director Mahir Bey had come from Der-Zor, but it was not clear what position he had had there, why he had come to Damascus, how he had become director, as the Director General of the Refugees Settlement Office was absent, having gone to a distant town called Nablus on personal business.

"If you really want to know Mahir Bey's past, you can find out by asking him directly," the policeman said, ending his report.

"No, let it rest for the moment," Julia said. "If necessary I'll approach Behidj Bey again in the future. Please give him my respects."

After the policeman had left, Julia went to Wahab's mansion to let Kirk and Seyfi know what she had found out and, at the same time, to seek their advice as to what to do about this deadlocked situation.

The poor girl didn't know what dreadful news awaited her there!

The maid who opened the door, seeing her, told her, with tears in her eyes, of Kirk's and Seyfi's arrests on the night she had left, Seyfi's escape on the way, and Kirk's imprisonment.

It was as if a sharp-edged iron implement had been thrust into the unfortunate girl's heart. She remained there, bewildered for a moment and then, suddenly screaming with fear, she rushed into the living room to find out the details of what had happened from the people living there.

Seyfi's mother, aunt and fiancée were sitting in the room in deep despair and worry, when Julia came in, distraught with concern.

"What a terrible calamity!" she cried, her throat tight from sobbing.

"Come and sit down, my girl," said the noble Arab ladies, immediately surrounding her and sitting her down in an armchair. "Kirk's been arrested, but there's no need to worry. The police can't prove him guilty."

"But what happened?" the unlucky girl said, her face wet with tears.

Mrs Makbouleh related what had happened, adding that they and the servants had been questioned by the police, and had been released under surety, on the condition that they appear in court if they were called.

"What did you say in your statements?" Julia asked, trembling.

"Altogether innocent and harmless information," Mrs Makbouleh replied. "For example, when they asked how Kirk knew Seyfi, we answered that they'd got to know each other at the Dardanelles. As to why Kirk was in this house, we said that we had a debt of gratitude to pay and that's why he was a guest. When they asked whether we knew that Seyfi was a rebel, we said we thought that he was on leave, and that he'd come to Damascus to see his mother and fiancée. They then asked why Mr Libani had come to our house and stayed the night on the day he had been released, we told them that as he was a friend of the family, we'd provided him with hospitality. They were interested in you too and asked if you knew Mr Libani before; we said that you'd been introduced to him here."

"But how did the police know that I knew Mr Libani?" Julia asked, astonished.

"A secret policeman had followed Mr Libani on the day he was released, to see where he went and whom he saw. The policeman had seen Mr Libani come here and stay the night. The next day he'd seen you come here and your departure in his company a few hours later. On the other hand the police knew of my sister's and Fehimeh's arrival here from Baghdad. Thinking that plots were being hatched in this house, they felt they had to search it."

"Has Seyfi escaped? Where is he now?"

"We don't know. He can't write to us of course, so that he won't betray himself. But anyway he didn't do the right thing by killing the policeman."

"Killing a policeman?" Julia asked, shaken.

"Yes."

"But why?"

"They had a fight with the police in the street," Mrs Makbouleh replied tenderly. Kirk fell down with a wounded knee. Seyfi wanted to pick him up and escape. Just then a policeman arrived. Seyfi, seeing the danger, fired and ran away."

"What's happened to Kirk?"

"They took Kirk in his wounded condition to hospital, then to prison."

"I hope they won't accuse him of killing the policeman!" Julia exclaimed, suddenly having a dire thought.

"Fortunately the dying policeman confessed that the person who shot him was the prisoner who ran away."

"I'll go to the prison and see what's happened to Kirk," sighed Julia, getting to her feet.

"We don't think that he'd have said anything to the police that was different from what we said about his working with Seyfi," Mrs Makbouleh said. "It was as if the poor boy was prophesying when he one day told us that if we suffered misfortune, we should all reply to the police questioning with the same answers. Go, my girl, assure him that we did as he suggested and that we won't add anything to what we've said before the court. We heartily hope that his innocence will be proved and he'll be set free."

"That hope is ours too," declared Seyfi's mother and fiancée, who'd been listening gloomily to the conversation.

"Only, my girl," Mrs Sabiha said, "my sister forgot one important thing. The police asked us where Kirk knows you from. We said that you knew each other from your country. If they should ask you about that, you must keep the circumstances of your meeting secret."

"Of course I will!" Julia breathed, "Because on the day the circumstances become known, that's the day of Kirk's death sentence."

"Miss Julia," Fehimeh said, accompanying the Armenian girl to the door, "of course you won't forget to come here often and to bring good news about yourself and Mr Kirk. If we have any news, we'll let you know."

* * *

Leaving Wahab's mansion, Julia went straight to the central prison in Damascus.

The elderly prison guard Officer Ballal came up to her and asked what she wanted.

"Kirk," Julia said, in a trembling voice.

"Do you have police chief Sherif Bey's permission?"

"No."

"You'll have to go and get it."

Filled with bitter sorrow and worries, Julia went to the Public Security building and presented herself to Sherif Bey. "Two days ago a young man named Kirk was arrested," she said, making superhuman efforts to restrain her inner feelings. "I went to the prison to see him, and they told me I had to have your permission to do so. Would you be so kind as to grant it?"

The chief of police, deeply impressed by the supplicant's beauty and boldness, looked quizzically into her eyes for a moment, then asked, "What is the prisoner to you?"

Julia had never expected such a question.

"My fiancée," she suddenly replied easily.

"Your name?"

"Julia."

Sherif Bey looked through several sets of papers on his desk and said, with a polite smile, "Please sit down. It was good that you came. We were already looking for you." He then pressed the bell on his desk and told the servant who entered to fetch secret policeman Haidar.

The secret policeman entered shortly afterwards and, seeing Julia, cried, "There, sir, that's the woman who entered Wahab's mansion on Wednesday, then left with Haroun Libani. How were you able to find her?"

"There was no need to bring me face to face with a policeman," Julia pointed out with bold calmness. "If you'd asked me directly, I could have told you that I was the woman who went into Wahab's house."

It was the first time in his life that he had seen an Armenian woman who spoke fearlessly in his presence. "Very well, Miss Julia," he said with a mysterious chuckle. "As you've expressed willingness to tell the truth, tell me why you went to that house three days ago."

"I went to see my fiancée."

"What was your fiancée doing in Wahab's house?"

"He was being entertained by his friend's aunt."

"Were you acquainted with your fiancée's friend and his aunt before you went to the house?"

"No."

"Your fiancée had been living in that house for three months and, in all that time, had never gone out. How did you know he was there?"

"He'd heard about me and had me called."

"Where do you live?"

"In the city, near the Armenian church."

"How come the house servant who left in the evening to call you returned with you at midday the next day?"

"That means that the servant didn't come to get me directly."

"So where did he go?"

"How do I know? Maybe he went to see his family."

"You said that you visited your fiancée in Wahab's mansion. When had you been parted from him?"

"We lost touch with one another about 20 months ago in Aleppo."

"Do you know Haroun Libani?"

"Yes, I met him by chance in Wahab's mansion."

The chief of police, considering the questioning sufficient, turned to the secret policeman and said, "Haidar Bey, take the lady to the holding center. When we feel it's necessary, well question her again."

"Excuse me, sir," Julia pointed out coldly, "I didn't come here to go to the holding center, but to be able to see my fiancée in prison."

"Yes, yes, you'll see him later."

Secret policeman Haidar came close to Julia and clasping her by the shoulder, said, "Please follow me, Miss."

"Please sir, you've no right to arrest me," Julia protested to the police chief. "If you need my testimony, you'll take my address and when I'm called, I'll go to the court."

"And if you don't go?" Sherif Bey cried.

"Why shouldn't I? After all, I'm going to give testimony in favour of my fiancée."

"It's safer for you to be at the police's disposal."

"So you want to keep me for months in the police station, until the day of the trial?"

"I'll keep you in my house, Miss," the police chief cajoled her with a wolfish expression.

"You're knocking at the wrong door, Sherif Bey," Julia said coldly. "I can't go anywhere. I came to ask for a permit to see my fiancée."

The chief of police saw that he had quite a complicated situation on his hands and added, "Miss, I want to know where an Armenian woman gets such boldness."

"Do Armenian women look so small to you?" Julia asked. "No, sir, you can't keep an innocent woman hostage in your house."

"I'll put you under my feet and grind you up like a clod of earth, do you understand?" yelled the police chief, who suddenly got angry.

"You can, but you'll regret it afterwards."

"I'll be sorry to have killed an Armenian woman?"

"I'll only say this to you sir; if you don't give me a permit, I know where to get it." Julia took a step towards the door.

"Haidar Bey, don't let her leave!" Sherif Bey cried angrily. "I'm going to make her understand how to insult a police chief!"

"Please, sir, it's you who are insulting me. You want to use force on me. The right to complain is mine!" Julia cried.

A ferocious glint appeared in the police chief's eyes. "Very well, Miss, complain," he said sarcastically. "You're faced with the Director of Public Security."

"Don't forget, sir, there's a higher official than the director of Public Security in this city, and I can present my complaint to him," Julia said.

"So you'll present it to the governor...?"

"No, to a higher personage than the governor, to Djemal Pasha."

"Keep your tongue between your teeth, foolish girl. Don't you know that anyone who uses his name doesn't remain unpunished?" the police chief chided.

"Yes, and the person who insults someone under his protection doesn't remain unpunished either," the young lady answered.

It was as if Julia's words fell like the blow of a club on the heads of the two Turkish officials. They had heard of an Armenian girl under Djemal Pasha's protection, and there was no doubt that she was in front of them.

"I'm sorry, Miss, it was a misunderstanding," the police chief muttered, instantly changing his rough attitude. "But why didn't you say before that you were under the pasha's protection?"

"Because I didn't realize that to obtain one of my just rights I'd have to use the pasha's name," Julia cried victoriously.

"You've no idea, Miss, what a thankless position this is," Sherif Bey said with a pitiable appearance. "A thousand different people enter here every day. Each one has a request. We can't deal with all of them. They shout, they complain… we're human beings, we get angry, and occasionally wound honorable people."

Talking in this way, Sherif Bey wrote two lines on a piece of paper, signed and stamped it, and, presenting it courteously to Julia, said, "Please accept this, Miss. This gives you the right to visit your fiancée every day, at whatever time you like. I hope that this special favour will help you forget the wound occasioned by the misunderstanding." Then, turning to the secret policeman, with typical Turkish official caressing gallantry, he added, "Haidar Bey, escort the young lady right to the prison.!"

"No, don't put yourselves out," Julia said, taking the paper and leaving. "I know the way."

* * *

When prison guard officer Ballal saw the permit that was in Julia's hand, he immediately got to his feet and bowed from the heavens to the ground. "Please, Miss," he said, leading the Armenian girl to a waiting room, "Sit here. I'll call your fiancée."

"My fiancée? Who told you that Kirk is my fiancée?" said Julia, surprised.

The prison guard looked at the piece of paper in his hand and, without saying a word, went towards a narrow, damp cellar. Then he opened the door to the cell and respectfully greeted the only inmate, "Mr Kirk," he said, "your fiancée has come to visit you."

"My fiancée?"

"Yes. May God will it, your fiancée."

"I hope it's not a mistake. I don't have a fiancée," Kirk said.

"Oh, you young people! Are you making fun of me?" cried the elderly prison guard, showing him the permit. "There you are. It says that the young lady bearing this permit may come here to visit her fiancée whenever she wishes. This is a permit that's not given to even one in a hundred thousand."

Kirk understood who it was visiting him. So, with a cry of joy, he rushed out of the cell and ran towards the bars of the cage.

"Julia…!"

"Kirk…!"

Both names seemed to burst out together.

"Oh, I'm so grateful that you've not forgotten me," exclaimed Kirk, holding Julia's hand that was trembling with emotion through the bars. "Thank you, a thousand thanks!"

"There's no need to thank me," Julia replied, looking at her rescuer with affection. "I heard of the misfortune just a little while ago and ran here. Tell me, how's your wound?"

"It's not painful today. What news of Seyfi?"

"He's not been caught yet." Then Julia told him of her visit to Wahab's mansion and about the answers those living there had given the police.

"Good, so they've not forgotten their lesson," Kirk murmured, satisfied.

"There's another reason to be pleased," Julia said. "The policeman who was killed said, before he died, that he'd been wounded by Seyfi. The person who started the fight was Seyfi. I think that the court can't find any proof and you'll be free in a few weeks." Then she told him how, when she had gone to get the permit, she had, by mistake, presented herself as his fiancée, for which she asked him to accept her apology.

"No, Julia," Kirk cried tenderly. "That answer of yours to the police chief as to why you wanted to see me wasn't the result of confusion, but the genuine voice of your heart, to which I also concur, saying, 'I love you... you're my fiancée.'" Kirk, with feverish movements put Julia's hand to his burning lips and kissed it heatedly. Julia, light-headed with joy, returned Kirk's affection, kissing his forehead. In this manner, behind the prison's coffins, they pledged their ill-starred love that had begun in such unfortunate circumstances about a year before.

* * *

When Kirk returned to his dark cell, he thought how wonderful it was to have a companion for life. If Julia hadn't been outside, who would look for him? Who would think of him? Who would be concerned for him? Who would look after him?

Seyfi's mother, aunt and fiancée would look after him like a mother and sister. But in order not to give rise to confusion, they couldn't visit the prison and he, for days, weeks and perhaps for months would be isolated without seeing a friendly face.

"I'm going to make a complaint to the police chief, asking why you're held in a cell reserved for murderers, as the dead policeman had confessed your innocence," Julia said as she was leaving. "Your crime is only that of disobedience, of you not wanting to go to the police station. If necessary, I'll go to the pasha."

"No, don't do that," Kirk said. "Because if he takes an interest, the problem will take a different turn. It's better to suffer two or three months imprisonment, rather than to take the matter outside police jurisdiction."

"Very well, but by appealing to the police chief, I can have your cell changed and make your imprisonment easier."

"Do that if you can."

And Julia left with a meaningful squeeze of hands, a smile on her lips, and hope in her heart.

Now Kirk realized how dark and gloomy his life would be if Julia didn't light up his dark sky with her radiant love and hope.

Would that day come when Kirk would be free and, taking her in his arms, would forget – even for a moment – all his woes and troubles?

Would that blessed day come?

Kirk lay down on the damp mattress and, his gaze lost in mysterious dreams, continually repeated to himself, "When, when will that day come?"

The Witness

Three months passed in the prison, each hour and day being one of soul-destroying waiting and anxiety.

During that time, thanks to Julia's approaches, Kirk's cell and prison conditions changed, but the uncertain state of his imprisonment didn't, since his files had not been presented to the court.

The police, using all their resources, were continuously looking for Seyfi, the real actor in the drama, and only with whose arrest would a great deal of light be thrown on Kirk's past and his links to Seyfi.

While accepting that Kirk had saved Seyfi's life at the Dardanelles, and that the latter was paying a debt of gratitude by having him stay in his aunt's house, why hadn't Kirk ever left Wahab's house during the three months he had been staying there?

Seyfi's voluntary incarceration was understandable, but what reason did Kirk have for avoiding police surveillance, and why had he tried to escape after he was arrested?

But as well as the police's suspicions were founded, he couldn't be kept under lock and key for months without real charges being brought. So, after three months of useless imprisonment, the police had to hand Kirk to the criminal court in the hope that, during the course of questioning, he would be caught in a net of inconsistencies.

Kirk, knowing that he was going to criminal court, was really pleased, because it meant that he was being accused of a civil crime while, if he was handed to the war tribunal, it would have meant that there was an accusation of treachery against him.

After preliminary questioning, the judge Ali Reza Bey asked Kirk if he had any objection to the accusation brought by the police against him.

"No," Kirk replied coldly.

"So tell us under what circumstances were you in Wahab's mansion on the night of the incident."

"The circumstance was that I was Seyfi's friend."

"Were your bonds of friendship so strong that he gave you hospitality for three months in his aunt's house?"

"Yes."

"What were the reasons preventing you from leaving the house at all during that time?"

"There was no reason. I didn't want to leave my friend alone, and I'd nothing to do outside."

"Were you never curious as to why he didn't go out into the street, as an officer on leave is free to move about?"

"He wanted to enjoy a peaceful life at home after two and a half years of hard service."

"Where were you three months ago?"

"Damascus."

"Before that?"

"In the Havran desert."

"How did you meet Seyfi?"

"By chance in the city."

"Didn't you ask why he wasn't spending his leave in his birthplace, Baghdad?"

"He said that he'd come from the Palestinian front and was to return there. To save time he'd written to his mother and fiancée to meet him in Damascus."

"Why did you want to run away from the police on the night of the incident?"

"I don't know why Seyfi wanted to; I just followed his example."

"When your friend was running away, didn't you ask what the reason was?"

"I didn't have time."

"Why did you follow his example?"

"I don't know, perhaps by instinct."

"Had you any reason to be frightened of the police?"

"As an Armenian, I suffered a lot at the hands of the police during the deportations. For that reason their appearance terrified me."

"Who killed the policeman Shaban?"

"I don't know, I'd been wounded before he was killed."

The judge consulted with his two advisors and then, addressing himself to the policemen escorting Kirk, ordered, "Take him to the prison. That's enough for today."

* * *

Kirk appeared before the court four times after that. Witnesses were heard – the inhabitants of Wahab's house – but it wasn't possible to find any proof to accuse him of being Seyfi's accomplice.

Kirk was happy. Julia was even more so who, visiting the prison every day, encouraged her fiancée, saying that he would receive a 'not guilty' verdict soon. "Even if they condemn you for resisting the police," Julia would say, "your sentence can't be more than three months. You've already been in prison for five. So in three days, when the final trial takes place, you'll definitely be free."

"In three days! In three days!" Kirk would sigh from the depths of his heart. "Oh! If only the three days would pass!"

But the three days passed like an eternity, and Kirk, on an October day, went to the criminal court to hear his verdict.

He was seated once more between two policemen when, in deep silence, the general prosecutor read the following charge: "Mr Chairman, the accused Kirk's close friendship with the rebel Seyfi is beyond doubt. The accused Kirk ascribes this friendship to his role as saviour at the Dardanelles front and the obligation that Seyfi felt towards him. Although the story is romantic, we've no reason to doubt it's veracity, if the accused Kirk's subsequent actions didn't go against the spirit of his statements.

"Mr Chairman, I'll point out three things to you, to prove that the accused Kirk was more than simply a friend to Captain Seyfi. First, his reunion with Seyfi. Captain Seyfi, who is wanted by the government as a traitor, couldn't walk the streets freely to meet the accused Kirk. But as he has met him, it means that the meeting happened well before Damascus. Why shouldn't they meet? One Armenian, the other Arab – both enemy races of the government – why shouldn't they find one another and join up to plot against their enemy government?

"Secondly, why has the accused Kirk stayed closed up in Wahab's mansion for three months? Did his concern not to leave his friend alone prevent him from going on the streets, or was it that he was frightened of being recognised and arrested?

"Thirdly, on the night he was arrested, why did he try to run from the police? We know that the leader of the rebels, Captain Seyfi, had serious reasons to do that. He's condemned to death in absentia, and immediately upon being caught, he'll be shot. Did the accused Kirk have the same reasons, or did he try to run because of a concern not to leave his friend alone?

"Mr Chairman, all this reasoning establishes, beyond all doubt, that the accused Kirk was not only Captain Seyfi's friend, but also his accomplice. Therefore I accuse him, and the rebel commander Seyfi, with the charge of getting a cavalry company to rebel in Diarbekir. Apart from this I regard Kirk responsible for the murder of the policeman Shaban. So I demand the same punishment for him that was so justly given in the case of his accomplice the rebel Captain Seyfi."

After the completion of the prosecutor's speech, the chairman of the criminal court asked Kirk if he had anything to say in his own defense.

"No," Kirk replied. "I've nothing to add to what I've already said. I'll just say this: I've never been in Diarbekir, so I couldn't have been there to help Seyfi to get the cavalry to rebel."

The judge once more consulted his advisors, and a moment later, in solemn tones, said, "Bearing in mind that it's not been proved that the accused Kirk was the rebel commander Seyfi's accomplice; bearing in mind that no firearm was found on the accused, and according to the policemen Saadek and Abdul Rahman's testimony he wasn't the aggressor; bearing in mind that according to the dead policeman Shaban's statement that he wasn't the killer, the court finds him not guilty of the accusation and crime ascribed to him. But noting that he had carried out an attack on officers of the law in pursuit of their duty the court, in accordance with the disposition of the criminal law, sentences him to three months..."

Just then there was confusion and noise at the door of the court. "A moment! A moment..."

"What's all this noise?" the judge asked, stopping his verdict.

"Listen to me, your honor..."

The man who said this and ran panting towards the judge was the director of the Kadem refugee camp Mahir Bey. "Listen to me, your honor... Give me a moment to get my breath back... I'm a witness..."

A horrified silence enveloped the courtroom.

Everyone's gaze was focused on the thin-faced little man who, with his dramatic entrance, had interrupted the declaration of the court's verdict.

Kirk, who had heard the verdict of three months' imprisonment with joy, suddenly felt a death-like coldness, seeing Death's Door killer number two.

"I, Lieutenant Mahir," the witness said, after pausing for breath, "accuse Sub-Lieutenant Kirk with the crime of treachery against the fatherland."

A dreadful shiver went through all those present.

Julia, who was standing with her mother in the front row of seats, so that she could be the first to embrace Kirk, remained frozen where she stood, as if turned to stone.

Now in her ears that were going deaf she could hear the echo, like the buzzing of a poisonous mosquito, of the accusation levelled by the deputy commander of Death's Door, whose every word was like a red-hot skewer thrust into her heart.

"About 16 months ago," the Armenian-eating monster said, "I was serving in the military post between Der-Zor and Mosul named Black Rock, under the command of Captain Khalid. As the court knows, similar posts are established in the desert to maintain government communication with the frontiers and the battlefront.

"I feel it unnecessary to speak about the military value of these posts here, because only the military authorities can appreciate their importance. I only want to tell the court the fact that this accused was the rebel Seyfi's comrade, who incited a cavalry company to rebel in Diarbekir.

"During their escape towards Basra, they attacked our post and, without reason killed Corporal Reza and five soldiers, seriously injured Captain Khalid, imprisoned us – 19 people – in the cave under the Black Rock and finally blew up the post with explosives.

"All of us were buried alive in the cave and were going to die from terrible tortures if our commander, Captain Khalid, getting out from under the ruins, hadn't come and opened the door to our tomb.

"These cursed criminals, naturally, after carrying out their crime, escaped. However, a few days later they were surrounded by a government force that was following them. During the battle that followed, they killed six more soldiers. 14 of them died, three were taken prisoner and the others managed to escape. The gentleman here and the rebel commander Seyfi were among those who escaped."

It was as if the court building shook at hearing this devastating revelation.

"I was convinced of the accused's treachery to the fatherland!" cried the general prosecutor with a victorious smile.

Shortly afterwards the president of the court made the following announcement: "Seeing that according to Lieutenant Mahir's accusation the crime ascribed to Kirk is of a military nature, this court doesn't find that it can deal with this case, so all the files will be transferred to the war tribunal."

* * *

Kirk couldn't sleep that night.

The accusation levelled against him had only one punishment – death.

They would hang him, because he had committed a crime: an unforgivable crime, destroying the vipers' nest, the bloodthirsty criminals lair.

The fear he had in his heart had finally become reality. Not only hadn't Mahir and his friends not perished, their accursed leader wasn't killed either.

So all his efforts had been in vain, seeing that the 3,000 refugees who had been spared Death's Door had been killed in the general massacre that had taken place a few months later.

Kirk, with his hands thrust into his trouser pockets, his head on his chest, walked up and down his cell like a wounded tiger.

More than for his own death, he was hurt that he would die and leave Julia, who had no one, and his thousands of fellow-Armenians who had formidable enemies like Khalid, behind him.

Tired from pacing, he sat down for a while with his back to the prison's cold wall and thought for a long time. Then, agitated, he got up once more and feverishly prowled his cell.

He continued until morning, when the prison guard came to him. "Mr Kirk," he said politely, "get your things and follow me. Your cell is being changed."

Without speaking, Kirk collected his things and followed the prison guard.

They went down some steps, walked along a narrow corridor, went down some more steps and stopped in front of a low iron door.

The prison guard opened the door with a large key, and invited Kirk to enter.

This was a small cell, three quarters of its height was below ground level, the remainder above the surface. Light entered through a narrow window near the ceiling that opened onto the prison yard. The walls and floor were stone, covered with mould, whose musty smell made the atmosphere unbreathable.

"Walk!" the prison guard said, pushing Kirk in the back with his finger. "Don't be frightened, the room is not that dark; your eyes will soon get used to it."

Kirk groped his way in and stood in front of the inner wall.

Officer Ballal put the shackles that were fixed to a long chain secured to the wall around his neck, wrists and ankles, then closed their locks and said, "The chain is quite long. If you feel fed up, you can wander around the cell."

Then, closing the door, he went away with the heavy tread of a pallbearer.

Kirk remaining alone in the cell, remained still and quiet for a long time. It was as if he was a beeswax statue, and didn't even blink his eyes that were fixed aimlessly on an unknown point.

At about midday the large key turned in the door's rusty lock. The prison guard had come, bringing with him a piece of dry bread and a pitcher of water.

"Officer Ballal," Kirk asked, opening his mouth for the first time that day to speak, "did my fiancée come to see me yesterday evening?"

"She did. But there was an order from Sherif Bey. We took her permit from her and refused to let her see you."

"Thank you."

The prison guard put the bread and pitcher on a wooden stool and left.

Kirk, thoughtful, resumed his statue-like position.

About two hours later he heard the sound of two people's footsteps – one light, the other heavy – that were coming in his direction. Suddenly his heart began to beat with unusual speed. Julia was coming, without doubt.

Indeed, shortly afterwards a small square slot opened in the door and, in the semi-darkness he saw his adorable angel's face. "Julia…"

Kirk ran madly towards the door… but he had hardly gone a step when he remained motionless, his body bending forwards, while his neck, arms and legs were restrained, pulling against the chain.

"Kirk, don't worry," Julia said in a voice trembling with anguish, "I'll find a way of getting you out of this place. If necessary, I'll go to the pasha."

"No, Julia, don't do that," Kirk cried.

"What shall I do then? You've no idea how difficult it was to get to see you. Yesterday, after the trial, I came here to see you as usual. Apparently there was an order from the police chief and they took my permit away. I went to see Sherif Bey, to get permission to see you. He was very busy apparently... he couldn't see me. I went again today, and was able to see him. When I said that they'd confiscated my permit, he said, 'My girl, your fiancée is accused of being a traitor to the fatherland, and I advise you to sever your links with him. If the pasha hears that you're in contact with a traitor, he'll remove his protection from you.'

"I begged and begged him and eventually he gave me a permit for one visit. I think, Kirk, that the pasha's intervention is necessary to get you out of this deadlock."

"That's not possible, Julia. The pasha can't alter my fate," Kirk said sorrowfully. "You'll lose his esteem for nothing."

"You're so wrong, Kirk," Julia protested. "First, don't say that the pasha can't do anything. Here in Syria neither the sultan, nor Enver or Talaat can do anything against Djemal Pasha's will. Although the Arabs sarcastically call him 'the emperor of Syria', they have the right to do so, as there's no higher authority in Syria. As for your second point, that I'd lose his esteem, tell me, of what use is my special position if I can't free you?"

"Don't ignore the pasha's protection, Julia. First, no one can hurt you and, second, you can, through your authority, carry on helping the refugees the way you are now."

"I'm going to help myself and everyone else and not you?"

"My situation is different, Julia."

"But what are you going to be here? Do you know what the punishment for treason is?"

"Yes, I do."

"No, no, Kirk, I don't want to lose you. I'm going to the pasha, fall at his feet..." The poor girl wasn't able to finish what she wanted to say; the words were strangled in her throat.

"Julia," Kirk begged tenderly, "if you love me, if you want to obey me, don't go to the pasha. I insist on this. You don't understand military matters. Apart from not helping me, it will undoubtedly harm you."

"In that case, when they call you to the war tribunal, deny Mahir's accusations. Say that he's confused you with another officer. Deny it, Kirk. They can't hang someone on the evidence of one witness."

"One witness? What happens if the other 19 witnesses appear in front of me...?"

"Kirk, wouldn't it be a good idea if we retain a lawyer?"

"A lawyer in front of the war tribunal...! Julia, you're a child!"

"So what do you think you'll do? Are you going to surrender to the executioner's sword without defending yourself?"

"Of course I'll struggle. But if I'm defeated, then I'll have two regrets: the first is losing you and the second is that I didn't kill Khalid."

* * *

The following four months Kirk spent in that deathly prison cell were the very worst of his life.

During that time he was only called to the war tribunal once where, after a short examination, he was taken to the prison once more. It was decided that he and Seyfi, being officers, and the latter having rebelled, certain papers had to be brought from Constantinople and Diarbekir.

In that time, he only had the good fortune to see Julia three times who, without Djemal Pasha's intervention, had succeeded in obtaining a permit from the police to visit her fiancée once a month.

Every time Julia's beautiful face appeared in the dark slot in the cell door, it was as if bright sunlight had dawned in the dark and musty cell. Like a plant without sunlight, he was sentenced to wither if, once a month, that sun didn't rise over him.

Every time she came, she extended her hand, always loaded with parcels, through the little door. Kirk could hardly touch it with his lips. The secure chains squeezed his neck to strangling point, and he was forced to retreat a step to draw breath.

Julia would anxiously ask if he had been called before the tribunal. On his negative reply, she would ask if she should approach the pasha, to at least have him change the circumstances of his imprisonment. When he refused, she would give him news of the things that happened outside and, because the three minutes allowed had elapsed, she would withdraw her head from the door and, after murmuring words of encouragement, would leave in the company of the prison guard.

As soon as the little door was closed, Kirk would begin to count the minutes, hours and days to the time he would next see her face again.

One day two soldiers with fixed bayonets, in the company of the prison guard, came and stood in front of him. "Get ready! The trial is today!"

The elderly prison guard removed the shackles. The soldiers manacled Kirk and, with him in front of them, took him to the war tribunal.

Kirk, having been in that evil place, knew the way. He went between the soldiers with fixed bayonets, who were standing guard at the entrance, like shadows on the stairs and in the corridors, and entered the courtroom. High-ranking officers sat at a horseshoe-shaped table, all of them stern-faced with piercing eyes. But the sight of a particular disgusting man, who had been invited there to bear witness against him, made him shudder more than the officers' threatening appearance.

That puny person was Mahir.

The tribunal president – a military man with the rank of general – after examining the files in front of him for a moment, asked the accused, in a dry and clipped voice, "Do you still insist that you had no part in the rebel Seyfi's rebellion?"

"Yes."

"Have you never been in Diarbekir?"

"Never."

"Did you, in any way, in writing, or through third parties, tell Captain Seyfi to rebel?"

"No."

"Mahir Bey, do you recognise the accused?" the president asked, turning to the witness.

"Yes, Mr President."

"When did you see him?"

"About twenty months ago."

"Tell us under what circumstances you saw him."

Mahir repeated the accusations he had made before the criminal court.

"What was the name of that military post?" the president asked, having listened to the story carefully.

"It was called Black Rock."

"What division was it attached to?"

"Der-Zor."

"As an officer linked to Der-Zor, under what circumstances are you here in Damascus?"

Mahir never expected that question. He suddenly paled, and stammered, "As an official, Sir."

"Your task?"

"I'm the police commander of the Kadem refugee camp."

"Are you a military man or a policeman?"

"Military."

"How is it that a military man who has a position in Der-Zor can be a police commander in Damascus?"

"When our post was destroyed... when... when... the post was destroyed..." Mahir was unable to find an answer. Confused, he shrugged his shoulders and, for the first time, realized what an enormous mistake he had made coming to the tribunal and betraying himself.

When that puny being made his accusations before the criminal court, it seems that he hadn't thought that it might be necessary to make extensive checks on the accuser to hang an Armenian. But since then events had taken such a turn that he had fallen into the hole he himself had dug, and there was no doubt he would be suffocated in it, if he failed to find a rational explanation to justify his move. "When... when the post was destroyed," he stammered, bewildered and stupefied, unable to finish what he had said.

"...You didn't surrender yourselves to the military authorities and each one of you went your separate ways, didn't you?" the chairman asked, completing his statement. "Who knows how you engineered things to take over that comfortable position at Kadem refugee camp!"

And while Mahir, in a hopeless position, was staring at the chairman's face, the latter ordered the secretary, "Write to Der-Zor. Have the files on the Black Rock post sent to me immediately. Also to the Damascus police command, so that they inform us at once how Mahir Bey was called to that new office." Then, speaking to the sentries, he said, "Mahir Bey is under arrest. Take both accused men to the prison."

* * *

One day Julia had, as usual, come to the prison to see her fiancée. Almost a year had passed since he had been arrested.

"What news?" Julia asked, her heart beating.

"None," Kirk replied. "They still haven't called us. It seems that the files haven't arrived from Der-Zor.

"Deny it, Kirk. As Mahir is a deserter, his testimony doesn't mean much. His comrades, fearful of being arrested, won't come to bear witness against you.

"It's not possible to escape by denying it, my love. The only way is for the real Death's Door to be revealed. Maybe in that way I can reduce my crime."

"That will be the day you lose, Kirk, if you were to confess."

"I'm already lost. At least the monster in the next cell will get his just punishment."

"Is Mahir here?"

"Yes, but let's leave that beast alone. What news of Seyfi?"

"It's thought that he's in Djebel Druse. His mother and fiancée returned to Baghdad. Mrs Makbouleh's house is under constant surveillance."

"What are you doing? How's your mother?"

"We work and pray."

"Miss," the prison guard said, looking at his watch, "three minutes is up. Although I don't want to stop your conversation, I'm frightened of my responsibility. Please leave, you can continue it next month."

"Next month…!" Julia murmured, her chest tight with restrained sobs, as she went away from the little door. "Will I find him alive next month?"

As she was deep in thought and was walking the length of the corridor, she saw two soldiers with fixed bayonets turn the corner and come towards her. To see where they were going, Julia stopped out of curiosity, when one of the soldiers said, "Miss, it's forbidden to stop here. Please leave the corridor."

"What's happened?" Julia asked, annoyed.

"We're going to take the prisoners."

"Where?"

"The war tribunal."

"May I accompany them?"

"No one can enter the war tribunal."

The poor girl, very worried, left the corridor and waited in a corner of the courtyard with the hope of seeing Kirk again. She didn't have to wait long. A short time later she saw the man she loved most shackled to the one she hated most… walking in front of the soldiers.

* * *

The war tribunal chairman said, talking to Kirk, "Colonel Hamdi Bey has understood from questioning the soldiers he has captured, that during their escape towards Basra, a sub-lieutenant named Kirk had joined them and, on his suggestion, they had looked for five days for the Black Rock military post that Armenians apparently call Death's Door.

"Kirk and Seyfi personally destroyed the post, killing six men, heavily wounding the post commander, and imprisoning 18 soldiers and

Lieutenant Mahir Bey, who's present and seated in the accused person's chair. Having a skirmish with government forces some days later, they killed six more, then escaped and disappeared. So, do you still deny that you're the above-mentioned Kirk?"

"I don't deny it, Mr Chairman," Kirk replied with the air of a brave man who was ready to face death. "But I'd like to make a small correction."

"Please!"

"We didn't destroy a military post, but the nest of a group of robbers," Kirk said. "They – pointing at Mahir – under the military label, without being military men, had established themselves in that den, where thousands of Armenian refugees were led, under the threat of bayonets and whips, for the girls and women to be raped, the people to be imprisoned alive in that black cave, then their belongings and money to be stolen.

"At that time I'd only just come to Der-Zor. I heard that they had put a 3,000-person caravan on the road to go to Death's Door.

"They'd already taken five 1,000-person caravans and destroyed them. There was no force that could stop them. The government took no interest in the fate of unfortunate Armenians. Refugees were brought to the desert like leprous dogs and left there. Anyone could massacre them as much as they liked. The government not only didn't prevent that sort of crime happening, on the contrary they encouraged those perpetrating the massacres by its indifference to the removal of an unwanted element as soon as possible.

"It was on that day that I met Seyfi who, with his rebel cavalry company, was traveling south through the desert. I'd saved Seyfi's life at the Dardanelles front and because of that earned his gratitude. So I asked him to help me save my 3,000 fellow-Armenians from the hands of their executioners.

"Seyfi nobly agreed to my request, especially when he was convinced that he would have dealings with robbers without any sort of position or status. After searching the desert for five days, we were finally successful in finding the cursed place called Death's Door, and at exactly the time when it's bloodthirsty owners were going to put their tortured victims into it.

"We immediately arrested those evil-hearted criminals and their leader, this gentleman who, without a shred of pity, ordered the soldiers to bayonet all those women and children who didn't want to walk to the place of their deaths.

"We'd already arrested three camel driver soldiers, who were taking about ten of their camels, loaded with stolen clothing, to be sold in Der Zor.

"Entering Death's Door we saw that horrifying cave, where 5,000 naked bodies had been piled on top of each other by the body snatchers. We saw two soldiers who were taking a half-dead girl there, to throw her on a pile of corpses. We also saw the post commander, former Captain Khalid, who wanted, like a hungry wolf, to tear to pieces another Armenian girl who opposed his will.

"When we were convinced that it was not a military post, but a refuge for army deserters – the camel driver soldiers had confessed to this, adding that they were protected by Colonel Hamdi, who had his share of the loot and kidnapped girls – we acted just as our consciences dictated."

"Let's accept that you were dealing with a group of robbers," the chairman said, "who gave you the right to mete out justice in a country where there's a government?"

"The government didn't protect the Armenians," Kirk said.

"Did you act according to your conscience when you deserted from the army?"

"Excuse me, Mr Chairman, I didn't desert from the army. They disarmed me because I was Armenian. They used me for a time in a labor battalion; then they took us to be massacred. There were 4,000 of us. I was the only survivor, having received a stomach wound made by a scythe and my body falling into the waves of the Kizil Irmak. That's how the army rewarded me."

"The army knows how to reward as well as punish," the chairman growled, with quiet anger. "Sit down!" Then, speaking to the other accused, he continued, "Lieutenant Mahir, through questioning it's been understood that the Black Rock has never been used for military purposes, therefore your and your friends living there – with the knowledge and agreement of Colonel Hamdi – constitutes a most serious offence against military discipline. Have you anything to say in your defense?"

Mahir's face took on the colour of lead. His hands and knees were shaking and his teeth chattered. The evil-hearted ruffian, apart from looking stupidly at the chairman, had nothing to say.

"Sit down!" the chairman said in an emphatic voice. "Your silence is proof of your guilt."

"I… I… I'm sorry, Mr Chairman I'm… very sorry that…"

"Sit down, sit down! I'm very sorry too."

Half an hour later the tribunal gave the following verdict against the two accused: "The tribunal, judging Sub-Lieutenant Kirk, regards him as an accomplice of Captain Seyfi, who's been condemned to death in absentia, and responsible for the deaths of 12 soldiers, 6 of whom were killed doing their duty. The tribunal condemns the aforementioned accused, who's already confessed his guilt.

"The tribunal, judging Lieutenant Mahir, regards him as a military deserter, as is Captain Khalid and his accomplices, the 18 surviving soldiers who, without having any official function, used the Black Rock post as a military post. The tribunal condemns Lieutenant Mahir who's present, and his above-mentioned accomplices who are absent, to death."

After reading out the verdicts, the chairman turned to the secretary and said, "Order the military authorities to arrest the absent condemned men and to bring Colonel Hamdi, under escort, here." Then, turning to the soldiers with fixed bayonets, he ordered, "Take the condemned men away."

In Front of the Wall

Julia, seeing Kirk taken to the tribunal, didn't leave the prison so that she could see him on his return and learn the outcome of the trial.

Although it was forbidden to leave visitors for long in the prison, Officer Ballal let her, as they had become friends since Kirk had been imprisoned.

Every time Julia visited her fiancée, she never forgot to bring the elderly prison guard gifts. When Mrs Makbouleh's servant brought Kirk food parcels, he handed the guard generous presents so he would look after Kirk well.

Officer Ballal was grateful to Kirk for the presents that he received thanks to him. He therefore didn't want to refuse Kirk's fiancée's request, especially as he had heard that she had a high-ranking protector.

So when Julia asked him to grant her, for that day only, a special favour, Officer Ballal took her to his room, allowing her to rest there for a time. Sitting on two worn chairs, they talked for a long time about the probable outcome of the tribunal. Officer Ballal, leaning on his years of experience, didn't see a bright future for Kirk, but didn't want to mention what he feared, so as not to upset his young guest.

After waiting for quite a long time, they saw the two prisoners who, manacled arm to arm, were coming in their direction in the company of soldiers with fixed bayonets.

Julia looked anxiously at Kirk's expression to try to guess the tribunal's decision, but couldn't determine anything, because he looked both happy and sad. "What verdict did the tribunal give?" she asked breathing the question when the prisoners reached her.

"All the criminals of Death's Door in absentia and this man next to me have been sentenced to death," Kirk said in a satisfied tone of voice.

"And you?"

A bitter smile appeared on Kirk's face. "Julia, I'm happy that, at least with my death…"

Julia couldn't hear any more. It was as if the ground slid from beneath her feet. Suddenly her knees gave way and she fell in the doorway, horrified, shattered, her whole body turned to gooseflesh.

"Don't be afraid, my girl," the old prison guard said to her, after returning from putting them in their cells, "it's not so easy to hang a man. The sultan and the minister of war have to endorse the death sentence. It may be that they overturn the sentence."

"No," sighed Julia, in a pained and mournful voice. "The sentence of the war tribunal is irreversible. They'll execute him by firing squad."

"But Miss, as you say that you're protected by a high-ranking personage, why don't you approach him?" Officer Ballal pointed out after a while. "Maybe through his intervention the sentence may be changed to life imprisonment."

"Kirk forbids me to approach him," Julia muttered, dolefully. Then, suddenly jumping up, "No, he's not going to stop me any more. I'm going to approach the pasha this very moment."

"The Pasha?" exclaimed the elderly prison guard, annoyed. "Is Djemal Pasha your protector?"

"Yes, but why are you annoyed?"

"Oh dear, Miss, your protector has great influence, but he's not in Damascus at the moment."

"Where is he then?" Julia asked anxiously.

"No one knows where he is," Officer Ballal replied. "The British have advanced on the Palestine front. It's thought that he's gone to that front on an inspection tour."

* * *

It's impossible to describe the mental anguish that Julia suffered during two weeks of life or death moments.

Every minute and every hour she thought that the executioners, having received the endorsement of the death sentence, had gone to the prison to get Kirk to take him to his place of execution. She spent her nights in delirious nightmares, seeing her love sometimes hanged, sometimes shot, then beheaded. Kirk would look at her with supplicating eyes, while she could do nothing except be a witness to these terrifying scenes.

Julia would open her eyes like a madwoman. Her heart would beat very fast, and her body would be bathed in sweat. Despite completely waking up, the terrible drama would continue in her imagination and she'd utter dreadful screams, while her mother, Mrs Iskouhi, would hold her hand, encouraging her not to be frightened, that she was at home and was only dreaming.

She would rush every morning to the pasha's office to find out if her protector had returned from his journey. When she found out from the guards that he hadn't, she would hurry to the prison to find out from Officer Ballal if Kirk was still there. She would draw breath at the elderly prison guard's assurance. She would return to the pasha's office in the evening, then the prison, and so lived through the most emotional and anxious 15 days of her life.

One evening she had gone once more to the pasha's office, where she learned that he had returned from his inspection tour. She approached an officer, to ask if she could see him. "I'm sorry Miss, but it's strictly forbidden to see him."

Julia waited hopelessly in the street so that she could present herself when he came out. But hours passed and her protector didn't emerge.

There was a military conference in the reception hall. Messengers silently came and went; everyone's faces had expressions of great anxiety that reflected extreme circumstances.

At nearly midnight the pasha came out of the office building in the company of two high-ranking officers. His expression was happy; it would appear that the conference had a favourable outcome.

The pasha, seeing Julia, who was standing a little away from his official car, asked her with some surprise what she was doing there at that time of night.

"Please excuse me, Pasha," Julia said, falling at her benefactor's feet, "I've a favour to ask."

Djemal Pasha smiled through his beard. Have you come about your refugees again?"

"No, Pasha, this time it's for me" – and Julia, after briefly telling him what had happened, asked, in a sobbing voice – "Free him, Pasha, only he can make me happy."

"Very well, I'll look into the matter personally," the absolute ruler of Syria said, getting into his car.

"Pasha! Tomorrow may be too late! Please order that…"

"I understand, I understand."

Djemal Pasha silenced Julia with a gesture and gave a note to her, adding, "Give this to police chief Sherif Bey. No one can do anything to your fiancée before my review."

* * *

Julia kissed her protector's hand and, clutching the precious order in her hand, ran to the police station.

"What do want at this time?" asked the duty policeman, barring her entry.

"I want to see the police chief," the Armenian girl replied, recovering her breath.

"The police chief is at home; come here tomorrow."

Instead of going away, Julia stood at the corner of the street. It was as if a dreadful premonition had entered her mind. It seemed to her that the confirmation of Kirk's sentence had arrived from Constantinople and the police chief would carry it out without knowing about the pasha's order. It appeared to her that the safe way to prevent a tragedy was for her to remain there, to give the police chief the order as soon as he got to the police station. "Kirk was in the prison yesterday evening, so he's there at this moment," she said rationalising it to herself. "Without the police chief's permission, no one can take him out of prison. If the chief of police hasn't yet arrived, he can't have given any orders. So, even if the sentence has been confirmed, it can't be carried out before he gets here."

While thinking like this Julia waited and comforted herself, thinking she had saved her beloved's life from immediate danger.

The darkness gradually gave way to daylight, and one or two people passed by, when a policeman came over to Julia and asked why she hadn't gone home.

"I'm afraid," Julia said, "that Sherif Bey may get to his office before me and, without knowing of the Pasha's order..."

"What written order from the Pasha?" the policeman interrupted, curiously.

"That preventing my fiancée being shot."

"Did Djemal Pasha give that order?"

"Yes."

"Addressed to Sherif Bey?"

"Yes, but why are you surprised?"

"I'm surprised because you're waiting here for no reason."

"Why?"

"Did you tell the Pasha that your fiancée was sentenced to death by the war tribunal?"

"No, I only told him that he was condemned to death."

"I thought so. Because the Pasha, thinking that your fiancée was condemned to death by the civil court, gave the order to the police for the execution to be delayed. But the police can't interfere in military matters and, if the confirmation of the sentence has arrived, the military authorities will carry it out without letting the chief of police know."

Julia's face paled. "What do I do now?" she murmured in a low voice, almost losing her senses.

"Your appeal to the chief of police is useless, Miss," the policeman said. "You must approach the military authorities to delay your fiancée's execution."

"Where are the military authorities?"

"It's difficult to find where they are. The shortest way, if you've suspicions that the sentence will be carried out tonight, is to go to the prison and wait for the officer and soldiers who'll come for the condemned men. Present them with the order. When they see Djemal Pasha's signature, they won't be able to take your fiancée anywhere."

Hearing the policeman's words, Julia was gripped by a terrible shudder. It was as if she had received a heavy blow to her head; everything went dark before her eyes, her knees gave way and her heart started beating very quickly. Not able to stand, the poor girl had the inner urge to fall to the ground in a dead faint, but thinking that even one moment's delay could be fateful, she made supreme efforts and was able to go forward in a mad dash, presenting a live picture of grief and anxiety.

* * *

In the 15 days since he was condemned to death, Kirk had practically lost the habit of sleep. Lying on his bed, he remained still, buried for hours in his thoughts. After a long vigil, he would occasionally succumb to a sort of slackness and, hardly having forgotten the world for a moment, he would once more open his eyes in the grip of a fit of nerves and hopelessness.

In his bitter thoughts he would sometimes say to himself how good it would have been if the blow with the scythe that had ripped open his stomach had been deeper and spared him all the misfortunes that followed.

His being saved from death that he had ascribed to good fortune, now seemed to be another result of his bad luck. His 4,000 comrades-in-arms, who had died at once and who had not seen these black days, were the fortunate ones.

If only he had died on the banks of Kizil Irmak!

But then he thought that if he had died, who would have freed the 3,000 refugees who, like a flock of sheep, were going to the slaughterhouse? Who would have saved Julia from being torn to pieces by that bloodthirsty hyena? Who would have destroyed Death's Door and, indirectly, have its monstrous owners condemned to death?

So if his not dying three years before had been a misfortune for him, at least it was fortunate for one part of the mass of his long-suffering fellow-Armenians. And even if he had only saved one person from the slaughter, wasn't it worth living, even if that living had been like a poisoned chalice?

But he had one inconsolable pain, apart from his final parting from Julia and not punishing Khalid: he was put on the same level as the person most hated by his people; his being shackled arm-to-arm with Mahir and taken to the war tribunal, his being condemned to death with him in the same tribunal and possibly being shot with him by firing squad before the same wall; mixing his pure blood with that of a Turk's evil-smelling blood.

Kirk couldn't sleep that night, nor lie down. Dragging his heavy chains behind him, he moved about the cell like a lion wounded in the heart. Every time the chains struck the stone floor, it was as if a voice whispered from the other side of the grave "this morning... this morning... this morning..."

That morning there was banging on his cell door. It was Officer Ballal, telling him to wake up. The elderly prison guard, to allay his friend's fears, had come ahead of the soldiers with fixed bayonets to prepare him for death, without thinking that his visit at an unusual time explained everything.

"Have they come to take me?" Kirk asked the prison guard, who entered the cell after a moment.

"Yes, your friend as well."

"My friend?"

"In other words your neighbour, Mahir Bey."

At the same time an officer and two soldiers appeared at the cell door.

Kirk didn't change colour at all. His first thought was for Julia, from who he was to part without even a good-bye kiss. When the poor girl came at the end of the month for her usual visit, who knows how much she would cry, finding that her fiancée had already departed this world!

After the prison guard put the wrist shackles on, he removed the chains, and then went to Mahir's cell.

This puny beast, who was sleeping, woke up as a result of the push given by the prison guard, and gave a scream of horror. Seeing the soldiers with their bayonets, he began to gabble meaningless sentences. "I... I... served my country... before God and the people... I've done my duty... I... I..."

Without replying to his mumblings, the prison guard put his wrist shackles on and released the chain.

The soldiers brought Mahir out of his cell and into the corridor shortly afterwards and tied his left arm to Kirk's right.

It was as if his arm had been bitten by a snake. Kirk's whole body became like gooseflesh from loathing then, with his head turned he away, walked in front of the soldiers with firm, confident steps. "Goodbye," he said to the prison guard, taking his leave of him. "Thank you for the care you've taken of me, Officer Ballal. I've one final request for you and hope you carry it out. When my fiancée comes in two weeks time, please tell her that I went to meet death with my head held high, and will die with her pure love in my heart and her sweet name on my lips. Goodbye, my elderly friend."

While Kirk was leaving the prison with proud and manly steps, Mahir, by his side, was crying, like all beings with evil souls and moaned, grunted and, due to his being overcome by fear, could not even open his mouth to say farewell.

"Dying's a bad thing, isn't it?" Kirk wanted to say to the unfeeling Turk, but he controlled himself so as not to have the abominable task of speaking to that abject person.

* * *

Julia got to the prison half an hour after Kirk's departure.

"You're too late, Miss," the prison guard said bitterly. "He's gone."

"Where?" Julia asked, bewildered.

"Don't you know? But in that case why did you come here early?"

"I came because I have a written order from the Pasha to prevent my fiancée from being shot," Julia cried, trembling.

"An order from the Pasha?" Officer Ballal exclaimed, horrified. "You'll have to hurry Miss, they took your fiancée to be shot" – and seeing Julia's terror – "don't worry, the sentence can't have been carried out yet. Wait,

I'll telephone the barracks… the execution is going to be carried out there."

"Please, Mr Ballal, hurry!" Julia said, almost fainting and falling onto a chair.

"Give me the order."

The elderly prison guard rang the barracks and shortly afterwards, with indescribable agitation and alarm, he gave the order, "Hello! Hello! Is that army command? This is the central prison. Listen, Djemal Pasha has ordered that the condemned man Kirk's execution be postponed. You don't believe me? How is that? I'm prison guard Officer Ballal. If you don't know who I am, let me speak to Saadi Bey, he knows my voice. Saadi Bey's not there…? Who is…? Refet Bey? Right, call him. Hello, Refet Bey…? Yes, it's me… Of course I've got the written order. Yes, it's signed by the Pasha… I'll send it with a policeman to you…. Please, delay the execution, or the Pasha will destroy us all."

* * *

A squad of soldiers lined up and took up their positions in front of a half-ruined wall some distance from the barracks. Suddenly the officer in charge shouted, "Take aim!"

The soldiers lifted their rifles and pointed them at the chests of the two condemned men, whose eyes had been covered with black cloths, and who were standing in front of the wall.

The officer was preparing to give the second order when he saw a cavalryman galloping towards him, shouting with all his strength, "Stop! Stop! Stop…!"

The officer, surprised, stopped and waited for the horseman who, arriving a moment later, handed him a piece of paper.

The young officer read the paper and walking towards the two condemned men, asked, "Which of you is Kirk?"

"It's me," said the condemned man on the right.

The officer undid the blindfold over Kirk's eyes and said, "Come here!"

Kirk didn't understand what was happening.

He'd hardly got out of the field of fire when the officer gave the second order, "Fire!"

There was a thunderous volley.

At the same time an abominable body folded on itself and fell to the ground in front of the wall.

PART IV

PART IV

I Want to See My Cilicia

The movement started with an attack by a small group of Armenian volunteers. Gradually gaining strength, they swept aside, like a broom, the bands of bloodthirsty hyenas who were eliminating the last survivors of the Armenian massacres which had spread throughout the Arab lands.

The flag of freedom was raised from Arabia to Damascus, from Damascus to Aleppo, and from Aleppo to Adana.

The agony was over. The black clouds covering the Armenian horizon were dissipated bit by bit before the storm created by the victorious army.

The wonderful sun of freedom had risen. Like a phoenix rising from the ashes, the surviving Armenians made their way in groups to the borders of historic Cilicia to create a new fatherland and to begin a new life.

New homes were being built everywhere, new families created, new businesses started. Everyone had the desire to forget the dreadful memories of the past, enjoy the present happy time, and get ready for tomorrow's magnificent victory.

Untold thousands had wished to see these wonderful days, but very few had the good fortune to see their ideal realized. The others had fallen, exhausted, on the road to Golgotha, victims of the burning hatred and fury of human beasts, or the death-spreading wretchedness of the deserts.

Kirk and Julia were among the lucky ones who, surmounting all obstacles, had managed to reach a free harbour.

As we know, Kirk had survived the sentence handed down by the war tribunal by a miracle. After that, before Djemal Pasha had time to deal with his case, the British Army, with lightning speed, had advanced from Salteh and Nablus and captured Damascus.

High-ranking Turkish officials, as well as military men and police, hearing of the British advance, had rushed to escape, leaving government buildings, barracks and the prisons to their fate.

Taking advantage of the chaos, the people had attacked the prisons, smashed down the doors and released all those poor people who had been condemned by Turkish judges and held in them by Turkish officials, mostly for non-existent crimes.

Kirk was among those freed and had hardly left the prison when he found his saviour Julia and, at the head of the crowd, his bosom-friend Seyfi, who had only arrived the day before from his voluntary exile and was one of the organisers of the popular demonstration.

It's unnecessary to describe their joyful, loving meeting here.

Shortly afterwards, at Seyfi's invitation, the engaged couple went to Wahab's mansion, where they found an ecstatic welcome provided by Mrs Makbouleh.

Seyfi and his aunt tried to insist that Julia brought her mother and that they all stayed in the same house until traveling was possible. But the engaged couple, not wishing to put them to any trouble, declined the offer with thanks, and went to their own house to live with Mrs Iskouhi.

Seyfi, saying goodbye to Kirk and Julia a week later, had left for his birthplace, promising to always write to them and invited them, after they had arranged their affairs in their fatherland, to go to Baghdad, to stay as guests of his mother and his wife.

Two weeks after their parting, Mrs Makbouleh had left for Egypt – where her husband's wealthy relations lived – to stay there for a time and rest. The noble Arab lady had extended them the same invitation, asking Kirk and Julia, when they came to Damascus, to visit her and stay in her mansion.

Travelling was possible a few months later and Kirk, Julia and their mother – Kirk also called Mrs Iskouhi mother – joining the caravans, had come to settle in Adana, as Julia's father's estate and farms had remained intact, while Kirk's and Mrs Iskouhi's homes had been destroyed.

Entering the city, they were overjoyed to see the Armenian Legionnaires, who, alongside French soldiers, victoriously went about the city.

The Turks, panic stricken, had made themselves scarce. Those who had bought abandoned Armenian property immediately handed it over when the rightful owners appeared. Many even paid for the wear and tear they had caused to buildings and furniture.

But their joy became even greater when they went to reclaim Julia's father's house and, turning the corner, saw scaffolding in front of it and, on the scaffolding, an old man who was occupied applying white rendering to the outside.

Kirk and Julia uttered cries of astonishment and ran to the old man.

It was the deaf-mute servant Samuel, who not only had arrived at the house before them, but had also prepared it for residence.

* * *

Samuel' return to his birthplace – whose name he didn't know – was an unbelievable story akin to a miracle.

We know that Julia found him lying on the ground covered in blood on the Death's Door battlefield, and in her horror had thought him dead; in reality he wasn't dead, as Kirk and Seyfi had found traces of blood but not his body. This is what had happened.

Samuel came to before Seyfi and Kirk had looked for him and, checking his body, found that a bullet had badly injured him in the groin. The blow had been so hard that when the poor old man had fallen down, he had hit his head on a sharp rock, lost two teeth and fainted as a result.

Recovering his senses, Samuel had got up and, dragging his injured leg, had started to look for his mistress. But only dead bodies could be seen on the deserted plain.

Assuming that Julia had thought him dead and escaped with her rescuing officers, he had limped in the direction he had seen the soldiers retreat before he was wounded. After going for some distance, Samuel had sat, tired, on a rock. Then he saw a string of pack mules that, after following the horses for some time, had stopped, considering themselves safe from rifle fire. The deaf-mute had gone and sat on the lead mule and, dragging the others behind him, continued on his way, without knowing, however, where he was going.

He would have become lost in the limitless desert if the mules hadn't unknowingly turned south. Travelling that night and all the following day, he reached the Euphrates. Seeing the river, he dismounted and threw himself into it like a madman and drank his fill. Then, having emerged onto the bank, he fell down in a dead faint.

Hours later, when he opened his eyes, he saw that the mules had disappeared. First he thought that they had wandered off but, when he found his pockets empty, he realized that it was a fellah's work.

Despite this he was comforted with the thought that there were human habitations in the area. Anyway, what would he do with money – money that Kirk had given him as a precaution – if he had no way to spend it? Where there were ways, it was possible to work and live.

Samuel had satisfied his hunger by eating grass and roots and had followed the river current. With his deaf-mute's brain he thought he had found the River Sihoun (Ceyhan), and that if he followed it, he would reach his birthplace, Adana.

But, weeks later, instead of taking him to Adana, the river had taken him in the opposite direction to a large city that was probably Baghdad. Seeing large houses and wide roads he had thought for a moment that he had reached the city he sought, but was quickly disillusioned, when he saw people in strange clothes who, as the completion of his misfortune, didn't have white skins. "Oh! There are so many cities in the world," he had said to himself. "I've seen so many since we were deported."

When he was walking the streets, a railway line had caught his attention. This line also went through his city, so if he got a train, he would be able to go to Adana.

Having thought it out, he carried out his plan immediately. Hardly had the train started when a ticket inspector had appeared. Samuel, using hand gestures, explained that he hadn't got a ticket. The official, shaking his head, had gone away, but half an hour later, when the train had got to a station, he had returned and told him to get off.

Samuel, thinking he had got to Adana, had joyfully jumped off the train, but when he had left the station, he saw that the official had played a bad joke on him. From then on he had followed the railway line, always with the absolute belief that his birthplace couldn't be very far off, as the same line went through it.

Samuel had walked for months like this, lying down where he had got to and staying at each village or station for a few days or sometimes weeks, working as a porter. People, pitying his dumbness, always gave him bread and work.

Every time someone had asked him where he was going, he always replied in the same way: "I don't know the name of the city… but it has a railway like this there…"

Passing through Mosul, Nisibin, Ras-ul Ayn, Arab Pounar and Djaraboulos, one day he reached Aleppo.

Seeing the clock tower in the square, Samuel had remembered the city and, going through winding streets, had found the Armenian church, which he had visited several times the last time he had been in the city.

None of the thousands of refugee families, that had previously slept on the ground, ill and hungry, were in the church's courtyard. Had they all left or died? Samuel didn't know and didn't want to know. There was only a priest in the empty courtyard. Crossing himself, he had gone to him, saying that he was a son of the Armenian Church.

Then, seeing that the good cleric was interested in him, Samuel had "told" him his story, asking him to send him to his birthplace.

The priest had shook his head and said it wasn't possible.

"Why not?" Samuel had protested angrily. "I want to go home. Who can prevent me?"

"Have patience, blessed one, have patience," the priest had said gently. "When traveling is possible, then you'll come with us."

And Samuel had patiently waited, without hope, until one day the victorious Allied army had entered Aleppo.

Joining the first caravan going to Cilicia, he was once more sitting in a railway carriage, and had watched, with his nose pressed to the windowpane, the passing mountains, plains, villages and towns, day and night.

Every time the train stopped in a station, he had got his bag – one that he had had with him since Baghdad – and got out, thinking he had reached Adana. But seeing his mistake, he had run back and got into the train once more.

Refugee Armenians had pitied his bewildered state and, to find the name of his birthplace, had asked for explanations.

Samuel had given the same answer using hand gestures. "There's a river in the middle of it… a bridge… trains… it was big…" Then, thinking that further details would help his fellow-Armenians understand, he had described how their house had three stories, that it had a garden at the back, that in a corner of the garden there was a hen house and so on. Then he had described the furnishings in his room, the clothes on the line, the polished brass vessels in the case and the new fur coat hanging on the wall.

When the travellers asked what he had in the strange bag, from which he would never be parted, Samuel had 'answered': "Pieces of bread… when I get to the city, I'll give them to my chickens."

And finally, one day, the train reached Adana. Samuel, seeing, from a distance the familiar houses and streets, had begun to clap his hands and jump up and down like a boy, showing the city to those around him. "Ehbe… Be… Ehbe… Be… It's here, it's here!"

As soon as the train had stopped, Samuel, holding the bag close to him, had thrown himself out of the carriage and hurriedly ran forward, occasioning smiles of pity and mercy on the faces of those there.

Brother Samuel, reaching the Aghasian's house, had seen that strange people were living in it, while he had thought that Julia with her rescuing officer would already have arrived and settled there.

"Get out quickly!" he had 'shouted' crossly. "My mistress and the officer will be coming here… I must clean the rooms."

The people who were renting the house, who were Turks, panicked when the deaf-mute suddenly appeared. The head of the family, saying, "Very well, we're going," had sat Samuel in front of the door and gone to the market.

Half an hour later he returned with an old man, who was probably the new owner, as when he heard of the return of it's former owners, he had a displeased expression on his face, thinking of course that what he had bought for a small price would be lost.

The tenant and the new owner haggled and argued for some time. Samuel had understood that the tenant wanted some of the rent paid returned, while the owner refused. At one point they stopped their argument and asked Samuel, "When will your mistress arrive?"

Samuel whistled like an engine, to make them understand that they were coming from the market immediately.

"Was there an officer with her?"

"Yes," – and moving his finger like a knife across his throat – "kekh… he's got a big sword."

At Samuel' answer the new landlord's face darkened. Shortly afterwards the tenant and the new owner came to an agreement and both went to the shop, probably to bring the balance of the rent. An hour later the tenant returned with a cart… By evening the house was empty.

Samuel joyfully entered the emptied house and rushed to his room, asking himself what state it would be in. The poor man was thunderstruck when he saw its bare walls and floor.

Thinking that the tenants had moved his furniture to another room, he had gone and opened the reception room, bedroom, breakfast room and all the other rooms one after another, on all three floors. But whichever room he entered, he had not found any trace of his furniture, nor the house's velvet-covered armchairs, expensive carpets or woven silk beds. On the contrary, all the rooms – apart from the rooms on the first floor used by the tenants – presented the appearance of dereliction and destruction, with the plaster falling from the walls, broken windows, and torn oilcloth-covered floors.

Samuel had gone into the garden to give his much-loved hens and roosters some food. But alas! He found a wilderness there; the fountain had dried up, the flowers and trees gone, and the hen house half demolished and missing its inmates.

The faithful servant sat at the entrance to the garden with his much-afflicted head in his hands, mourning his masters' smashed happiness for a moment. Suddenly, as if he had a premonition, he jumped up and, finding a broken fern broom, began the work of cleaning the house.

For the whole day he swept the house from top to bottom, then the garden. The next day he brought water in a battered tin vessel and washed the doors, floors and staircase. He understood a little carpentry and had some money saved. He bought tools and gradually repaired the door locks, the staircase handrail and replaced the broken windows.

One day he had whitened the walls in the rooms with plaster paste, another day he had polished the marble tubs in the kitchen with sand. On another he cleared the garden of dried grasses; subsequently he cleaned the fountain of the remains and dirt left from dried moss.

When he had finished the work on the inside of the house, he had erected scaffolding outside it one day and was engaged in whitening the front when he saw his mistress, who was coming with the young officer.

Samuel was certain of that return. He immediately jumped down from the scaffolding and hugging his master and mistress with his dirty hands, 'told' them how all the furniture had been stolen, that there were no clothes on his line, or the brass vessels in the case, or his fur coat hanging on the wall.

* * *

After settling down in Cilicia, Kirk and Julia married and, after putting their affairs in order, began a voyage that was, rather than a honeymoon, a journey of learning.

Kirk wanted, before he planned what he wanted to do, to find out, in places where there were numerous Armenians, what their needs were. So, setting out with Julia, he first went to Mersin, then Tarsus, Sis, Dort Yol and Iskenderoun (Alexandretta).

In this last town, however, an incident occurred whose effects would once more disturb Kirk's newly established peaceful life.

One evening he went out with his wife to a theatrical presentation for the benefit of Armenian orphans.

There was still half an hour before the curtain was due to go up, but the theater was full to overflowing with a mixed crowd. Couples and Armenian Legionnaires were to be seen everywhere. Everyone's eyes sparkled with great happiness.

Kirk, looking at the merry crowd from his seat in the box, was thinking how this freedom was a wonderful thing, that, with the wave of a magic wand, it turned emaciated remnants into a vibrant people. How wonderful to have a free land and authority!

Suddenly the sound of an anthem and clapping disturbed his thoughts.

"The orphans! The orphans!" the people in the foyer cried, clapping. "Long live Armenia! Long live Cilicia! Long live France…!"

Then a group of cleanly and neatly dressed orphans, led by trumpeters, entered the auditorium and took up their allotted places. Everyone directed admiring glances in their direction. At that moment everyone was excited by the same idea: that the children who wandered about, hungry and thirsty, in the desert – who died in hundreds from hunger, sunstroke and exhaustion – were now free from the danger of death and would grow up strong and fit in their free country, and then become the next generation.

"The nation's lucky children!" cried Kirk, meaning the orphans. "They lived through so much; and now they are able to see this victory."

"Let's pray that their bright sunlight isn't covered by black clouds again," Julia murmured.

Just then an incident in the auditorium caught Kirk's attention. Two Algerian soldiers were making an Armenian woman in front of them uneasy with their asides and gestures. First she stayed quiet then, her patience exhausted, she asked them to leave her alone. Taking encouragement from the woman's protest, they began to laugh deep in their throats and coarsened their disgraceful jokes.

An elderly Armenian, who was seated near the orphans, seeing the soldiers' bad manners, approached them and, after asking them to behave, led the woman to a distant part of the hall, thus ending the incident before it got serious.

Kirk, seeing the man's intelligent act, looked carefully at his face and suddenly exclaimed in amazement upon discovering that the peacemaker was the one-time protector of Armenian virgins, Charles, who had disappeared in such mysterious circumstances at Bozanti.

"It's Charles," cried Kirk, jumping to his feet. "Julia, do you remember, when I talked about Sara I told you how he saved her from the Armenian spy Nouri Osman's claws? Would you allow me to invite him here?"

"Of course, it'll be a pleasure to be introduced to that self-sacrificing Armenian," Julia replied with pleasure.

Kirk ran from the box and rushed down the stairs into the hall, and caught his one-time friend by the arm. "Charles, my unequalled friend, how wonderful to see you again!"

"Kirk...! I'm delighted to see you alive and well!"

The two friends threw themselves into each other's arms and embraced.

"But what are you doing here?" Kirk asked, finally speaking.

"I heard that Nouri Osman was here and came here on two day's leave," he said through clenched teeth. "But unfortunately the news was false, so I'm returning to Adana tomorrow."

"Are you still after Nouri Osman?" Kirk asked, surprised.

"No, I lost track of him long ago," Charles said, "but I'll tell you about that later. Now, tell me, what are you doing here?"

"I've settled down in Adana too, and I'm now on a journey."

"It's surprising that we've not run into each other in Adana. I'm the orphanage supervisor there."

"Are these orphans your little ones?"

"No, they're local ones. When I heard that there was a function, I came to see them. But tell me, what are you doing in Adana?"

"I'm not doing anything at present. I'm married and, before I start a business, I want to find out the state of the people and local conditions."

"You're married...! I must congratulate you and wish you every happiness, my friend. So you found Sara...?"

Kirk's face suddenly darkened. "Charles, you can't imagine what a horrible death the poor girl suffered," Kirk said with a very sad voice. "But we'll talk about that later. Come, let's go to my box; I must introduce my wife to you."

They went together, keeping their feelings in check with difficulty.

After Charles had been introduced and the story of her and Kirk's meeting briefly related, he told them of his disappearance that Kirk was interested to hear.

"You were right it seems, friend, when you said I was wrong not to kill that traitor who denied his own identity in the Tarsus train. That meek spy had expressed his regrets at what he'd done and swore an oath, simply to extricate himself from a difficult situation.

"Do you know what game he played with me? As you may recall, I'd warned him that I would watch his every move and on the first occasion that he betrayed his oath, I'd stab him to death. Nouri Osman, to reveal my identity, spent a month to work out who was constantly near him.

"Although I'd taken great care not to be seen by him, occasionally circumstances arose that forced me to be near him. It would appear that this hadn't escaped the dog's notice. It was a few days after you left. I was returning to my hut late one night through deserted gardens when I heard quick footsteps behind me. I looked round to see it was him.

"'Stop! I've got business with you!' he cried, in a menacing voice.

"At the same time I saw he had a pistol in his hand, and that his eyes were shining with a flame of devilment.

"'Nouri Osman, don't come any closer,' I said.

"But I'd hardly said those four words when I heard the sound of a shot, then another, then a third. Then I felt my knees give way and I fell down.

"'Nouri Osman punishes those who get in his way like this,' the vile being victoriously shouted, running towards me to see if I was dead. But I wasn't dead. No matter how wounded I was in the stomach and chest, I still felt that I had the strength in my arm to stab him in the chest with my dagger as he bent over me like a bloodthirsty vampire.

"The following morning passers-by had found our bloody bodies in the middle of the street, lying next to each other. Briefly – because I can see that the curtain will go up shortly – there was a long trial. The miserable wretch, turning everything around, accused me of being a chauvinist Armenian who had stabbed him to exact vengeance for his having changed his religion, and adding that he had replied with his firearm.

"I defended myself before the court, saying that he was the attacker. 'If I had attacked him,' I said, 'he would have wounded me from close range, but the doctor's report establishes the fact that the bullet was fired from a distance.'

"The base traitor replied that he'd fired at me when I was attacking, but was some distance away.

"I said that as I hadn't reached him, I couldn't have stabbed him, so he must have been lying when he said that I'd wounded him first. But no matter what I said, the judge found me guilty for attacking a soldier. According to Turkish justice, a soldier has the right to hold an Armenian, throw him to the ground and kill him, but an Armenian apparently has no right to raise his hand against the soldier to defend himself.

"On the basis of this wonderful reasoning, I was sentenced to one year, eleven months and four days imprisonment. I still haven't understood the strange length of the sentence. In other words the judges had so carefully weighed my crime that they found that it was worth one year, eleven months and four days, rather than a round two years.

"When I came out of prison, I found that outside there were no Nouri Osman, no Khalid, no governor or police chief. There weren't any Armenian refugees left to plunder or imprison anyway. I worked for a time as a laborer on the railway. I then managed to get to Adana, where I remained until the entry of the victorious army.

"But we'll see one another again," Charles said, rising to his feet. "The bell, telling us the curtain is going up, has sounded. I'll go to the auditorium... I'll see what the children are doing."

"Come to my hotel before you return to Adana tomorrow," Kirk said, giving him the address. "We'll have lunch together."

* * *

The performance that night was very successful.

The actor and actress took many curtain calls amid the enthusiastic clapping of the audience. At one stage the enthusiasm was such that no one wanted to leave, and everyone begged Miss Aida, the actress, to sing "Armenia".

Although she was tired Miss Aida, not to disappoint the crowd, came on stage and sang, in her attractive voice, the anthem requested, electrifying the atmosphere.

The song had hardly finished when unending applause nearly raised the roof and the audience demanded the special song starting with the words, "When the gates of hope are opened... When the gates of hope are opened..."

The actress Miss Aida didn't refuse this request either and sang:

"I wish to see my Cilicia,
The land that's given me sunlight..."

The hall erupted once more with clapping and hurrahs. The audience, after hearing this second anthem, was highly delighted and well satisfied. Everyone was about to leave when the two Algerians – the ones who had tried to create trouble with the Armenian lady – suggested to Miss Aida that she sings the "Marseilles".

Some of those present correctly pointed out to the soldiers that it wasn't possible to sing a cappella song in a national function, especially as it had been closed.

"If the function had ended, why did the actress sing the anthems you asked for?" the Algerians protested.

"She sang them to satisfy the entire audience's request," several people replied. "She's tired now and can't sing a third song."

Instead of being satisfied and quietening down, the black soldiers raised their voices and began to shout, as Armenians looked askance at them, who had come to protect Armenians.

With the row growing in volume, several Armenian Legionnaires rushed to the Algerians to calm them and get them to leave the hall peacefully. But the black soldiers, thinking that the Legionnaires were going to arrest them, immediately took out their pistols and told them not to come closer.

Suddenly about ten arms held the two soldiers' arms and wrists like iron pincers. At the same moment a sergeant named Keith rushed up to the scene of the trouble and, after ordering the Armenian Legionnaires to let the two men alone, told the latter that they were under arrest, and had to go to barracks with him to account for their lack of discipline.

The Algerians holstered their weapons and, walking in front of the Armenian sergeant, quietly left the auditorium. In the street, however, they had hardly walked twenty paces when, after punching the sergeant in the chest, they began to run away. They pulled out their pistols and began firing at passers-by and the Legionnaires following them.

Hearing the sound of firing, about ten French and Algerian soldiers appeared from nearby streets. Believing the runaways' statement that the Armenians were pursuing to kill them, they warned the latter to halt. The Armenian Legionnaires protested that the men running away were the guilty ones and they should be arrested first.

"Surrender or I fire!" a French military policeman shouted, threatening the Armenians.

"Arrest the men running away," Keith ordered, arriving a moment later. "Don't believe their lies! Don't let them escape!"

Armenian volunteers in the barracks, hearing the details of their brothers' deaths, mutinied. The French have surrounded them in the barracks and have demanded the Armenians' surrender. The Armenians have refused. The French have threatened to shell the barracks and bury the Armenians under its ruins."

"Charles, are you joking with us?" Kirk and Keith exclaimed angrily.

"What joke, boys? I'm telling you the truth. But I didn't finish what I had to say. The police have examined the garden of the house where you killed one Algerian and heavily wounded his two friends. The owner, a Christian Arab, made a statement to the police that, hearing the noise of the battering at his door, he had run to the window and seen you two. But because he didn't know you, he described your faces. After the French police had left, a Turkish neighbour went to the Christian Arab and said that he had followed you and seen you enter this hotel. He suggested that the Arab betray you, but the latter, frightened of vengeance, refused the Turk's suggestion. When I heard that, I went to the Turk and threatened to kill him if he betrayed you. Frightened, the Turk promised to keep quiet, but you can't depend on his silence; maybe tomorrow he'll act like a dog and betray you anyway. The safest thing for you both to do is to leave the city."

Kirk and Keith couldn't believe their ears but, regaining their coolness, they wondered what there was to be surprised at, as it was possible to expect anything from the French.

"When I tell you to leave, don't think I mean that you should return to Adana," Charles said a moment later. "Because if that wicked Turk betrays you, the police can find out Kirk's name and address from the hotel owner and immediately arrest him."

"So where shall we go then?" Kirk said, frowning.

"The safest place is Marash," Charles said. "The British are there. Go and stay there for a month until the situation clears."

"Mr Charles," Julia asked, having listened to this conversation silently and with her heart palpitating, "if my husband and Mr Keith are arrested, what punishment will they receive?"

"We've a precedent, my girl," Charles murmured sadly. "Two more bodies will be added to those of Guyon."

Part IV. Chapter 2

Black Clouds

Kirk had planned to return to Adana from Iskenderoun to spend the winter there, but then, in spring, decided to make a much longer voyage of inspection in the Hadjin, Marash and Aintab regions.

But events had taken such a turn that he temporarily delayed his return to Adana and, on the same day, he left in a driver's car for Marash, naturally taking Julia and Keith with him.

Charles returned to his orphans in Adana on the same day, promising to keep his friends informed of developments.

Reaching Marash, Kirk rented a large house in the Armenian quarter, inviting Keith to stay for as long as he wanted to remain in Cilicia.

Keith thankfully accepted the offer, and became attached to Kirk, who had saved him from the hands of the enraged Algerians, with feelings of gratitude and affection. Kirk returned the affection, finding in Keith a noble Armenian imbued with high-minded feelings who, leaving his work and rest behind him in America, had come to serve his people and nation.

Ten days after reaching Marash, they received a letter from Charles, in which the latter described how the legionaries who had rebelled in Iskenderoun had surrendered, and how those enthusiastic young men, broken-hearted, had resigned from service under the French flag.

In his letter, Charles also added that he visited Mrs Iskouhi and Samuel often, that the French police didn't bother them, meaning that the Turk in Iskenderoun had kept his word.

The first part of the letter angered Kirk, Keith and Julia. The final part, however, pleased them with the thought that their problem would soon be forgotten and they would be able to return to Adana.

Their situation was exactly the same when one day they received a second letter from Charles. The French police had raided the Aghasian house one night and, after searching every room, had fiercely questioned Mrs Iskouhi and Samuel as to the whereabouts of the owners of the house. Mrs Iskouhi had said that they had got married and were on their honeymoon, probably in Constantinople. The deaf-mute, crossing himself, had reproved the French, trying to ask them if they weren't ashamed of themselves, trying to arrest Kirk, as they were Christians like the Armenians. Although the deaf-mute's answer had amused the voluntary exiles in Marash, they couldn't hide their concern that the situation, instead of improving, was becoming more serious.

Indeed, Charles' third letter completely proved it. The French police had questioned Mrs Iskouhi and Samuel for a second time and had threatened to imprison them if they didn't tell them where Kirk and the sergeant accompanying him were. Mrs Iskouhi and Samuel insisted on what they had said before, adding that Kirk hadn't written to them, while they didn't know the Armenian sergeant at all.

Kirk, thinking that the French police may torture the two poor old people because of him, wrote back to Charles, telling him to put them in a carriage and send them secretly to Marash.

A week later Mrs Iskouhi and Samuel arrived in Marash and embraced their loved ones, having missed them very much.

After their mother's and the deaf-mute's arrival, the correspondence with Charles ceased for some time. Concerned, Kirk wrote to his friend, asking why he had not written.

Instead of an answer, his friend himself arrived.

* * *

It was an evening in May. Exactly a year from the day when Kirk had been taken out of Damascus prison to the barracks to be shot.

Before the evening meal was finished, when they were seated round the table talking about the horrors of those days – comparing them to the present unsettled time – the door bell rang.

At Kirk's look, Samuel ran to open the door. The guest entered and shook hands with the deaf-mute with a smile. He was preparing to shake the dust off himself when Kirk jumped up and running through the door, cried, "Welcome, Charles, why are you in this state?"

"May I curse the French," Charles replied, wiping the sweat off his brow with a large handkerchief and then embracing his old friend. "I too escaped and came here."

"But why did you escape?" Kirk asked, annoyed.

"I'll tell you. But please give me a glass of water. My throat's very dry."

Kirk led his friend to the kitchen. Charles washed his hands and face and, after drinking two glasses of water one after another, went into the dining room with his friend.

"I can see that the air in Marash agrees with all of you. So, tell me, how are you? Are you comfortable?" he said, affectionately squeezing everyone's hands.

"Yes thank you," Kirk said, speaking for all of them. "But tell us what happened."

"I killed two Turks," Charles said calmly. "If I hadn't escaped, the French would have exiled me to Guyon.

"Don't tell me that this has become Arshagavan; escapees all coming to Marash!" Kirk exclaimed.

"The situation is gradually getting worse," Charles said, becoming very serious. "The Turks went away and the French arrived. The policy they adopted towards Armenians has hardly changed."

"That's true," Kirk concurred, nervously drumming his fingers on the table. "We see the proof of that every day. But tell us, did you kill the Turkish spy in Iskenderoun?"

"No. That knave, frightened of the results of his betrayal, has run away," Charles replied. "The Turks I killed were different."

"Who were they?"

"Two arsonists" – and he raised his voice – "All of you, listen carefully to what I have to say. One day the Turks are going to destroy the orphans."

No matter how unbelievable it sounded, it created great grief and anxiety in all those present.

"Don't be surprised at what I say," Charles continued with glittering eyes. "The French have spoiled the Turks very much. You'll hear one day that the Turks will have either set fire to the orphanage or killed the orphans with swords."

"But are we going backwards?" Kirk asked anxiously. "This is very bad. Please tell us what happened."

"Two weeks ago," Charles said, "when I was doing my usual night time rounds in the orphanage, I was preparing to return to my room. As I was leaving the dormitory, I saw two people talking in the street, occasionally looking around them and sometimes looking at the orphanage.

"I'd hardly noticed them when I saw another person, coming from the direction of the station, join them. It was as if he'd given the men standing there a signal. The three of them began to quickly walk away in the opposite direction. The three men's behaviour wouldn't have seemed unusual if, a few minutes later, a night duty policeman hadn't appeared from the other end of the street. 'I wonder,' I said to myself, 'if their swift departure had anything to do with the appearance of the policeman or not?' If it did, then it meant that they were plotting something bad that had been foiled by the policeman's arrival. But what could their plan be? The orphanage wasn't rich for them to think of robbing it.

"To satisfy my curiosity I turned the light off and waited in the dark, to see if they returned. I wasn't disappointed. A quarter of an hour later the three mystery men appeared at the end of the street and, while two of them came below my window and looked with interest at the building, I noticed the third keeping a lookout at the street corner.

"Just then the policeman's whistle was heard. The three men disappeared like ghosts and didn't come back that night. I told the director what I'd seen the next morning, and asked him to provide me with a weapon, as I thought that, for some reason unknown to me, they wanted to break into the orphanage.

The director sent me to the governors, the governors sent me to the National Union, and the National Union sent me to the Prelacy. I repeated at each place what I'd seen the previous night and told them of the necessity for me to have a weapon for self-defense. At the prelacy they said that the government had strictly forbidden Armenians to carry arms, so I should be alert and, if the thieves were to reappear, to let the police know by telephone.

"Seeing that it was impossible to make these people understand, I went and found a friend who was a gunsmith and, explaining my concern, begged him to loan me a pistol for a week. 'What do you mean lend you one for a week?' my noble friend asked and, opening a drawer, took out a pistol and put it in my hand. 'This is a gift from me to you. How many cartridges do you want?'

"'Ten will be enough,' I said.

"'Add a zero to that from me,' my friend said, handing me a box of one hundred. 'Use them and then come again, Charles. If what we have to do remains in the hands of these "cotton-wool" men, God help us!'

"I thanked the gunsmith and taking the gun and cartridges, went back to the orphanage. I said nothing to the orphans of course, so as not to disturb them. But I had a helper named Arakel – a simple lad, but very brave. I took him to one side and explained what was happening and advised him to be alert at night. I told him to come to my aid if I called him.

"'What with, a broom handle?'

"'No,' I said, 'my weapon is enough for both of us. Just be ready to help me.'

"A greater part of the night had passed when I saw the same shadows coming in our direction. Two of them came and stood below my window as they had before, while the third stood at the corner of the street, watching for the night duty policeman.

"I watched quietly from behind a curtain to see what they were going to do. I didn't have to wait long. One of the thieves, with great speed, suddenly jumped onto his comrade's shoulders and from there onto the orphanage wall. Hardly had he climbed onto the wall when he bent down and, extending his arm, pulled his companion up. In less than a minute the two criminals had come over the wall.

"Seeing the thieves' entry, I ran out of my room and called Arakel. I saw them from a window in the corridor trying to open the door to the wood store with a key.

"'Good Lord, why do they want to steal our wood in spring time?'

"'Follow me,' I said to my helper, pulling him by the arm. 'We must give them a very good welcome.'

"'Wait and at least let me get my thick staff.'

"Arakel and I went down to the ground floor and, passing through the entrance carefully, stopped at the corner of the wood store for a moment to hear if the thieves had been able to enter it. Indeed, they were inside it and at that moment were engaged in splashing a liquid on the wood.

"'I don't understand this devil's work,' whispered Arakel. 'Why are they wetting the wood? By the time winter comes it'll be dry again.'

"'For God's sake,' I said, telling my helper off, 'can't you smell anything? They're spilling oil to make the wood flare up.'

"'What…?' Arakel let out such a cry of horror that the two arsonists, terrified, started to turn back. But I didn't let them use their weapons. I suddenly fired the pistol I had in my hand several times. The criminals, uttering screams, fell onto the bundles of wood on which they'd tipped oil.

"In the morning I went to the prelacy and told them that two robbers had come and that I'd punished them in the only way I knew, because if

I telephoned the police, by the time they arrived, the orphanage would have been a mass of flames.

"Instead of congratulating me, the people there rebuked me, saying that they'd have trouble with the government.

"'I made the government's work easy,' I said, 'cleaning up criminals who were planning to take the lives of 500 helpless orphans.'

"'You're right, but don't you know that the French are very strict in these matters? They don't want an Armenian to touch one hair on the head of a Turk.'

"'I know, and it's because of that that the Turks dare to burn down our orphanage,' I said. 'The two criminals' bodies are still in the wood store. Let the French know; let them come and see what the "innocent victims" under their protection were doing.'

"'Of course we'll let the police know. But don't let anyone see you,' they told me. 'We'll see what happens.'"

I'll be brief. The police went and found the bodies. Despite the absolute proof of the Turks' guilt, they demanded that I be handed over, basing their demand on the Turks' objection that I'd killed them to take revenge on the victims, and to justify myself I'd set up the scene.

"The National Union's and prelacy's protests were in vain. The French believed the Turks more than us. I knew what they were going to do to me if I was arrested. So I wore my gun and came straight here."

"You did very well, but running away from a crime is not a solution," Kirk said, as if he was reciting a proverb, and fell into deep thought.

* * *

Kirk had come to Marash for one month, on the basis that French policy towards Armenians would quickly change and he would be able to return to Adana to work on his plans. But winter passed, it was spring, spring ended, the summer finished, it was autumn but there was still no sign of any improvement.

The long life of exile, with its lack of a definite limit and comfort would have gradually bored Kirk if he hadn't got his two inseparable friends, Keith and Charles with him. After he had settled in Marash he had met, by chance, a young man named Serop, whose life he had saved in front of Death's Door and, through him, Richard, who was the son of one of the notable people in the town.

They usually spent the day in Richard's shop, talking and discussing the day's events that were gradually becoming more worrying.

One day all five of them were sitting in Richard's office, when a gigantic 45 year-old man, dressed as a farm worker and well tanned by the sun entered. "Excuse me," said the newcomer, addressing Richard, "you don't know me – my name is Andrew, and I'm a muleteer from Fendidjak, but I'm now a farm worker in a village about three hours from here – but I know you, because I've often seen you with the British officers of the occupying army. I know that you're a patriotic and selfless person, so I came to let you know something important."

"Please, sit down," Richard said, marvelling at his great build, bright eyes and clever forehead. "The people here are more patriotic and selfless than I am. You can speak with every confidence in front of them."

"What I've got to say is very brief," said the former muleteer form Fendidjak, still standing. "What I've got to reveal is not altogether a secret, as everyone knows about the *Milli* movement. But I felt it my duty to tell what I've seen.

"Yesterday morning I was working in the field. I saw a car on the upper road that passed at speed and entered a Turkish village about half an hour distant. I was surprised and wondered who would have come by car to that village. To satisfy my curiosity I went there and heard from a shepherd that I know that it was a Turkish officer, who was in civilian clothes and traveled around the villages to get the local population to revolt against the local government.

"The *movement*, growing and growing in volume, has now reached our borders. Tell the British; let them work out a solution, or we'll come to a terrible end. Goodbye, sirs." Saying this, he took his leave of the shop owner and his guests and, like a man satisfied with having done his duty, left the office.

After Andrew left, those present talked for a long time about the disguised Turkish officer's proselytising within Cilicia's borders and finally decided to inform the military governor, with whom Richard already had personal dealings.

To this end, taking Kirk as well as the chairman of the National Union with him, the following day Richard went to the military base and explained the situation to the British commander.

The British commander, after listening carefully to the Armenians' reasoning, laughed at his guests' unwarranted fear and, chuckling, said,

"Don't worry, gentlemen. The Turks can do nothing now. We've defeated them and, if necessary, we'll do it again."

"Please excuse me sir," the chairman of the National Union said, "you defeated the Turkish army, but you mustn't lose sight of the fact that the Turkish people are in a position to raise other armies."

"Are those people mad?" the British officer cried scornfully. "Didn't the Turks see our victory? Didn't they feel our might and understand our authority? When they couldn't stand up to us with their German and Austrian allies, are they now going to rise against us in their forsaken and disorganised state? Go back to your homes and carry on with your work. You've been very frightened and see imaginary enemies everywhere. The Turk is dead and can't rise again."

"The Turk isn't dead, but has only fainted from the blow he received," Richard pointed out. "Now there's a *movement* to revive him."

"But the people aren't blind to follow a few adventurers," the British officer replied carelessly.

"Sir," Kirk said, speaking in his turn, "if you will allow me to tell you about a small incident that I saw, I'll show you how the Turkish people follow and fall into every kind of adventure."

"I'm listening," the governor said, recovering his usual coolness.

"Five years ago," Kirk said, "I was in Sivas to study. That year there was an election for a parliamentary deputy and the local Committee for Union and Progress party had a Turk who'd been in prison many times and who had a murky past, elected in some illegal way.

"To protest against this invalid election, the opposition party head collected together all the vagrants and porters from the marketplace and, dividing a purse of money between them, told them to go to the square in front of the government building and shout, 'We don't want it! We don't want it!' whenever he was going to read his speech.

"The protesters went towards the government building with their flags and drums. On the way groups of curious people joined them and a considerable procession was created.

"When they reached the square, the leader got up on a high rock and began to read his speech in a deep voice. Every time he stopped at a full stop, the people shouted together 'We don't want it!'

"The governor, hearing the protesters' noise, sent police to find out what they didn't want. The man who had been reading, seeing the arrival of the police, jumped down and disappeared. So too did a significant part of the crowd, following their leader. The police however, managed to arrest seven people and took them before the governor.

"'What is it you don't want?' he asked the arrested men.

"'We don't know,' they replied, shamefacedly. 'Everyone was shouting, "We don't want it", so we shouted too.'

"Sir, this is the Turkish psychology," Kirk continued, "They are ignorant and like all ignorant people they're dangerous. They believe anything without examining it or using logic. When the officer traveling around in the car says, 'Follow me, we're going to destroy the British', all of them will follow, without asking if they've enough strength to do it. They're so ignorant that if the officer tells them, 'The army of the entire British Empire consists of 10,000 men, while we've got 10,000,000 soldiers', they'll believe that too, because they haven't got the ability to tell a lie from the truth."

Kirk's words were logical. The Turks were ignorant and would blindly follow their leaders, without taking into account that they had been defeated in the war and were weak.

Despite this, the British commander, after a moment, asked, "Let's suppose it's like that. Are you in any danger?"

"Not today, but tomorrow…"

The British commander stopped him with a smile. "You're safe now, aren't you? Go away; we'll think about it tomorrow."

* * *

One day, due to political events, those who were going to think about tomorrow, deserted Marash and departed, handing the city over to the French.

The spark that was derided by the British commander, gradually got bigger, became a fire and, spreading, reached the borders of Cilicia, threatening to blaze up and turn the surviving Armenian people, who had only just been able to rebuild their homes and dress their wounds, into ashes.

Black clouds covered the horizon and the bewildering ghost of death once more appeared in front of everybody.

The news of massacre, robbery and destruction in provinces that hadn't been freed, and where Armenians once more had the misfortune to return to and settle, gradually became known. Every Armenian heart began to tremble. The Turks had become wilder and even more ferocious.

The spreading fire one day reached the gates of Marash. The surrounding villages were filled with bandits and provoking elements. Armenian peasants left their fields and vineyards once more and sought sanctuary in the city, bringing with them dreadful stories of torture and massacre.

The ring tightened even more. The city became less safe. Individual killings and night attacks – especially in the city's outskirts – became commonplace.

The Turks, getting bolder by the day, openly declared that they would drive the French out and save their fatherland from under the heel of the occupying army. They promised security of life, property and honor to the Armenians if they helped them rid the country of their enemy.

The Armenians informed the French of this. Like the British, they laughed at the Turks' bragging, suggesting that the Armenians refuse the Turks' offer, in which they saw a ploy to set the two Christian nations against each other. "We've come to protect the weak nations," the French general said. "There's not a power on earth that can remove us from where we are."

But despite the French general's boasts, grave events followed one another. One day a mass of bandits entering the city hoisted the Turkish flag over the citadel. On another day, they openly distributed arms to the Turkish and Kurdish mob. On yet another day they sealed off the city's streets, cutting Marash off from the rest of the world.

Seeing the impotence of the French to prohibit these exploits, the Turks grew even bolder and, one day, deriding the victors, took their rusty swords and went into the streets, to begin the cleansing of Cilicia with the 40,000 Armenians in Marash.

Under the Protection of the Powerful

It was a cold and grey day – the 21st of January 1920, the third day after Christmas – when a despairing cry went up, "Run away! Run away! The *chetteh*s are coming…!"

It was the Armenian shopkeepers who gave the warning, seeing the cowardly stabbing of patrolling Armenian and French policemen in the market. They began running to their homes, while the Turkish mob, led by bandits, pursued them, continually firing and yelling at them in a terrifying manner.

Those who had the luck to escape the massacring mob shut themselves in their houses and, securing the doors and windows, waited with weapons at hand, to defend themselves, their families and their honor.

But the battle didn't commence immediately.

The bandits, seeing the means used by the Armenians to defend themselves, hesitated for a time. Being greater in numbers the mob wanted to wait for a few days to see what position the French would adopt towards them. Eventually however, when they became convinced that the French wouldn't do anything for the people they were protecting, they plucked up their courage and gave the signal to fight, starting with burning Armenian houses with bundles of twigs soaked in oil.

The scene was dreadful. The Armenian quarters, set on fire on all sides, burned like great furnaces. The wind, very strong at that moment, fanned the fires and spread them everywhere. The buildings burst into flame one after another and collapsed with great creaking noises.

Human shadows clung to one another in the flames, sparks and smoke.

It was a fatal battle waged between Turks and Armenians. There were mortal battles on every side, everywhere; on roofs, in yards, under walls. The one who lost had no right to live any longer.

The massacring rabble sometimes retreated, treading on its dead and wounded, and sometimes advanced, walking over Armenian bodies. Then it would retreat once more, then attack and, like storm-tossed waves, would strike and be struck, shatter and be shattered, splinter and be splintered.

And the battle continued like this all day, all night, the following day and the days after that, with the Turks sometimes victorious, and sometimes the Armenians.

* * *

It was the eighth night of the battle.

Not far from the ruins of the Armenian quarter of Tsorametch, inside the ruins of three or four wooden houses – the stone foundations of which were still standing at the edge of the street about half a man high – around twenty Armenian fighting men were seated around charcoal braziers, talking quietly and smoking, while others, each hidden in a corner, yawned and dozed.

A little distance away, in the place assigned to their leader, Kirk, wrapped in a wide coat, was also sitting near a fire and desultorily watching his lieutenant who, sitting opposite him, was occupied with cleaning a rifle.

The silent stillness of a cemetery surrounded them. Everywhere there were the four walls of individual burnt houses, downed roofs, smashed doors, tree trunks turned into charcoal, and piles of rubble. This was like a large wound opened in the breast of the city as far as the eye could see.

An Armenian church, a strongly built house, or a stone-built pavilion could be seen here and there at their full heights in the desolation of the ruins – the only buildings not consumed by the fire. Thousands of people had taken refuge in these buildings, escaping from the terror of fire and sword.

The Armenian fighters and legionnaries, under skilled leaders, having dug trenches around these buildings and raised barricades, fought with spades, hoes, stones and teeth against the fanatical Turkish mob and bandits who, after reducing Armenian houses to ashes, wanted to set fire to the Armenian churches still standing, and put the poor people inside to the sword.

How long could that unequal battle between the Armenian people and the Muslim mob last? While the enemy continually received help from outside and renewed its strength, the Armenians, cut from the outside world – even from one another – grew weaker day by day.

Reflecting on this scenario, Kirk's thoughts turned to his wife. She had taken refuge in the Holy Mother of God church, like 2,000 other women, old people and children. He had only had one opportunity to see her since the fighting began.

She felt a little unwell. She had been dizzy a few times and felt sick. She was lying in front of the altar on a small carpet. Her mother watched over her, constantly awake, while the deaf-mute, crossing himself 'prayed' in front of the Crucifixion.

"Andrew," Kirk said, hoping to drive away his vexed thoughts for a while by talking, "have you got a wife and children?"

"No, commander," his lieutenant replied, who was the same former muleteer from Fendidjak.

"You're lucky not to be married," Kirk sighed.

Andrew smiled bitterly and said, "I was married and had four children."

"So where are they?" Kirk asked absently.

"The Turks killed them," the former muleteer replied.

The conversation was destined to end in silence. The silence of the night was then broken by a sentry's warning voice saying, "Who's that?" followed by a sharp scream, "Don't! Don't...! I'm Armenian."

Kirk quickly turned to the sound and saw a youth of about 15 years old, without a coat who, with his hands in the air, was begging the sentry not to fire at him, while the latter, lowering his rifle, rebuked him, saying that his thoughtlessness could have led to a serious accident.

"Hey, youngster! Come here!" Kirk shouted at him. "Who are you and what are you doing at this time of night?"

"My name is Armen, sir," the youth said, coming towards Kirk and blowing on his frozen hands at the same time. "I came to find out what state you were in."

"Who sent you?"

Armen, confused, looked at the ground and then, like someone guilty, said, "Nobody sir. They wouldn't let me fight because I'm too young, so I decided to become a messenger to help my people."

"Come here," Kirk said, leading the patriotic boy to the fire. "Sit down and get warm."

Armen approached the fire and sat for a long time with his hands and face towards it.

"Where are you from?" Kirk asked, after looking at his guest for a while admiringly.

"I'm from Marash, sir."

"Where are your parents?"

"My parents died in exile. I'm an orphan."

"Armen," Kirk said, putting his hand on the brave-hearted youth's shoulder, "do you know how dangerous it is to go around in the dark among the ruins at night? Let's leave aside the fact that you're not protected by warm clothing. Don't you think about the enemy's bullets that are fired in every direction killing people who don't think and are outside the defenses?"

"I know, sir, that's the reason I go out at night and take great care that I'm not seen by the enemy."

"Then you don't have the password. You could be killed by bullets fired from Armenian positions, which was going to happen here if our sentry had acted more quickly."

"Very well, sir," Armen said, with a pleading look. "After this I'll be careful. Please give me a password."

"I'd advise you that, when you come to our defenses, you whistle like this: hoo, hi, hiu, hiu, hiu... The 'hoo' quietly, the 'hi' five notes higher and the 'hiu's one note down from the top, but long."

"Like this: hoo, hi, hiu, hiu, hiu..."

"Yes, exactly like that. Now tell me, where you went and what you saw," Kirk said, immediately becoming friends with the youth.

"I've been to quite a few places," Armen said, beginning his report, "the same worries and pain are everywhere: overcrowding, illness, lack of food and military supplies. Let's take the Latins' monastery. About 4,000 people have found sanctuary there. The French only give a handful of wheat for the children, who number over 300. Hundreds of schoolboys and girls, who were in class when the fighting started, are still there and separated from their parents and relatives. There are many among them who've not eaten anything for days. The adults have been hungry for a long time anyway."

"Isn't it possible to get aid to them from outside?" Kirk asked, thinking deeply.

"The building is isolated within the surrounding ruins, sir," Armen said. "The Turks, taking up positions in a nearby mosque, continuously fire at all those who want to get to the monastery or escape from it. When

I was there, the Armenians thought of opening a tunnel to establish contact with the French camp ten minutes away. But I don't know if they succeeded."

"What else did you see?"

"The people in the Holy Cross Catholic church are somewhat lucky. They still have two days' food."

"How many are they?"

"About 2,000. There are also about 1,500 people in the nearby Protestant church. The day before yesterday Mr Keith killed two cats to feed the sick. The French confiscated them, saying that because they are fighting, they need food more."

"Are they really fighting?"

"On the contrary. They haven't fired one shot at the Turks. It's the Armenian fighting men who, in positions in the surrounding houses, constantly throw the advancing mob back. But in all the things I've seen, the worst scene is in the cathedral. In the prelacy over a hundred fighters are lying wounded. The doctors are doing one operation after another, cutting off arms and legs. The ladies of the Red Cross have stopped work, bewildered, because they've neither medicines nor cotton. On the other hand there are 4,000 people in the cathedral and in one or two buildings in the vicinity. Poor Charles doesn't know which one he should help."

"If there's no help, our end will be very bad," Kirk murmured, turning to Andrew who, deep in thought, was listening to young Armen's heart-rending news.

"The French have betrayed us!" Andrew cried with a look of distaste on his face. "How are we going to continue to fight if we can't get provisions and military supplies?"

"I know where there are military supplies," Armen said. "I went to the Holy Mother of God church and told them. But Mr Richard said that unfortunately he couldn't utilize the opportunity as their positions are unsuitable."

"But where are the supplies?" Kirk and Andrew asked, extremely interested.

"The chettehs have camped behind St. Toros church," Armen replied. "They've about ten mules loaded with military supplies with them."

"That is good news," Kirk declared. "How many chettehs are there?"

"There are 50 – 60."

"Sir," Andrew said, jumping up. "Give me 20 men, and I'll go and teach those robbers a lesson."

"I can't let you have twenty men because if the enemy attacks suddenly from the opposite positions, the 17 of us here will be in a very weak position," Kirk pointed out. "Can you do what's necessary with ten?"

"That's too few, sir. Give me at least 15."

"Very well. Take five men from our rear right wing. Serop is there; greet him for me and he'll give you the men you need."

Then Kirk issued an order and, collecting the fighters round him, said, "Comrades, as you know, we're all suffering from a lack of supplies. There are some fighters among us who haven't even got five cartridges..."

"I've only one..."

"I've only got three left."

The person who's got the most is Andrew," Kirk continued. "I personally have 13 left. As our position is on the firing line, I think that we won't be able to defend ourselves for more than half an hour with what we've got if we were subject to a fierce attack. Fortunately the enemy doesn't know about our weakness and has recently hesitated to attack us. That hesitation won't last long. At the first opportunity he'll collect his forces and begin an assault. Before that terrible skirmish happens, we've been lucky to get some good news. Our young messenger says that a detachment of chettehs with a considerable amount of supplies have camped behind St. Toros church. I need ten men, as well as five from Serop's group, to go, under Andrew's command, and capture those supplies from the bandits. The task is dangerous, but our and our loved ones' lives depend on it. Who wants to join that group?"

"Me! Me! Me!" could be heard from all sides.

"Think carefully, men. Maybe you won't come back."

"We're ready to die!" the Armenian braves cried decisively.

"I'll take this opportunity to remind you to use your cartridges sparingly," Kirk said. "Until you're sure that each bullet will kill one of the enemy, don't fire."

"I'm the most economical, sir," said an older fighter from the corner. "Until I can bring two people to heel, I'll not fire."

* * *

Hearing the neighing of a mule, Kirk opened his eyes. He had stretched out for a time near the fire to rest.

Immediately straightening up, he saw Andrew who, leading a mule
loaded with military supplies by the reins, was coming towards their
positions, crouching every so often behind the half-ruined walls. A
second fighter followed Andrew, also leading a mule, then a third, a
fourth and, behind that, two people without, however, either one leading
an animal.

"Six men!" Kirk murmured sadly. Then, raising his voice, he asked
"Andrew, where are the others?"

"They fell, sir," the man from Fendidjak replied, sighing and giving his
animal to the first fighter. "Two men from Serop's group too. We
captured seven mules. We brought four and gave the other three to the
others, so that they could eat the meat as well as use the loads."

"Was the fight hard?"

"Not really. We caught them between two fires and attacked suddenly.
No more than nine or ten escaped. By the way, I forgot to tell you,"
Andrew said, sitting near the fire, "Serop says hello. He's captured three
chettehs and, from their confessions, has understood that their
commander is someone called Captain Khalid. He said 'if you tell your
commander Khalid, he'll understand'."

"Khalid?" Kirk said, growing pale. "Where is he?"

"In the citadel of course," Andrew said, pointing at the enemy
positions. "But why did you go pale, sir? Who's Khalid?"

"The Death's Door executioner," Kirk muttered through his teeth with
terrifying hatred. "Now I understand why our people from St. George's
here were burnt alive in the lime kilns. That beast's head should be
smashed in, or he'll not leave one of us alive in Marash."

"We'll destroy him, sir," Andrew said, calmly rolling his moustache.
"Don't worry, as long as our provisions and supplies last."

* * *

It was the fifteenth night of the battle.

During the week the Turks attacked the fighters protecting St. George
three times – they regarded them as an obstacle to the encirclement of the
Holy Mother of God church – but they were driven back each time with
heavy losses.

Kirk was pleased because his soldiers had plenty of supplies and were in
a position to oppose the enemy's assaults for a long time.

He was in his usual place by the fire, seeing out another white winter's night, when he suddenly heard the youth Armen's whistle from behind a pile of rubble close by.

"Hoo, hi, hiu, hiu, hiu…"

"Where are you, boy?" Kirk shouted, gladly calling the young night-time messenger to him. "You've not appeared for a week. I was concerned that you may have had an accident."

"Sir," Armen said, going near the fire and warming himself, "it's very difficult to go from one place to another. It sometimes happens that I have to wait for six hours behind a rock until I can't be seen by the enemy and hide behind the next one. They've fired at me nine times in the last two weeks and I've escaped without harm nine times."

"Bravo Armen!" Andrew called from his corner. "When you grow up we'll make you commander-in-chief of the Armenian army."

"Talk to me, my friend," Kirk said, sitting next to Armen. "What news have you brought us?"

"The situation of the Holy Mother of God church is very dangerous, sir," the young messenger said. "The Turkish mob, under the leadership of the chettehs, has tried to surround the church for several days. The Armenian fighters' supplies have been used up. Several people went to the cathedral to get bullets from the French camped there, but the French refused to help. The people in the church, hearing that their fighters had returned empty-handed, were panic-stricken and, frightened of a Turkish assault, poured out of the church to take refuge in the cathedral. The Senegalese soldiers opened fire on the crowd and drove them back to their previous refuge. Quite a few people were killed and injured."

"Dreadful!" Kirk muttered, suddenly seeing his ill wife before his eyes. What had happened to her in the church? Even if she'd not been a victim of the Senegalese soldiers' fire, wasn't her life in danger in the Holy Mother of God church that had been the target of the Turkish bandits and mob?

Kirk's first thought was to get his rifle and, taking all the dangers into account, rush to his wife's defense. But he then thought that he couldn't leave, as his role in the forward defenses was to protect not only his wife, but also everyone's wives and children.

"What bitter fate," he said, sighing from the depths of his heart, "To be killed by the enemy, to be killed by a friend. But I don't understand why the Senegalese soldiers fired on the Armenian people."

"Because the cathedral is very crowded," Armen said. The French don't want to make the situation worse for those already in the cathedral by adding to their numbers."

"Were there many dead? Were there women among them?" Kirk asked, with a shudder of hatred.

"Yes, women and children too."

At the same moment a trumpet's long and short notes could be heard coming from the enemy positions.

"It's the signal for assembly," Kirk said, simultaneously forgetting the thought that tortured his mind and running towards the hole opened in the wall. "It appears they're getting ready to attack."

"I'm not frightened any more. If they're coming, they'll have something to see," Andrew said, adapting his sight through another hole. "I can see the trumpeter's head, sir. Shall I fire?"

"Only the man's forehead appears above the barricade," Kirk said. "Wait for him to raise his head a little more."

"What he's showing is enough for me," Andrew said, pushing the muzzle of his rifle through the hole in the wall.

"Take careful aim, Andrew, don't miss."

"Don't worry sir!"

Hardly had Andrew finished speaking when the dry sound of a shot was heard, which was followed by a brief trumpet note, "Toot!"

The trumpeter, exhaling his last breath into the trumpet mouthpiece, disappeared behind the barricade.

"19!" Andrew said, pulling his rifle back and stroking his whiskers with the palm of his hand.

"What's that?" asked Kirk, interested in the count made by his soldier.

"The number of kills I've made, sir," Andrew said brightly. "I'm taking revenge for my wife and four children."

* * *

Despite the trumpet signal given for assembly, the lack of movement in the enemy camp surprised Kirk. "That's strange," he said, moving his head away from his viewpoint. "What happened to those men? It's as if all the men opposite have died together." Then a sudden thought came into his head. "Andrew, I don't think that there's anyone in those positions. Maybe they're providing a diversion to keep us here, while they're going, or have already gone by the road at the back, to the church of the Holy Mother of God."

"If you'll permit me, sir, I'll go and find out," Andrew said with wonderful coolness.

"That's a good idea. But be careful."

"Don't worry, sir." Taking his rifle and slithering his way through the piles of rubble, Andrew went towards the enemy's positions.

Kirk watched his lieutenant until he could see him no more. The he carefully examined the enemy defenses, and suddenly saw the brave soldier from Fendidjak who had killed the trumpeter stand on the parapet, put the trumpet to his lips and blow a blast. He then pointed in the direction of the Holy Mother of God church, trying to say that there was no one behind those defenses and that Kirk and his men were staying there for nothing.

"Comrades!" called Kirk, immediately gathering all the fighters around him. "Forward! The church of the Holy Mother of God is in danger!"

* * *

When the fighters from St. George arrived at the church with their rear forces, they saw that a bloody battle was taking place between the local Armenian fighters and a powerful mob accompanied by bandits of over twenty times their number. The mob, bent on massacre, had almost surrounded the Armenian church on three sides and had set the nearby school on fire. Kirk and his soldiers' thunderous appearance turned the mob into a terrified crowd, giving new energy and spirit to the church's exhausted defenders.

The Armenians had hardly extinguished the fire in the school when the bandits set fire to the priest's house. The fighters went in that direction. A hand-to-hand battle took place in the flames. Bullets whistled, swords flashed and the sound of axes could be heard. Every time a blow fell, a young life faded away, a dream was shattered.

At the hottest moment of the battle Kirk saw his friend Richard who, having fallen by the blow of an axe, was lying under the fighters' feet, murmuring words that couldn't be heard above the deafening noise of the mob and the fighters, as well as the wailing of the people in the church.

At the same moment he saw the pockmarked face of a monster with loathsome features, and his whole body shook. It was Khalid, the bloodthirsty master of Death's Door, the hyena always thirsty for

Armenian blood who, holding a great sword, was encouraging his chettehs by continually shouting in a hoarse voice, "Strike! Strike without mercy! Kill the infidels!"

"Death to the criminals!" Kirk shouted, going towards his wild enemy.

More than twenty fighters immediately followed their leader.

Khalid and the ten or so bandits around him suddenly finding themselves surrounded, tried to retreat, but it was too late. The Armenian fighters threw themselves like lions at them and stabbed them all to death.

"You'll not escape me this time!" Kirk yelled, putting a bullet in his enemy's head. "It's a waste of a bullet, but there, take it! Here's another to carry out the war tribunal's verdict!"

It was as if an enormous weight had been lifted from his heart, and Kirk felt unusually relieved at seeing his enemy's death. But there was no time for joy; the bandits' comrades attacked in greater numbers and surrounded the Armenian fighters in their turn.

Other Armenian fighters came to their aid and, while hundreds of men fought hand-to-hand, arsonists from the mob climbed onto the church roof and, spreading petroleum about, set fire to it.

The people hiding in the church ran through the flames screaming with terror, some with their hair and dresses alight. Those who managed to leave the confusion were killed by murderers wielding axes waiting outside the doors.

The Armenian fighters, seeing their families being smoked out, increased the swiftness of their blows and rushed towards their loved ones who were being burned alive.

The mob and bandits, achieving their aim, didn't want to continue the fight, so moved to one side to watch the panic-stricken unfortunates from a distance and hunt them for sport later.

Kirk, seeing the arsonists leaving the church doors, rushed inside to find out what state Julia was in.

A great many women and children were piled up, dead. Some were crushed under rubble fallen from the roof, some were half burnt and turned into cinders. Because the church was built of stone, the internal wooden fittings had burnt out quickly, but that "quickly" was enough for most of the people inside to be suffocated.

Kirk, stepping over the bodies, went towards the altar, where he knew his wife had been lying on the first day of the massacre. Not finding her among the bodies – nor her mother nor the deaf-mute servant – Kirk was encouraged for a moment, thinking that perhaps Julia, escaping the Senegalese soldiers' rifle fire, had managed to take refuge in the cathedral.

With that thought he began to run out of the smoke and ashes of the church when, just inside, in front of the door, the clothes of an old man, lying on his face, caught his eye. Suddenly it seemed that his breath caught and his eyes stood out. It was the deaf-mute Samuel and, lying next to him, was his wife, also on her face, as well as, next to her, Mrs Iskouhi.

Both old people had taken Julia by the arms, as if they had tried to help her escape but, seeing the waiting axe-wielding men, hadn't ventured out and had fallen there, suffocating.

Kirk knelt next to his wife. It seemed to him that she still showed signs of life. Who knows, maybe the proximity of clean air and her youth had saved her life.

Encouraged by this thought, he picked her up and left the building quickly. He had hardly gone five or six paces when a volley of shots spattered around him. A moment's hesitation would have meant the loss of everything. Fortunately Kirk didn't hesitate. On the contrary, he gathered all his strength and, with miraculous movement, ran forward.

* * *

It was the sixteenth day of the battle.

Thanks to first aid, Julia's life had been saved and she was lying in a building next to the cathedral that was being used as a hospital. There, in a faint voice, she told her husband – whose right hand was bandaged and was sitting near her – how her illness had prevented her from leaving the church, and how her mother and Samuel had so selflessly looked after her, remaining faithful to her until the end of their lives.

Recalling those terrible moments, Julia was very moved, but she couldn't weep as the tears had dried in her eyes.

"Julia, forget that dreadful past now," Kirk encouraged her, taking her hand. "You can be sure that we'll be free soon."

"What if we're not?" Julia whispered – revealing for the first time that she was expecting a baby.

"Don't worry, my love," Kirk comforted her. "The doctor said you've still got a week. Relief forces from Adana should be here before then."

"I don't know. A bad premonition worries me," Julia said in a strange, trembling voice.

"Put aside that childish thought," Kirk scolded her in a sweet tone. "There are doctors and nurses here to… make sure you're comfortable."

And they continued to exchange affectionate and loving words, until Charles and Andrew appeared.

"May it be over now!" they exclaimed, congratulating Kirk and Julia. "We're very pleased that you both emerged from the fire alive. But Kirk, what happened to your hand?"

It was Charles who asked the question.

"It's not important. I had to pay a small price for get rid of bloodthirsty Khalid," Kirk said. "It's a knife wound. But please sit down. What's the situation?"

"The situation is still not clear," Charles said. "The Turks burned the Holy Mother of God church, but couldn't get any further. The Armenians are defending themselves in the other centers heroically, and that includes at our church. Talking specifically about this area, our supplies are plentiful, but the overcrowding and the crisis over food worry us very much. The Turks have cut off the water recently. We repair the pipes, they destroy them. We'll see what happens in the end."

"What have you got to say," Kirk said, turning after a moment to his lieutenant. "Where were you, friend? In the confusion I didn't have the opportunity of seeing you."

"We were busy with the mob," Andrew said, modestly lowering his head. "I'm sorry that we lost Serop, sir."

"Don't call me sir again, Andrew," Kirk said in a bitter voice. "There are no fighting groups or fighters left. Alas, we lost all our brave men."

* * *

It was the seventeenth day of the battle.

Awaking from a deep, restorative sleep, the like of which he had not had for over a fortnight, Kirk had recovered his energy and, handing Julia over to a nurse he knew, he left the "hospital" to inspect the cathedral and other places for a short time.

But it wasn't possible to move about. There wasn't a place in the church's courtyard that wasn't occupied. Everywhere there was noise, confusion, movement, whispering. Little children screamed, sick people moaned, children shouted, the devout, kneeling in corners, read prayer books.

The people who had been able to take refuge in the church building and the rooms in it were fortunate. The rest were in the yard, under open skies, subject to rain and frost.

Everyone's face had the deathly seal of hunger and sickness on it, while their eyes had the sorrow of merciless massacre and deep disillusionment in them.

Kirk, moving among these remnants of humanity, wept. A person had to have iron nerves to stand the pain and death of these people, his fellow-Armenians.

"Sir," a mother begged him, thinking that he was an inspector checking what their state was, "Don't you have a piece of bread that I can give my sick son?"

"Compatriot," another stammered, "please, do you have a covering for us? …We're trembling with cold."

Kirk couldn't go any further into this ocean of suffering humanity and turned back. When he was near the Prelacy building, he saw the people taking refuge in the porch had their heads up, looking to the sky, as if they were looking for something. Curious, he also looked up and thought that he heard a buzzing from a great distance that sounded more like the regular beat of a motor than the noise made by an insect.

There was no doubt that an aeroplane was approaching. But belonging to which side? Could it be a dove bringing the news of freedom? Or was it a carrion-eating buzzard that was going to spread death and destruction?

With their hands shading their eyes, the people looked for a long time, living indescribable moments of anxiety and agitation. Finally the aeroplane appeared in the sky above the courtyard and immediately joyful exclamations came from everyone's lips, "It's French… It's a French aeroplane…!"

And while the old and the infirm hugged one another with tears of joy, Kirk hurried to the hospital, to tell his wife that the hour of freedom was near.

* * *

It was the twenty-first day of the battle.

The situation on the day following the arrival of the French aeroplane was completely turned upside down. A French military column reached the besieged people and, camping outside the city, began to shell the Turkish quarters.

The Turkish mob and bandits who, after burning the people in the churches of St. George and the Holy Mother of God, were preparing to burn the people in the cathedral, the Protestant church, the church of the Holy Cross, the Latins' monastery and other places, now ran away in terror to put out the fires that were consuming their own homes.

The shelling lasted, without mercy, for three days and nights. On the fourth day the Turks put up a white flag and went to the French to beg them to stop firing.

The news of the Turkish surrender went from one position to another and, in the evening, the Armenians embraced and congratulated each other on escaping certain death.

"Congratulations, Julia!" Kirk said, giving his wife the good news. "Didn't I tell you not to lose heart...? These dark days will be over very soon."

Julia put her head on his chest and cried with happiness. "When, when will we leave here?" she sobbed with a weak voice.

"The French won't allow us out of the church yard," Kirk said, stroking his wife's hair. "But tonight, if an armistice is signed, I hope that tomorrow morning I'll be able to take you to the American hospital" – and smiling after a moment – "Julia, do you know what I'll name the baby, if it's a boy?"

"Alex or, if it's a girl, Alexandra?"

"No. If it's a boy, Vrej (Vengeance), and if it's a girl, Vrejouhi."

The conversation between husband and wife was interrupted with the arrival of guests. In any event, was solitude possible in a place where people were crowded on top of one another?

"So, you two, what's this? Talking like a couple in love!" Charles exclaimed, with a humorous tone in his voice. "Look and see who I've brought to see you!"

"Keith!" Kirk cried, jumping up and squeezing his friend's hand. "How wonderful to see you alive!"

"I'm delighted to see you alive too," Keith said in a voice full of emotion. "Kirk, I was going to commit suicide if something happened to you, as it was on my conscience that you left Iskenderoun because of me ..."

"Please, close the subject," Kirk said, seating his friend next to him. "I did my humanitarian duty in Iskenderoun. If, because of that, we came here and suffered, that's not our fault. Don't forget, Keith, the poet's words, 'Death is the same everywhere'."

"Our friend Kirk is as good a fighter as he's a moralizer," Charles said in a jolly tone of voice. "Now that you've had your lesson, Keith, tell us how you spent the twenty one days of the siege with your French 'friends'."

"Exactly as a dog and a cat would if they were put in one bag," Keith said. "Brother, it's not possible to come to an understanding with these people. Despite the fact that they were surrounded like us, they neither fired at the Turks, nor would they let us fire. They took the food from the hands of our women and children, appropriated the best parts of the building for themselves, told the children off, and hit them if they cried from fright. Just as you, escaping from Adana I came to Marash nine months ago, and then escaped from their clutches and came here."

"Good. Did they recognise you?" Kirk and Charles asked, curiously.

"No, because of another 'crime'."

"But tell us what happened."

"The day before yesterday I was walking behind the French positions," Keith said, telling of his 'crime', "when I saw that the Turkish mob, hearing the sound of the bombardment, had ran away towards the valley, very frightened.

"A machine gun, in its place on the ramparts, caught my attention. A soldier, shot in the forehead, was lying beside it. I immediately went and sat in the dead soldier's place and, turning the muzzle of the machine gun in the mob's direction, began to fire at it. As the machine gun fired, the Turks were sprinkled like mulberries on the ground.

"Just then a French corporal, drawing his gun, came up to me, saying, 'You pig of an Armenian, what right have you to interfere in our military affairs?' I didn't tell him that I'd once been a sergeant in the French army. I only told him that I wasn't a pig and had the right to take vengeance on behalf of my thousands of burnt fellow-Armenians.

"'Be quiet! Come with me! You'll receive the punishment you deserve,' he said.

"'Get away from me, or it'll be the worse for you,' I said threateningly.

"The Frenchman, seeing my threat, went to call his friends, while I continued my work until I finished the entire belt of cartridges. Then I got to my feet and went to our positions. Half an hour later I heard that the French were looking everywhere for me. So as not to create an incident, for two days…"

Before he had finished his story, Kirk suddenly set off. He had heard a thin, weak sound from the street.

"Hoo, hi, hiu, hiu, hiu…"

Shortly afterwards Armen and Andrew entered the room, the latter crying happily, "Hey you son of the devil, where were you? You've not appeared for a long time."

The young messenger opened his mouth to speak, but suddenly, clutching his chest and uttering a strangled moan, fell to the floor.

"Blood!" Kirk called, quickly making his way to the young man. "Armen, tell us what happened."

"The Turks…" Armen whispered, half opening his eyes and giving Kirk a bitter smile.

"Yes, yes, what happened about the Turks?"

"The Turks set fire to the Protestant church…" Armen stammered in a voice that could hardly be heard. "The Armenians, making a hole in the wall, took refuge in the Catholic church… The Turks torched the church of the Holy Cross too… The Armenians wanted to escape to the Latins' monastery…. The Turks, with axes…"

"Poor boy, he's rambling," said those present sympathetically, looking at one another.

"Armen! Armen!" Kirk cried, stroking the young messenger's forehead. "Tell me, who wounded you?"

"They chased me… The mob is coming… Sir…"

At the same time a shrill cry went up and uproar was heard from the distant Armenian positions.

"To arms! To arms! To arms!"

Kirk, Keith, Charles, Andrew and many other fighters, surprised by the noise, handed the wounded youth over to the women who were there, and hurriedly left the room. But they had hardly reached the street when they stopped with horror.

The mob, with torches lit on the end of long poles and making ferocious noises, was coming towards them, while behind them, in the distance, the burning French barracks filled the whole horizon with flames and smoke.

The Disastrous Retreat

No matter how tragic the result, it would have been interesting to know how the victory gained by such sacrifice ended in such a shameful defeat.

After three weeks of fighting, the Turks, under a white flag, had gone to the French authorities to ask for an armistice. They were minded to surrender because they thought the French military column had come to reinforce their local forces.

When they heard, however, that the column had come to secure the retreat of the French forces surrounding in the city of Marash... they resumed their half-completed work, but this time more boldly, as the defenders of the Armenians not only were leaving – that is deserting the very people they were protecting – but they were exhausted by the long battle carried on by the Armenians.

The defenders of the cathedral, seeing the French defeat, felt completely disillusioned. Then, seeing the mob's advance, they immediately realized the truth and ran to their positions to defend their lives and honor.

The fighting lasted all night with great ferocity. The Armenians, surrounded on all four sides, forced the infuriated mob back with incredible bravery that, like a maddened, foaming flood, the mob continually attacked the church's defenses.

Towards the morning the Armenians managed to cut through the cordon surrounding them and suggested to the people that they escape out of the city, following the retreating French... while they would buy time by keeping the enemy occupied as much as possible.

The women and children, hearing the order to escape, became extremely alarmed and, pushing one another, came out of the rooms.

At one time the confusion and panic in the street was such that the escapees crowded together at a corner, forming a dense mass. At that point, many fainted from the pushing and fright, while others were trampled.

"Calm down! Walk slowly! Don't hurry...!" Charles, who was overseeing the clearance, advised, "Don't forget that you can do nothing more than what you're fated to do... Pray to God..."

"We curse that God," thousands of voices cried. "Curse! Curse! Curse...!"

"Don't lose heart, boys! Hit them! Hit them!" Kirk shouted from a short distance away, encouraging his comrades. "If we can hold out for half an hour, we'll have ensured the people's retreat. Hit them! Hit them constantly!"

"Hit them!" Andrew, Keith and all the heroic Andrews of Marash's legendary battle echoed. "We're going to die, so let's die bravely, let's die in the struggle, having avenged ourselves... Hit them, boys, hit them mercilessly!"

* * *

Half an hour later, when the Armenian fighters had fired their last bullets, they abandoned their positions and ran to catch up with the retreating people.

But hardly had they escaped the mob's pursuit, left the city and joined their loved ones in the open plain, when horrible cries were heard from the front of the caravan. "The chettehs have cut the road... let everyone look after themselves..."

It was as if a bomb had fallen from the heavens, whose masses of shrapnel spread in every direction. The Armenian fighters saw with horror that each of the 4,000 people they had saved ran in different directions, screaming with terror.

Father, mother, wife and child didn't exist. Every person, by instinct, thought only of the salvation of their own soul.

The bandits and mob, seeing the dispersal of their victims, immediately formed a circle to trap them in a ring of steel.

But no matter how careful they were not to let anyone out of the ring, there were a few escapees who succeeded in getting themselves out of the general melee before the ring was completed.

Kirk was one of those rare people who escaped and, with matchless selflessness, carried his sick wife out, despite Julia's pleas that he should leave her and save himself as it appeared impossible for both of them to escape in that way.

But Kirk took no notice of his wife's pleading. On the contrary, he comforted her, saying that she shouldn't be frightened and that he would protect her until his last breath.

After going a considerable distance from the danger area, he stopped for a moment to draw breath. Hearing his fellow-Armenians' despairing cries, Kirk was tempted for a moment to turn his head and look. If only he hadn't! The frightening scene of massacre, the like of which he had not seen – in the massacre of Kizil Irmak there were no women and children – weakened him and froze the blood in his veins.

At the same time he saw a giant in Kurdish clothing seated on a mule and holding a large broadsword rushing towards him. Kirk had no means of fighting this armed killer, but even so he put down his precious burden and, standing in front of her, waited, firmly deciding to jump at him at the first opportunity.

But fortunately there was no need for fighting. The giant jumped off the mule and, putting his hands in the air, shouted, "Mr Kirk, don't be afraid, it's me, Andrew!"

"Andrew...!" Kirk exclaimed joyfully. "But friend, what do you look like?"

"This is number 41, Mr Kirk," Andrew replied victoriously. "He wanted to kill me, but I moved quicker" – and holding Julia in his powerful arms, he put her on the mule – "Mr Kirk, hold the other side. We've no time to waste. We must escape from here."

Kirk obeyed his faithful soldier mechanically and, continually spurring the mule on, they escaped, until they were lost from the sight of the killers.

"Andrew," Kirk asked, after regaining his coolness, "do you know what happened to our comrades Keith and Charles?"

"I didn't see Keith, Mr Kirk, but Charles died in my arms," Andrew replied gloomily.

"Poor Charles!" Kirk said quietly, deeply affected by the news.

"The poor man had a very painful death," Andrew said in an agitated voice. "He was wounded in the chest, and rolled about near me, roaring dreadfully. I opened his clothes to see what had happened. A bullet had smashed the large cross hanging round his neck, and the pieces were driven into the bones of his chest. I never understood who that strange man was who carried a bishop's cross. Did you know him, Mr Kirk?"

Kirk remembered the oath he'd sworn in Bozanti and replied, "No, I didn't."

* * *

After moving on for two hours, they came to a small group of 14 escapees – two men, eight women, three small boys and a baby strapped to it's mother's back – who were sitting at the side of the road, exhausted.

"Why have you stopped here?" Kirk asked as he went up to them.

"We couldn't follow our friends," the poor people replied, "we didn't have the strength."

"Where are they?"

"They went with the French."

"With the French? How come? Aren't you escapees from the cathedral?

"No, we'd found protection in the Latins' monastery," the Armenians said, "We heard one night that the French were leaving without letting us know… We immediately collected our coats and covers and followed them. When we were going through a tunnel the Turks cut the road and massacred all those who were at the rear. We were at the front and were saved."

"How many people were in the rear?"

"More than 2,000. The Turks massacred everyone who was in the Protestant and Catholic churches and who wanted to join us."

"They did the same to the 4,000 Armenians who'd found refuge in the cathedral," Kirk declared in a sad voice. "Only about 100 survived. We're some of the few lucky ones" – then speaking to the women – "Get up, sisters, let's go. Stopping here is dangerous because when the killers finish their work, they could follow us."

"You go. We won't be able to continue the journey," the women and children answered regretfully.

"Give us your baby, I'll carry it on my lap," Julia said, speaking to the woman with the baby.

"Thank you madam," the latter replied, seeing Julia's poor state. "I don't want to impose on you."

"Don't lose hope," Kirk said, encouraging the exhausted travellers. "Get up, let's go, the French can't be far away. Although they left during the night, they couldn't have moved very quickly with a large crowd. I hope we'll meet them before nightfall."

The caravan walked for about an hour. Coming round a hill, they met another group of about 30 people who, drowsy from the cold, were lying on the road.

"What are you doing here?" Kirk asked, approaching them.

"We're waiting for death," the poor people sobbed in a pitiable tone. "We've been hungry for days, we've no strength left. We can't walk any more."

* * *

By the evening the small caravan of people, passing through uninhabited areas and always avoiding the presence of the murderers, reached the bank of a river safely.

"The river isn't too deep," Andrew said, well acquainted with the local geography. "There are shallow places where it's possible to cross, provided that we hold each other's hands as the current is strong and, if you weaken, it'll knock you down."

"Isn't the water cold?" the little boys and girls asked, trembling.

"It is cold, but we've got no choice. We won't be safe from the chettehs until we get to the other side."

"Take your clothes off and hold them on your heads," Kirk advised the people, "so that when you come out of the water you can put them on dry and be protected from the cold."

While the poor people were hesitating about undressing in the cold weather and going into the freezing water, they heard rifle shots and, turning round, saw 10-12 horsemen who were galloping towards them, continually firing and yelling.

They were murdering bandits who, after apparently destroying the Armenian population of the city, had spread out and were combing the mountains and plains for stragglers to pursue.

"The river! The river!" Kirk shouted, egging the people on and providing the first example, "Follow me!" Julia, Andrew and others, who were brave enough to get into the water, followed Kirk. Those who hesitated and stayed on the bank were later killed by the bandits who, without making the effort to dismount, cut open the heads of the poor, terrified, exhausted and stupefied people with axes.

The bandits, having killed their prey in this manner, tied their axes to their belts and took up their rifles. They then lined up along the river bank and fired at those swimming, uttering loud, inhuman cries every time they saw the person they had shot disappear beneath the water.

Kirk and Andrew, seeing that Julia, seated on the mule, was very exposed to the bullets, got her off the mule and, taking her arms, took her through the water, sometimes swimming, sometimes wading through the shallow places.

"Don't be frightened, Julia, have patience for a little while longer," Kirk said, constantly encouraging his wife. "We've already gone through three quarters of the river… As soon as we reach the other bank, we can consider ourselves safe."

But Julia didn't speak. She had long fainted from the cold, fear and the terrible pains caused by the advanced state of her pregnancy.

"Don't give up hope, Mr Kirk," Andrew said, this time encouraging his leader. "If…"

"Yes, if…?"

Kirk hadn't heard the whistle of the bullet that entered Andrew's neck, emerging from his forehead, felling the giant instantly, just as he had killed the trumpeter on the enemy barricades at St George's church.

"Poor hero," Kirk muttered, seeing his faithful soldier, his head under water, creating red bubbles where he had been. "Poor hero! The Turks, after killing your wife and children, got you too."

Then, without wasting any time, Kirk held his wife's body very tightly and, gathering all his strength once more, stumbled forward.

* * *

Months earlier, when one day Julia had declared that she was going to be a mother, Kirk had been very happy.

What dreams they had dreamt for the future of their child when, as man and wife, they had been sitting together in wicker armchairs in the garden one evening! How they would love it, how happy they would be when they saw the child growing up day by day, tall and strong. "Born in freedom, grown up in freedom, our children will never believe all the tortures we suffered under the rule of tyranny," Kirk had said to his wife. "They'll think, when they hear the stories about the massacres and deportations, that they're all legends. But when they've grown up, and they check and see that the stories are true, how they'll bless us for protecting them from any repetition through our sacrifice and blood."

"As we would have blessed our parents and forefathers if they, through their lives and struggle, had been able to spare us all this trouble," Julia pointed out.

It seemed as if those words had been exchanged centuries before.

"Of what use is Armenian procreation?" Kirk thought, looking at his wife who, recovered from her fainting fit, was lying on the cold ground in a hopeless state. "Of what use is it, if it's not to provide another victim for the Turk's knife or pleasure?"

What had been the fate of the Armenians, be they young, be they youthful or old? What had happened to the 30,000 Armenians of Marash who were there only yesterday or the 3,000,000 Armenians living in Turkey a few years ago?

What highly educated and learned young people there were among them and what educated and beautiful young ladies! What promising schoolchildren and youths! Weren't their wishes and ideals, aims and plans ended with one blow of a sword or a bullet?

And to think that he was going to have a child, adding another to the legion of enslaved who would one day curse their parents – as they had cursed their own – for bringing them into this world.

"Julia," Kirk said, interrupting his thoughts, seeing her in convulsions, "can't you walk for another quarter of an hour? I hope that when we pass the hill opposite we'll reach a warm house."

"Who's going to provide us with warm hospitality? The people who massacred us?" Julia said, suffering great pain.

"Don't say that, my love. There are still sympathetic hearts in this world... Anyone who saw your state, whatever race he belongs to, couldn't close his door in our faces."

"You'd be right about the human race," Julia whispered. "But alas! We're surrounded here by beasts in human form."

Kirk was confused, not knowing what he could do to take his wife to a nearby village. He had no strength left to carry Julia – he had already carried her six times since crossing the river – and he could never leave the sick woman alone on the mountain and go to seek help.

Most of the night had passed. The strong, bitter wind blew, hardening their wet clothes that made them cold rather than warm, until they were like pieces of wood. The howling of wolves and the barking of jackals could be heard in the distance.

"Julia," Kirk begged, taking her frozen hands in his, "try, my love. Get up. Let's walk slowly. I'm sure we'll find a village, a house, a hut near here where we can forget all our troubles around a warm fire."

"Oh! Will I see that happiness?" Julia sobbed softly. "To have a warm room… to lie on my back… to close my eyes and sleep…"

"Don't lose hope, Julia. If you have the will, you'll find that rest."

"Kirk," sighed Julia, in a semi-conscious state, "I feel so wonderfully sleepy… Let me sleep here… You go to the village…"

Her words gradually became inaudible.

"Julia! Julia!" Kirk cried, shaking his wife, "Please don't sleep. Wait, I'm going to take you in my arms again to move on." And Kirk tried to pick her up.

"Oh! The pain," Julia shrieked, holding her sides and rolling about. "Kirk, please don't touch me." Then she screamed heart-rendingly and sobbed, "Mother! Mother…!"

* * *

There is no greater sorrow in this world than that felt by a person seeing a loved one's pain, especially when he or she feels powerless to do even the smallest thing to ameliorate it.

There never was a worse torture than that suffered by Kirk that night, in those frozen plains, when his wife, having escaped from fire, sword and water, closed her eyes forever, writhing with the pains of childbirth, while the snow fell carelessly and the jackals and human beasts barked in the distance.

Within the Boundaries of Hell

Kirk found himself in an unexpected position when he became conscious the next morning.

He was buried up to the neck under hot manure inside a low, dark stable. An elderly couple were sitting next to him, and a little distance away was a cow, a calf and a colt. The picture of Bethlehem would have been complete if his wife and new baby had been there. But alas, they weren't.

Just as the sieve-making couple had crossed themselves with joy when they saw Kirk wake up from his death-like sleep, so the elderly couple did the same, giving thanks to God that they had succeeded in bringing back to life the half-dead traveller lost in the snowbound plains.

The old woman immediately got up and, bringing a cup of boiled milk, asked Kirk to sit up and drink it. Then, after Kirk sat up with the old man's help and drank the milk, the couple moved him into the next room that was nicely warm thanks to the fire burning in the grate.

Kirk didn't understand, as there was a fire in the house, why his hosts had buried him under the manure in the stable. His mind was so full of questions that he didn't know which one to ask first to satisfy his curiosity. "But are you Armenians?" he asked first of all, not believing his eyes.

"Yes, we're Armenians. My name is Toros," the old man replied, sitting next to his guest.

"How have you stayed alive?"

"No one's attacked our village up to now because the Turks know that all the villagers, frightened of bandit attacks, brought in their harvest and animals and went to Marash. They're not interested in empty villages and their few elderly residents at the moment, when a little distance away there's a large city to plunder and it's population to massacre."

Kirk shuddered at the thought that there was an Armenian family in the proximity, when he and Julia had fallen, exhausted, in the empty plain. "How did you find me?" he asked, his throat tight from anxiety.

"I'd gone to cut wood in the morning," the old man replied with a sad sigh. "I saw your and your wife's bodies buried under the snow. You were still alive. I put you on my donkey and brought you here."

"What about my wife?" Kirk said, almost crying.

"She was dead," Toros said sadly. "I went with Kaspar Amou and brought her body here and buried her in our cemetery."

* * *

Kirk enjoyed Keri Toros' and his wife Ashkho's hospitality for two months. He spent nearly all of the first month in bed because he had contracted pneumonia. Without medicines or doctors, Kirk hovered between life and death for a long time until, thanks to his hosts' unselfish sacrifices, his life was saved. He spent the second month convalescing.

The Turks didn't bother the Armenians during this period. After conquering Marash, they were preparing to take Aintab, Hadjin and the other cities populated by Armenians in Cilicia. Villages with their few inhabitants represented a negligible value for them.

Even survivors of the Marash massacre returned to the village. Kirk heard from them that after the Turks had taken over the city and massacred the people who resisted in the Armenian quarters, they had left some Armenians in a few places alive, although even now the Turkish police tortured them, falsely accusing them of joining the French and using weapons against them.

Kirk also heard that about 1,000 people who had retreated with the French had frozen to death on the road by the time the remainder had reached Selahieh station three days later.

The worst news amongst all this was that the road had been closed. Turkish nationalist forces had camped at every point along the border and it wasn't possible for anyone to enter Cilicia without endangering his life. In other words Kirk had once more remained on soil under the control of Turkey and, as an Armenian, had lost his liberty and security.

Two months later when, having recovered his strength, he said goodbye to his noble-hearted hosts, he didn't know which way to go to leave the borders of hell.

He automatically went to the cemetery where he had gone every day since he had recovered, taking spring flowers for Julia's fresh grave. Having once more collected flowers from the plain and placed them on his wife's grave, he, as usual, went to a corner to be alone and buried himself in his thoughts for hours.

Kirk thought of the terrible ups and downs that had happened in his eventful life in such a short time.

It was five years ago, on a similar spring morning, when he was fighting at the Dardanelles front against the British, and where he received, for the first time, his baptism of fire. How happy he was then! He had no worries or sorrows. His home and place were safe, his loved ones alive and well. It was only longing for them that pained him.

A year later however, on another spring day, having lost everything, he was going to the deserts of Der-Zor, to fight against a beast in his lair.

Three years ago, once more on a spring day in Damascus, he had been reunited with Julia, whom he had rescued from Death's Door.

A year later, his eyes covered with a black cloth, he was standing in front of a firing squad.

Last year, with Cilicia was freed, he married Julia and achieved all his ideals.

But this year…!

It seemed to him that the happiness he had enjoyed for a time was a delusion that he had dreamt one night as he slept in the desert of Der-Zor. In that dream he had seen Julia, the advance of the victorious armies, and the executioners' panic-stricken escape.

He had seen all that in a delusion and, delighted in a simple way, thought that he was living the truth. But now, awakened from it, he saw that it was the continuation of his former life, the same death-breathing, parching wind that blew, …the same destructive scythe that was reaping.

In this world of truth, where he had had the second delusion of being born, Kirk saw that life ended like the first: his home and family had been destroyed once more.

At least before he had had hope; he had suffered, hoping that one day the war would end, that the stormy night would be followed by a brilliant dawn. Now his only hope had been smashed, so what sun would he wait for? Which saint should he rely on? Which Christian government's promises should he believe?

"A world of lies and duplicity! Treacherous and rapacious humanity! Shame on you! A thousand shames on you!" Kirk exclaimed, venting all his heart's bitterness.

Suppressing his feelings with superhuman patience, he got to his feet, gave a pious kiss to his wife's grave and, his heart deeply wounded, left the cemetery.

* * *

Like a lion imprisoned in an iron cage – continuously pacing back and forth, occasionally pausing in the space between two posts, thinking that it can escape through it – Kirk wandered through Kemalist Turkey for a complete year, thinking that he had found a way to leave it. But it was impossible; every exit was securely closed!

The hopes that the Allies would intervene to improve the situation gradually disappeared. There never was such a terrible year in terms of mourning, pain and disillusionment as 1920. As the Turkish star rose, so the Armenian one dimmed.

The ink on the Treaty of Sevres had hardly dried when a dragon-like murderer named Topal Osman appeared, who arranged bloodbaths in Marsovan, Amasia, Yozghad, Eudocia, Samsun, Kirasun, Sivas and other towns and cities.

Massacres, exile and deportations took place in Constantinople, Kastamonu, Afion Karahissar, Eski Shehir, Duzdjeh and Arslanbeg as well.

The Turkish nationalists, not yet sated from spilling so much Armenian blood, attacked the newly-formed Republic of Armenia and did the same to hundreds of thousands of innocent people there too.

The Powers watched all these massacres with their arms folded and, as a reward for all those crimes, promised the executioners that they would revise the Treaty of Sevres and evacuate the areas occupied by the Allied powers.

Kirk finally gave up the idea of going to Cilicia. Hadjin fell after a nine months siege. Aintab had fallen long before. The French were preparing to leave Cilicia. At the same time the Italians were planning to leave Antalia, while the British retreated to the borders of Constantinople, leaving the defense of the great masses of Christians in the hinterlands of the Ionian and Marmara seas to the Greek army that had been defeated twice by Inonu.

Hearing that the Greeks were preparing to go on a major offensive, Kirk went to a border town in the hope that, during the first moments of the advance, taking advantage of the Turks' confusion, he could get through the border.

At the end of April, when he was wandering towards a village in the Geyveh area, he met an elderly but very fit old peasant who, with a small bag on her back, was coming in his direction.

"Excuse me sir, but are you Armenian?" the elderly peasant asked with unexpected boldness, looking at Kirk's face.

"Yes," the latter replied, heartily pleased that he had met someone who spoke his mother tongue.

"You're Miss Julia's fiancée, aren't you?"

Kirk turned deathly pale. "That's right," he said, in a bitter voice. "Where do you know me from?"

"From Damascus," the Armenian woman said, gratefully squeezing Kirk's hand. "You may not know me. My name is Sister Khatoun. Miss Julia gave us refuge in her house. I heard your story from her and later saw you after you were freed from prison. How is that noble girl and her good mother Mrs Iskouhi? But why are you so affected, Mr Kirk, did something unfortunate…?"

"Yes, a dreadful misfortune…!" Kirk sobbed, with a cry of regret. "I lost both of them in the massacre in Marash last year."

"Oh! My God!" Sister Khatoun cried, crossing herself. If only I could have died and not heard that dreadful news. How were the beasts able to · kill that delicate young lady and her matchless mother?"

"Who would the beasts save?" Kirk sighed, with an expression of distaste and hatred.

"I'm frightened that it's going to be our turn Mr Kirk," the peasant woman replied. "Did you know that they're taking all the Armenian young men into the army?"

"I didn't know," Kirk said paling. "Why?"

"So they won't work with the Greeks. The police are arresting all the men they see and, using conscription as an excuse, are exiling them to the interior. It's good they've not seen you."

"That's why I keep away from the towns. What state are people in?"

"The police aren't bothering the people at the moment, as they haven't got the list of men returning from the deserts, to be able to demand them from their houses. But they say openly to our faces, 'We sent you to Arabia. Why have you returned? We don't want you'."

"They've become the rulers of the country. They'll do a lot more yet," Kirk growled through his teeth.

"Our hopes are pinned on the Greeks," Sister Khatoun said with feeling. "If they, going over to a powerful offensive, don't capture this region, we're all sentenced to death." Then, after hesitating for a moment, she went on, "Mr Kirk, Miss Julia did a great deal for me. I'd like to repay some of that to you. Come with me. I'm going to take you to a secret place."

"A secret place…?" Kirk asked, amazed.

"Yes. Do you see those mountains? There are 16 young Armenian men in a secret cave there, to escape the threat of massacre, exile or hanging. No one knows they're there, apart from us who, (referring to her bag) sometimes take salt, sugar, tobacco and other necessities to them in turn when we visit them. Follow me. If you fall into the hands of the *Milli* (Turkish nationalist) people, that'll be the day you'll die."

"Thank you for the favour you're doing me," Kirk said, "but I don't want to be a burden on you."

"You won't be a burden," Sister Khatoun said. "I'm already taking food for my nephew. After this I'll take double the amount for you."

"Is your nephew there too?"

"Yes, Krikor is the boys' leader. All of them are patriotic Armenian lads. When they hear who you are, you can be sure that they'll idolize you, Mr Kirk."

* * *

Passing along narrow paths and always going up the side of a mountain, by the evening Kirk and Sister Khatoun reach a cave in a lost leafy thicket that, at one time, served to hide smuggled tobacco and, in 1915, as a hiding place for a group of Armenian fighters.

A number of men looking like woodcutters were at that moment preparing their evening meal. One was skinning and preparing a rabbit, four or five were removing the feathers from hunted birds, while others were preparing skewers.

Sister Khatoun's arrival with an unknown young man was the cause of much joy and, at the same time, curiosity, among those present.

"Welcome, Sister Khatoun, welcome!" was heard from all sides.

A young man with a thick head of hair, who was occupied baking lavash bread, hurried forwards to welcome the newcomers.

"Krikor," the peasant woman said, addressing the latter, "I've brought you a young man and you'll like him very much. I've told you many times how Miss Julia saved our lives in Damascus. Mr Kirk was her fiancée, then her husband..."

"We're delighted to meet you," Krikor said, shaking Kirk's hand.

"... But Mr Kirk's value is not that he was Miss Julia's husband," Sister Khatoun continued. "This gentleman was the Armenian officer who destroyed Der-Zor's Death's Door and saved 3,000 Armenian refugees' lives."

"Well done Kirk!" all the fighters shouted together, who had momentarily left their work and gathered curiously around the newcomer.

"This is the gentleman," Sister Khatoun said, "who in Damascus had the commander's lieutenant from Death's Door shot by firing squad, and as I just learnt, killed the actual commander of that place in Marash himself who, at the head of Turkish chettehs, had come to put the Armenian population of Marash to the sword. 20,000 Armenian were massacred there, among whom alas, was the young lady, Miss Julia, who saved our lives."

The happiness that for a moment had been seen on the faces of those present, suddenly disappeared, giving place to expressions of sadness, anger and hatred.

"Mr Kirk escaped by a miracle from the Marash massacre and, since then, has been traveling about Turkey hoping to find a way of getting out of the country," the peasant woman said, ending her introduction. "I'm delighted that I had the pleasure of meeting him on my way here. I took him by the hand and brought him here. I hope you'll excuse my going against your ban."

"What are you saying, Sister Khatoun? On the contrary, we'd have been angry if you hadn't led a brave person like Kirk here," all the fighters cried, becoming animated once more.

They then invited Kirk and Sister Khatoun to sit at the head of the table.

Kirk was very affected by his fellow-Armenians warm welcome and could only say a few words to show how grateful he was.

"Hey, aunt, tell us what news there is from below," Krikor said to his relative after a while.

"No news at all," Sister Khatoun sighed. "The commander of the Turkish cavalry has announced that they'll water their horses in the archipelago."

"But Sister, horses don't drink sea water," they all exclaimed, laughing throatily.

"You must understand the cleverness of the Turks," Sister Khatoun said with a smile. "The British prime minister has asked Kemal's delegation to tea and promised them that he'll free the exiles on the island of Malta."

"Let him free them; there's only a few mass-murderers," the fighters said angrily.

"The Armenians have killed the monster-born Talaat," the peasant woman said at the end.

"That is good news," the fighters said joyfully. "Why didn't you tell us before, Sister Khatoun?"

"What's the use, my boys," the Armenian woman said, groaning. "I told you before, one mass-murderer dies, and in place of him a thousand more grow."

* * *

Kirk thought that he was among the brave fighters of Marash, so like them were these fighters with their fearless natures and unreserved selflessness.

The poor peasants didn't know what to do to comfort and rest their honorable guest. They took him hunting with them and taught him the skills required to set traps for wild animals, or went down secret paths to the valley and showed him marvellous ways to catch fish.

Kirk joined in their work every day as one of the group and willingly did the duties assigned to him, be it carrying water or collecting plants or fruit.

But no matter that his life in the company of these selfless fighters was safe and like a game, he could not rid his mind of his sorrow for Julia or the disillusionment borne by all his race.

He became more and more melancholy as time went on, just as he had in the mountains of Djebel Druze.

Hardly had a month gone by when he fell ill with a consuming illness – malaria, which affects all those unused to the climate. Kirk, one day, would fall into bed shivering and suffering a high temperature. The next day he would feel a little better, but the following day it would start again, and like this, continue.

During this period of illness, Kirk had a nightmare crisis. In his dream he saw twenty bombers that flew from every direction to bomb the villages and towns. Tongues of flame rose to the heavens from all sides. Bombs rained down and sent huge shards of earth, stone and iron into the air.

The frightened people fled from the towns, seeking salvation in the open plains.

Fields, gardens and forests were burning around the people trying to escape. The aircraft continuously dropped bombs that made great craters beneath their feet.

From a distance an air fleet arrived, forcing the avenging aircraft to fly away. A tremendous aerial battle took place above and below the clouds. Those that were hit fell to earth and were destroyed. So the first, second and third fell to earth. Then the fourth, fifth, sixth and seventh. The others bravely continued fighting. Five more planes fell. Then seven.

Then only one remained against hundreds. But eventually it too was damaged and, like a wounded eagle, it hurtled down to the ground on fire and smoking, to be destroyed.

But the pilot hadn't died. He had hardly emerged from the burning aircraft when many bayonets surrounded him.

The encircled hero took out his pistol and fired at the enemy. When the last bullet had been fired, he saw a soldier with his bayonet running towards him. The pilot hit him on the head with the handle of his gun…

"Ow…!"

Kirk opened his terrified eyes and clutched the fist he had hit the wall of the cave with during a mad fit. Covered in sweat, he was panting like a bull that had been running, and couldn't at first understand what had happened, or where he was.

He was in total darkness and the sound of an aircraft continued to be heard in his ears.

Kirk couldn't understand if he was in a dream or reality. If he was in reality, what was the sound of a machine he had heard in his dream?

To solve the mystery, Kirk called Krikor to help him, who was sleeping next to him. Not receiving a reply, he wanted to nudge the group leader, but when he extended his arm, he found his hand touched nothing.

Kirk called his comrade sleeping the other side, but he too had disappeared. "Hey! Boys, where are you? Why don't you answer?" the Armenian officer shouted, surprised.

"...."

Suddenly he had an idea. The noise of the aircraft could still be heard. There was no doubt that a real aircraft was flying in the sky and the fighters, hearing the noises, had gone outside to see which country it belonged to.

Kirk's conclusion was right. When he staggered out of the cave, he saw his friends, like white ghosts in their whit underclothes, standing in the dark arguing.

"It was Greek."

"It was Turkish."

"No, it was Greek."

"No, it was Turkish."

* * *

A week after the aircraft had flown over them, Kirk opened his eyes one morning to see unusual confusion and activity.

"Get up, friend!" Krikor called, running to him happily. "Get up! We're finally saved. Come and hear what Sister Khatoun is telling us."

Kirk quickly got off his mattress and, running towards the mouth of the cave, saw his Armenian benefactress who, panting, was telling how the Greeks, suddenly advancing, had captured these areas, and how Greek planes were bombing Eski Shehir, while Greek battleships were shelling Samsun.

Although Kirk didn't have the heart to rejoice – that nerve had died in him – he couldn't suppress his happiness, looking at his friends, who were joyfully congratulating one another, just as the unlucky people in the cathedral in Marash had done when they had seen the arrival of the French aircraft.

"So, God heard our prayers," Sister Khatoun cried, raising her eyes to the heavens. "Thank the Lord! Thank His power!"

"Or the power of Greek cannon," a fighter playfully cried from a short distance away.

An hour later, having prepared their belongings into parcels and tied them to the ends of staves – that they carried like rifles over their shoulders – they were coming down the mountain singing and joking.

Fortunately Kirk didn't have a temperature that day. Leaning on one or other of his friends in turn, he reached the outskirts of the village comfortably. Seeing the parting of his friends one from another – each going to his own home – Kirk turned to them and, as if he had a supernatural premonition, said, "Comrades, before I say goodbye to you, I'd like to thank you for the brotherly care you gave me. I'd like to take this opportunity to make a small suggestion that I've garnered from my life's experiences, although at great price. Don't depend on victory in war. Armies are like tides, always flowing and ebbing. Never pin your hopes on the Greeks. They're here today; tomorrow they'll wipe the dust from their feet and return to their country, just as the French, Italians and the British did.

"One day you may once again come face to face with our race's deadly enemies. Try not to see that day. Sell whatever you have and go to Constantinople. Work to go to Armenia from there. That's where our hope and future is. The Armenian people can't put down roots and flourish on other soil.

"Once I gave the refugees who were being driven to Death's Door a command. I give you the same one now, 'Escape'. This is a marvellous opportunity to settle your affairs and leave."

No matter how bitter Kirk's words were, the peasants found them true and went to their homes agitated, thinking how false the happiness that was their due actually was. Yes, the Greeks could retreat. They must sell their houses and animals and once more take up the refugee's staff. Until they settled in their forefathers' fatherland, there would be no peace for them.

"Kirk," Krikor and Sister Khatoun said, taking their friend's arms, let's go to our house. Until you recover from your illness, we'll make preparations and then go together to Armenia."

Kirk, feeling unable to continue his journey, couldn't refuse his benefactors' invitation, and they went together to his hosts' house.

But when he set foot in their house, he could never have foreseen how soon his prophesy would turn into reality.

* * *

The Greek army, hitting determined resistance form the Turkish nationalists, soon began to fold in on itself.

Bandit groups operated ahead of the Turkish army, burning, destroying and committing massacre.

The Christian population of Marmara's hinterlands escaped in panic like people living at the bottom of a volcano seeing the fiery, roaring eruption.

The escapees gradually descending from the mountains, plains and slopes resembling rivulets, joined together and formed a great caravan that, just like a river current, flowed towards the sea, towards Izmid, and from there hoping to get to Constantinople.

Kirk, Krikor, Sister Khatoun, Krikor's young wife and three year-old son were in this bewildered caravan, whose leadership Krikor had taken up, being well acquainted with the secret paths of the region.

Walking day after day they passed through uninhabited mountains and plains and virgin forests. Every time they saw human bodies and burnt villages on their journey, they diverted from their way, metaphorically remembering the poet's words 'the chettehs have passed this way'.

Only one day was left before they reached Izmid when Krikor, who had been watching the bandits who had been following them for some time, noticed that they had closed road.

"The road's closed ahead of us; to go back means death; we can't go right or left because there are Turkish villagers there. What do we do now?" Krikor asked Kirk.

"There's only one thing to do," he said without hesitation, "we must choose the lesser of the two evils. In other words, instead of having to deal with the chettehs and soldiers, we must give precedence to the peasant."

"In other words to the axe and chopper?" Krikor asked nervously. "Kirk, I know the Turkish peasants of this area very well. They're not far behind the chettehs in terms of ferocity."

"As you know them, isn't it possible to promise them money to let us go through?" Kirk pointed out.

"It's not a bad idea," Krikor said, after thinking for a moment. "Two hours over there there's a Circassian tribal leader by the name of Musa Bey who, before the war, used to do business with my father and who was given hospitality in our house many times. Let's go to that village. If he's alive, I hope he'll help us."

"Where'll we get the money from?" Kirk asked.

"We can't demand anything from these poor people, as they're all naked and barefoot," Krikor replied. "I've got 110 gold coins with me; I'll use them to save our people."

"Well done, my friend!" Kirk exclaimed briskly. "Let's go straight away and make the necessary arrangements."

Then Kirk and Krikor led the people to the bottom of a deep valley – where no one would think that people might hide – and, after instructing them to wait there calmly for their return, they set off to Musa Bey's village.

Fortunately the elderly Circassian hadn't died. Seeing Krikor, he remembered his father, the merchant Markar Agha, and promised to get the caravan out of the danger zone with the help of 10 horsemen, if they paid him 200 gold coins as a ransom.

"Musa Bey, I've got 110 gold coins," Krikor said, pleading. "Please accept it for my father's sake and let us go through. There are 744 of us; you'll have all their prayers."

"I won't exchange 744 infidel prayers for one Mohammedan one," the Circassian declared, cold-heartedly. "Either accept my suggestion, or leave."

"But where will we get the rest of the money from?" Krikor stammered. "All of them are poor peasants."

"If 744 people can't get 90 gold pieces together why are they living?" the elderly man asked with a satanic smile.

"You know the reason, Musa Bey. All of them are from poor families who have returned from the desert. They'd hardly sorted out their economy when they were once more forced to leave everything and escape."

"My final offer: bring 150 gold pieces."

"Very well. Take this 110 gold pieces; we'll pay the remainder when we're out of the danger area."

"Without receiving all the money, I'll not move," the Circassian said implacably.

"Let's go," Krikor said, turning to his friend. "Until we can get the 40 gold coins, we won't be able to persuade this man."

"You go and get the money," Kirk said in a low voice. "I don't trust this robber. He could follow us and find out where the caravan is. I'll stay here."

Kirk's farsightedness saved 744 people from a great disaster.... Hardly had Krikor gone when three bandits, spurring their horses, approached the Circassian's house and asked him if he had seen a caravan of *kaffirs*, whose trail they had lost four hours previously.

There's no doubt that the fickle old man, breaking his word, would have given a positive answer if Kirk hadn't been sitting next to him. But he shrank from doing so because of the Armenian's presence and, after hesitating for a moment replied, "I haven't seen them. They must have gone by the top road."

After sending the bandits on a false trail the knavish robber nudged Kirk's knee and said, "Son of an infidel, pray to me, you escaped easily."

Krikor returned three hours later tired and out of breath. He took a handkerchief from his bosom and, handing it to the Circassian, said, "Sir, please be content with this. Whatever we had, I took and brought here."

"What's in it?" the old man asked.

"128 gold coins, 37 medjidiehs, some change and 60-70 earrings, rings and bracelets."

The shameless Circassian opened the handkerchief and, after examining the contents for a time, exclaimed, "You son of an infidel! What you call earrings, rings and bracelets are all silver... But never mind, there is your father's memory. I'll get you all through the danger area. Come with me."

On the Open Sea

The confusion on the quay at Izmid was very great.

Turkish bandits had reached the city gates. The Greek army, regarding any defense as useless, was emptying the city, putting the people on steamships, specially brought from Constantinople.

The fear of imminent massacre and the thought that there wouldn't be enough ships was so great that each person, with the object of saving himself, embarked on any ship, without knowing where other family members were.

Loaded ships departed. As the number of ships decreased, the confusion and terror on the quay increased proportionately.

The last ship was about to weigh anchor when the last Greek soldiers embarked on a fast cruiser and disappeared.

At the same time new groups of refugees arrived at the quayside who, seeing the preparations being made by the last ship to sail, began to shout in heart-rending tones, "For the love of God, wait! Take us with you... The chettehs are pursuing us, we'll all be killed...."

The ship's captain – a brave-hearted, noble Greek – felt he couldn't leave over 700 people to the vengeful, ferocious bandit groups, so he lowered the ship's ladder and took all of them on board.

A quarter of an hour later the ship had weighed anchor and gone.

They had hardly traveled half a mile from the shore when the escapers saw the Turkish flag unfurled over the city and the quays filling with a mass of people.

They were Turks – armed with knives, axes and rifles – who were shouting angrily and shaking their fists at the retreating ship, while others were taking bundles and parcels left by the refugees from one another, stealing their contents.

"We arrived at exactly the right moment," Krikor said from the upper deck of the steamer, looking at the tempestuous rabble on the quay. "If we'd been another quarter of an hour late, none of us would have remained alive."

Kirk – to whom these words were directed – was closely watching two dots on the sea – two human heads, one male, the other female – that were swimming towards the ship, while the Turks were firing at them from the shore.

"Look there," he cried, holding his friend's arm with horror. "There's a swaddle tied to her back too."

At the same time the steamer's seamen noticed the escaping couple and immediately threw lifebelts to them. The woman had almost reached one when she cried with pain and disappeared under the water. The husband, who had not seen his wife's disappearance, held onto the lifebelt and shortly afterwards was brought on deck in a semi-conscious state.

Kirk, watching that young man, whom they were trying to bring back to consciousness, thought that he was seeing his own life in a magic mirror.

There were so many similarities between the events that had taken place in such a short space of time. It was as if the things that happened at Marash were happening in the province of Nicomedia. The same false happiness, the same escape, the same pursuit, the same firing by a mob bent on massacre from the edge of the river or the edge of the sea; and then the same semi-conscious young man, losing his wife and child.

Weren't his and this young man's and all the young men's stories microcosms of his nation's history? Thinking that by swimming, the ocean had been crossed, isn't the Armenian nation, held in a powerful net of retreat, once more going back, back towards the foaming waves?

Leaning on the iron railing on the upper deck, just as Kirk was deep in these thoughts, there was a sudden violent jerk, followed by a frantic scream.

Kirk didn't take long to find out what had happened; the ship, very much overloaded, had grounded in the shallow channel.

* * *

About 30 chettehs came to the ship by steam launch and ascended the deck.

An officer with a rough, savage face issued a short order to his men. The bandits, their rifles held threateningly, spread throughout the ship and, after taking up important positions, gave a warning to the people. "No one move from where he is!"

The bandit leader with two followers went to the bridge. Bandits with fixed bayonets had already disarmed the captain, the first mate and the engineer.

"What nationality are you?" the officer asked, giving the men tied up a hostile glance.

"We're Greeks," the Captain said coldly.

"You're prisoners of war," the chettehs leader said shortly. "Has your ship broken down?"

"No, it's run aground."

"Who are your passengers?"

"Refugees."

"Robbers, you mean!" the hyena yelled with a criminal look. "They robbed Turkish villages and now they're trying to escape!"

"Did these naked and barefoot people carry out robberies?" the captain asked quietly.

"Yes, they not only carried out robberies, but also killed people. If they're not guilty, why are they running away?"

"They're running away because they're frightened."

"Why are they frightened? We're not beasts to tear them to pieces… Their flight means that they've committed crimes and are scared of judgement."

"No, commander," protested the captain bravely. "They're frightened of precedent."

"There's no need to argue," the bandit leader scolded. "Now tell me why you can't bring the ship to the quay."

"We can't get clear off the bank we're grounded on without a tug."

"Moheddin Bey," the beast ordered, turning to one of his followers, "have a tug brought here immediately. I also want you to arrest all the seamen and bring them here. And you, Medjid Bey – speaking to the second bodyguard – imprison the male travellers in the hold and collect the women and children on the upper deck."

"Yes, sir."

The two adjutants respectfully left and, while Moheddin Bey was giving the appropriate orders to the chettehs, Medjid ordered the people: "The men down below, women and children up above!"

"Why are you separating us?" asked a Greek married priest innocently.

"Here's the answer!" the barbarian yelled, emptying his pistol into the priest's forehead. "Let this be a lesson to you! Anyone who hesitates will suffer the same fate!"

The people who saw the killing of the innocent priest began to scream and cry, moan and sob.

"If you don't keep quiet, we'll shoot all of you here!" Medjid threatened in a loud voice. "Be quiet and do what we say immediately!"

The crying and screaming stopped at once. Two women, who didn't want to be parted from their husbands, were badly beaten, while their loved ones were killed before their eyes.

"Crying, pleading and resistance are all forbidden," Medjid roared, turning his weapon on the people. "Do you see this? So do what we tell you without making a noise."

The men went into the hold hopelessly. Some of them, for fear of being killed, couldn't even say goodbye to their wives and children.

Shortly afterwards the bandit chief, having finished questioning the captain and the seamen, came to the hold to look at those held there. After examining several people's faces closely, he ordered, with a hate-filled growl, "Tie them in groups of 20 with thick ropes. They'll tell the war tribunal of their numerous crimes."

* * *

"These men aren't going to try us, but are definitely going to kill us," Krikor said after the chettehs had gone.

"Not only us, but also our wives and children too," lots of voices said.

"Lads," Kirk said in his turn, "can we undo the ropes with which we've been tied up?"

"What with? They left nothing we can use," a Greek youth said.

"For example, we could rub the ropes against the great iron nails in the walls until they wear through."

"Assuming that we can do that, what are we going to do then?" several people asked.

"It's not worth talking about the advantages of having free hands," Kirk replied, "especially when our enemy is sure that they're tied."

"That's true," Krikor agreed. "Our guards pay less attention to us. So when the opportunity arises, we can take advantage of their carelessness."

"But what sort of opportunity?" a few pessimists asked. "They're going to take us to the shore and, as soon as we set foot on it, ten times our number will attack us."

"But there's still hope that, if a few hundred die, the rest will be free," Kirk said. "If they take us out of the city, there's even more chance we'll escape with fewer losses."

"How?"

"Of course they'll not assign as many chettehs as there are Armenians. 30-40 could finish us off, each killing a group of 20 of us assigned to him. Now, imagine what could happen if our hands were free and, on a given signal, we attack that limited number of executioners. If each group disarms the murderer assigned to it, we'll all be free."

"That's not a bad idea," all the bound men agreed in a convinced tone. "We're going to die anyway, at least this way we'll be able to try our luck."

"If we act coolly, we'll succeed," Kirk said, encouraging his friends. "Come on, let's start work! Just be careful that your bonds aren't completely severed. Wear the inside part through and get it to the state that we'll be able to snap them with a small effort."

* * *

An hour later the only tug to be found in the port of Izmid approached the ship. Many boats accompanied the tug, all of them full of armed people. Seeing the crowd on the ship's upper deck, they shook their swords, chuckling madly and making death threats.

The tug immediately got to work to pull the ship off the sandbank, but it proved unequal to the task.

The bandit chief, seeing that it wouldn't be possible to bring the ship to the quay, ordered the people rowing the small boats to take the murderers back and return empty, to transfer the ship's passengers back to shore. "Thank you for your patriotic fervour," he said, speaking to the mob in the boats. "Go back to the quay and wait for instructions."

"Hurrah for Suleiman Bey!" the mob of killers replied joyfully and rowed back.

Half an hour later seven empty boats returned to the ship.

"First the men," Suleiman Bey said, turning to his bodyguards. "Put one group of twenty men in each boat and, under the guard of two soldiers, take them to the shore."

"Come on then," Moheddin and Medjid shouted into the hold. "Seven boats have arrived. 140 of you come up."

"Let those who are ready follow us," Kirk said, walking with his group towards the hold ladder. "Please keep cool. Remember that all our lives depend on each one of us remaining calm."

Seven groups of young men climbed the ladders without a sound and walked between two files of bandits with fixed bayonets. Each group, under the guard of a pair of ferocious-looking murderers, entered a boat and sat down.

Immediately a boat received its load, it set out for the quay, where a motley crowd had collected shouting dreadful curses, while a Turkish Muslim cleric was praying from a minaret, praising Allah for allowing him to live to see this happy day. "Allah ekber... Allah ekber..."

One of the bound men, seeing these joyful preparations made by the hoja and the people, lost his nerve and threw the bandit sitting next to him into the water with one punch. Another two did the same to the other bandit.

Although all this took place in an instant, because it happened without the knowledge of the other boatloads of bound people, the latter were unable to follow their comrades' example before the chettehs had the time to resort to their weapons.

The boat Kirk was in capsized in the ensuing hand-to-hand fighting that took place. The bandits in the other five boats managed to regain control of the situation and, keeping the prisoners quiet by using the threat of arms, nevertheless fired at the 40 escapers, of whom 20 swam while the remainder rowed the boat. All the swimmers and the boat went in different directions.

The mob, incensed by the sight of people in the water, ran along the edge of the port, screaming and shouting, and waited for the swimmers heading for the shore to reach it...

Others, armed with rifles, leapt into small boats and pursued the escapers, to hunt them like wild ducks. Shortly afterwards, Suleiman, the bandits' leader, taking about ten men with him, joined the hunt in the steamboat, chasing the escapers who were rowing the boat they had captured. The bandits left on the ship added their continuous volleys too as they saw the escapers swimming towards them.

The young Armenians and Greeks, fired at from all sides, swam without losing hope with all their strength. Those among them who had the misfortune to be hit by bullets sank below the surface of the Marmara's green waters proving once more, with their horrible deaths, that history repeats itself, especially with regard to the history of the eradication of the Christian communities in Turkey.

* * *

When Kirk reached the shore, the massacre-bent mob hadn't yet reached where he was, although their terrifying howls and cries could be heard nearby.

Without stopping for even one moment and without knowing where he was going, he instinctively ran away from the approaching crowd, when a voice caught his attention: "Compatriot, not that way!"

Kirk looked round and saw a young man who was wet like him and who was escaping in another direction, waving to him to follow at the same time.

Kirk immediately changed direction and ran after his fellow-Armenian without saying a word. He was very surprised, a little later on, when they had passed the danger zone, to find that his companion was none other than the unfortunate husband who had swum from the shore and, at the moment of deliverance, had lost his wife and child.

"I don't know why I'm still living," the young man said after resting a little, when he had recovered the breath to speak. "I don't know why I make the effort not to die, when I've no reason to live any longer."

"I ask myself the same question every day," Kirk said, sighing sadly. "I too don't know why I struggle to prolong this life of torture."

"I'm a wretched person," sobbed the young man, covering his face with his hands. "After losing my wife and child in one day, I still cling to life."

"Me too," Kirk breathed. "I saw the misfortune that happened to you, the same as happened to me in far worse circumstances. But get up, let's go. We'll talk as we walk."

"Fortunately the streets are empty," the young man said, getting to his feet. "The entire Turkish population of the city is down at the shore to watch the 'entertainment'." Then, after a short silence: "Your entering a dead end street leads me to think that you're not from here. Am I right?"

"I'm very grateful to you for cautioning me," Kirk said. "Yes, I only came to Izmid today, escaping ahead of the Turkish army. Are you from Izmid?"

"No, I'm from Eski Shehir," the young man replied. "When the British left the town, I left hurriedly and settled here, hoping that the Greeks would capture Eski Shehir and I'd become the owner again of the wealth I left there."

"With whom did you leave it?"

"I left the goods from my shop with a Turkish friend. That thief promised to send me the money..."

"And he didn't? I don't understand; why did you trust the Turk?"

"I was already forced to leave all my goods. I thought that if I left them with the Turk, even if he didn't honor his promise, I'd be able to retrieve them when the opportunity arose."

"Fine. As you were in Izmid, why didn't you leave by ship in good time instead of staying here until the last minute?" Kirk asked, curiously.

"There never was anything said about abandoning the town," the young man replied, choked. "They made the announcement that special ships would be arriving from Constantinople only this morning, and that we should leave immediately. We made our preparations to leave in deep shock and in a spirit of hopelessness and thousands of us ran to the quay. The port was already full of Armenians and Greeks from the surrounding villages. The word was that the Turkish army and the murdering chettehs who advanced ahead of it would be entering the town in one or two hours. So you can imagine the scale of the panic and pushing and shoving that took place when the people were ordered onto the ships.

"I lost my wife, who was carrying our three month-old child, in that disorder. Thinking that she'd been able to go on board ship with the crowd, I too embarked on the first ship and started to look for her. Not finding her there, I disembarked with great difficulty and looked for her on a second.

"It was at the last moment that I heard from a compatriot that my child had been crushed in the crowd and my wife had been escorted by a Greek soldier to a pharmacy. I immediately left the ship and ran to the pharmacy. My compatriot's information was correct; my wife was there, and the pharmacist was busy binding up my child's wounds.

"Seeing me, the Greek soldier left for the cruiser, advising me to take my wife and child immediately to the last ship. A quarter of an hour after the Greek soldier left, we tied the child on my wife's back and, with me carrying our bags, went to the quay.

"But when we reached the shore, we saw that the ship had just left the quay, while the Turkish mob was running from the end of the street, yelling and cursing madly. There was only one thing we could do: jump in the water and swim for the ship. That's what we did. You know what happened after that."

Kirk related his escape from Marash in the same situation and the heart-rending circumstances of his wife's death.

"My misfortune is so like yours," sobbed the young man. "How did you stand so much sorrow? I don't think I'll be able to live after this."

A bitter smile appeared on Kirk's face. "I thought like that too, but I'm surprised that I'm still alive," he said, comforting his friend. "There's great truth in the saying that time heals all wounds."

"It's true, but I'll feel guilty for the rest of my life. My wife, as if she had a presentiment, begged me, every day, saying, 'George, let's not stay here, let's go to Armenia', but I didn't listen to the voice of reason, and persisted in staying in this cursed country, tied to my land and work."

"Your late lamented wife seems to have been very hurt by the Turks," Kirk pointed out.

"Yes, she was very frightened," sighed George. "She would tell of the terrible massacre in Erzerum and how only she and about another ten Armenian women escaped."

"Was your wife from Erzerum?" Kirk asked with a sudden, moving recollection.

"Yes, but why do you ask?"

"What was your wife's name?"

"It was Shnorhig. But I don't understand why you've lost colour."

"I paled because I had a fiancée who also escaped the massacre in Erzerum by a miracle."

"But a little earlier, when you were telling me your story, you said that your wife was from Adana," George pointed out.

"That's true, I married her after Sara died."

"Which Sara?"

"My fiancée, Sara Sarkisian."

"Was Sara Sarkisian your fiancée?" George cried suddenly, amazed. "But who said she had died?"

Kirk, indescribably troubled, looked George in the eyes and, in a trembling voice, asked, "Do you know Sara?"

"Of course. After the armistice, when I met my wife in Aleppo, I also met her. They both worked in the Red Cross hospital."

"So Sara's in Aleppo?"

"No, Constantinople."

"Where in Constantinople?"

"I don't know the address. She always wrote to my wife."

"Let's not be wrong about this, friend. The Sara I'm referring to was the one who was caught in the explosion in the train tunnel in Amanos about six years ago."

"It's that very Sara I'm talking about. I know her whole story. I know how she was kidnapped in Tarsus when she was with the Americans there, by a traitor to his nation called Nouri Osman. How she was rescued by the intervention of a noble Armenian and how she worked on the railway as a porter. And how she escaped by a miracle from the tunnel disaster, and was forcibly married to a Kurd..."

"With a Kurd?" Kirk asked with a horrified cry. "What are you saying?"

"Don't worry, Mr Kirk," George said, calming his friend down. "Your fiancée is a girl of Armenia and that same night... But that's a long story and I'm very tired. I'll tell you later."

* * *

The two friends continued their journey, alternately walking and then sitting down, without however, knowing where they were going and why.

"How do we get out of this hell now?" Kirk said continually, and whose longing for freedom had grown many-fold after knowing that Sara was alive. "Until we find an escape route, the sword of Damocles will always be hanging over us."

"I've got 40 gold coins in my belt," George said. "Can't we use them to find a way?"

"There's only one way left," Kirk replied. "We must try our luck in the ports on the Black Sea coast."

"What can we do there?" George asked anxiously.

"We'll hire a sailing boat and or..."

"And or what?"

"Do you remember that eight days ago that Greek warships were shelling Samsun? If they shell it again, we can hide on one of the European ships during the commotion."

"But I've no hope that after their shameful retreat, the Greeks will go on the offensive once more."

"Don't say that! As they've announced that they're minded not to relinquish Izmir, they're forced to continue fighting and secure their borders."

Exactly three weeks after this conversation, a part of Kirk's supposition came true. Constantine's soldiers, having begun a great offensive, not only recovered the territory they had lost, but also captured Eski Shehir, throwing the Turkish nationalist army back over the River Sakaria in a state of chaos.

Although the Greek warships didn't shell Samsun after this unexpected victory, the inhabitants of houses along the shore of that port awoke the same night from their sleep in terror to the sound of rifle fire.

Running to the windows, they saw – in spite of the darkness – a large Italian ship at anchor in the open, stormy sea and a boat being rowed towards it, followed by a steamboat.

The steamboat was carrying Turkish policemen who, keeping the other boat in view using a large lamp, were continuously firing and whistling at it, telling the escapers to surrender. In the mean time the latter – three Armenians and two Greeks – without paying any attention to the threats, rowed quickly, slicing through mountainous waves, sometimes rising to the crests and sometimes disappearing into the troughs.

All they could hear in the dark was the sound of the boat pursuing them and the whine of the bullets over their heads. Every other sound was lost in the roaring of the waves and the tumult of the storm.

"Be brave, boys!" Niko – a bold Greek seaman – yelled. "Every time we reach the crest of a wave, lie down in the bottom of the boat. Don't be afraid, the bullets won't hit us."

The other fugitives obeyed their leader and so reached the Italian ship unscathed.

Shortly afterwards Niko skilfully navigated the boat around the ship's stern – so they were protected from the bullets – and, with incredible swiftness, secured the boat to the hook on the end of a rope that was tied to the ship's handrail.

"Follow me, boys!" he cried, climbing the rope towards the deck.

The second and third escapers followed the Greek. The fourth had climbed halfway up when the steamboat rounded the ship's stern and a bullet was fired. The flame from the gun had hardly been seen when the escaper climbing the rope let it go with a strangled scream and fell into the water.

The fifth escaper, who was still in the boat, knowing he was going to be a target for the policemen's bullets, threw himself at the rope without hesitating. Bullets splattered on the side of the ship. One finally wounded him in the arm. The poor man was going to fall into the water, not having the strength to climb up, when suddenly a friendly hand, disregarding every danger, pulled him up.

* * *

Shortly afterwards, when the escapers had disappeared behind the cabins, the Turkish police brought their steamboat alongside the ship and boarded it in the same way.

The Italian captain and seamen, hearing the sound of rifle fire, had emerged from their cabins to see what was happening on their ship.

"Four men have boarded your ship. We've come to demand that they be handed over to us," the policemen's leader, in reply to the captain's question.

"Can you tell me what crime they are accused of?" the captain asked, examining the Turks scornfully.

The policemen's leader was abashed. He didn't know who the escapers were to make false accusations against them.

"Why don't you say anything?" the captain asked, his arms folded across his chest. "Did they kill someone? Burgle a house? Rape a woman? Or were they smugglers?"

"No, they're escaping to Constantinople."

"Is escaping to Constantinople a crime? Your king lives there," the captain pointed out.

"We don't recognise the jurisdiction of Constantinople, where the government has entered the crooked service of the Allies," the policemen's leader replied.

"The government of Constantinople doesn't recognise you, who are rebels against the king's authority," the captain answered. "If you were honorable men, you'd have come to my ship and politely asked for the handing over of the 'escapers'. You've no right to kill people who are under the protection of my flag. Please leave my ship or I'll have you arrested and, as murderers, take you to Constantinople in chains."

The Italian captain could carry out his threat. The police hung their heads in shame then, without saying anything else, retreated to their steamboat and disappeared into the darkness.

It was only on the following day, when the ship weighed anchor and began to sail majestically through the now calm waves, that the escapers were able to believe that they were free and were going to Constantinople.

* * *

28 July 1921

I heard that my friend Yervant, escaping on an Italian ship, had arrived in Constantinople yesterday.

I went to Kum Kapu, to his relative's house where he was staying, to welcome him.

Yervant's first question to me was: "Vahram, what happened to the diary you were keeping?"

"I'm still making entries in it. Why?" I asked.

"Let me introduce you to a man who can give you a lot of information for your diary," said my friend, taking me to a young man who, with his left arm in a sling, was sitting near the window.

"I'm delighted," I cried. "What's your name?"

"Sub-Lieutenant Kirk."

ALSO BY VAHRAM DADRIAN
an incredible diary of the Armenian Genocide

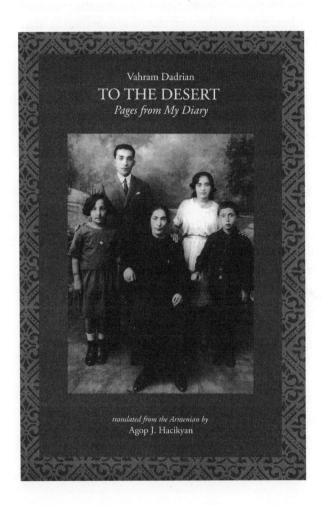

To the Desert: Pages from My Diary (Gomidas Institute, 2003) translated from the Armenian by Agop J. Hacikyan and edited with an introduction by Ara Sarafian.

To order or for more informóation please contact
info@garodbooks.com